Prais

WHITE HEART OF JUSTICE

"High stakes and powerful magic collide... Noon's voice is wry and genuine, encompassing her sharp sense of self." —*Publishers Weekly*

"Kudos to Archer for creating such a compelling heroine and mythos!" —*RT Book Reviews* (4 stars)

"Archer has a gift of creating characters with depth, growth and confidence that will leave all urban fantasy lovers wanting more." —*Night Owl Reviews* (Top Pick)

"I spent the entire novel compulsively reading, racing to the finish to see what would happen." —*Bitten by Books*

"The best so far... I SERIOUSLY CHEERED... an action-packed piece of excellence." —*Happy Tails and Tales*

"A must read for fans of urban fantasy and dystopian fairy tales where Armageddon is only the beginning, not the end." —*The Reading Café*

"A thrilling adventure that brings Noon and her Guardian Angel Rafe literally to the gates of Hell, inspired and exhilarating... well-written and believable... unexpected but pleasing..." —*The Qwillery*

"The series focuses on Noon's developing magical power, relationships, and many adventures in the unforging, demon haunted world of Halja." —*Bibliomania Book Reviews*

"A homage to Noon's independence.... *White Heart of Justice* delves deep into a quest of magic, freedom, redemption and love." —*Tower of Babel*

"[Noon's] growth over the course of these books is immense and heartfelt." —*That's What I'm Talking About*

"Action, adventure, romance, humor, suspense, danger, deception...Pick up the entire series and give it a read... Fans of fantasy and paranormal novels will definitely enjoy." —*What the Cat Read*

FIERY EDGE OF STEEL

"Archer delves deeper into the enticing and magical world of *Dark Light of Day* in this original and clever urban fantasy." —*Publishers Weekly*

"The second Noon Onyx story is an astounding adventure tale... This is proving to be a really fresh and fascinating series!" —*RT Book Reviews* (4 stars)

magic, creatures, and ... adventure.... An excellent balance between fantastical action and romance." — *Bibliomania Book Reviews*

DARK LIGHT OF DAY

"A spectacular debut novel." —USA Today bestselling author *Faith Hunter*

"A brilliant character who struggles against fate to find her place in the world. Set against the backdrop of university life, there is an abundance of adventure, mystery and passion!" —*RT Book Reviews*

"Delightfully dark and unique." —*Bitten By Books*

"Archer is now down on my 'never miss' author list." —*Night Owl Reviews*

"[A] fascinating story line... Archer has created a dark world that will grab your attention from the very start." —*The Reading Café*

"Well written and fast paced urban fantasy with unique characters and a multi-layered plot." —*A Dream within a Dream*

"Ari is powerful, dangerous... and sexy, but he can also sometimes be sweet and sensitive.... Loved Noon's Hyrke friends, Ivy and Fitz too!!"
—*Feed Your Fiction Addiction*

The Noon Onyx Series by Jill Archer

DARK LIGHT OF DAY
FIERY EDGE OF STEEL
WHITE HEART OF JUSTICE
POCKET FULL OF TINDER

POCKET FULL
OF TINDER

JILL ARCHER

BLACK WILLOW BOOKS

POCKET FULL OF TINDER

Copyright 2016 by Black Willow, LLC

All rights reserved.

To contact the publisher,

please address your inquiry to:

P.O. Box 381

Shrewsbury, Pennsylvania 17361-0381

PUBLISHING HISTORY:

Ebook edition/December 2016

ISBN: 978-0-9979138-0-4

Paperback edition/December 2016

ISBN: 978-0-9979138-1-1

Cover art by Rebecca Frank

www.jillarcher.com

PROLOGUE

He'd been traveling for weeks, following the river westward. A great aerial beast with a broken wing trying to follow the curving lines of a bigger, blacker beast on terra firma. Beneath him, the Lethe River twisted and writhed. Every left turn was agonizing. The wing, bent at an unnatural angle, caught wind where it shouldn't. The drag was enormous. He often felt as if he were drowning, his wings clasping at the edges of a whirlpool whose edges grew taller and steeper as it closed in on him. And then he'd have to *push*, soaring up into the air again with labored breathing that sounded louder than a blue whale's blowhole.

As he neared New Babylon he kept a keen eye on the water, searching for boats and sails and men. Men who may not have seen a drakon in decades, perhaps longer. Men who would sound an alarm and alert others to his presence. It was the type of homecoming he wished to avoid.

So he'd flown at night and timed his arrival with the new moon. All below was black and gray. Far off there were tall ships lit by lanterns, but closer (thank Luck *closer*) was his goal – Bradbury's docks.

A man without fire or an electric torch would have been blind. But to a drakon, the world seemed drawn with charcoal and smudged with starlight. Another night, with a different wing and the company he sought, he might have thought it beautiful.

He smelled the river and the city, the scents of men and the rich food they liked to eat. Loud, boisterous voices rose from the waterside inns, saloons, and taverns. He clenched his jaw and banked left across the water toward Etincelle, straightening again – or at least trying to – before he got too close. With a last, desperate push *up* he rose above the Lethe, beating his inefficient wings against the midnight sky, until he found warm air to ride down, circling… waiting… watching for anyone who might still be at the docks. He did not want to be seen in drakon form.

He landed less gracefully than he would have liked, skidding to a halt just before hitting a crate that would have tumbled into the Lethe had he not finally found purchase on the dock with his claws. With a last glance around, he shifted.

Wings collapsed. Snout, jaw, and teeth were reabsorbed. Claws disintegrated, turning to dust. Tail wriggled and twisted, curling inward, like a snake eating itself. Lungs and heart halved. And then halved again. Head pounding, body shaking, Ari fell to his knees, his right palm pressed against the dock, his left arm cradled uselessly against his side.

He was home.

Sticking to the darker parts of alleys and streets he'd known since infancy, he made his way to the Carmine rowhouse, picked the lock with waning magic, and quietly slipped through the door. Avoiding the creakiest boards in the hall, he made his way to his old bedroom and found clothes – a pair of worn canvas pants and a ripped tunic that Joy had mended. He'd find a pair of boots later. He was tempted to fall into bed immediately, but shifting hadn't taken away his hunger or his memory of how good New Babylon's food had smelled.

Less carefully and much more hastily, he walked to the kitchen and was just about to open the ice box when his mother's voice stopped him.

"Aristos, I raised you better than that. Open that door and you could ruin half of what's in there."

He dropped his hand from the ice box's handle and turned around.

Joy Carmine stood in the doorway of her kitchen clad in a turquoise nightgown. Her white hair was unbound and her pink eyes concerned once she saw the tunic he was wearing. She likely recognized it as one she'd stitched up not long ago. She walked over to him and gently lifted his left arm. It gave the impression of two elbows, each locked at an odd angle. She raised her gaze to his face.

"She found out, didn't she?"

An hour later, Ari was seated across from Joy and Steve at the Carmines' kitchen table. Steve was dressed in worn but well-mended clothes and everyone, despite the hour, had a mug of beer in front of them. The leftovers from at least three different meals (collops of rabbit, onion pie, and broiled sturgeon) were now in Ari's stomach and he'd told them of the trip to the Shallows: how he'd been the unintended target of a revelation spell, that Noon had broken up with him after learning he'd been hiding his true nature from her, and that he'd spent the last two months wallowing in his misery and the swamps of the eastern hinterlands.

Steve received the news with a hard look. All three of them had disagreed from time to time on whether and when Ari should embrace his demon heritage. Drakons were unusual and rare creatures, more feared than revered. Throughout his childhood, there'd been a careful balancing of interests. Early on, there'd been some talk of trying to find another home for him, but Joy had never been for it and besides... who? Where? No legend had ever spoken of a drakon being raised in a happy home. There were no stories of law-abiding *regulare* drakons, only villainous *rogare* ones, which seemed to seal Ari's fate. Joy was determined his life's course would be different. That *he* would be different. Almost from birth, he had been discouraged from shifting into his true form.

Before he was even a year old, Joy had convinced Steve not to reveal the extent of Ari's abilities. After all, drakons were maligned and misunderstood. And it wasn't as if they were breaking any rules. Unlike Maegesters, demons were under no obligation to live any particular type of life. So he'd been taught to value his magic. To control it, and use it only for worthy purposes. As a Maegester might.

His first lover, the Patron Demon of Waves and Waterbirds, had known the full extent of Ari's abilities. But she'd never understood his choice to reject his full rights as a demon or his emotional attachment to the Carmines. Halja's Hyrkes were supposed to be his followers, not his family. That last word was always said with a huff of impatience, as if Ari were too young to understand how the world worked. Cliodna may have been one of the loveliest creatures Ari had ever seen (her true form was that of a shapely, starlight-colored swan, so unique to the demon world it had its own name – *rara avis*), but her signature had forever felt like wet feathers to him – cold, damp, and full of quills. Lying with her had been like sleeping on a bed of water-logged hay. He'd broken it off with her long ago.

"Maybe it's for the best," Steve said. "A *human female* with waning magic? Who also happens to be the executive's daughter? Nouiomo Onyx is like a white wyvern. Singularly unique, but dangerous. You should have stayed with the white swan."

Ari made a derisive sound, but said nothing. In one respect his father was right. If he'd stayed with Cliodna, he would not feel as hollow and empty as he did now. Leaving Cliodna had been a relief, but leaving Noon had been almost impossible.

"What will you do now?" Joy asked. "Is returning to St. Luck's out of the question?"

He nodded—

A loud banging on the Carmines' door interrupted their discussion. Abruptly, everyone stood up. Steve frowned and started toward the door. Ari moved as if to follow but Joy stopped him. "It's the neighbors," she said. "When they find you—"

"—We've talked about this," Ari said, tamping down his impatience. "You can't see the future. No one can."

She met his gaze grimly, refusing to flinch from the truth she thought she saw. She'd always been like that. It wasn't just Joy's immunity to magic that had allowed her to raise a drakon. But he refused to let her words – or her improbable visions – convince him that he didn't have a chance. That *they* didn't have a chance….

He'd always believed that Luck could be persuaded by his will. That he could have what he wanted as long as he wanted it badly enough. But now… wanting Noon… and knowing that she didn't want him…. His mother's mention of happiness wasn't an accident. They both knew full well that if he wanted Nouiomo Onyx, he could "have" her, as any demon might. But Ari didn't just want her body; he wanted her heart. He wanted to be happy.

With her.

Always.

Or at least for the rest of Noon's hopefully long-lived life.

He left as smoke and shadow. It wasn't a form that came naturally or easily to him. But as he slipped through the Carmines' open transom window, he knew he'd made the right choice. Below him, too anxious and edgy to notice a wisp of smoke trailing out of the house and into the night, was a mob of fishermen, dock workers, and river whalers. They stood in the street, clustered around Steve, clutching torches, lances, and harpoons.

"Ari's not here," Steve said, sounding unconcerned. "He sailed east toward the Shallows month before last. But the runner will bring back one of the executive's Maegesters before long and *he* will search the docks. Even if what Donny saw *was* a drakon, don't try and hunt it down. You'll only get yourselves killed. Go home." The men shifted on their feet, eyeing the sky nervously. When they still showed no signs of clearing out, Steve prompted.

"A warm bed and your wife... or possible evisceration and incineration? I know which choice I'm making." When Steve turned back toward his door, a few of the men chuckled. After all, how likely was it that a drakon had come to Bradbury?

Thank Luck, that drakon would be long gone before sunlight revealed his claw marks on the dock. Big as plowed furrows and undeniable evidence that something large and deadly had landed there.

Part I

Humpty Dumpty sat on a wall,
Humpty Dumpty had a great fall.
Fourscore men and fourscore more
Couldn't make Humpty what he was before.

—ENGLISH NURSERY RHYME

1

TWO CRONES

The claw-and-ball had been chewed clean off. It lay on a patch of sunny parquet floor, just to the right of an antique, aubergine wool rug now covered with the splintered remnants of an eleventh-century pedestal table and one very large, ghastly looking, somewhat repentant barghest.

Nova's head rested on her front paws as her gaze shifted warily from me to Miss Bister, Megiddo's *dormater*, or house mother.

"Megiddo's lobby is not a kennel, Miss Onyx. That"—she motioned dismissively toward Nova—"*beast* can no longer be housed here."

I opened my mouth to respond, but Miss Bister continued speaking, her tone rising only infinitesimally, her back as stiff as Luck's lance must have been and her expression just as hard. She pointed toward the previously priceless, three-footed piece of furniture that was now a worthless, two-footed pile of kindling.

"No amount of money – or magic – can fix *that*, Nouiomo. It's beyond repair. I warned you. I made an exception to my 'no pets' rule because you never cause trouble. You never forget your key; you promptly pick up your deliveries; you change your own light bulbs; you double-bag your trash. You leave nothing behind in the bathroom; you don't monopolize the washing machines; you are exceedingly polite to the lift operator; you don't sing in the shower."

I suppressed a sigh. After a year and a half of painstaking effort, harrowing experiences, and endless hours of education, my worth had just been measured by the fact that I could change a light bulb. I'd mastered fiery magic, become an adept fighter, learned the law, killed countless demons (one regrettably, the others much less so), freed myriad immortals from an accursed, tortured bondage, and survived having my heart nearly destroyed by both love and an arrow, yet none of that meant bupkis next to the fact that I double-bagged my trash. And yet...

I couldn't really argue with Miss Bister either. Everything she'd said was true. And who was I to tell her what she should deem important? I respected that she valued domestic order and antiques. I did too, if not nearly as much as I valued the thing that now threatened our continued access to such. I glared at Nova, who swept one paw over her eyes as if she could hide from me and the evidence of what she'd done.

Barghests are giant hellhounds. They're bigger than bears, fiercer than rabid raccoons, and uglier than naked mole rats. Their teeth are the size of railroad spikes, their claws as sharp as a sickle, their breath as foul as sewage gas. But they are also affectionate, brave, and loyal. What barghests lack in magic, they make up for in devotion. And even though I was plenty mad at Nova for chewing up Miss Bister's table, I also knew it wasn't Nova's fault.

It was mine – for thinking the lobby of a demon law school dormitory would be a good place to keep her.

"Miss Bister, please," I said. "I'm truly sorry. I know I can't replace that exact table. But if you would just allow me to—"

"No," Miss Bister said simply. "Either the beast goes… or you do."

I stared at the small, frail, magicless woman in front of me, trying desperately to think of some way to fix this problem. Wasn't there something I could do, or say, or offer her that would make amends and convince her not to kick us out?

But all I could think of was how useless some of the things were that our society valued most. As Miss Bister had pointed out, neither magic nor money would help. If I was going to repair the table, I'd need to find another way. Which would take time. And that meant I'd need to find somewhere else for us to sleep tonight. Because if the beast was going… I was too.

"Yes, Miss Bister," I said. "I understand."

She narrowed her eyes, slightly suspicious of my now-gracious defeat since I'd just spent the last half-hour trying to persuade her to accept various forms of reparation. But then she nodded, handed me a couple of paper bin bags, and left.

I slid one bag inside the other and stooped down to pick up the slobbery remains of Nova's mangled chew toy. When I finished, she came over to me and nudged my arm with her head. She let out a woofy whine.

Was she *sorry? She darn well better be!*

I gave her a scratch behind the ears.

"Now that you've sharpened your teeth on my former *dormater*'s furniture, are you ready to eat some real food for breakfast?"

Nova growled her assent and I made for the door, carrying the double-lined bag on my hip. Miss Bister may have given up on her table, but I wasn't going to. I was leaving tomorrow for a six-month outpost residency. If I could find lodgings elsewhere for tonight, I'd have half a year to figure out how to fix Miss Bister's table. With Luck's blessing, I'd be back here for my final year at St. Luck's.

I exited Megiddo, hoping it wasn't for the last time, with a bag of soggy sticks, a shamefaced barghest, and renewed determination.

Culpa est mea, mi amice. The fault is mine, my friend.

Within minutes I had bought two A.M. Grab Bags #9 and a pound of scrapple at Marduk's, our school's underground pub, and walked over to Abaddon, one of the dorms next to Megiddo. I waited outside, alternately taking bites of bannock and bacon and tossing bits of scrapple to Nova. The students who exited Abaddon were only momentarily startled by seeing us there. They were used to seeing a barghest on campus by now and, so long as we weren't blocking the fastest route to coffee, they were happy to ignore us.

A short while later, a puckish young man with cantaloupe-colored hair came out. He looked nearly as sleep-deprived as I felt (no doubt because he'd spent the night carousing with his girlfriend, *not* because he'd been studying), but he grinned when he saw me.

"How's Francesca?" I asked.

He cocked a brow at me. "She's fantastic, as you would know if you hung out with us more often."

"I do hang out with you. I spend almost every day with you, Fitz."

"Study group and classes don't count, Noon."

I handed him the other grab bag from Marduk's.

"For me? What's the occasion? Did you read the cases for Armed Conflict today? Oh, probably not, since you're leaving tomorrow." He spied the remaining scrapple. "Can I feed her the rest? Where's Ivy? Did *she* read the cases for Armed Conflict?"

When I wasn't off campus tracking down *rogares* or near-irretrievable objects, I spent most of my time with Ivy, my Hyrke roommate, and her cousin, Fitz. Ivy wouldn't take the news that I'd be moving out well. She wouldn't be mad at me. Or Miss Bister. She would be mad at Nova. Which was why I was hoping Fitz might keep an eye on her while I finished the last two things I had to do before I left.

"Never mind," Fitz said. "I'm sure she's ready. So why're you up so early? Did you bring me a bannock and bacon too?" He peeked in the bag. "Is there any—"

Fitz pulled a small black jar out of the bag. There was no label, but every St. Luck's student would recognize it. The product of a back-room partnership between the manager of Marduk's and an Angel who had epicurean skills but no desire to work with wine, it was experimental and expensive. Fitz's eyes grew round as a bolt of lightning flickered inside the jar. He hooted with delight.

"You bought me a jar of Thunderbolt?" He twisted the top off, his tone reverential. Despite the clear morning, ominous thunder rumbled in the sky.

"You could save it for after finals, you know."

"*Sollicitudo, solitudo.*"

"'Worrying about tomorrow is a waste of today?'"

He grinned, raised the drink toward me, and downed it in one gulp. Students who had been ignoring us were suddenly drawn to him as if he were a

supermassive   black   hole   emitting   gaze-grabbing
radiation.

I glanced over at Nova and then back at Fitz as I
handed him her half-eaten loaf of scrapple. His hair
stood on end, buzzing with electric bolts of blue and
white.

I was a law student, not a math whiz, but I was
pretty sure the day's equation would be:

*Nova and a pound of pork + Fitz and a can of
Thunderbolt = What could go wrong?*

After leaving Nova with Fitz, I caught a cab to Siujan
Street. "Finish trousseau" was the penultimate item on
my To Do List before I left. Ordinarily, trousseaus are
for brides, which I most certainly was not. But in my
country there are other less marital, more martial groups
of people who gather trousseaus before leaving one
place for another.

I'd spent the last four months amassing a pile of
hand-crafted clothing and armor at Sartabella's, a very
upscale tailor's shop in Barter Hill. My oftimes
glamoured Guardian Angel, Fara, had recommended that
I begin (and end) my preparations for this semester's
assignment by shopping at Sartabella's. She'd made it
sound as though it would be as simple as making an
appointment to have my pants hemmed. But Sartabella
didn't work like that. It wasn't that Fara had to
recommend Sartabella to *me*, it was that Fara had to
recommend me to *Sartabella*. And, at first, Sartabella
had wanted nothing to do with me.

A Maegester?

Sartabella only worked with Angels.

A female Maegester-in-Training?!

Even worse. How was she supposed to design clothing for a woman who was so dark and dreadful? So grim and ghastly?

I'd reminded Sartabella that the sign outside her shop said she designed armor as well as clothing. What did she imagine her other female clients did in the armor she made for them? Did she think they used their spells to knit baby bonnets and tea cozies?

Certainly not. She knew exactly what her Angel clients did in the armor she made for them. Because *becoming* Sartabella's client wasn't the real hurdle, *being* her client was.

Once Sartabella agreed to work with a client, the two engaged in extensive thaumaturgic psychoanalytic fittings. Sound flaky? It was anything but. Sartabella was a consummate professional. But there was no denying that her methods were odd and deeply uncomfortable at times. Starting with that first day. She'd demanded that I take off a piece of jewelry and give it to her.

Will I get it back? I'd asked.

If you have to ask, you shouldn't be here, she'd answered.

Reluctantly, I'd handed over the only piece of jewelry I wore – the silver bracelet that my former Guardian Angel, Raphael Sinclair, had given to me. Sartabella had reached for it and the moment her fingers made contact with it, she'd looked surprised and troubled – two of the many emotions we'd experienced frequently during her unusual fittings.

Today was my last appointment with Sartabella. As with previous fittings, I had no idea what item of clothing or armor Sartabella would design and make for me as a result. My trousseau was nearly complete and I had no idea what was in it. It was only Fara's complete confidence in Sartabella, and mine in Fara, that compelled me to see these sessions through to the end.

Like many small, central New Babylon shops, Sartabella's was located on the ground floor of an old row house. I'd never been upstairs, but I knew that Sartabella lived up top. The outside was fairly nondescript – four marble steps leading up to a door that was so pristinely white it had to be ensorcelled.

Fara was waiting for me on the steps, unglamoured, which was a rarity for her but something Sartabella insisted on. (No one but Sartabella was allowed to practice magic in her shop.) Fara was dressed as I was, in canvas pants and a cotton tunic. Her brownish-blonde hair was knotted in a simple bun and she wore no make-up. Her scars were ever-present, as was her menacing-looking feline companion, Virtus, but her expression was light. If she was feeling any discomfort as a result of dropping her usual glamour, it didn't show. I paid the driver, ascended the steps, and paused briefly at the top.

"Ready?" Fara asked, her voice involuntarily and permanently pitched between a squeak and a croak.

I nodded, not trusting my own voice. If *my* voice shook, what excuse could I give? I couldn't claim to be the victim of an old botched spell like Fara. I could only be the victim of old-fashioned nerves, which was something Maegesters-in-Training were trained not to show.

We entered a foyer that was cool and dark compared to the midsummer sun outside, and soon stepped into Sartabella's fitting room, a beautiful, contemporary, elegant space painted in crisp cucumber and mint, sparkling silver, and moon-bright white. Inside the room were two dupioni-covered barrel chairs, a fitting platform, and five floor-length mirrors in a semicircle surrounding the platform. Since Sartabella wasn't there yet, I gave the fitting platform a wide berth and took a seat in one of the chairs while Fara did the same. We faced each other silently.

She gave me a knowing look. "So... big day tomorrow, huh?"

I was tempted to make some quip like Fitz's *sollicitudo, solitudo* maxim, but I was too keyed up to pull it off without betraying my anxiety so I went on the offensive instead.

"Are *you* ready, Fara? Did you learn Precision, Amplification, and Cohesion?"

"We both know you don't need those anymore, Noon. Asking me to learn them is a crutch. And a diversion. You never want to talk about the spells that I've found that might actually help you – like Acceptance, Moving On, Rapprochement, Avoiding Rebounds..."

I narrowed my eyes. "Avoiding Rebounds? Where'd you find that one?"

"Rafe."

I grimaced and faced a fivefold reflection of myself looking guilty.

But what did I have to be guilty about?

Rafe had left me. Walked out on our relationship before it even started, so that he could train with the Ophanim. Luck knew when I'd see him again. And as for Ari, the person I'd been rebounding from, he'd done worse to me than just leaving before things got serious. We'd been super serious, and he'd trashed our relationship with a big, fat demon lie.

"Rafe also suggested I learn the spell Finish What You Start, but then he had the most extraordinary change of heart. Made me swear – actually swear an oath – not to find it and cast it over you. What gives, Noon? Are you ever going to tell me why Rafe gave you his bracelet? Did he just feel bad about leaving to go train with the Ophanim? Or was there a more... intimate reason he gave you something to remember him by?"

I resisted the urge to hiss *shhhhh* because it seemed so childish. And yet I felt childish. Hiding secrets when I hated them. Yes, I'd kissed Rafe. Yes, he'd claimed he was in love with me. And, yes, I'd felt something for him too. But, under the circumstances, it was best not to dwell on what.

"Noon, I'm a witness to the biggest secret you've had since you tried to hide your magic – that your new employer, Lord Aristos, is really your old boyfriend, Ari Carmine. I don't think confirming my suspicion that you started something with Rafe – your ex-Guardian Angel – that he's afraid you'll finish is that big a deal."

Then I did hiss *shhhhh* and I didn't care how childish I sounded.

"The only spell I need, Fara, is a cloaking spell to hide my emotions. Because I don't want Ari"—I cleared my throat—"ahem, *Lord Aristos*, to feel them. Ever. And I don't want to talk about any of this"—I made a swishing motion with my hand—"ever again."

"You don't want to talk about Sartabella's ever again?" Fara said. She looked confused, but I couldn't be sure. Even without a glamour Fara's true expressions could be hard to read.

"No. I don't want to talk about Ari—"

"—well, that's going to be hard since you're going to be working for him starting tomorrow—"

"Or Rafe," I said through clenched teeth. Fara was being intentionally obtuse. My life was complicated, but she knew all of the major players and most of what had happened among us. "As a matter of fact, I do need you to find another spell." She perked up.

"The spell Keep Quiet. And then cast it over yourself."

She harrumphed ("as if *any* Angel would *ever* cast a spell like that over themselves") while I slumped in my seat, hoping Sartabella wouldn't be as late as she normally was. *Was it just me?* I wondered. *Because I wasn't an Angel? Or was Sartabella simply late for everything?* I sighed and stared morosely at the ceiling, resisting the surprisingly strong urge to spin in my chair.

When Sartabella entered the fitting room ten minutes later, I was a little more ratcheted up than usual. I wasn't worried about my magic getting away from me. That never happened anymore. And I wasn't worried that Sartabella might feel my jitters because she was an Angel and couldn't. No, I was worried about what today's fitting might reveal.

The aging seamstress clapped her hands together and motioned toward the fitting platform. "Up, *up*, Ms. Onyx, neither of us has all day. Last fittings usually only require something easy like a handkerchief or scarf, but every now and then, the fitting platform will call upon me to make a wig or a watch or something equally complicated."

She strode over to me, shooing me toward the mirrors, and took the seat that I vacated. As soon as I stepped onto the platform, the room transformed itself. The ceiling disappeared and was replaced with open sky. The smooth green walls became the crumbling ruins of an old stone keep. The floor was suddenly strewn with dirt, leaves, rocks, and rubble. And Sartabella's mirrors instantly morphed into a giant, three-story throne made from the bony skeleton of some ancient sea colossus. Its massive ribs encircled the throne's seat and its gargantuan skull hung over its top, jaw open, as if poised to swallow whoever stood before it.

Sartabella inhaled sharply and started coughing. Remembering previous fittings, I started to go to her but she held out her hand to stop me before I left the platform. "Always, *always* such interesting settings for your fittings, Ms. Onyx. Where are we?"

I glanced over at Fara, who would also recognize this place. Fara hadn't been with me for every fitting, but she'd come to a lot of them. I didn't know if she did it because she wanted to know more about the ward she'd be protecting this semester or if she knew that Sartabella's sessions were often harrowing and wanted to lend me her support. Maybe both. In any case, it was she who answered.

"The old keep at Stone Pointe in the Shallows, where Noon's first field assignment was."

"Were you her Guardian then?"

"No. Raphael Sinclair was."

"Ah," Sartabella said and then fell silent. I'd never been able to work out whether Sartabella knew Rafe beyond what I'd told her during my fittings. I glanced up, wary about standing under so many rows of razor-sharp teeth even if they were an illusion. Of course, my memory of what had happened in the old Stone Pointe keep contributed mightily to my sense of unease. Though she couldn't sense my state of mind with her magic, Sartabella was highly intuitive when it came to reading her clients' mental states. Instantly, she knew this place felt toxic to me and she demanded to know what had happened. As with previous fittings, I kept my answer short and basically told her *I had a run-in with a drakon here.*

I don't know how I managed to keep a straight face. "Run-in" didn't even begin to describe the horror I'd felt when I saw Ari involuntarily shift into a drakon right in front of me – or the devastation I'd felt when I realized that he'd been lying to me for months about who and what he was – or the fury I'd felt when I realized that he might have gone on lying to me *forever* if Rafe hadn't unintentionally revealed him to be a demon in our midst.

"Oops, my bad" didn't cut it when your sin was being a demon and you didn't tell your girlfriend about it.

On the fitting platform, I clenched my fists and banked my fire.

Sartabella, who missed nothing, frowned.

"Did the drakon try to kill you?"

"No." My emotional state caused me to answer more forcefully than I might have otherwise. But the word was no less truthful for its emphatic delivery. Ari had saved my life, not tried to end it.

"Did you try to kill it?"

"No!"

"But encountering it was traumatic for you."

"Wouldn't encountering a drakon be traumatic for anyone?"

"But for *you*, Ms. Onyx? I don't understand why this particular demon seemed so dangerous…"

"Well, at the time, I hadn't done all of the things I've done now."

"Naturally," Sartabella agreed wryly. She arched her brows and cocked her head, waiting for more of an explanation.

"Encountering the drakon was a surprise," I finally said, unable to even look at Fara now.

"Undoubtedly."

"And the… ah… well, the drakon killed another demon while we were there."

"And how did that come about?"

"He… bit the other demon's head off."

"Did he… eat the other demon?"

"No!" Another emphatic negative. I was becoming just the least little bit unhinged. These fittings often made me feel that way, but this one was worse than the others. Maybe Sartabella was practicing more magic on me than she'd declared, which would be highly illegal.

But just when I thought the tension couldn't get any higher, it crested and troughed.

"What happened after that?" Sartabella asked.

"He flew off."

"Not many demons fly."

I shrugged.

"Have you ever flown?"

"How could I have? *I'm* not a demon who can shift into a winged form."

"But you told me during another fitting that you rode a barghest shaped from waning magic."

"So?"

"I thought perhaps… after your encounter with the drakon… you might have tried it."

"Tried what?"

"Flying," she said, exasperated. "By riding a drakon shaped out of waning magic," she said, as if that sort of thing was attempted every day.

I stared at her. The idea had never even occurred to me.

"Why would I want to do that?"

"Have you ever wanted to do half the things you've told me you've done?"

I opened my mouth, but couldn't think of a thing to say. But Sartabella, being an Angel, was never at a loss for words.

"I think I know what your last item needs to be."

2

HELLFIRE AND DAMNATION

Halja was populated mostly with Hyrkes. But there were a significant number of us with magic, which came in three types: waning, waxing, or faith. Waning and waxing magic users were the descendants of Lucifer's army, which made us all sound like bloodthirsty banshees.

And some of us were. Just as some of those who practiced faith magic (or no magic) were. As I reminded myself nearly every day, my ancestors may have been violent, barbaric people, but that didn't mean I needed to be—or at least, not all of the time.

Waning magic users were usually men – Host sons who were sent to prestigious demon law schools like St. Luck's where they were trained as Maegesters. Waxing magic users, on the other hand, were usually women – Host daughters who were sent south to apprentice with a Mederi tribe. Mederies weren't violent or barbaric. And they definitely weren't bloodthirsty. No, they used Luck's chthonic forces to heal and grow.

So why had I, a Host daughter, been born with waning magic?

They say "be careful what you wish for" but maybe

it should be "be careful who you pray to." Twenty-two years ago, during a difficult pregnancy, my mother had prayed to the Angels' god, Mica, to save my twin brother and me. Of course, being Host, she'd pleaded to Luck too.

Maybe the Lost Lords fought over us in the womb. Maybe only one of them heard my mother's appeal, but was piqued that she'd tried to play both sides.

Who knows what really happened?

The only thing I knew for sure is that I didn't obsess about it the way I used to. Life was short, especially for Haljan Maegesters, and I wasn't going to waste mine worrying about things that had happened before I was born.

So what *was* I going to worry about?

My next assignment.

All second-year Maegesters-in-Training were required to do a six-month externship their fourth semester with a potential future employer. Most Maegesters secured positions with the Demon Council when they graduated, but some joined small practices that catered to minor demons with minor matters, while others found employment by working directly for a patron as their *consigliere*. Consigs were legal advisors, of course, but we were also a bit more. Oh, we weren't bodyguards or assassins... exactly. The martial aspects of the job were to ensure our *own* safety and impartiality. In theory, we represented the interests of *both* Council and patron, advising the patron on follower affairs, interactions with other *regulares*, tithes, sacrifices, and other commercial and municipal matters in accordance with Council policy.

Obviously, it was a job where conflicts of interest could arise.

Even more so in my case, since my externship employer happened to be my ex-boyfriend.

Who'd lied to me about being a demon (as hereinbefore mentioned) and who possibly (okay, probably) still had feelings for me. But there was no getting out of it. I'd agreed to go.

So how did I deal with all these complications?

By concentrating on:

My. Next. Assignment.

Ahem.

Rockthorn Gorge. That's where I was headed tomorrow. The bustling mountain town where Ari now resided as patron. The bustling mountain town where so many other demons lived, it was often called "a demonic anthill." Which was why the very last item on my To Do List before I left should have been "Get a good night's sleep" but was actually "Meet with faculty advisor." He'd left a note in my mailbox instructing me and my Guardian to be at Bone Hill in Myriostos, a tiny, cramped slum in New Babylon's southeast sector, by sundown.

After a twenty-minute cab ride from St. Luck's, a fifteen-minute rickshaw ride through the narrow streets of Ragland, and then an even longer walk through the inaptly named Paradise, we finally saw the gate to Myriostos – although "gate" was probably too grand a term for the rickety assortment of rusting rods that had been welded together at the beginning of two parallel lines of pilings rising up from the trash-strewn ground in front of us. Looking south along this unusual main street toward the Lethe, I realized that Paradise had not, perhaps, been inaptly named after all. Because anything,

compared to Myriostos, would have qualified as
Paradise.

Centuries ago this area had been outside city limits.
In fact, it hadn't even been land at all. It had been part of
the river and it was where New Babylon's waste had
been dumped – downstream and out of sight.
Apparently, a few hundred years had made solid, if not
stable, ground out of rubbish and rubble. I opened the
gate and stepped from Paradise into Myriostos.

To our left and right were an incalculable number
of stacked shacks and spliced lean-tos. My second
semester I'd traveled to a poor fishing community on the
eastern Lethe, so I'd seen Haljan poverty before, but
never anything like this. The Shallows had been full of
mud and rust and huts that were drafty and leaked. That
outpost had been dirty, even smelly at times, with a
distressingly unpredictable food supply. Its settlers had
battled disease and other medical emergencies with no
Mederi. But I realized, as I walked deeper and deeper
into Myriostos, how lucky they were compared to these
people. The Shallows settlers had land and lots of it.
They had fresh air and flowing water. They had room for
their children to run. They didn't have to light fires in
their highly combustible homes to cook their food.
Looking around, I guessed that, *rogares* or no, any one
of these New Babylonians would gladly have traded
places with any one of those Shallows settlers.

It seemed impossible, but the farther we walked, the
higher and more numerous the shanties on either side of
us were piled. I craned my neck, scanning the irregular
skyline. By evening it was no more than a thin, jagged
line of indigo crisscrossed by countless black wires.

Here and there, faces stared back at us – children
playing on stairs, women watching from windows, men
standing in doorways. Every now and then the unusual

quiet would be broken by a bang, a cry, or a shout. But there were no screams. The few people who passed us look more ragged than dangerous. As hungry and dirty as the settlers from the Shallows had been, but more exhausted. Compared to the fierce, resilient fishermen and their families, these "middensteaders" seemed listless and without hope.

Wolfram had told me that Bone Hill was a small mound located in the approximate center of the slum where its sinners were punished or executed. I'd just spotted a tottering pillory near its top when a trio of rough-looking men started walking toward us. They made me nervous. Not because I was worried they'd harm us, but because I didn't know what their intentions were. Fara and I were clearly outsiders – two women – without obvious weapons, wearing what looked like expensive clothing (Fara's mantle was an illusion, but how were they to know?). The last thing I wanted to do was shape a weapon here. It would be like striking a match in a neighborhood made of tissue paper.

Where was Wolfram?

Although they were roughly the same brawny size, it was easy enough to tell the men apart. One had a diagonal scar running from his right eyebrow to his left cheek, another had a long, braided beard, and the third was carrying an ax. The ax-wielder's scowl was the most menacing, but I kept my face impassive as he approached.

"Who are you?"

"Nouiomo Onyx. I'm supposed to meet Ralla Wolfram here at sundown."

The man's scowl relaxed into a frown, but then he looked up toward the sky and his expression became... worried, which seemed strange. I didn't look *that* intimidating. Maybe they recognized my last name...?

Even in Myriostos, residents were bound to have heard of Karanos Onyx, Executive to the Demon Council.

"Wolfram's not here."

I clenched my jaw, momentarily forgetting about the burly trio. My faculty advisor had been notoriously hard to track down this semester. In fact, I'd only ever met him one other time. He was NEVER around. And now he'd stood me up. Again.

In front of us, the men were eyeing the sky.

What were they afraid of?

Due to our earlier discussion at Sartabella's, my thoughts gravitated toward those few demon species in Halja that fly – the biggest of which was a drakon.

But here?

Ari was in Rockthorn Gorge, and drakons were nearly as rare as women with waning magic.

Before I could puzzle it out, the black wires above us started buzzing and crackling. The narrow slit of violet sky sizzled and the entire street flickered as the neighborhood's power turned on. Glow lights flashed then dimmed, then brightened again. Finally, the wall of buildings on either side of us flared with electric light. The air seemed to hum and sparks raced across the sky-top wires. They reminded me of fireflies – deadly fireflies capable of starting a real fire.

The men's gazes were also drawn to the sparks, following them as if hypnotized. *They were afraid of fire, alright, but not the kind that drakons bring.*

A shout in the distance reminded us that, even in Halja, one simple, charged particle can wreak just as much havoc as a demon.

The men started running and we followed. I felt a few defensive spells slip into place as we entered a building. Even with electric power, the light inside was poor and we lost the men almost immediately. Myriostos' tenements were worse than a labyrinth. The only things we saw inside the doorway were trash, graffiti, two sets of stairs, and nearly a dozen doors.

Another scream told us which direction to head – to our left, up the nearest set of stairs, round a corner, up another flight, through an open doorway, and out onto a rooftop. Then, a flash of movement. It was the men from the street.

"Cast Maiden's Thread over them!" I yelled to Fara. It was somewhat risky. Unless a crime was being committed, Angels weren't supposed to cast spells over a target absent their permission, but Fara didn't hesitate. Instantly, a gossamer-thin thread of light showed us which direction they'd gone.

More twists, turns, skidding on dusty surfaces... I couldn't help wondering if we were being led somewhere for some nefarious purpose. But as we raced across high, narrow boards, leapt from rooftops, and ran between spaces of dim light and darkness, two constants remained: the screams got louder and the light grew brighter.

By the time we arrived at the source of the fire, one entire room was engulfed in flames. Billowing clouds of soot puffed out. Every day I wielded precisely shaped weapons forged from fire... which were nothing like this. *This* was chaos. The fire in front of me seemed like a living monster, made as much from black smoke as orange-red flames.

Scores of people were on the rooftop with us. Some were throwing small buckets of water on the fire. Others were trying to drag a large hose up another set of stairs. Still others were nursing burns – theirs or others'. Two of the men we'd followed were among the crowd, but the glowing thread attached to the third—Fara's casting—led directly into the blazing inferno.

I ran into the flames, leeching oxygen from the air as I went. But the fire, fat on cardboard, plywood, reeds, and rushes, continued to rage. I pleaded to Luck that the whole block wouldn't be blown to kingdom come in a dust explosion.

Fara followed me in. I realized, later, how brave she'd been. Although her scars were due to a botched spell, they were the remnants of burns. It was hard enough for me to walk into a burning building. I can't imagine what it must have been like for her.

The heat inside was so oppressive it was difficult to process anything else. It felt like we'd walked into a kiln. I'd battled many opponents by now – each of them capable of generating heat, shaping fiery weapons, and throwing blasts of pure kinetic energy, but nothing I'd experienced either in the field or the sparring ring had prepared me for this. It felt like I was being burned at the stake, but I forced myself to concentrate on the search.

Where was the ax-wielding man? Was anyone else in here?

Fara and I slowed to a walk. *The floor could give way at any minute*, I thought. I could leech oxygen, but I couldn't fix broken bones. I also couldn't cool things that were already hot. Which meant that even though I was making good headway putting the fire out, the air was still singeing my lungs.

Beside me, Fara was casting something chilly and preternaturally badass. Without her spell casting, we'd surely have succumbed to the heat, flames, and fumes.

We found the ax-wielder in the next room, collapsed on the floor next to a woman and her child. Fara cast the rudimentary spell Carry over the man and woman and we slung them over our shoulders. I picked up the child and we made it out of the burning portion of the building exactly 2.5 seconds before it exploded.

Between our magic and the water, we were able to extinguish the fire. Fara healed those who had suffered burns and smoke inhalation and, miraculously, everyone survived. After making sure the newly homeless had places to shelter and sleep, we left.

After returning from Myriostos, we were sooty, sweaty, and exhausted. Fara headed back to the Joshua School to feed Virtus and I went to Marduk's to meet Fitz and collect Nova. I expected to see Ivy there too, so I girded myself for a tearful discussion about how I was no longer welcome at Megiddo.

There had to be some way I could repair my ex-dormater's table... make it what it once was?

But instead of Ivy or Fitz, I ran into Wolfram, of all people, who was sitting alone in a booth with a messenger bag and five empty beer bottles for company. He waved me over, motioned for me to sit, and hailed a waiter. He ordered another beer and I asked for bangers and mash with water.

"Water?" Wolfram said, pointing to the sign above the door.

> *Grapes are sweet*
> *Apples are neat*
> *But it's Barley and Wheat*
> *That can't be beat!*

"Come on, Onyx, it's my treat," and then he guffawed at his rhyme adding, "After all, we may never meet... again."

I groaned and rolled my eyes. "Like you care."

He shrugged and told the waiter, "Bring her a beer too. If she doesn't drink it, I will."

I leaned back in the booth and concentrated on Wolfram rather than what was happening around us. After all, I'd eaten in Marduk's hundreds of times whereas I'd seen my truant faculty advisor only once before now. His temples were more gray than I remembered, as was the scruff on his cheeks, but his stare was as sharp as his signature, which was mildly surprising since he'd drank almost an entire six-pack of beer already.

"Where were you?" I demanded, ticked off that he'd stood me up.

"Leaborough."

Had I misunderstood him earlier? About where to meet? Leaborough, a.k.a. Fleaborough, was another New Babylon slum. "I thought you said to meet you in Myriostos."

"I said you needed to be in Myriostos." He motioned to my singed clothes. "You obviously made it in time."

"In time for what?"

"To put out the fire," he said with exaggerated exasperation.

"You knew there was going to be a fire in Myriostos?"

He nodded. "There's a fire there almost every night. But I needed to be in Leaborough."

"Why?"

"Someone there came down with smallpox and I needed to take a Mederi in." He pointed to me with his beer bottle. "You can't let disease fester in a place like that. One infected person will soon be twenty."

"But you're a Maegester... a St. Luck's professor..."

"So?"

"Don't neighborhoods like Leaborough or Myriostos have patrons who look after their residents?" I was almost certain they did, even if I couldn't remember who they were. My former Manipulation professor, Quintus Rochester, would have been furious at my lack of recall. The one thing I did remember, though? Slum patrons were often called *rattenkönigs*, an old world term that meant "rat kings."

Wolfram murmured something snarky under his breath. Something about being raised in a castle and then moving to an ivory tower... I gathered he was referring to me and I stiffened. But before I could respond, he slapped his hand down on the table and yelled, "Did you *see* any sign of a patron's presence in Myriostos tonight, Ms. Onyx? No! Why? Because Myriostos' patron doesn't give a damn." And then he laughed.

"Why are you laughing? None of it is funny."

"No, of course not. But if you don't keep a sense of humor about Halja you'll quickly become maudlin, my dear, and then you'll be of no use to anyone. Do New Babylon's poor have patrons? Certainly, they plead and give sacrifices, such as they can, to someone, but the only practical help they'll ever get will come from the Council, not their patron. The Council *does* give a damn – or rather *a* dam. Specifically, a hydroelectric dam."

Comprehension dawned. My offer letter had mentioned a hydroelectric dam. At the time, I'd thought the idea ludicrous for at least a dozen reasons. Waning magic and machines didn't mix... Rockthorn Gorge was over a hundred miles away... it was a place of historic unrest... there had to be better, more direct ways to help Halja's magicless masses...

"Is that why you sent me to Myriostos tonight?" I asked. "To see how the Council's—Nonsensical? Absurd? I cleared my throat—"*ambitious* dam project will benefit New Babylon's less fortunate?"

He nodded. "The Council wants to replace Myriostos' current, slipshod, shite-built electric grid with a new one. The new grid's electricity would be supplied by the New Babylon power plant, *not* that rattletrap collection of basement generators the slum lord provides."

Huh. So Wolfram wasn't a total asshat. He hadn't been MIA this semester because he'd been skulking about in bars, he'd been MIA because he'd been battling fire, disease, and deadbeat patrons in neighborhoods no one else wanted to think about, let alone visit.

He laughed again. "You should see your face. It's like I told you Lucifer was a saint. You know the name of your school is an oxymoron, right?" and then he laughed even harder. Wolfram's sense of humor seemed dangerously close to fatally unhinged. Half of me wanted to scoot farther away in case Luck chose to strike him down, but my other half raised my glass to him.

"Finally, a St. Luck's professor who isn't going to lecture me on the benefits of beadledom or the merits of fiery martial arts."

"Wrong," Wolfram said. "Paper pushing and sword slinging are a Maegester's bread and butter. Don't ever forget that. But some of us can do more. *You* might be capable of doing more, Ms. Onyx."

"Like building a dam?" I said with more than a touch of skepticism. It wasn't that I didn't want to help the people of Myriostos – I did! It was just that I wasn't sure if building a dam in Rockthorn Gorge was the right way to go about it. "Don't 'the wise build bridges and the foolish build dams'?"

Wolfram stared at me for a moment, his signature fizzing like effervescent water. Then he narrowed his eyes and smiled. "Isn't your Guardian Angel supposed to be the one who quotes the Book of Joshua?"

I shrugged. Wolfram's stare lingered longer than it needed to, but eventually his amused look turned deadly serious.

"The dam project in Rockthorn Gorge might seem, at first blush, to be a folly, but I can assure you, dear acolyte, that it is not. Its completion is, quite frankly, the single most important goal of your residency. The Council wants it, the patron and people of Rockthorn Gorge want it, but the people of Myriostos *need* it."

3

DEMONS AND DISASTERS

My quote about bridges and dams wasn't just a proverb from the Book. It was also a specific reference to the hydroelectric dam project up in Rockthorn Gorge.

At one time, Rockthorn Gorge had rivaled New Babylon in terms of size, but the fractious nature of its inhabitants and its mountainous location prevented the exponential growth that had led to New Babylon becoming Halja's center of government and commerce. Nevertheless, the town was populous by outpost standards. Nearly seven thousand Hyrkes, forty-plus demons, and a handful of Angels lived there. They had a hospital, winery, bank, a half-dozen inns, and their own post office. Mail was carried in and out three times a week on the Midland Express, the single rail line to and from the town.

Of course, saying the Midland Express was a rail "line" was like calling a bumblebee's flight path "straight." The way north was a tortuous route climbing 6,382 feet in 139 miles. Most of it was narrow-gauge, steep-grade rails, but there were a few places where passengers had to disembark and board funiculars, which were specially designed rope-and-pulley cars. I'd never been, but Ivy (who'd been nearly everywhere) told me to "hold on to my hat." I didn't wear hats any more than I'd been north of Northbrook, but I caught her meaning. The last hair-raising portion of the trip occurred when the train crossed a soaring viaduct built across an enormous tiered waterfall.

Its name?

The Memento Mori.

"So if everyone wants or needs the dam, why has the project been so plagued with problems? My offer letter mentioned *rogare* attacks and a workforce mutiny. Are the work conditions there that bad?" I had a hard time believing Ari would allow Hyrke masons or miners to be attacked or abused if there was any way to prevent it.

"It's not really problems so much as problem – one very big one," Wolfram said. "The attacks weren't carried out by random *rogares* in an unplanned manner. They were premeditated attacks carried out by one *rogare* in particular."

"Who?"

"Displodo."

I grunted. "A hackneyed nom de guerre if ever I heard one."

Wolfram's mouth quirked but instead of laughing, he launched into lecture mode.

"Displodo is the name of a second century, northern folk hero. But he's not a 'steal from the rich and give to the poor' kind of hero. He's more of a 'target the town's infrastructure and blow it to bits' kind of 'hero.'"

"Then please tell me part of my assignment is finding him," I said. "At least tracking down *rogares* and dealing with them is one of the things I've been trained for. Building dams isn't."

At least that got a laugh. "It is, but it won't be easy. Council Maegesters have been catching and killing 'Displodo' since the apocalypse. The name is more of a rallying cry than a sobriquet. It's an identity that has been assumed throughout the years by multiple people to try to get what they want."

"Which is?"

"Freedom."

"From what? Rockthorn Gorge is an outpost. It's hard to think of somewhere freer than that."

"Displodo and his disciples want complete independence from New Babylon."

Ah, of course they did. What was that saying? One man's terrorist was another man's freedom fighter? "They want to be free of the yoke of the Council, don't they?"

Wolfram raised an eyebrow. "Let it never be said that you're unable to understand an opponent's perspective, Ms. Onyx. 'Free of the yoke of the Council'? Next, you'll be drawing propaganda cartoons for Displodo and his merry band of murderous separatists."

I scoffed. "No, I won't, and you know it."

The fact is, the Council's control often chafed me. But I also understood its purpose and intent. The Demon Council existed, at least in theory, to protect Halja's peace. When I made the decision to train as a Maegester, I made the decision to work under its authority, despite its shortcomings. Maybe that made me a hypocrite to some. But I wasn't one to throw out embers with cinders.

"Wait—what cartoons?"

"For the past year, Displodo has exclusively

targeted the Memento Mori dam project. He's blown it up three times, killing a total of seventy-eight Hyrkes and three *regulare* demons, including the former patron. Each time, he's left behind a cartoon – a drawing of himself amongst the wreckage. It's basically his way of signing his work."

Ugh. I made a face – the demons who were dispassionate were the worst – and was just about to ask Wolfram if he had copies of the cartoons when Fitz and Ivy walked in. I knew immediately from their mutual expressions of shock, sadness, and reluctance that they'd come to deliver bad news. No, horrible news. News I wouldn't want to hear.

I jumped up and accidentally banged the table. A few of Wolfram's empty bottles crashed to the floor. The sound of shattering glass was not uncommon at Marduk's, but the room went silent when they saw me rushing toward my Hyrke friends.

"Fitz, where's Nova?"

He looked confused. "Outside. With Fara and Virtus."

Oh, no. "Did Nova and Virtus get in another fight?"

"No," Ivy said, stepping in. "Nova's fine. So is Virtus. And Fara. It's…" She paused, looked around the room, and then lowered her voice so that only I could hear. "There was an explosion in Rockthorn Gorge this morning."

Suddenly, I felt unsteady on my feet. As if I were on the dock of a ship.

"The new patron?"

"Among the missing."

The moment felt surreal. What if the last time I saw Ari was the last time I would see him again *ever*?

"How do you know?"

"A courier from your father's office delivered this while you were in Myriostos." Ivy handed me a single sheet of paper with typewritten words on it.

DEMON COUNCIL
OFFICE OF THE EXECUTIVE

FOR IMMEDIATE DELIVERY
   Nouiomo Onyx
   New Babylon, Halja
   St. Lucifer's Law School
   Megiddo, Room 112

Regret to advise you, the Memento Mori viaduct and partially constructed dam in Rockthorn Gorge was destroyed again this morning after an explosion of unknown origin.

12+ laborers and tradesmen dead. Many others injured. Some still missing, including patron, who was last seen at the construction site.

Catch next train north and help stabilize situation. Further particulars and assignment modifications to follow.

We walked back to the booth where I'd been sitting with Wolfram and I showed him the message. His expression turned furious and his signature fiery. His fingers melted holes in the bottle he was holding, and beer leaked out onto the table. He slammed the bottle down, burned the remaining beer off his hand, and reached into his messenger bag. He withdrew a stack of flat leather pouches tied together with twine.

"Your dossier," he said, tossing it to me. His face gentled for a moment and he looked genuinely regretful. "I'm sorry I didn't make more time for you over the last few months"—his face hardened again—"but then again, I doubt it would have helped you. You know why I agreed to serve as your faculty advisor?"

I shook my head.

"Because you don't need one."

He yelled for the waiter then and told them to pack my food to go. It was by no means fortuitous, but Luck had arranged it so that Nova and I would have a bed tonight after all.

We'd be sleeping on the train.

I never drank the beer that Wolfram ordered me, but my memory of that night is hazy. Still, a few sensory impressions loom disproportionately large in my mind compared to their relevance, like the acrid smell of the steam locomotive's coal smoke, the cardboard taste of my mashed potatoes, and the somber sight of Fara's glamoured outfit – a midnight blue tabard with a white star emblazoned on the back.

When worn this way, the star was referred to as a mourning star rather than the Morning Star. It was an extraordinary show of solidarity for an Angel who still quoted the Book of Joshua from time to time, and, in fact, when I commented on it, she murmured, "'Lay down your arms and mourn with me.' Joshua, one, two." I nodded, my throat too tight to respond with words, and slipped past her into a railcar trailed by our bags and my trousseau chest, which she'd helpfully cast a simple levitation spell over.

Nova and Virtus took up positions opposite one another and promptly went to sleep. Fara read, first Joshua, then her spell book, and then *Rockthorn Gorge: Burial Site of Servius Rockthorn, Lucifer's Northern Warlord*. Meanwhile, I sat watching sunset-hued buildings turn to shadowy hills and dark valleys until, finally, my window became a rectangle of pure blackness I could no longer face. Miles and hours passed, the train swayed, and the elevation rose while thoughts of demons and disasters kept me from sleeping.

If Ari was missing (I refused to think about a worse alternative), which demon might be leading the search and rescue? According to the most recent volume of the *Demon Register*, there were only three demons in the area worth listing: the late Lord Potomus, past patron of the gorge; Lord Acheron, patron of his eponymous river; and Cliodna, the Patron Demon of Waves and Waterbirds.

Funny that the register only mentioned three demons out of forty. My guess was the others weren't patrons and thus the publisher hadn't thought them worthy of mentioning. But then I realized I didn't have to wonder who some of the others might be. Wolfram's dossier would have more information on the town's *regulare* demons.

A half-hour later, I found what I was looking for.

ROCKTHORN GORGE

DEMONS OF INTEREST

Aristos: Drakon. Demon Lord of Rockthorn Gorge. Administrative chambers and living quarters are in the Rotunda. Elected recently in an uncontested election after the last patron was killed.

Cliodna: Rara   avis   (swan).
Patron   Demon   of   Waves   and
Waterbirds. Main devotion site is
a   gilded,   mountaintop   sanctuary
for birds and artisans. The town's
miners   are   also   under   her
auspices.   Member   of   Aristos'
camarilla.

Yannu: Bunyip. Captain of the
Guard. Trains and supervises the
town's regulare retainers. Bunks
with the rank and file in Tower
#1. Member of Aristos' camarilla.

Acheron: Magnus stilio (giant
lizard). Patron of the Acheron
River. Overlord of the North.
Whereabouts unknown.

*Other   demons   in   the   patron's
camarilla*: Malphia, Eidya, Runnos,
Bastian.

Ari had a camarilla? Huh. Camarillas were an
antediluvian throwback. They were a group of courtiers
or *regulare* demon advisors. Suddenly, my mind was full
of questions. As *consigliere*, would I be a part of the
camarilla? Or did the Lord of the Gorge's consig advise
independently? Which would be more adversarial? To
compete for Ari's ear within the group or without?

Did I even have to compete for his attention?

Did I want his undivided attention?

What would these demons of interest think of my
past relationship with him if they found out about it?
Had he already told them? If so, which part of our past
relationship had he emphasized? *Amore*, *more*, *ore*, or
re? Would the members of his camarilla view me as a
consigliere, a fellow favorite... or worse – an ex-
favorite?

And then another thought occurred to me.

What if one of them was Displodo?

Rather frantically I started digging through the dossier's contents for more information on Ari's camarilla, but the only other item of immediate interest I found was a silver vial on a silver chain. It had been tucked into one of the leather pouches. I knew what it was – a dose of waerwater.

I'd used waerwater during my trip to the Shallows. Basically, it was a nearly-always-fatal dose of demon poison. Any *rogare* accused of a sin punishable by death had the right to request a trial by waerwater. If the demon lived, they were deemed pardoned by Luck. I had issues with the practice, but fastened the chain around my neck nonetheless. If I found Displodo, I'd be happy to offer him a trial by waerwater. And if he refused or survived – I'd kill him myself.

An hour after midnight we made the first switch from steep-grade railcar to funicular. Everything around us was dark, which meant I had no visual frame of reference, and my sense of disorientation increased with our elevation.

The moment we arrived in Rockthorn Gorge I could feel him. His signature was faint but unmistakable and I turned toward him as if I were a compass needle and he was magnetic north. Magnets usually made me think of metal and coldness, but Ari's signature was anything but. He'd always felt like the sun to me. Warm, bright, energizing... intoxicating. Something I was instinctively drawn to. And now his pull was as irrefutable as gravity.

I picked my way through the broken dam's destruction, fearing I'd find him trapped under a mountain of debris, but he was on his feet and rushing toward me. I stepped toward him, my magic swirling around me like a fiery vortex. Even before we neared each other, my signature erupted and its bubbly, billowy edges raced to meet his. Without thinking, I let our magic merge and that feeling of comfortable warmth and buzzy intoxication went supernova.

Ari's mulberry-colored eyes were just as deep and dark and undeniably hypnotic as I remembered. His hair was long and unruly, its mahogany color rich and slightly glowing, like banked coals. We spoke at the same time.

"I thought you weren't coming until tonight."

"They said you were missing."

His tone was incredulous and reverent, as though I was a comet who'd appeared in the sky sooner than expected, while mine was full of awe... and not a little restraint. We stared at each other, our signatures a melded, viscous, steamy mix of unshed emotion.

Who knows what might have happened next? I like to think I would have gained control of myself and my emotions, but possibly not. My reactions to Ari had never been one hundred percent manageable. He always made me feel as if I teetered on the brink of something boundless. Something that would consume me so completely that there would be nothing left of me, *only* it.

Love? No, we'd fallen into that abyss long ago.

Madness? Maybe.

In any case, thank Luck, the lurching of the train brought me back from the brink.

4

MEMENTO MORI

Despite my disorientation, or perhaps due to it, I'd fallen asleep. I shook off the remnants of my dream as the railcar slowed to a stop. Across from me, Fara stood and peered out of the railcar window. I could see nothing but blackness.

"Another funicular?" Fara murmured. "Or something else?"

"I don't know," I answered softly, also rising. I snapped quietly at Nova to stop her growling as Fara whispered the words to Nocturne, a spell that increased night vision, hearing, and smell; and Camouflage, a spell that lowered body temperature and shielded its target from echolocation. My right hand flexed, an instinctive precursor to shaping a weapon.

A few seconds later, the railcar door slid open with a bang. The conductor stood at the entrance holding a cross-bow, but it was pointed at the ground, not us.

Was I paranoid?

You bet I was. MITs who weren't often didn't graduate. There might be no reason to suspect an attack, but it made me more than a little edgy to be this far into Halja's hinterlands with no witnesses to our potential fate but the lone conductor of a steam locomotive and its single railcar.

"This is as far as I can take you," he said. "The gorge is less than a few miles from here. The viaduct was destroyed, but there's a set of stairs that leads down to the river. If you want to wait until morning..." His voice trailed off when I shook my head and jumped out, followed by Fara, Nova, Virtus, our bags, and my trousseau chest. I squinted and Nocturne kicked in, allowing me to see a set of rail tracks, the side of a forested mountain, and a foggy night sky. The air felt chilly and damp, but I'd hiked in worse and wanted to keep moving. If this was as far as the train could take us, we likely had an hour of walking to go before we reached the gorge.

"Luck be with you then," the conductor said. "I'll be up again once the viaduct is repaired. Oh, and watch out," he said, motioning behind us. "They don't call them hidebehinds for nothing."

Hidebehinds were a type of northern *rogare*. As their name suggested, they hid behind their prey. Like a few other demons I'd encountered (most notably, hellcnights), hidebehinds had specially adapted signatures. I'd only be able to sense one if I was facing it. So, obviously, the conductor's words caused a mild burst of alarm. I spun around, shaping a fiery sword.

But there was nothing behind me.

I swallowed my groan, resheathed my sword (as beautifully simple for me now as closing my hand), and relaxed my signature.

The railroad tracks stretched in front of us, gently curving right around an enormous mountain. On the left, the land dropped sharply. Except for the track, everything was covered in vegetation. No doubt a Mederi could have told us what all of the various species of plants and trees were, but to me, it just looked like greenish-black cover for things that might be lying in wait to kill us. The low-lying mist didn't help, but we set off immediately.

Our footsteps on the ground sounded, to my spell-enhanced ears, like a giant chewing on rocks, and my trumped-up sense of smell only aggravated me. As a waning magic user, I'd grown up avoiding greenery. I may have been exposed to considerably more of it in the last year and a half of my life than during the first twenty, but that didn't make the smell of damp earth, decomposing wood, or pine any less distressing.

Shortly after sunrise we reached the rim of the gorge. Even though I stood on solid ground and there was no immediate danger of falling into it, my stomach dropped as if I had. The gorge was *enormous* – a near-vertical drop into a dark chasm hundreds of feet below us. At the bottom, the Acheron River was dry. I knew from the materials in my dossier that the river had been diverted during construction. The plans and specs called for the viaduct to be converted into a dam. Gazing at the wreckage below, however, I knew the project had once again been set back. Pieces of the viaduct's ruined archways were strewn about the dry riverbed as if they were toy building blocks that had been kicked over by a child with a temper. But it hadn't been a child. It had been a bomber – one who'd killed twelve people, possibly more.

One who'd possibly killed Ari.

All through the night, I'd managed to ignore my growing panic. Ari was strong and powerful... robust and nearly invincible...

Wasn't he?

But standing at the edge of Halja's northernmost ravine, staring down at what looked like an army of ants rather than a rescue party made up of demons and men, I could no longer ignore my feelings. I was afraid. Not of falling into the gorge, but of what I might find at the bottom.

The stairs were as precarious as one could imagine. Barely wide enough for Nova, covered in loose scree, with no rail or rope. Even with Fara's levitation spell, the hike down took all our concentration. Her spell lifted an object mere inches off the ground, not feet. So one ill-chosen step and we'd have plummeted over the side. I didn't – couldn't – think about what might be happening at the bottom until we got there.

It took all morning.

Around midday, my foot finally settled on solid ground. For the first time since sunrise, I gazed beyond my feet. The gorge was no less impressive from below. Its rocky, variegated walls rose straight up into the air, infinitely higher than the stacked shacks of Myriostos. All around us were patches of dust, pockets of mud, stone debris ranging in size from an apple to a railcar… and men, women, and demons.

Their collective signatures assailed me. None were familiar. I'd managed to keep a lid on my hysteria by concentrating on getting down here, but now that I *was* here, and I still couldn't feel Ari's signature…

I spun around, cursing the fact that I still had trouble sensing signatures beyond physical barriers. My own signature flashed – more blinding light than burning heat. But it got the demons' attention. A score or more turned my way. Some were curious, others annoyed, but most were distracted by the ongoing search and rescue.

Victims of the explosion and viaduct/dam collapse lay everywhere. They looked like rag dolls, their limbs twisted, broken, and bent in unnatural ways. Skulls were crushed, bellies burst open, eyes stared glassily at a sky they couldn't see... there was blood everywhere. I realized then that most of the victims had perished in the fall, not the initial explosion. I looked up to where the Memento Mori viaduct had been not twenty-four hours ago and a cold, hard knot of fear formed in my chest.

How could anyone survive that fall?

Ari has wings, I reminded myself. But I knew that fact alone wouldn't have saved him.

Displodo will pay for this, I thought next, and was just about to suggest to Fara that we split up when a demon stepped in front of us. With scrawny legs, bulbous eyes, and a protruding stomach, he looked like someone I could easily take in a fight. But his signature felt tough and sinewy – like beef jerky. He grinned lasciviously at Fara and then frowned at me.

"An' who are you? Yer not welcome here, you know? Especially now. I'll take yer bondservant though." He turned toward Fara and gave her an even wider grin, intentionally baring four outsize incisors. "Put 'er to good use, I can," he said. He leaned toward her and snapped his jaw shut just a hair's breadth from the tip of her nose. I nearly singed him on the spot but Fara stopped me by murmuring "Peace, Nouiomo," and then she changed her glamour. Her blue tabard became a snakeskin robe, her braided, blonde hair became the tail end of a rattlesnake, and her cornflower-blue eyes turned golden with narrow black slits for pupils. She faced our assailant, opened her mouth, and hissed, revealing inch-long fangs and a forked tongue.

"You'll do no such thing, demon," she rasped. "This is Nouiomo Onyx, the patron's *consigliere* and ex-inamorata, and I'm her Guardian. You'll address her respectfully or I'll cast Venom, Necrosis, and Gangrene over you, you sleazy, mangy rag."

Oh boy. For her first formal act on my behalf, Fara had exceeded my expectations – and the bounds of discretion and propriety. I didn't blame her—this demon's signature felt as vile as a *rogare*'s—but I cringed nonetheless. It was dangerous for an Angel to threaten a demon. But the demon shrugged her off and turned to me. His scornful gaze raked me head to toe.

"*You* were the patron's inamorata?"

By then my patience had fled. I straightened my shoulders and held out my hand, palm side up. In the past, when I'd pulled off these little tricks to establish my magic and my authority, I'd always formed fireballs. They were easy, after all, and it had been only Hyrkes I'd needed to convince. This demon, I thought, required something more. He reminded me of a rat, so that's what I formed in my hand. It grew quickly, appearing there almost as if Luck himself had spawned it. Only the barest traces of smoke and fire betrayed the fact that it wasn't real.

The demon's gaze widened and his signature contracted. I doubted anyone in Rockthorn Gorge had seen waning magic shaped into anything more intricate than a two-piece bow and arrow, and certainly nothing that had its own sentience. Just so there would be no more misunderstandings, I clapped my hands together, snuffing out the rat. I smiled sweetly at the demon, opened my hands, and showed him a pile of ashes. I blew them into the air and stared at him.

"Rumor reached me that Lord Aristos was missing. Has he been found?"

The demon shook his head. His eyes were respectfully downcast but instead of disdain, his signature was now full of enmity.

"Where was he when the explosion occurred?"

"Standing on top of the dam."

After that, Fara and I split up.

By mid-morning, I began to despair. Debris was everywhere, most of it in piles much taller than me. There didn't seem to be much organization to the search efforts either. Hyrkes and demons alike wandered through the rubble looking for survivors and digging them out. I was tempted to use magic to blast through the bigger mounds of fallen rock, but was too worried I'd make matters worse. The last thing a buried, unconscious survivor needed was to be blasted with waning magic.

So I searched and I rescued, pulling victims out from under the wreckage one by one. Eventually, I hoped, one of them would be Ari – and that he'd be alive.

Around noon, I found him. He was standing on the other side of a massive chunk of the old viaduct. He had a bloody gash on his forehead and his right hand held the corners of a ripped cloak. It swirled around his bare legs and I realized that, under it, he was naked. But the realization was alarming rather than amorous. *He must have shifted*, I thought. *That's how he survived.* But he hadn't flown fast enough to avoid getting trapped under the falling debris.

Standing in front of him with an inscrutable look on her face was the most beautiful creature I had ever seen. More dazzling than even Fara, and Fara had pulled off some amazing glamours. Her hair was a gorgeous mane of milky white swan feathers and her face was flawless with arched eyebrows, high cheekbones, and obsidian eyes. She wore winged epaulets... and not much else. Even if her name had not been included on Rockthorn Gorge's "Demons of Interest" list, I would have recognized Cliodna, the Patron Demon of Waves and Waterbirds. My guess was, the white swan had been Ari's white knight – that she'd just rescued him.

My signature flashed and they turned toward me. I felt Ari's signature flare. Its edges raced toward me—

I retracted my signature, slamming it shut like a door. It was instinctive. Defensive. Cliodna's gaze passed back and forth between us twice before she finally dropped her hands from Ari's shoulders and stepped back. Her signature pulsed once, ominously, and then quieted.

Ari cleared his throat. "Cliodna, this is—"

"—Nouiomo Onyx." The swan demoness stared at me, her dark, glassy eyes unblinking. After an uncomfortable moment, she made a moue of distaste and turned toward Ari.

"She smells like her barghest."

The next encounter was only slightly less disconcerting. When the new arrival asked who I was, Ari paused briefly and then introduced me as a past Laurel Crown contender who would be serving as his *consigliere* for the next six months and possibly "in perpetuity" after I graduated. He then casually mentioned I'd be formally inducted into his camarilla later. I decided now wasn't the time to worry about either the initiation ceremony or what working for Ari *in perpetuity* might mean.

By nightfall, hundreds of torches and lanterns glowed in

the gorge. Orange spots were concentrated in three areas: down by the dry river bed, at the base of the gorge's northern wall, and at its top. Nephemiah Zeffre, Ari's Hyrke foreman, had miraculously survived both blast and aftermath, and he'd rigged a temporary hoist to lift those who were too injured to climb.

At the top, the railway continued on the other side of the now non-existent viaduct. A handcar was being used as a makeshift ambulance to shuttle people to the town's train station, which was another fifteen miles northwest. I'd asked Fara to accompany some of the more injured workers back to the hospital so that she could cast as necessary during the trip, but I vowed to stay until the last missing person had been found.

I spent my time after that clearing away more rocks, rubble, and debris so that trapped men could be pulled free, building a makeshift travois for Nova so that she could haul men and supplies to and from Zeffre's hoist, and providing light, warmth, and comfort to those still waiting to be healed... or to die. It was agonizing, but how could I complain? I hadn't lost anyone I loved.

Finally, Ari called off the search. All of the missing had been accounted for and everyone was anxious to get back to town. I waited until nearly everyone was out of the gorge before climbing up and catching a ride back with Ari, his Captain of the Guard, Yannu—I remembered his name from the list of camarilla members—and Ari's foreman, Zeffre.

Barghests and bunyips are both huge so there wasn't much room, but I managed to squeeze in between Nova and Yannu nonetheless. If the bunyip captain was surprised I chose to sit beside him rather than Ari, he didn't show it. I likely ruined any impression of strength or bravery, however, when my signature pulsed briefly and uncontrollably after I realized his double row of teeth, two arms-length tusks, and deep-set snake eyes were only inches from my face.

Ari sat across from me. He'd found clothes somewhere and had washed off most of the dirt, dust, and blood that had coated him earlier. Even so, he looked as worn as I felt. I wanted to ask a million questions – about Displodo, the explosion, possible suspects, clues, potential leads... about Zeffre and Yannu and the other demons on my "Demons of Interest" list... about Ari and what he'd been doing since I last saw him, and why he'd become patron of Rockthorn Gorge.

But I could hardly ask questions about possible suspects in front of possible suspects, and the more personal questions should wait... or possibly not be asked at all.

By the time I arrived in Rockthorn Gorge, I'd slept for only four hours out of the past forty-eight. I'm sure if the town had been ordinary, I wouldn't have remembered my first glimpse of it.

But it was anything but.

The two words that immediately came to mind when I saw Halja's northernmost outpost were *rugged* and *beautiful*. In its own way, it was a diamond in the rough – something dazzling and enduring carved out of something coarse and rocky.

A serpentine street lined with slate and clay tile-topped residences wound its way from the train station to the top of the mountain while a central set of stairs provided a narrower, and infinitely steeper, way up. At the end of each switchback were larger buildings: guard towers, a giant rotunda and, at the summit, an open-air pavilion. If the map in my dossier was to be believed, the pavilion was Cliodna's sanctuary, which meant the other building up there had to be the hospital.

"You know what we call those stairs?"

I turned toward Zeffre, who'd walked over to stand beside me, and shook my head.

"The Stairway to Heaven."

I smiled obligingly. *Apt*, I thought, craning my neck. Wispy clouds shrouded the mountain's peak. But Zeffre's next words made me realize that "heaven" was open to interpretation here in the gorge.

"The graveyard's to the left of the hospital," he explained, "and the vineyard to the right." He smirked, but it seemed self-deprecating. Ari's foreman had the kind of face one might describe as craggy or weathered, but his eyes were a crisp blue and his expression, post-smirk, was kind. He glanced back at Ari, who was speaking to Yannu and two other bunyips.

"We'd planned a different welcome for you, you know," he said.

I gave him a wan smile. "I don't need a formal welcome. I just need a place to wash and sleep. Preferably somewhere big enough to house my Guardian and our beasts...?"

"His lordship had the former *consigliere*'s chambers readied for you," he said, pointing to the rotunda.

"Isn't that where Lord Aristos' chambers are?"

Zeffre gave me a cryptic look. "Yes, but it's a big place and you'll be spending at least half your time there."

"Where will I spend the other half?"

"With my retainers," Yannu said, joining our

discussion. He bumped me with his magic, hard enough to make me stumble. His answer wasn't unexpected but I elected not to ask the obvious follow-up question *doing what?* because I was fairly certain his next answer would be *anything I tell you to* and then I'd be forced to say *we'll see* or *yeah, right* or *you wish*, and I just wasn't in the mood for chest thumping.

"When and where?" I asked instead.

"Tomorrow morning. Behind the rotunda." Yannu's signature pulsed with *power*, *push, prod*, and *poke*. He felt like a more militant version of every Maegester instructor I'd ever had, bar Wolfram. "Tenacity can show you."

"Tenacity?"

"Aristos' Angel."

Ari had a Guardian? How was that even possible? I thought Angels only worked for Maegesters...

The rotunda was Rockthorn Gorge's version of a patron's palace but by the time I got there, I was so tired that the only two descriptors I could think of were "big" and "round." A young woman, maybe a few years younger than me, met me at the door. She was dressed in a red and black checkered maid costume, which she'd paired with black boots, fingerless gloves, and black-painted nails that had been bitten to the quick. Under her left eye, a black tear had been inked onto her cheek.

"Did they find Aristos?" she asked.

"Yes, he's fine." *No thanks to you*, I thought. If this girl was his Guardian, she'd done a piss-poor job of it. "Are you Tenacity?" Almost every Angel I had ever met preferred white, bright, and flawless. They wore diamonds, not argyle. Suddenly, I felt like shaking her.

Did she have any idea how worried I'd been? How terror-stricken? How—

"I was going to jump out of a p—p—pie," she said and then burst into tears.

5

DEAD OF MIDNIGHT; NOON OF THOUGHT

Turns out Tenacity was Ari's court jester – or so she said. She neither looked nor acted like a formally trained Angel jester, which made me think her role might be a little more protean.

She told me she'd been down at the explosion site looking for Ari all day yesterday. But when night fell and he still hadn't been found, she'd gone to the hospital to help out, which is where she met Fara and realized we'd arrived early. Apparently, Tenacity had planned an elaborate welcome for us, which involved her jumping out of a giant pineapple patisserie. I didn't have the heart, under the circumstances, to ask her where she'd come up with the idea, why she thought it appropriate, or whether Ari had known. Despite the absurdity of it all, her tears seemed genuine. I think she hadn't realized how worried she'd been until after she heard that Ari was okay.

In any case, she calmed down soon after her outburst and gave me a tour of the public spaces of the rotunda and my chambers. By far the largest and most impressive space inside the rotunda was the atrium. It was a cavernous, echoing dome full of marble statues, bronze effigies, and bone idols. At the apex of the dome was an oculus that, depending on the weather, allowed either shafts of light or drops of rain to enter. Interestingly, there were no birds anywhere in the structure, and I wondered if Cliodna had something to do with that. *Maybe all of the winged creatures roosted with her?* Except for Ari, of course.

Beneath the oculus was a fountain and in its center was the atrium's biggest sculpture – an enormous statue of the town's founder, Servius Rockthorn, Lucifer's Northern Warlord. He held a *tabula ansata*—an ancient writing tablet—in his left hand and a fireball in his right. I wondered what was inscribed on the tablet – a warning or a welcome? – and then refocused on Tenacity, who was explaining our respective roles. She slept elsewhere, but spent her days here doing all the things I wouldn't be doing.

"In other words," she said, "you handle all the 'pen and sword' type stuff and I handle stuffing all the skeletons in the closet, washing everything but the kitchen sink, and performing tricks for his lordship." A zing of... *something* I didn't want to identify... bloomed in my signature, but then she winked and followed it up with two handsprings and a tuck, which I took as further clarification – carnival tricks, not carnal.

At the end of the hallway, Tenacity blew me a kiss and waved goodnight. Frankly, the thought of Ari with her – or anyone else – made me sick to my stomach.

Just as the thought of Ari and me together again terrified me.

Just before midnight, I finished my ablutions and put Nova out for the night. I was passing back through the rotunda's atrium on my way to the chambers I'd been given, when a voice spoke from the dark.

"Did you come to fulfill your promise, Noon?"

I whirled around, half a second away from shaping a sword, but pulled back when I saw Ari standing beside one of the pillars surrounding the fountain. His face was shadowed and his signature was taut with banked emotion. I frowned, as much from confusion as from his nearer presence. He stepped toward me, into the circle of dim moonlight shining down from the oculus, and motioned to the lantern I held.

"You promised when you came to the gorge you'd bring me life and love."

I opened my mouth to deny it. I hadn't said that exactly.

"I told you I'd bring you a lit candle," I said slowly, firmly, remembering. My promise had been made at a place and time that had seemed very far from where and when it would have to be kept.

"But you said it on Bryde's Day," Ari said, stepping closer. "That's what a lit candle means then. Or have you forgotten?" I refused to step back. I didn't want to start off the next six months by retreating. What kind of precedent would that set?

But the combination of darkness, privacy, and *me* seemed to bring out Ari's latent predator impulses. How had I thought this residency would go? It seemed preposterous now, watching Ari advance on me, that I'd thought I could be professional about our relationship or (even more laughable) that I could control him. Without thinking, I snuffed my lantern out, plunging us into near blackness.

"It's no longer Bryde's Day," I said.

I guess, subconsciously, I'd thought to take my

promise back somehow, or at least show Ari that I wasn't prepared to deliver on it just yet. But extinguishing the tiny flame and uttering those words only seemed to blast away the last of his restraint. He closed the distance between us immediately but I retreated just as fast, falling back until I bumped into a pillar.

Ari stood in front of me as he had countless times before, his chiseled features nearly as set as those on Rockthorn's statue. He rested one hand against the pillar and then leaned toward me. I tensed and closed my eyes. My heart beat erratically in response to his breath on my neck. But my actions were no precursor to a kiss. I wasn't trying to be coy.

I genuinely did not want him to touch me.

A year or so and more ago, I'd bared my heart to him and he'd ripped it out. Not with a drakon's sharp teeth but with a man's silent tongue. *You should have told me*, I thought. Because then I could have avoided what I felt now. I loved him but I was petrified of making myself vulnerable to him again.

We stood like that, inches apart but not touching, for what seemed like half the night. Then Ari made a sound of disgust (with himself, I think) and frustration (with me, to be sure) and lowered his arm. He stepped back and then motioned for me to follow him.

I'm not going to lie. I was unbelievably hesitant about doing so. But it seemed as if some sort of détente had just been established. Ari had shown me that, while he was a demon who desperately wanted me, he was also a man with iron control.

I followed him into a lesser outer hall furnished with wooden tables, upholstered sofas, and a wool rug. Their colors were muted until Ari lit the sconces with his magic and then shades of crimson, copper, dappled stone, and speckled fawn emerged. He walked over to a table and I joined him, still wary enough to keep it between us. Only then did I notice that he was still wearing a cloak – and that it hung oddly on him.

"Take your cloak off," I demanded. He looked surprised, confused, and then annoyed.

"No," I said quickly, "that's not... I mean..." I cleared my throat and schooled myself. He'd offered a truce of sorts a moment ago. A temporary emotional ceasefire, and I didn't want to break it with carelessly chosen words. So I traded my concerned tone for a courteous one and asked what I should have asked before.

"Did you injure your arm?"

"Yes."

"Why didn't you have a Mederi heal it? Or heal it yourself"—I dropped my gaze, suddenly unable to meet Ari's—"by shifting."

When I looked up again, Ari was still staring at me.

"It's an old injury," he said.

"What do you mean, an old injury? It wasn't something that happened yesterday?"

"No," he said and waved his hand in a dismissive gesture that told me he wanted me to drop it. But I wouldn't. I was here to be his consig, which meant I needed to know what he was talking about. How could it be an old injury? He hadn't had it last year. I narrowed my eyes.

"When did you injure it?"

"It doesn't matter," he said, impatiently. "That's not what I wanted to talk to you about."

"But it's something I need to know about."

He said nothing.

Ari's not wanting to talk about it made no sense. How big a deal could it be? Even a mediocre Mederi could rebreak it and set it right. Unless…

"You didn't break your arm, did you? You broke a wing."

This time, he was the one who looked away.

"Why didn't you shift back?" I said, my voice soft. I understood now what a big deal it was. A demon can be healed just as a human can, but they usually self-heal by shifting. If Ari had been injured as a drakon, however, and didn't shift into human form until after the broken wing bones fused, then the bad break would carry through. I wanted to ask him then if I could see his arm, to assess the damage, but the question suddenly seemed improper, as if I was overstepping. If I was here working for any demon other than Ari I wouldn't have dared – at least not on the first night.

"So how do you want to do this, Noon?" His voice was efficiently crisp and businesslike.

"What do you mean, 'this'?" I asked. I didn't mind talking shop at midnight, especially after what had happened, but he was going to have to give me something more specific than *this*. "Do you mean hunting down Displodo, ensuring the safety of your work crews, guard rotations here at the rotunda, or something else?"

"I mean us."

I bit my lip, but then said in a steady voice, "There is no us."

Ari clenched his jaw and met my stare.

"As long as we are both alive, there will always be an us. I left you alone, like you wanted. You got rid of my *signare*. How, I don't know. But none of that means there isn't an *us*. So now that we're working together again, I want to know how you want it to go."

I...

Oh.

I swallowed.

Uh...

Was my plan really for us to dissemble?

Luck, that sounded pathetic even in my head. I couldn't say it out loud.

"I thought you'd say that. So *I* have a plan," Ari said.

Of course he did. It wasn't that Ari was incapable of letting me take the lead. It was that the last time I'd taken the lead my decision had indirectly led to our breakup. *Would I make the same decision if I had it to do again?*

Yes.

Probably.

Of course.

Maybe.

Ari smiled. "Frigore Luna is in three months. Acheron will be coming to the gorge for the celebration. Between now and then, you train with Yannu, patrol with his retainers, and work with me, all while pretending we meant nothing to each other before. Because that's what you want, isn't it?"

I gave him a weak smile. He knew me too well.

"And after Frigore Luna?" I asked. "What then?"

Ari gave me a cunning look and then retrieved a clear bottle from one of the sideboards. He set it on top of the table. Inside was a reddish black liquid and on the outside was a small label with "Black Gilliflower" handwritten on it. My eyes widened. Nicknamed "Veracity," it was a type of ensorcelled apple wine the

Angels made. It compelled honesty. Dissembling, while drinking, was impossible.

Ari laughed when he saw that I recognized what it was.

"I say we drink this. Together. Later that night."

He arched a brow and glanced at Rafe's silver bracelet, which I was wearing on my wrist. He obviously knew there were things I hadn't told him. And despite the fact that we'd broken up because of his Big Demon Lie, he was never shy about pointing out that I too had trouble revealing hard truths.

"Why not drink it now then?" I asked recklessly.

But Ari shook his head.

"I haven't seen you in *ages*, Noon," he said. His voice held an unfamiliar note and his signature felt abruptly different than the man I'd dated... loved. This person – this patron demon – sounded sly and beguiling. He walked around the table toward me. "I want a chance to... enjoy you... before you tell me things I don't want to hear."

"Enjoy me?"

"Uh-huh." He stepped closer.

"I'm not going to sleep with you."

Wow. Did I just say that? Maybe the mere presence of Black Gilliflower compelled bluntness. What had happened to the concern I'd had just sixty seconds ago about propriety?

But Ari seemed to revel in my candor. He grinned as if we were back on track.

"That's your choice," he said, once again leaning toward me. I let him, feeling less vulnerable now that I wasn't pressed up against something. "But it doesn't mean I'm not going to try to convince you to."

"That's hardly how people act when they don't know each other."

"But I'm a demon," he said, blowing a puff of soft, hot smoke against my lips. "Remember?"

"I'm not trying to forget," I whispered. "I'm trying to forgive."

6

PERTHIUS

They say true irony is hard to define. Fine. I say it's dealing with three Angels in the first fifteen minutes of your first full day of work for a demon lord.

Tenacity woke me just before dawn. Thankfully, Nova hadn't tried to gnaw on any of the rotunda's statues the way she had on Miss Bister's table, but she had left a big pile of bear bones outside the door, and Virtus had hidden a half-eaten deer behind one of the larger boulders on the hill. Ari's jester insisted I clean them up before breakfast or go without. A complaint was on the tip of my tongue—hadn't Tenacity said that *she* would stuff all the skeletons in the closet?—but I remembered my last morning at Megiddo all too well. My midnight rendezvous with Ari had left me feeling tense and edgy, but sleeping in one of the guard towers with Yannu's retainers would have left me feeling completely blown. I couldn't risk Tenacity kicking me out the way Miss Bister had.

The next Angel I sidebarred with was Fara, who wanted, once again, to make a case for casting spells over me that I didn't want. Over a meal of cold deviled river crabs and hot stinging nettle tea, Fara pressed me to allow her to cast either Tabula Rasa ("Who says there are no second chances to make a first impression?"), Center of Attention (I had a feeling Fara was projecting more than just her magic when she suggested it since her glamour this morning was a feathered animal print jumpsuit), or Two Wrongs & Then Mr. Right. When I glared at her over that one, she just huffed and said, "Maybe your problem is magic users, Noon. Didn't you tell Sartabella you only dated Hyrkes before Ari and Rafe?"

"Rafe and I didn't date," I said, my words clipped.

"What *did* you do?"

I ignored Fara then in favor of managing Angel #3 – the dressmaker herself, who wasn't present in the gorge but whose presence was very much woven into each of the garments in my trousseau. Everything but the last item she'd designed for me had been neatly folded, wrapped in paraffin paper, and packed in the wooden chest that we'd brought with us from New Babylon. Sartabella had told me that the paper helped her enchantments last. Each of her packages had a label, but instead of saying what the item was, it merely specified the event I'd need it for.

Since Ari had provided few details on what his Captain of the Guard's training would be like other than a continuation of my St. Luck's physical-magical readiness drills, I pulled out the package in my trousseau labeled "Sparring" and unwrapped it. Inside was a note:

Today, you must be Perthius not Daimoneda.

Perthius had been a fifth-century Maegester who had rescued Daimoneda, the executive's daughter, from being sacrificed to Megaptera, a giant drakon, although the only people who believed that story were children… and apparently spellcasting couturiers. The real problem, however, wasn't that Sartabella had used a "princess and dragon" type myth as inspiration for what I'd just unwrapped, but rather that Perthius would *never* have worn something like this. My jaw dropped as I beheld what was sure to be skintight black scaled armor. Emblazoned on its front was a scarlet drakon.

Instantly suspicious, I asked Fara, "Did you know what my sparring gear was going to look like?" Her jumpsuit would look like a plain brown wrapper next to this and yet... the two suits looked as if they were part of a collection. I narrowed my eyes at her and she blinked back at me. I swear, only Fara could look like an ingénue while dressed in leather and leopard print. I wore the damned armor, though, because it was either face Yannu in that or wear the canvas pants and cotton tunic from yesterday, and we all knew what they smelled like. Better I look like a badass than smell like a barghest.

I exited the rotunda's rear doors and walked out onto a large patio where Yannu was waiting for me.

"Welcome to Rockthorn Gorge's sparring ring," he said, motioning beyond the patio's edge to the remains of an old amphitheater, which had been carved into the mountainside behind the rotunda.

My gaze followed Yannu's gesture, and I craned my neck. At the top of the crumbling steps and stone benches, hundreds of feet above where I stood, was Cliodna's sanctuary. Compared to the ruins on the slope, it looked lofty, elegant, and beautiful. Built into the rocky outcroppings on either side of it were much newer observation platforms. They appeared to be the only level, stable areas between the rotunda's patio and the sanctuary's terrace.

Great, I thought. Fighting on the remnants of the

amphitheater's stands would be like fighting on a sharply tilted, oil-slicked marble floor.

Another difference? Yannu told me that he conducted his training via melee, not matches. That got my attention. I knew Rockthorn Gorge's *regulare*s hovered right at the edge of rule-breaking, but demon melees were a far cry from my strict St. Luck's training.

"Fara, me, and our beasts are a team then," I said, thinking that I wanted to fight alongside people I knew for the first melee. I heard a few snickers, which highlighted the third difference – the audience was bigger.

At St. Luck's, readiness drills took place in the dungeon, because the faculty couldn't chance having its mostly Hyrke student body get hurt. But, according to Yannu, Lord Aristos didn't "coddle his humans," so Rockthorn Gorge's Hyrkes were allowed to decide on their own whether they wanted to watch or not. And, from the looks of the crowded observation decks, at least a few dozen of them did. They'd come armed with shields and were standing close to low walls, but how much cover could those provide? Their presence made me almost as nervous as the demons I'd be fighting.

The fourth difference was that I'd be fighting against other female waning magic users. They were demons, not humans, but in my entire academic career I'd never spared with another "girl," although I imagined that any of the demonesses in the ranks facing me would gladly have killed anyone who called them that.

Finally, we got to something about training that sounded familiar when Yannu said, "Angels aren't allowed to aggressively cast against *regulare* demons."

I nodded my understanding, and Yannu laughed.

"I'm going to put you up against Malphia, Pestis, Kalchoek, and me," Yannu said. "See how you do.

Wanna pick different teammates?" He paused and looked over at the rotunda. "The patron said he'd fight with you, if you wanted."

Yannu's last words hung in the air as I tried to suss out their underlying meaning. Was Ari's offer an honor, or an unintentional insult born of his old habit of always trying to protect me? Yannu's comment that Ari didn't coddle his humans probably wasn't Ari's choice of words, but I knew he respected self-sufficiency and independent thinking – at least in others. He'd only ever been conflicted about those traits in me.

I could never decide whether to help you stand on your own two feet or sweep you off them. I realize now, it was never my choice to make.

Well, he was giving me a choice now.

I shook my head. "No change to my team."

Yannu shrugged. "Suit yourself."

There'd been some tittering and a bit of hubbub when I'd first walked out. At first I'd thought it might be my old handicap – the fact that I was a human female with waning magic. But after I saw the nearly equal number of demons and demonesses in the ranks, I realized that wasn't it. *It was the damned armor*, I thought, *and the blasted scarlet drakon.* Fara hadn't had to cast Center of Attention. All eyes were already on me. I was the patron's new consig. Everyone wanted to see how I'd fare in a fight. And dressed like this, I'd better show them I knew what the hell I was doing.

Did I though? Luck and all his legions, I was just about to WILLINGLY pick a fight with four demons. With only my Guardian and beasts to back me up.

I briefly conferred with Fara and she cast up Virtus,

Nova, and me with various boost, buff, and bump spells, as well as our old standby Impenetrable.

Yannu motioned that my team should take the "high" starting position in the stands while his team took the "low" position on the rotunda's patio – the amphitheater's stage. When I moved into place and faced the demons we'd be fighting, I was glad I hadn't argued. Yannu was as big as a water buffalo, his skin was thicker than my armor, and his signature felt as immovable as a cartload of wet clay.

Pestis completely creeped me out. She reminded me too much of other demons I'd dealt with who'd had both neurotic and necrotic tendencies. Her eyes were lidless and teary and her skin gleamed with what I hoped was sweat, but the worst was her gaping mouth – because every time she opened it, flies swarmed out.

Malphia, on the other hand, was quite pretty. With shiny, bluish-black hair, cobalt eyes, and strong features, she looked almost human. The only monster-like thing about her was her signature. It felt horrible, like a sticky, toxic, cobwebby shadow she couldn't wait to smother me with.

And then there was Kalchoek – the demon we'd first met at the destroyed Memento Mori dam site. He was the demon who'd traded barbs with Fara – the one she'd called a sleazy, mangy rag. He seemed to have grown five times his size despite being downhill from me. He pointed at me, made a slicing motion across his throat, and then clicked his teeth together as if he were nibbling on something. Kalchoek was nothing if not categorically disgusting.

My signature pooled with *expectancy*, but I did nothing to disperse it. I was anxious and, truth be told, not a little afraid, although I was better at hiding it now.

"Melees are often painful, always dangerous, but

only occasionally lethal," Yannu said.

Were his words supposed to make me feel safe?

It didn't matter. I was long past the point when I could ask for Ari's – or anyone else's – help.

"Your fire must cauterize your opponent's injury," Yannu clarified. "And no deadly blows. The first team to be surrounded loses. Got it?"

I nodded and then...

It began.

Per our plan, Fara scrambled up and over. She took cover behind a large boulder that was some distance away from the observation decks on that side of the amphitheater. Nova edged toward Pestis, her normally sloppy gait replaced with a few tense, deliberate tracks, while Virtus wasted no time attacking Kalchoek (I think he was still pissed I'd burned his deer carcass). He launched at the beady-eyed, sharp-toothed demon looking determined to prove that his bite was definitely bigger. They disappeared to my left in a ball of stony dust. It was just as well, because I had my hands full defending myself against both Yannu and Malphia.

I'd like to say I was good enough to have shaped two swords and fought them both simultaneously while standing still, but I'm not. My magic is strong, and my body is a lot stronger than it used to be, but let's get real. A bunyip. For crying out loud. Fighting Yannu was like fighting a devil hippo. And fighting *both* Yannu and Malphia... *Oh, vae!*

Instinctively I fired up a knife and shield and managed to raise it in time to deflect a ringing blow from the bunyip just as Nova lunged at Pestis. But the Lady of the Flies blinked spasmodically, disappeared, and then reappeared a few feet from where she'd been. Nova sailed through the air and landed a dozen steps lower in a shower of scree. She sneezed, and I had only a second to register that it wasn't dust up her nose. It was horseflies. I hoped Fara knew a spell that could help her. Pestis looked like a demon who would need to be controlled with something a bit more proactive than Fly Paper.

A moment's distraction was all it took for Yannu and Malphia to move uphill and flank me. Too late for me to stop them. In St. Luck's dungeon it had never mattered where we stood. North, south, east, west. Right, left, whatever. There was no up or down. There was no sun. The MITs I'd sparred with back home had endlessly circled before attacking. Not here.

Yannu came crashing down on me and it was all I could do not to turn tail and run. I felt a spell slip over me, likely Aegis, and somehow, amazingly, I survived a direct hit from Yannu's flaming broadsword. We parried, feinted, cut, slashed, and burned our way across, up, and then down the amphitheater ruins. They had nearly driven me back down to the patio before I decided to swallow my pride and duck beneath the next blow instead of meeting it. I fled uphill a few feet, back to my starting point, and turned on them.

"I thought you said no deadly blows." Sounding petulant was preferable to sounding petrified.

"If you're more than just a moll, you'll survive. If not…" Yannu shrugged. Rage pulsed through my blood and my magic turned white hot. Calling me a moll was way worse than calling me a girl. Moll meant camp follower or whore.

Don't lose control, I counseled myself. *Channel your emotions into your magic.*

But incandescent fury was not enough.

Because Yannu stepped back and Malphia stepped up.

Fighting Malphia womano a womano was like fighting a daymare. Her insidious magic crept along the edges of my signature, poking it, scratching it, and then slicing it and slipping inside. Small dark wisps of darkness whispered lies that sounded like cruel truths and it became difficult for me to tell the difference.

I was a heartless murderer.

My brother was a ghoulish necromancer.

My father was another demon in disguise.

My mother didn't love me.

Ari didn't love me.

Rafe… had never loved me.

The sky above me darkened and the people disappeared. And there was just me, standing amongst the rocky outcroppings of a mountain that had stood long before Armageddon and Lucifer and his Northern Warlord and the town he'd founded ever existed, and which would be standing long after we were all gone. There was just me and the mountain and those lies or half-truths or whole-truths. The feeling of desolation and isolation I experienced was so complete, my fire flickered. How hard I'd once wished to get rid of it. How hard I'd worked lately to master it.

The mountain disappeared.

Remember that old riddle, if a tree falls and no one hears it, does it make a sound?

What if an entire world fell and no one was left?

Would there be sound?

Light?

Fire?

It seemed not, because mine was getting snuffed out by the silence. My fiery knife and shield became one tiny flame and all I could see was the four-inch circle of light it created. My breathing slowed, my heartbeat slowed... Three inches... two inches...

I felt another spell slip over me then, one I'd never felt before. It was as fierce as my mother's hug when I first came home after declaring my magic at St. Luck's... as intense as the fiery blast that had followed my marking Ari with my *signare*... and as ardent as the look in Rafe's eyes when he'd saved me from dying over and over and *over* again.

It had to be Love, there wasn't a single other spell that could have affected me that way. And Fara had just cast it over me, saving me from a dark, lonely end.

The silence was suddenly broken by snarling, growling, and grunting. I heard the scuffling of boots on stone. I felt the wind on my face. And I squinted at the sun. Small rocks and pebbles dug into my knees and I realized I had fallen in front of Malphia—although, if it weren't for her signature, I might not have even recognized her. Pretty Malphia had vanished. Thick, black spider veins now crisscrossed her face, and fetid, toothless gums filled her mouth. She raised her sword as if she were about to lop off my head. Ari emerged from the rotunda and charged toward us. His magic felt deadly, but its rage wasn't directed at me. It was directed at Malphia.

Looking back on it, I'm still not sure what she would have done. Would she have swung her sword regardless of the consequences? Or would she have lowered it, respecting Yannu's edict about no deadly blows? All I know is, I wasn't going to wait to find out. I didn't want to die and I sure as hell didn't want Ari killing her for me.

I hurled a giant fireball at her, knocking her off her

feet and into the air. She sailed downward and crashed onto the patio's stone pavers. I whistled to Nova and Virtus, their signal to bring their prey to me. My hope was that they could shepherd Pestis and Kalchoek onto the patio and then somehow I'd shove Yannu down there and we'd call it a day.

Ha. Hmm... Yeah, it didn't really happen like that and I have only myself to blame. But, honestly, until Yannu, I'd never fought a bunyip before. Lord Potomus, Rockthorn Gorge's former patron, had been a bunyip. And, according to my dossier, the ranks were full of them. Which led me to wonder why the hardy, pragmatic residents of the gorge had picked Ari, a young, unknown drakon, to be their patron.

Why not Yannu?

Nova and Virtus came when I whistled, of course, but that only helped the bunyip round *us* up. By the time the four of us assembled on the patio, Malphia was up. I glanced at Ari. His gaze bore into mine but he made no move to join the fray, thank Luck. I knew now I wasn't going to die. Not with Ari here. But I also didn't want to lose in front of him. Losing is almost all he'd ever seen me do. It galled me now to think that, after a year and all I'd been through, from his perspective, it would look like nothing had changed.

So I formed a fiery four-barrel pepperbox and pointed it at Yannu.

"Call your dog off," I told him, waving the gun toward Kalchoek, who was now trying to chew on Nova. I could tell she didn't appreciate it and I was getting fed up. To his credit, Yannu didn't seem to blink over my weapon choice, although everyone else did. Even Malphia stepped back.

"Call *your* dog off," he said.

"She's not a dog."

"Neither is Kalchoek."

I shrugged. "Then call your demons off."

If Yannu backed down now, it would be a draw. Neither of us would win, but neither of us would lose. No one had been surrounded. I'd just formed a fairly sophisticated weapon that, when fired, might blow up the old amphitheater's stage, stands, and everyone standing on them. Past Maegesters who'd tried this had only ever succeeded in detonating themselves and their immediate area. But who knew? I could be the one who shaped a pistol that finally worked. After all, I was the only MIT I knew who could shape sentient creatures out of my magic. Why not working firearms? And this one had four bullets. How convenient.

"I think I'll call your bluff instead," Yannu said.

"Suit yourself," I said, smirking. I raised the gun toward Kalchoek and – POW!

The world went black.

But I didn't shoot Kalchoek. Or blow us up. Nor was it Malphia's dark magic at work again. It was Fara's awesomeness. This was our last desperate bid to win. The spell was called Bitter Black and it stank like gunpowder.

The temporary blackout allowed Nova, Virtus, and me to escape from the midst of Yannu's team before they surrounded us. When the smoke cleared, the vague outline of my coup de grace took shape. Virtus went after Pestis and Nova attacked Malphia. I don't know if it was because she was sick of getting flies up her nose or if it was because Malphia was the one who'd come the closest to killing me. Regardless, Fara then cast our final planned spell – Cryptid – over them. Nova grew two more heads, lion claws, and a scorpion's tail and Virtus morphed into a werecat. My plan wasn't perfect. Cryptid didn't make Nova impervious to Malphia's mind-magic, nor did it make Virtus immune to flies, but I was counting on the element of surprise. We only needed a few seconds to turn the tables…

Where was Kalchoek?

I'd lost sight of him when Fara had cast Bitter Black, and now I realized he wasn't here. A hard knot of icy fear gripped me. I swung my head from side to side. I couldn't see him. All I saw were myriad demons, endless broken stairs, countless boulders…

I couldn't sense him either. But I was suddenly very afraid I knew where he was. I met Yannu's stare. His expression was as hard and merciless as the rocks and stone ruins surrounding us.

Fara.

I scrambled up to the boulder she'd hidden behind and rounded it. She was lying prone beneath Kalchoek, stiff as a board, her glamour gone, her *potentia* drained. He sat on her back with one clawed hand in her hair and the other on her chin, holding her in place while he sniffed, snuffled, and drooled words in her ear. Whatever he was saying was scaring her. And I didn't need to feel her signature to be able to tell its effect was worse than if he'd bitten her or blasted her with magic. I remembered all too well that, initially, Fara had been more frightened of demons than me. During our trip to the Shallows she'd obsessively carried and quoted the Book of Joshua. But unlike me, she'd never complained or tried to shirk her duties or responsibility. In time, I'd come to realize that beneath her superficial gloss, Fara was a deeply devoted person. She was more selfless and brave than I could ever be, which was why the sight of her lying numb with fear beneath Kalchoek didn't just make me see red, it made me want him dead.

I threw a burst of magic at him that was incalculably more powerful than the one I'd just thrown at Malphia. I didn't care if it was lethal or not. I didn't want to eviscerate Kalchoek, I wanted to incinerate him and then obliterate his ashes. Luckily for him (and perhaps for me too), he leaped away just in time. I rushed over to Fara and knelt beside her, but she turned on her side and wouldn't look at me. She wasn't crying. She was just... silent and still. Alive, but wounded in ways I couldn't see, even though she wasn't glamoured.

Something inside me snapped. I shaped a knife that was so hot it burned blue and sprang toward Kalchoek, imagining all the ways I was going to gore him with it. But midway between the ground and him, someone tackled me. We slammed to the ground, the wind temporarily knocked out of me. But my fury fueled my magic and I wrestled with my opponent, the burning blue of my knife setting my entire signature alight. Viciously and instinctively, I slashed at my assailant, but he caught my wrist and held it tight.

"Noon – stop!"

Those words and that voice... His signature swirled around and over me. His body pressed on top of mine. His hand gripped my wrist. He released his hold once he saw that I knew who he was, but that only made it worse. All the heat from my magic seemed to rush toward my face and I shoved him off of me and stood up.

By that time, Fara had regained some of her composure and I went to stand beside her. This first melee had not gone the way I'd wanted it to. Not one little bit. But I refused to cower or act as if I was the one who'd done something wrong. I met Ari's stare hoping like hell that my face looked as stony and cold and unfeeling as Yannu's had just a moment ago.

The bunyip lumbered up to where we stood. I was sadistically satisfied to see no less than a half-dozen cauterized burns on his hide. He motioned to Fara, who was still avoiding direct eye contact. "I could have given the order for her to be attacked the moment the melee started," he said. I clenched my jaw, but held my magic in check. "She's a liability. All Angels are because they're weak."

I nearly choked, remembering Fara facing the demons at Ebony's Elbow and the Stone Pointe keep. And I remembered Rafe – not just the demons he'd faced, but the spells he'd cast. The way he cast them. I'd always had the feeling he'd shown me only the tiniest fraction of what he could do. And then I remembered the Angels I wished were weak, like Holden Pierce and Peter Aster.

"Angels aren't weak," I snapped at Yannu. "You just limited the spells she could cast."

The mountain seemed to go quiet. The fifty-odd Hyrkes watching from the observation decks were still.

"*I* limited the spells she could cast?" Yannu asked. "Or Luck? Aren't you training to be a Maegester? You should know the law."

I held Yannu's gaze, my face expressionless, my magic banked, my temper controlled. Nova came over and nudged my hand. Virtus sauntered over and sat next to Fara. Almost absentmindedly, she stroked his head.

"Looks like you're surrounded," Yannu said. "You lose."

I scoffed. "I'll only ever lose once – when I die.

"Yes, I know the law. St. Luck's taught me well. And I know the most important rule – follow the rules. *Praeceptum primum, praeceptum solum.* But you know what rule I learned on my own? *Si fortuna et angeli tui tecum sunt, nemo tibi obstare potest. If luck and your Angels are with you, no one can be against you.*"

It's more than risky making up your own rules in Halja, doubly so when your rule suggests luck is more powerful than Luck. The quiet seemed to extend beyond the mountain. But then Yannu laughed and looked at Ari. "Your ex-inamorata did well, Lord Aristos. She might even last six months as your *consigliere*."

7

ROTA FORTUNAE

Fara and I managed to hold our heads high until we got inside the rotunda. I led her through the atrium, past the fountain, and into my chambers. Tenacity was in the study room, but she wasn't cleaning. I paused at the doorway, in no mood for a joke about domestic chores, but then I saw what she was doing – gardening. Sort of. She stood in front of my desk, which was piled high not only with papers but also razors, folding bones, beads, seeds, pins, pens, inks, and dyes. There was even a small guillotine.

She turned to face us wearing a short dress that was covered in colorful paper flowers. In fact, there were paper flowers everywhere – on the desk, chairs, floor, bookshelves, in Tenacity's hair, on her wrist. They were strung on garlands hung across the window and they were "planted" in a new window box. Tenacity's face was grave, a marked contrast to her bright cheerful creations. She walked over to us as a ballerina might, en pointe, curtsied to me and then offered Fara a folded piece of paper. If we were looking for a non sequitur to distract us from what had just happened, Tenacity couldn't have come up with anything better. After a brief glance at me, Fara accepted it. Tenacity leaned toward her, surprised her with a quick hug, and then drew back.

She pirouetted, made a sweeping gesture toward the room's new décor, and bowed.

Fara looked down at the piece of paper she'd been given. It was a whirlybird – a paper fortune teller. On the outside were four colors; on the inside, eight flaps.

"Go ahead," Tenacity said. "See what it says."

Fara held it out toward me. I chose *orange* and then *three* and Fara opened the flap. It was a quote from the Book of Joshua.

"Fall down seven times, stand up eight."

– Book of Joshua, 5:12

Despite everything that had just happened, and the real physical pain I was still feeling, I laughed. "I think I fell down more than seven times," I said.

"Nineteen," Tenacity said, nodding. "But you got up twenty."

I grunted my reluctant agreement, took the fortune teller from Fara, and offered it back to her. She chose *blue* and *seven* and I opened the flap.

"The first thing we do, let's kill all the rats."

– Henricus Sexto, Part 2, Act 4

This time, my laugh was unrestrained. Even Fara was smiling. *Henricus Sexto* was a popular street play about a mythical outpost lord, who has to deal with all sorts of chicanery and shenanigans. It was low comedy at its best.

"How did you know which colors and numbers we'd choose?" Fara asked. I could tell she was impressed. "Which soothsaying spell did you use? And what spell helped you make all this? The only growing spells I've heard of have to do with grape vines."

Tenacity's face fell. "Oh, I don't know any spells."

Huh?

"But you're an Angel, aren't you?"

She looked uncomfortable and then shrugged. "I believe in the teachings of Joshua, so the demons call me 'Angel.'"

I frowned.

What kind of answer was that? Did she pray to the Savior or plead to Luck?

I started to ask but then decided against it, too afraid her answer would be "neither" or "both." Rockthorn Gorge seemed to dictate a very different "first rule, only rule" than I was used to. Instead of *follow the rules* it seemed to be *make up your own*.

***

TERROR IS DREADFUL BUT NECESSARY.

I stared at the cartoon Zeffre had just shown me. It was a rough, crude drawing but no less effective for its rudimentary style. In the background was the gorge, the destroyed dam, debris, and victims. In the foreground was a black-robed figure whose facial features were obscured by a hood. The repulsive words of the caption were signed with a single initial – the letter D.

I grimaced and handed the paper back to Zeffre.

We were sitting on stools at a wooden bar at The Horn & Tail, a pub on Third Street with stone floors, dark paneling, and bitter pale ales. Outside, a slow drizzle was falling and the fog had come back. Evening was creeping up on the town, and some passersby now carried lanterns.

After our brief tête-à-tête with Tenacity earlier, I hadn't waited for specific instructions from Ari. I probably should have, but frankly, after our tumble in the sparring ring, I hadn't trusted myself to be calm around him. So I'd told Fara to check in at the hospital and I'd gone looking for Ari's foreman.

Over the past four months, Zeffre and I had traded a handful of letters, which made him more of an externship advisor than Wolfram had ever been. I figured my investigation should start with him. I'd found him down at the dam site and he'd given me a tour of the wreckage and the town.

According to Zeffre, this outpost had once been a lonely castle built on the precipitous face of Mount Occasus to the west. Servius Rockthorn had brought his family and a few demon legionaries to settle here after Armageddon. Within a few centuries, however, gorge settlers had moved to the relatively less steep slope of adjacent Mount Ortus. Today, all that was left of the original Mount Occasus settlement were ruins and the Magna Fax, which, despite its name, was not a fiery meteor or a giant torch or even a big light. It was simply a large cannon.

Meanwhile, despite periodic attacks by Displodo, the newer town built on Mount Ortus had thrived.

"Displodo has destroyed the dam four times over the past year," I said, pointing at the cartoon. "Why?"

"It's a symbol of New Babylon's interference in gorge affairs."

"Don't most people want the dam? Its construction has created hundreds of jobs. Its completion will generate revenue for each of the three major patrons up here: Acheron, Aristos, and Cliodna."

But Zeffre just laughed. "Let me guess, someone in New Babylon told you that?" When I didn't respond, he nodded for me. "Look, I don't know what the exact terms were, but it doesn't matter. Whatever they were, I'm sure Acheron wasn't interested."

"How do you know?"

"Because I know Acheron."

"Do you follow Acheron?"

"No. I follow Aristos."

"But you haven't always. Do you follow other demons?"

His eyes crinkled but I couldn't tell if he was amused or annoyed. "How is that relevant?"

I shrugged. "I was just wondering if you adore any other demons here in the gorge."

"Ah," Zeffre said, "I get it. You're wondering about my loyalties. You're thinking I might be throwing suspicion on Acheron so you don't look too closely at whoever else I might follow."

I gave him a look that told him that's exactly what I was thinking, and he snorted.

"First off, I'm not accusing Acheron of anything. I'm just telling you things he would want you to know. It's no secret he opposes the dam. It will completely block the natural flow of his river. Second, you may be Lord Aristos' *consigliere*, but you're a Council MIT. Word on the street is that you're also the new lord's *ex*-inamorata. Don't call my loyalties into question when yours are still up for grabs."

I almost dropped my jaw – the man's audacity was incredible – but I stopped myself just in time. *What had I expected? That Ari's foreman would be milquetoast?* Zeffre was testing me, that's all. Just like everyone else here.

I scoffed and pointed to my bloody lip, which still hurt. "Yeah? Well, I'm the one who bled for him today, Zeffre, not you."

After a moment's hesitation, Zeffre raised his glass to me and drank.

"So if not Acheron or an unnamed separatist, then who?" I asked. "Who else would want to assume the mantle of Displodo in order to sabotage the dam project?"

Zeffre shrugged and I thought that was it. That this cheeky old man was finished telling me what was what – at least for today. But then he jabbed at the cartoon with his finger and said, "He was there."

"Of course he was there—"

"—No, I mean afterwards," He looked around the room to see if anyone was listening. They weren't, but he leaned closer anyway. "Displodo didn't just blow up the dam, he was there during the search and rescue. He walked among the dead and the dying."

My blood chilled as I stared at the drawing. No need to ask Zeffre what he meant. I *saw*.

"How many demons were present at the search and rescue?" I asked softly.

Zeffre grunted and made a vague gesture. "A lot. But not Acheron. He wasn't there."

"Other than Cliodna, who else from Lord Aristos' camarilla was there?"

The old man turned to me and met my stare. Even in the dimming light, his eyes were a bright, robin's egg blue. "All of them."

"Which of them knew Aristos was going to be there the day before?"

Zeffre sighed and repeated his previous answer, but then he lowered his voice even further and said, "They also knew Lord Potomus was going to be on the dam the day *he* was killed."

"How's that possible?" I asked. "You're talking about two different groups of demons."

But Zeffre shook his head. "The camarilla passes to

the next patron, just like the rotunda does. Lord Aristos' camarilla was Lord Potomus' camarilla."

We sat in silence for a few more seconds and I wondered whether I could trust Zeffre... whether Ari should be trusting Zeffre. Finally, I threw some coins on the counter and stood.

"You think Displodo is one of the demons in the camarilla, don't you?"

He nodded once, but it was enough. I patted his shoulder on the way out.

"Thanks for the tour... and the warning."

By the time I returned to the rotunda, the sconces and chandeliers had all been lit and Fara was back from the hospital. I fed Nova, plopped down on my bed, and started mentally sorting through coping strategies for tonight – my formal introduction to Ari's camarilla. Considering how this morning's melee had gone, and the fact that I'd just learned that one of them was likely a murderous traitor, I couldn't wait to break bread with them. But when Tenacity came in a few minutes later she assured me that, while the affair would be formal and symbolic, it wouldn't be long. In fact, we wouldn't even sit down.

"So it's not a dinner?" I asked.

Tenacity laughed, but she sounded more anxious than amused. "Not exactly... I mean, it's not every day that his lordship adds someone new to his camarilla, right?"

Right... So what, exactly, had I gotten myself into? Since my dossier had been light on details, I asked Tenacity what I could expect.

"Well..." she stalled, as if wondering how to

describe such an arcane event, "the whole thing takes place around a *rota fortunae*—"

"A *rota* what?"

"A wheel of fortune."

"Like your whirlybird?"

"Oh, uh, no." Again, that laugh. "Not really. It's a round table that spins. After your introduction, you'll walk up to Lord Aristos and shape your best weapon. Something like that pepperbox you shaped this morning, but a little less... explosive? But don't point whatever it is at him. Instead, place it on the table, bow to him, and take your seat."

"That doesn't sound so bad," I said. But Tenacity's anxious look turned to one of guilt. "There's more, isn't there?"

She nodded. "Once everyone's in place, Lord Aristos will spin the table and then... everyone gets their *just deserts*."

"Let me guess," Fara said. "Their *just deserts* won't be dessert?"

Tenacity smiled sheepishly at Fara. "Do you know any spells that will make blood pudding, boiled cockscomb, or marmot meat taste good?"

Fara made a face and shook her head. Tenacity turned toward me with a grave look. "Just remember, each of the dishes is a delicacy here. Symbolically disarming yourself and then accepting whatever dish fate serves you is a way of showing not just fealty to his lordship but also experiencing kinship with his camarilla."

Kinship? With a pack of demons? Ha!

I had one last question.

"Did you make whatever I'll be eating tonight, Tenacity?"

When she nodded, I told her that no matter what it was, I was sure to love it. Then she reminded me I didn't know what the other five dishes were.

She grimaced. "I'll leave an extra mint on your pillow," she promised, which made me laugh. Would I have gotten turndown service and extra mints if I'd stayed in the guard towers with Yannu and his retainers? I thought not.

After Tenacity left, Fara got down to the business of helping me get ready. She'd be on show too, of course, but only for a few minutes while she introduced me and, besides, her outfit was a glamour, as always. *I* was the one who insisted (much to Fara's frequent dismay) upon wearing real clothes to these sort of events. So, after a brief dunk in a deep copper tub, I found the package that Sartabella had labeled "First Night" and put on what was in it. Immediately, I was glad I hadn't actually worn it on my first night here. Who knows what might have happened had Ari cornered me in the dark while I was wearing *this*?

The gown covered almost everything, but somehow still managed to look risqué. Cut from red, black, and white silk, it was floor-length with long drape sleeves, a cinched waist, and plunging neckline. There was no lining, so it clung to every curve. But, surprisingly, it didn't show off my mark.

Like every other waning magic user, I had a demon mark – a splotchy spot of skin right above my heart. I'd always been told that Luck put it there, I guess to mark me for some nefarious purpose. But Ari was the one who taught me that our marks could be used for a more romantic – even erotic – purpose. Some waning magic users could brand their beloved's heart with magic. A branded mark was called a *signare*. Not everyone could do it, he'd challenged, but somehow I was able to brand

Ari's demon mark with my *signare* within a few days of his declaring his feelings for me. Eventually, I'd let him do the same to me and, for months, our mutual *signares* had proclaimed to the demon world that we were taken.

I sighed.

Bliss was an illusion when you lived in Halja.

Ari's *signare* on my heart was long gone now. The casualty of a curse and maybe something else. All I knew was that I didn't want to think about it tonight, which was why this dress was perfect. Out of sight, out of mind, right?

Minutes before I was due in the rotunda's great hall, I twisted my hair up in a chignon, slipped the silver vial of waerwater around my neck, and asked Fara to cast a simple healing spell over me – to get rid of the last of the burns and bruises from the morning's melee.

The rotunda's great hall had curved walls, two fireboxes, an enormous round table in the center (the *rota fortunae*, I gathered), and the aforementioned pack of demons. I sensed Ari's presence immediately, as well as a barrage of other signatures. My gaze swept the room. In addition to Ari, Cliodna, Yannu, and Malphia, there were three other demons I hadn't yet met: an argopelter, a selkie, and a sinister-looking man who could have been Malphia's worse half. I may not have practiced eating blood pudding with a smile, but I had memorized the members of Ari's camarilla. So I knew the argopelter was Runnos, his exchequer or money man; the selkie was Eidya, his New Babylonian liaison; and the dark wizard was Bastian, his Angel/Mederi emissary, who managed the hospital, vineyard, and wine cellar.

Tenacity preceded us into the room with a series of cartwheels, handsprings, and flips, her blonde braids, shiny black boots, and spiked belt, cuffs, and collar glinting in the candlelight. She stuck her last landing in front of Ari and pulled a torch, a match, and a flask out of her sleeve. She lit the torch, took a swig from the flask, and blew a great big burst of fire into the air. Of course, to a room full of demons, her stunts were hardly impressive, but I was glad to see that Ari, at least, appreciated her gesture. He thanked her quietly, she motioned to us, and Fara stepped up.

Introductions usually fell to Angels, and Fara had been working on this one for months. She'd refused to share it with me ahead of time, telling me that, if I trusted her with my life, I should darn well trust her with my introduction. Fair enough. She started with the usual litany of people, places, and things, announcing that I was "Nouiomo Onyx of Etincelle, second year Maegester-in-Training and *Primoris* of St. Lucifer's school of demon law, daughter of Karanos Onyx, executive of the Demon Council, daughter of Aurelia Onyx nee Ferrum of the Hawthorn Tribe, and sister to Nocturo Onyx, a Mederi who goes by the name Nightshade."

But then she went off-script as only an Angel could, weaving a highly entertaining tale about my exploits over the last year or so. I would have accused her of embellishing except that everything she said was true. I really had discovered Luck's long-lost tomb, fought alongside Grimasca, the Grim Mask of Death, drowned in Ebony's Elbow, survived a *suffoca ignem* curse, killed Orcus, Patron Demon of the Verge, liberated the *mortem animae*, and brought back *Album Cor Iustitiae*'s scabbard, which I'd generously given to the Divinity to repay a debt but also to "seal the bond of peace between the Host and the Angels." Fara stared defiantly at each of the demons then and I repressed the urge to grin and wink at her.

Reactions to my intro were mixed. Yannu's eyes had widened and then narrowed when he'd heard about Orcus, Runnos had looked positively avaricious over the scabbard, and Bastian had seemed bored. Ari's reaction was the only one I couldn't be sure of. He'd clamped down on his signature almost as soon as Fara had started. I'd told him when I accepted this job that I wasn't the same person he used to date. And he'd told me it didn't matter – but how could it not?

Fara and Tenacity took their leave and I gave my full attention to everyone else's introduction. None of them had Angels as heralds, but their deeds were almost, if not more, illustrious than mine. As I listened to Ari endlessly enumerate everyone's coups and feats of derring-do, I was glad Fara had spared none of mine. There were a few titles that were missing from someone's bio, though, namely *bomber*, *murderer*, *seditionist*, and *traitor*. But my emotions were thankfully in check so I doubted if any of my suspicions showed in my signature or on my face. Finally, it came time to symbolically disarm ourselves. Since Cliodna went first and Yannu second, I had a feeling we would lay down our arms in order of seniority.

Cliodna, clothed in a robe of white feathers, fired up a wee piece of jewelry – specifically, a poison ring, which nearly made me choke with laughter. Poison was known as a woman's weapon, after all, and Luck forbid anyone accuse Lady Cliodna of being anything but. Yannu predictably forged a sword. It was a beauty though, a long saber with a heavily sculpted gold pommel. He laid it beside Cliodna's ring on the *rota fortunae* and the two weapons hissed and spit in the semi-darkness of the stone room. Malphia went next, shaping a wisp of black shadow. It snaked through the air, over to the center of the table, and twisted around Yannu's sword and Cliodna's ring. I had to give it to her; Malphia's weapon was creepy.

Runnos formed a wooden club. At first glance it appeared to be an uninspired choice, but then he smashed it down on the table, briefly shattering the fiery weapons and temporarily dispelling the shadowy one. Bastian shaped a quarterstaff and Eidya a dagger and then, suddenly, it was my turn to approach Ari.

By this time, everyone else was standing around the *rota fortunae* waiting for us. I turned toward Ari and gave him my undivided attention for the first time since last night. Sometimes, it amazed me that he'd been my boyfriend. I suppose, in hindsight, the fact that he was a demon seemed all too obvious. What's that saying, "Love is blind?" No kidding, because Ari radiated power, magic, and gravitas. He had all the charisma a demon could possibly want to make his followers adore him. How could I have ever thought the person standing in front of me was just a man?

He wore a knee-length black cloak over gray pants with black boots and an enigmatic smile that could pass for rueful or insolent. His chestnut-colored hair was as thick as a barghest's but as smooth as a selkie's, and his maple-colored eyes had just a shade too much cranberry in them for him to be human.

Seriously, how dumb was I?

But I knew, standing in front of him now, that I hadn't been dumb as much as defenseless... helpless... powerless to resist my feelings for him. Because it hadn't been Ari's looks that made me fall in love with him. It had been his vulnerability, infrequently glimpsed during the briefest of moments – the time he'd been nervous about asking *me* out, the time I'd caught him reading sonnets penned by a hopeless romantic, and the time he'd told me there was nothing that he wouldn't do for me, except for the one thing he should do – let me go.

But he had. He'd let me go. And now I was back and I was expected to "disarm" in front of him.

Could I? Would I?

The last thing our relationship needed was more of my submission. I wanted to show the Lord of the Gorge that my body, magic, mind, and heart could be immune to him, but I also wanted to show *Ari* that I was there for him. That I'd help him "guard the guards."

In the end, it was Tenacity's advice that helped me decide. She'd told me to "shape my best weapon." Well, my best weapon was often my ability to commiserate and empathize. I wasn't a natural-born killer like everyone else standing around Ari's wheel of fortune.

So I chose to give Ari something different – a miniature fiery drakon similar to the fiery rat I'd formed for Kalchoek. But this time, it was too big to sit in my palm. It perched on my hand as if I were a falconer and it was a goshawk. In honor of Tenacity's earlier display, I let it breathe fire into the air and then I released it. But instead of sending it to sit on the pile of weapons Ari's camarilla had formed, I sent it straight toward him. He held up his good arm and my small beast flew right onto it. Instead of bowing, I lowered my head for a moment and then raised it, meeting Ari's gaze. Emotions so fast and fleeting they were indiscernible raced across Ari's face. But then he settled on a smile that could only be described as cocksure and together we turned toward the *rota fortunae*.

8

HONESTY

It looked like braised chicken.

How bad could something that had been cooked in wine be? At least I hadn't gotten the fried river scorpion.

Once we were all standing around the table, Ari had made a perfunctory toast "to the grapes," which was a reference to us – what was left of Luck's legions – and sacrifice. Then we'd lifted our glasses and drank while Ari spun the table. The whole thing had felt a little surreal, as if I was playing a game in some sort of demon saloon. Considering that my assignments often felt like bets wagering my life and the lives of others, I'd been near giddy with the thought of participating in an activity where the stakes were merely gastronomical as opposed to astronomical. When the table stopped, I'd removed the lid from my *just deserts* plate pleased to find that, when it came to low-stakes gambling at least, Fortuna was willing to smile on me.

I sliced into the tiny, stewed bird and took a bite, marking the official moment when I became a member of Ari's camarilla. I hadn't expected to feel different, but I was relieved nonetheless when the only sensation I experienced was the stinging heat of red pepper on the tip of my tongue. My eyes watered momentarily and I fought the urge to sneeze.

The formal event was as brief as Tenacity had said it would be. Within a quarter hour we'd finished and exited into the rotunda's atrium. Tenacity was playing a harpsichord and Fara was waiting with Nova, Virtus, and a few people I didn't recognize. Bastian made a beeline for Fara, spoke with her for a few minutes and then left, presumably to check in with whichever Mederi was on night shift at the hospital. But everyone else stayed, breaking off into smaller groups. Based on their behavior, I was betting the strangers were inamoratas.

Oh, goody, I thought. *More strange demons to meet.*

But then I reminded myself that I should use this uncomfortable après-event for its intended purpose – to get to know Ari's camarilla.

Runnos, Eidya, and their mates cornered me early on to discuss all manner of things: immigration of residents from New Babylon, the state of education in Rockthorn Gorge, the Memento Mori viaduct and future dam, what it was like to work for my father, even inn and restaurant recommendations in Etincelle. Runnos had wanted to hear about the Laurel Crown Race and, in particular, my search for *Album Cor Iustitiae*, the famed White Heart of Justice. I stuck to the bare facts and then asked about Cliodna's artisans and the armor they made, which was one of the gorge's top exports. Despite the bureaucratic and, at times, pedantic nature of our discussion, it wasn't unpleasant, just L-O-N-G.

I talked with Yannu and Malphia next. I wish I could say that our discussion was short and sweet, but it was more like short and strained. Yannu critiqued my performance during the morning's melee and then started quizzing me about the pepperbox. *Could I shape other types of handguns? Had they ever worked? What happened when I fired them?* His cross exam was so relentless I was forced to admit that this morning's pepperbox had been my first. It was either that or lie, which I didn't see much upside to. He would find out about the limits of my magic eventually. He reminded me of Rochester, my first magic instructor, who'd had no qualms about his teaching methods possibly killing me. Sure enough, Yannu ended the discussion by asking who I'd pick for my team tomorrow.

"Sticking with your beasts and your Angel, Onyx?" he asked, motioning to Fara, who was talking to Ari a short distance away.

"Always," I said.

"Anyone else?" Malphia asked. She cocked her eyebrow and gave me a meaningful look. I suppose choosing Malphia would have been a good idea. After all, she was the one who'd almost chopped my head off. If the melee had been a Gridiron ranking match, she would have beat me hands down. But the way she used waning magic was anathema to me and I wanted no part of it. So I said I'd pick Lord Aristos if his offer was still open.

"Perfect," Yannu said, grinning, reminding me of the way Nova looked just before she tore her prey limb from limb.

***

Around midnight, Cliodna approached me. Remembering her earlier comment that I smelled like a barghest, I girded myself for another insult. But instead she said, "I can see now what he sees in you."

Playing dumb and answering with "Who?" or "What?" would just insult both of us. But saying "I can see now what everyone sees in you" seemed a tad too confrontational, no matter how true. And here I'd been worried that my dress was too clingy and low cut. At least I was wearing one.

Sometime after the *rota fortunae* ceremony, the Patron Demon of Waves and Waterbirds had disrobed. She now stood in front of me clad in nothing but a jeweled bikini top and booty shorts, although, to be fair, she'd paired her swimsuit with knee-high gladiator boots and giant swan wings – real ones – which kind of looked like a cloak...

When would I learn? There was a reason none of the demon languages had a word for modesty!

Grumpily, I admitted to myself that Cliodna looked radiant. She was the "risqué" I'd worried about being.

"I was sorry to hear about Lord Potomus," I said truthfully. "I heard he was a fearless, stalwart, and devoted patron."

"He was also bullheaded, territorial, and inflexible." She sighed and slipped her arm into mine before I even realized what she was doing. I tensed and she must have sensed it, but her body and her signature stayed loose and fluid. She led me from the outer edge of the atrium where all the sconces were toward the moonlit middle. Her stride was slow and easy and there was no trace of the odd volatility she'd exhibited the first time I'd met her. If anything, her signature pulsed with curiosity and attraction. But I wasn't quite as naïve as I used to be, so I was glad when Nova got up and followed us as we strolled amongst the sculptures and statues.

"I want to hear everything about you," Cliodna said, patting my arm. "How you shape your magic into winged creatures; how long you've worked with that lovely girl, Fara, and her gorgeous sweeting; why on earth you chose a monster that looks and smells like that"—she turned around and pointed at Nova—"for yours." I tried to extract my arm from hers, but she held tight. "I want to know when you'll come see my sanctuary and meet my artisans. I want to know when we can start designing armor for you. Or jewelry. Or anything else." She stopped walking and turned toward me, taking both of my hands in hers. She held them up at my sides and took a step back, almost as if we were dancing, and swept her gaze over me. After a moment's assessment, she dropped my hands, slipped her arm through mine again, and resumed our walk.

Again, there was nothing in her signature to suggest that she was a threat. And yet...

"Did you outfit Lord Potomus' *consigliere?*"

She made a disparaging noise and then spat out rather more forcefully than was required, "No! Scapolite was old and ugly. He wouldn't have been any fun to..." Her voice trailed off as if she'd sensed she'd gone too far. Said too much. Suddenly, I had a feeling I knew what her last words would have been – *dress up*.

Cliodna might look like she was twenty-five, but she was actually twenty times older – old enough to have seen well over a dozen generations of humans live and die. Maybe if I'd seen the number of deaths that she had, I might be reserved in my attachments as well. Still, it didn't exactly sit right with me that she viewed me as a life-sized doll, more pet than person.

I had a feeling the more I got to know Cliodna, the less I would like her. But I didn't want to alienate her just yet. That would make keeping an eye on her doubly difficult. I had a sudden flash of inspiration.

"It's not armor or jewelry, but there is something your artisans might be able to help me with. It's something that was very dear to someone back home. It was damaged. Perhaps they could repair it?"

Cliodna's expression soured. "My artisans design one-of-a-kind pieces. They do not repair junk."

"Oh. I see. Well, I haven't much hope for it, it's true. I just thought, since your artisans are known to be the best in Halja…"

As we neared the atrium's silvery core, its warm candlelit edges faded and Tenacity's plucky harpsichord notes devolved into somber echoes. Cliodna's expression became resigned.

"Fine," she sighed. "Bring whatever ruined piece of trash you like so long as you come. I meant what I said. I want to hear all about you. As I'm sure you do me. After all, it's not every day that two of Lord Aristos' exes get to swap stories."

I felt it then, that volatile flash that I'd felt when I first met her. Her signature flared like a match being struck and then, just as quickly, blew out. But I could hardly process the *what* of it because I was still reeling from the *why*.

"You and…?" I couldn't even finish the sentence. I had no idea what emotions were reflected in my signature. I'd known Ari had dated women before me, of course. I'd even met one of them and we *had* swapped stories. Nice ones, though. Because she'd been wonderful. Yes, I had been jealous of her at first, but I'd been unable to sustain it in light of Ari's obvious feelings for me and the woman's incontrovertible kindness. But *Cliodna*? I wasn't jealous, I was appalled. How could Ari have…?

She laughed. "I see he didn't tell you. Well, that's probably because he wants you back. He told me so, you know. We talked a lot about you. But there were *so* many questions he wouldn't answer. That's why you must come to my sanctuary and tell me yourself. I will make you a promise, Nouiomo Onyx. No matter what role you assume here in the gorge, *consigliere* to the patron or more, I will give you the finest armor and the largest chest of jewels Halja has ever seen – in return for your promise that you will convince him to return to my bed upon your death."

Her eyes burned bright and my stomach somersaulted. I recognized demonic fervor when I saw it. I shook myself free of her and stepped back.

There was so many things wrong with her offer. But first and foremost was, *did she really think I would accept it?* There were only about a million Haljan legends involving poisoned dresses, robes, crowns, and scepters given to poor, unsuspecting adversaries. And this was the demon who'd just shaped a poison ring as her best weapon!

If Cliodna was truly trying to do away with me, she'd have to do better than this.

I laughed. "I could never make such a promise, even if I wanted to. What the patron does with his life is his business – before or after my death. As for the latter, he likely won't have to wait long, but my demise won't come about because I was too greedy or too stupid to say no to a trunkful of poisoned baubles."

I expected Cliodna to be angry then, that her demonic fervor would reach a new terrifying peak. But to my surprise it evaporated immediately. She actually smiled, and all traces of animus were swept from her signature as if blown out by a mighty cathartic wind.

"Yannu said you wouldn't go for it," she said matter-of-factly. "But I had to try. Melees aren't my style, you know?"

I didn't know what to say. *Which parts of what she'd just said were true? Had she and Ari been lovers? Had the hostility I'd felt in her signature been real or a ruse? Now that I'd survived this test, would she be thinking of even more clever, diabolical ways to kill me?*

Luck, how I hated working with *regulare* demons! At least with the *rogares* you knew where you stood. With demons like Cliodna, the question of friend or foe changed every day, every hour, every moment. Who was it who'd said, "The only difference between a *rogare* and a *regulare* is that the *regulare* hasn't been caught yet"?

So here's the thing. I totally lost it later that night. After all my earlier passing of tests and impressing demons like Yannu and boldly standing up to demons like Cliodna, I lost it with the one demon I really needed to keep it together for – Ari.

"Why did you serve grape wine tonight?" I asked, eyeing the bottle of Black Gilliflower that I'd taken out from under Ari's sideboard. "Why didn't you serve this to each of your guests and then ask them whether or not they had anything to do with blowing up the Memento Mori viaduct and dam?"

After his camarilla had left and Fara had gone to bed, I'd told Ari that I needed to speak with him. Then I'd led him in here to the place where he'd reminded me he was a demon before almost kissing me. To the place where he'd so forthrightly claimed he would try to seduce me.

Yeah... Not. Gonna. Happen. Seduction required a clueless partner, which I wasn't any longer.

It hadn't even been twenty-four hours and Ari had made no major moves, but I wasn't going to wait. I was going to knock that cocksure expression off his face and force him to be honest with me. I wasn't sure I wanted to start over with him, but I knew for certain that I did *not* want to continue as we'd started.

I was perversely pleased to see that my question made Ari uneasy. He grimaced and perched on the edge of an upholstered chair. Then he blew out his breath and surrendered – to my opening volley at least.

"Because it doesn't work on demons."

I'd suspected as much, but it still made me furious to hear it. I guess the only good thing was that Ari hadn't tried to beat around the bush about his answer. He'd 'fessed up to the fact that he was more interested in hearing my secrets than revealing his. Still, my desire to slap him was so strong, my fingertips crackled with fire.

"You slept with Cliodna?"

I could almost hear his inner groan. *Yep, these conversations suck, don't they, Ari? Well, deal with it. Feel these petty human emotions like the rest of us.*

"Which one of them told you?"

"Does it matter?"

He stood up. "No," he said, running his good hand through his hair. He started pacing. "Does it matter that it's true? I don't need to drink Black Gilliflower to admit it." At least he had the guts to look me in the face then. But I gave no ground and pressed on immediately, my tone clipped and my signature at a very tightly controlled boil.

"Why didn't you tell me?"

"Because it was a long time ago. I don't love her. She knows that. I love you. She knows that too."

I didn't say anything.

"Noon, we've never talked about the people from our pasts before."

"Maybe we should have."

"Really? Do you honestly want to hear about mine?

Because I don't want to hear about yours."

"Then why suggest the Black Gilliflower? Now you're just lying to yourself. But you know what, Ari? Like you, I don't need a glass of ensorcelled wine to admit there's someone in my past. And it wasn't a long time ago. But *he* wasn't trying to kill us. He only ever tried to save us."

I felt the uptick in Ari's signature as he realized who I was talking about – Rafe.

"You left us in the Shallows," I continued, my voice softer, almost as if I still couldn't believe it, "and then... *everything* happened. The Stone Pointe keep collapsed, but it might as well have been my entire life. We barely made it out alive. And then we spent *two months* in a rowboat getting home. Do you remember what the eastern hinterlands are like, Ari? *Do you remember how many water wraiths live there?!*

"And then another month waiting for any sign of you... where you might be... whether you were alive or dead or just never coming back. I finally lied for you. Lied to my father and the faculty and to everyone we know – except for Rafe and Fara. I told everyone you disappeared. And I got on with my life. I only thought about you every single minute of every single day. And then... I finally didn't. I only thought about you once an hour and then once a day and, by then, I'd not only proved I'd earned my *Primoris* rank but I'd fought my way through the Gridiron matches to become St. Luck's Laurel Crown contender. See how far bitterness and heartache can take you?"

Ari was looking miserable now, but I was just getting started. He'd brought this on himself with his dishonesty and duplicity and smug smiles and self-righteous declarations of seduction.

"You want to know how I got rid of your *signare*?"

My voice was no longer soft. It was harsh with recollection. "I was cursed. And then I nearly died. Oh, not like the night the keep collapsed or the countless times the wraiths nearly killed us. Or even all the times I'd *felt* like I'd died, but it was really just another Laurel Crown contender beating me up or burning me. *NO*. This 'nearly died' was for real. Brunus Olivine shot a *suffoca ignem*-laced arrow straight into my heart. Finally! *Finally*, something happened to me that was worse than finding out you'd lied to me."

Ari stood a few feet away from me hunched under his cloak, his good hand clenched into a fist and a ferocious expression on his face. If I wasn't already far, far past the point of no return, it might have given me pause. But as it was, I merely took a breath and kept going, my anger still seething.

"By the time I got your letter – you know, the one that said it was probably best that you left me alone? The one that said I should stay close to my Guardian? – he'd already saved me more times than anyone could count. In fact, it's fair to say that *Rafe* brought me back to life.

"So you know what I did with your letter? *I burned it*. Until there was absolutely nothing left of it. Not a single trace."

I stood fuming. Had I intended to tell Ari this much? There were other things, actually, that were more important. Rafe had told me I should *tell him everything*. But did any of what I'd just said matter to anyone but me?

I lost a little steam then and gestured helplessly, toward who or what I don't know. I think I was just remembering the rest of Fara's introduction earlier tonight. Was a rehash of everything I'd accomplished really necessary to make the point I was trying to make? No.

"I don't need you anymore, Ari." I stared at him, still fired up enough to feel no fear. His eyes had blown past mulberry and cranberry and now were red-hot. "I came up here to help you, but to do that you need to be honest—"

"—I left you in the Shallows because you told me it was over." Ari's voice was low and rough and tinged with not a little madness. "You said you couldn't be with me anymore and I believed you, because I felt your anger and your fear and your repulsion in your signature. I wanted *nothing more* than to stay, but I knew if I did, it would only make things worse. Possibly drive you away forever. Make it impossible for you to forgive me. So I shifted, and left, like you wanted. But I didn't go far. I made it to the other side of the Blandjan and then... I just dropped out of the sky. Crashed into the brush. Broke my wing. And lay there."

He was deadly still now, his eyes no longer red-hot.

"For how long?"

He shrugged and avoided meeting my gaze.

"Ari? Honesty, remember?"

"I don't know," he said in a flat voice. "Weeks? Months? All I know is the weather was different and I'd nearly starved to death by the time I shifted back. I wouldn't have bothered if I hadn't known it was the first step in getting back to you."

His signature was masked, but I had a feeling it was because he was trying to shield me from something rather than hide something from me. It suddenly occurred to me how bleak and lonely and hopeless he must have been feeling. He must have blamed himself—

"The broken wing likely stopped me from abducting you and flying off to some cave in the hinterlands."

Was he serious?!

"You wanted honesty."

His gaze finally met mine and I could see that he was a man tormented by his bestial side. He took a shuddering breath, looking nearly defeated.

"Please don't say you don't need me anymore. Because I need you. You burned your *signare* into my heart too, Noon, and *it's still there*. I've never loved anyone the way I love you. I've never wanted anyone the way I want you. I want you in my bed and in my life, and whatever I have to do to get you there, short of abducting you – maybe – I will do."

I nearly ran to him then. I almost forgave him totally. I was *this close*. And, if it hadn't been for Cliodna and the Black Gilliflower – and if he'd left out that mind-blowing abduction comment – I probably would have. (Did his *maybe* mean he was still fighting that urge? As if he'd ever be successful. I'd like to see him try.) But, a moment later, I was glad for my reserve. Because there were things Ari still hadn't revealed to me. Namely, himself. He still hadn't shown me his mangled arm.

Or calmly shifted in front of me.

I walked over to him. "After the melee tomorrow, let's patrol the gorge. Just us. We can look for any sign that Displodo might be a *rogare* and talk more then, okay?"

If he was disappointed by the fact that I didn't respond to his declarations, or if he was surprised that my voice now sounded normal, he didn't show it. He nodded, looking contemplative.

"Until tomorrow then," he said and I left, eager to escape the temptation to do something I'd later regret.

9

STONEWALL

*G*et up! You have to do the dishes."

Wha...?

My whole body ached, my vision swam, and my thoughts sloshed around in my head like the broken boards of a barrel that had been tossed over a waterfall.

Who was shaking my shoulder?

I tried to slap her hand away, but she easily evaded and shook me harder.

"Don't you remember?" She asked in an utterly annoying sing-songy voice. "I wash everything *but* the kitchen sink. That means whatever's in there is your job. So *get up!*"

I rubbed my eyes, briefly wondering where all of Ivy's pictures were, and then remembered where I was. The chambers I'd been sleeping in were far more luxurious than Room 112 of Megiddo, but apparently not even a sumptuous four-poster bed with velvet curtains, feather pillows, and five-hundred-count sheets could make me feel as if I hadn't drunk an entire barrel of Black Gilliflower on my own, which was completely unfair since I hadn't even had a sip. I hoped that damned bottle was resting in the bottom of a trash bin somewhere.

Of course, I was so tired I probably would have crawled in there with it if it hadn't been for Tenacity, who was sitting on the edge of the bed smacking my leg. "I'm kidding," she said. "About the kitchen sink. I cleaned that out last night – and what a job it was! Nothing like ending your day mucking offal out of a two-tub terrazzo sink." She clasped her hands together, raised her head as if giving thanks to… who exactly I'm not sure, and sighed blissfully. Then she looked down at me, her expression serious.

"You melted your alarm clock, you know," she said, her voice now deadpan. "And *that* you will have to clean up yourself."

I groaned. How many alarm clocks was this now? I pulled the covers up over my head only to have her rip them off me. Jeez. Thankfully I didn't sleep in the buff.

"Do you treat all the patron's guests like this?"

"Only the ones who burn things by the side of their bed in their sleep."

The crowd was bigger today. I wasn't sure if it was because word had gotten out that yesterday morning's melee had been interesting to watch or because everyone wanted to see the patron spar, which I gathered was not a normal occurrence. Regardless, there were about three times as many Hyrkes gathered on the observation platforms this morning as there had been yesterday.

Yannu introduced me to the team we'd be sparring against. Unsurprisingly, since she'd been my biggest weakness yesterday, Malphia was its captain. But the fact that I'd found Yannu to be a formidable opponent hadn't escaped his notice either. In lieu of sparring directly against me this time, however, he'd added not one, not two, but three other bunyips to Malphia's team. Each and every one of them was as large and dense, both physically and magically, as Yannu had been. In fact, it was almost as if he'd cloned himself. Not only did their signatures feel almost indistinguishable from his but their names were Yuri, Yarin, and Yavin.

Malphia's final team member was a hidebehind named Vannis. Hidebehinds were mostly *rogares*, and to this day I have no idea what motivated Vannis to join the ranks, but it wasn't so he could chum around with his fellow *regulares*, that's for sure. He seemed to dislike everyone. Over seven feet tall and whip-thin, he looked like a bear who'd been stretched on a rack. He was lanky and loping and covered in black, bristly hair. When I turned my head, he faded into heat haze and his signature disappeared.

Terrific. One distraction and he'd be all but invisible.

My team was exactly the same as yesterday, except for the addition of Ari. He'd emerged from his chambers after breakfast dressed in battle gear and an easy smile – almost as if he were looking forward to the burns, blood, and sweat we'd all be covered in by the end of the morning. His signature was gauzy, even shimmering, and the edges of it bubbled around mine like liquid sunlight.

"Same rules as yesterday," Yannu said, "except that the team with the first captain to be incapacitated loses." He grinned at me, his two huge tusks poking through his lips. His thoughts were clear.

I'd be easy meat.

I swallowed and refused to look at Ari, too afraid either he or Yannu would see it as a sign of weakness.

As he had yesterday, Yannu gave us a few minutes to confer.

"Stay where I can see you," I told Fara shakily. *Expectancy* was already pooling in my signature and it was making me jittery. "Climb up on one of the boulders. Cast Impenetrable over yourself. Nova and Virtus can circle its base and defend you. That should keep you protected and preserve your *potentia*."

She scoffed. "Noon, I'm *your* Guardian, remember?"

"Yeah, but I need you ready to cast whatever it was you cast over me yesterday that saved me from Malphia." I bit my lip, a nervous habit I wished to Luck I'd been able to banish. I doubted any of the demons would intentionally try to kill us during the melee... but then again, who really knew? If one of them was Displodo, the melee would provide the perfect opportunity for them to try to kill both the patron and the Council's investigator. And, even if Ari and I weren't in mortal danger, how bad would it look if we lost with half the town as witnesses?

Malphia, three bunyips, and the near-invisible hidebehind. Holy Halja!

Ari had been unusually quiet. Back when we were working together, he'd never missed an opportunity to voice his opinion – or at least give me some sign if he thought my plans weren't going to work. It was a trait that had always annoyed me. His know-it-all attitude had chafed. But now that I had a little bit more experience and skill, I realized not asking his opinion on strategy here would be plain dumb. He was the one most familiar with these demons, after all. And we were running out of time. I turned to him. He had the oddest expression on his face. I couldn't tell what he was thinking.

"Well?"

"You don't have to worry about Malphia," he said. "At least not if we share and swap magic like we used to. Open your signature. *Relax* and use me as your anchor. Malphia's magic is strong but there's no chance she'll be able to attack you the way she did yesterday if we work together." He paused, giving me a chance to say no.

Did I have a choice? I'd been feeling Ari's signature along with every other waning magic user's since I first arrived. But I'd never opened up completely. For one, I didn't like feeling all of them. And two, completely open my signature to Ari? Share and swap magic with him? Every waning magic user on the mountain would then know how we felt about each other. *Ari* would know how I felt about him. And I'd know how Ari felt about me, although he'd made it pretty clear last night.

Still…

Being told something, no matter how emotional the delivery, was very different than experiencing it.

"Ready?" Yannu called.

I took a deep breath and nodded at Ari, not trusting myself to speak. His expression turned serious then and he quickly told us the rest of his plan. We broke off and joined the others at the bottom of the old amphitheater.

"You lost yesterday," Yannu told me. "So you can start high again."

Fara immediately cast us up using both older and newer favorites. Then she, Virtus, and Nova fled for the relative safety of the sidelines while Ari and I shaped swords and squared off against Malphia's team. Yannu signaled and, suddenly, the air was full of clanging, scuffling, growling, and grunting.

I lost Vannis almost immediately. I couldn't see

him. I couldn't sense him. If not for that, I might have delayed cracking open my signature completely, but doing so was almost instinctive when I realized he'd disappeared. Besides, I'd told Ari I would, and now wasn't the time to be waffling or second-guessing myself.

So, just as I was lunging toward Yavin (Yuri?), I relaxed my signature. It was weird for my brain to be telling my magic to soften, slow, and expand while simultaneously telling my muscles to brace, quicken, and contract. For a moment, both my fighting and my magic felt sluggish and uncoordinated. Then, with a *whoosh* of blistering heat, Ari's magic saturated mine. Instantly, I felt infused with feelings of *solidarity*, *relief*, and *exultation*. As if Ari had been waiting for this moment – the moment we could join forces and attack an adversary without any of my old hesitation – for his entire life. Almost effortlessly, the two of us pushed back three bunyips. I wouldn't have believed it possible if I weren't the one advancing on them. Their sunken eyes seemed to pop out of their heads in disbelief.

Out of the corner of my eye, I saw Malphia's expression change from cruel to confused. As it had yesterday, her magic had been hovering at the edges of mine, poking, scratching, slicing, trying to gain the entry that I'd so easily just granted to Ari. And he'd seized it, without reservation, while at the same time offering me unfettered access to what seemed like a bottomless pit of power. Although that bottomless pit didn't mean I was able to see Vannis, who still eluded me.

Ari's plan called for me to wait until Vannis attacked me. He'd been sure he would. I was the team captain. Incapacitating me was the goal. Vannis was on Malphia's team but he preferred to work alone and, most importantly, the only subtle thing about him was his invisibility, not his tactics. Once Vannis attacked, Ari'd said he wanted me to shape a bunyip.

"Can you do it?" he'd asked.

"Not for long," I'd replied.

Ari had quickly explained, as if I hadn't known already, that the point of these melees was for his Captain of the Guard to assess our strengths and weaknesses. Yesterday, Yannu could have immediately given the order to attack Fara, but he hadn't. Why? Because he'd wanted to see me fight. So, even though Ari had a plan for incapacitating Malphia, he advised me to wait before I gave the order to do it. Why? So I could show Yannu more of what I could do, which was shape fiery beasts in addition to weapons.

My fiery bunyip was sure to lure Malphia into the fray, and at that point, it would be up to me how long I wanted to fight before giving the order to take her out. The only thing I shouldn't do is lose sight of Vannis once he attacked me.

Fine, I'd said, as if there was nothing to it.

After all, Ari's plan was a good one – no, it was a great one.

Which is why I should have known it was never going to go the way we wanted it to.

Was it my pride that got in the way? Was I so hell-bent on showing Yannu – and Ari – what I could do that I didn't see the danger?

Vannis didn't attack me. He attacked Ari. Stabbed him in his left side – up under his damaged, useless arm – with a dagger. I only know this because Vannis stood there after, holding his Luck-forsaken bloody blade and smiling, until he was sure I saw him. Then he disappeared again. Ari swayed, his good hand pressed against an exponentially-increasing patch of red, and then fell to his knees.

Yuri, Yarin, and Yavin bore down on us then and everything went to hell. The magical maelstrom between Ari and I died out and his magic choked. That frightened me because it made me worry his wound might be fatal.

"Fara!" I yelled, pointing to Ari. "Stanch, left side. Then cast Aegis, Impenetrable, and every other shielding spell you know." Then I leapt away, hoping the bunyips would follow me. But of course, since Luck never seemed to favor me when it came to big stakes like this, only one of them did.

Not chancing *potentia* waste or a mistake, Fara ran to Ari's side rather than casting from afar. Nova and Virtus went after the other two bunyips – Yuri and Yavin? Who the hell knew? – I didn't care. I blasted the bunyips with electric bolts, but it was like blasting rubber boats. Nothing happened.

Meanwhile, Malphia's dark magic was slithering along the edges of mine, and Yarin was raining blows on me right and left. It was only a matter of time before he simply railroaded me and then stomped on me. Fara's glamour flickered and faded. Her *potentia* nearly drained, she slumped against Ari, who was now struggling to get out from under her.

My boost and shield spells started to give way and I felt Ari's signature change. He'd been radiating *frustration*, which I'd thought odd in light of his injury. I'd have expected him to be pulsing with *pain* and *rage* like I was. But *frustration* morphed into *desperation*. I was given the most fleeting glimpse of his current emotional state when my words from last night rumbled in my head.

I don't need you anymore.

Ari had said he wanted me to show Yannu what I could do, but this whole time Ari had been trying to show *me* what *he* could do. For me. What we could do together.

But his plan backfired.

When Ari realized he could no longer help me win the melee, something inside him snapped. Complicated human emotions gave way to more basic, primal ones like *kill*, *mine*, and *take*. His magic bubbled back into him as if fed by an enormous preternatural spring. With dawning horror, I realized what was happening – Ari was shifting.

The rational part of me was glad. Shifting would help Ari heal faster. But the irrational part of me was afraid. Keeping him alive was my priority, but at what cost? This creature wasn't going to merge his magic with mine. It would do what it wanted. Fara stumbled back and Ari's gaze met mine. It was no longer familiar. Fiery-red eyes, set in a head with a long snout, enormous teeth, and horns, stared back at me. Instead of a man, Ari crouched before us now as a drakon, fully healed except for a maimed left wing, muscles tense and ready to spring.

Malphia immediately went down on one knee and bowed her head, but the bunyips merely turned toward him, considering.

Were we going to continue the melee now? Surely, a truce would be called. Ari needed to calm down and shift back. I couldn't control him like this. It felt as if *he* couldn't even control himself like this.

I glanced at the observation decks. Many of the Hyrkes had fled, but a few brave souls had stayed, including Zeffre, who stood beside Tenacity on the nearest platform. Yannu was some ways away but he had a calculating expression on his face, as if he'd been planning for this. He nodded to his bunyip retainers, but instead of attacking Ari, they turned back toward me.

I clutched my sword and my stomach burned.

Where was Vannis?

Yarin raised his sword and Yavin and Yuri came running. My boost, bump, and shield spells were gone. Ari's magic was no longer available to me. A hidebehind assassin lurked somewhere near, three bunyips were bearing down on me, and one very large, uncontrollable drakon was one step away from killing someone and/or just scooping me up and flying off with me.

It seemed preposterous, but it was very real. Ari's massive drakon heart seemed to beat with only three clear thoughts: *kill... mine... take.* His thoughts were so primal, the object of each desire wasn't even named. For the drakon, there was no Yarin, Yavin, or Yuri. There was no Malphia, Vannis or even Nouiomo. There were only enemies and a treasure, which he was sick and tired of not having all to himself.

My own signature must have pulsed with shock, dismay, and not a little fear. Just before Ari launched himself toward me, I gave the order to end it.

"Stonewall! Now, Fara!" My voice faltered a bit. "Ari though, *not* Malphia."

Admitting defeat – and possibly shaming Ari – wasn't at all what I'd wanted to do this morning.

Like the good Angel she was, Fara complied and cast Stonewall over Ari. It had been his idea, but who would have guessed we'd have to use it on him instead of the other team's captain? Instantly, a stone wall, tall and round as a two-story tower, enclosed him.

"I surrender," I called over to Yannu. "You win," I told Malphia. Not wanting to fuel Ari's fire any longer, I ruthlessly tamped down my feelings of bitterness, frustration, defeat, and disappointment. I took a breath, waiting to see what would happen.

Would the surrender be accepted? Would Fara's

stone walls hold Ari?

Malphia rose and glanced at Yannu, who was eyeing me with a narrowed gaze. I couldn't tell if he was pleased or disgusted with what I'd just done. Finally, he gave the cessation gesture and the bunyips retreated. I exhaled as he walked over to me.

"Angels aren't allowed to aggressively cast against *regulare* demons," Yannu reminded us, his expression dark.

"Stonewall isn't offensive. It's defensive. And Ms. Vanderlin didn't cast it over the patron, she cast it around him." In some ways, it was a semantics game. One that was nerve-wracking to play without Ari by my side. In our current conditions, neither Fara nor I could defend ourselves against Yannu. And we'd just incapacitated the one demon who would have.

Yannu stared at Fara for a long time before turning back to me.

"Looks like you lost again, *consigliere*."

"I surrendered. And, besides, it wasn't a fair fight."

Yannu cocked a brow at me. "Is that so? At least we weren't the ones who cast an experimental, potentially dangerous spell over this town's demon lord."

"We? 'Fess up, Yannu. You cheated by helping the opposing team win. Malphia wasn't its captain, you were."

Inwardly, I gulped and cursed myself for speaking without thinking. *Dumb, Onyx, dumb.* You don't accuse a *regulare* demon – especially a Captain of the Guard – of cheating.

But Yannu just shrugged. "I'm everyone's captain."

Behind us, Stonewall disintegrated just as Vannis reappeared. I tensed as Ari, a man once again, emerged naked and faced the hidebehind. But instead of trying to attack Ari again, Vannis took a knee and bowed as Malphia had.

Yannu lowered his voice so that only I could hear.

"I'm not sure what Aristos' greater weakness is – his left wing... or you."

10
WALKABOUT

They say that smell is the oldest and most powerful sense we have. And this is mostly true, even for members of the Host. Certainly, metaphysical things are best sensed with our magic, but with the purely physical, we're no different from Hyrkes. And the smell of Ari – calm, peaceful, relaxed, contented Ari – sprawled so close to me brought back a flood of warm memories: playing mancala with him at his adoptive family's home in Bradbury... sleeping in on Saturdays in his dorm room at Infernus... even studying together at Corpus Justica, which had almost always led to other, less cerebral, pursuits.

He smelled the same. Some combination of vanilla, anise, and hot muscly man that I'd once been completely and naively overwhelmed by. To be fair, Ari's human form wasn't a lie. Most demons have several forms. But whatever human shape they take is theirs. It's not an illusion or a glamour. They can't change it. It's who they are – or at least it's *part* of who they are.

After this morning's melee, Fara and I had retreated to our rooms. I hadn't known if Ari would still want to patrol the gorge with me, but I figured, under the circumstances, that waiting at the rotunda was probably better than heading off somewhere else.

Fara had spent an hour at her desk, writing up field notes and journal entries. Then she'd declared that, if all I was going to do was sit around all day, she was heading to the hospital. Then I'd waited... and waited... and wondered if Ari was angry with me for having Fara cast Stonewall over him.

Around midday, however, Tenacity had come into my room to inform me that his lordship wanted me. She'd given me a saucy wink then, which I'd ignored, and told me she'd packed a picnic lunch for us. Curious about where Ari might be taking me, I'd scrubbed my face and located a package in my trousseau marked "Walkabout." Soon after, my bloodstained armor had been exchanged for soft canvas pants and a comfortable tunic. Thinking of the mid-summer heat, I'd tied my hair back and stepped into the atrium.

Tenacity had hooted at my appearance.

"What?"

"You should wear pigtails."

"Why?"

"Because then you'd look even less intimidating," she'd said, guffawing. "It's hard to believe you're the same person from this morning. No one would be afraid of you looking like that."

"Should they be?"

She'd rolled her eyes. "Yes!" And then Ari had entered dressed in something similar and Tenacity had nearly lost it.

Our stated purpose was to look for any sign that Displodo might be a *rogare* who was hiding somewhere outside of town, but our excursion was also a chance for Ari and me to discuss suspects and clues. I'd been in the gorge for two days now. And I'd spoken to Ari privately each night. But those discussions had focused on the *us* I'd denied existed. Today, I was determined to further my investigation.

We spent the next hour and a half hiking along a blackened trail that skirted the northern bank of the Acheron. Mount Occasus' peak rose in the distance and, the closer we got to it, the steeper the trail became. After I'd turned around for the seven hundredth time, Ari had assured me that there was very little chance of encountering a hidebehind. He likened them to shooting stars. They were out there, but they wouldn't show themselves during the day.

"Vannis did," I said, not bothering to hide my hatred.

But Ari only smiled and said, "I'm not worried about him so you shouldn't be either." I wasn't entirely convinced, but I let it drop, not wanting to spoil what was otherwise a serenely beautiful hike. All afternoon, we'd neither seen, nor sensed, anything out of the ordinary.

In time the narrow trail led us to a broad, open ledge. Built into the right angle between the ledge and the sheer rock face of the mountain was an old stone castle, six stories high, roofless and crumbling. At first it reminded me of the Stone Pointe keep, but once inside, I realized the two buildings were very different. Here there was no mud or muck, no disgusting bone throne or human refuse. Its proportions were normal too, not monstrously gargantuan. This wasn't a place where giants had once lived. According to Ari, it was the original home of Servius Rockthorn and his family. This had been Rockthorn Gorge's first castle – its first "rotunda."

Ari spread a blanket over the building's floor, a

combination of broken pavers and dry dirt. Then he emptied his pack. A few bottles of water and a dozen or so small paper bags fell to the ground. I sat down near the blanket's edge and reached for one, hoping it wouldn't be full of *just deserts* leftovers.

How long passed after that with us merely sitting, sipping, and eating, I don't know. The bags turned out to be full of the most innocuous, almost boring, food items: tree nuts, beef jerky, and hard cheese. The silence between us might have been awkward if it weren't for the fact that it allowed us to hear the warbling of bluebirds and the occasional, farther off, cry of an eagle or griffon. After all, tension was pretty hard to maintain when the air was full of bird song. So, little by little, I began to relax. Truly relax. To a soft, mellow state that I hadn't felt since before I'd arrived.

Ari seemed to bask in my mood. He sprawled out on his back, alternatively chewing and simply gazing up at the cloud-covered sky. His signature radiated *tranquility*, and it had seemed like, in that moment anyway, if I'd suggested we forsake everything for each other and just spend the rest of our lives doing nothing but this, he would have agreed with alacrity.

Maybe that's what he was waiting for. For me to suggest such a mad and selfish scheme. Thank Luck the smell of him – spicy, sexy, dangerous, yet familiar – brought me back to reality. Ari peered over at me.

"How are Ivy and Fitz?"

I smiled. "They're well. Ivy is Assistant Editor for the Riparian Law Journal now and Fitz is dating Francesca."

"Francesca Cerise?"

I nodded, grinning.

"What happened to Babette?"

"She threw him over for Cornwall Dun."

Ari grunted and then laughed. But his laughter seemed to die early, accompanied by the briefest whiff of wistfulness. *Did Ari miss St. Luck's?*

I'd never thought about it before, but why wouldn't he? Why would he have signed up for three years if he hadn't at least liked some part of it? He'd enrolled there before he'd even met me.

"I'm sorry," I blurted out.

Ari frowned and his signature seemed to snap and retract. "For what?"

"For Stonewall…" I took a deep breath. "And for Revelare Lucere."

Revelare Lucere had been the spell Rafe had cast that had revealed Ari to be the demon he was. I hadn't intended to apologize for telling Rafe to cast it. Or for telling Fara to cast Stonewall today. And I probably would do everything all over again the same way if given a second chance. But that didn't mean I wasn't sorry for some of the consequences. Like the fact that Ari could never return to St. Luck's as a student. Or the fact that I may have undermined his authority today, which was the opposite of what I'd come here to do.

But he didn't seem angry. His signature was no longer radiating *tranquility* but he was far from fired up. He sat up and faced me.

"Life would be a whole lot simpler without the Angels, huh?"

I pulled my knees up and wrapped my arms around them. "Life would be a whole lot simpler without demons," I countered. But I cocked an eyebrow at him and smiled so he would know I was only half-serious.

He grunted and looked away.

"Ari…" I said, wondering where to start. We

needed to discuss Displodo and the camarilla and the possible connection between the two, but there were a few preliminary things I was wondering about, like: "How did you end up here? Why Rockthorn Gorge?"

He blew his breath out. "Remember first semester when I told you I knew Cliodna?" I shook my head slowly, trying to remember. But Ari waved off my lack of recall. "It doesn't matter." He paused, thinking. I didn't sense he was trying to avoid telling me something as much as he was simply trying to figure out the best and easiest way to share his story.

"My parents haven't always agreed on what future I should have," he said. I murmured in sympathy and wondered if that was the case for all parents. Mine had certainly disagreed about which direction to steer me.

"My parents raised me as a human," Ari continued. "Not as a Hyrke, of course,"—he laughed then, I guess because he still thought the fact that I'd been raised as a Hyrke was at least nominally ridiculous – as if he was in a position to criticize! – "but as a human member of the Host with waning magic. My mother taught me discipline and control and I was sent to occult schools so that I could learn the ways of the Host from the perspective of its human members."

I nodded. I knew that Ari, unlike me, had attended Host schools before enrolling at St. Luck's.

"When I reached adolescence, however, my father started encouraging me to seize my demon destiny." He scoffed. "As if there is such a thing. Unlike humans, demons aren't born with a birthright. They aren't spawned as the patron of something. They have to forge their identities and followings from whatever openings are available. I told him I didn't want to be the patron of anything. I didn't want followers. But he said that was only my mother talking." Ari's voice grew soft. "My dad pointed out that even Matt, my younger brother, would be gone in eighty years, maybe less. What would I do then?"

My throat grew tight. Lots of people talked about immortality as if it would be a blessing. Didn't they realize how lonely it would be? Demons weren't immortal, but they lived for so much longer than we did, they might as well be.

"There were discussions. There were fights. In the end, it was agreed that I'd contact your father about becoming a demon executioner. Since I have zero tolerance for *rogares*, it was a job I was good at." He paused then, perhaps giving me a moment to complain. In the past, I'd made all sorts of noise about his violent history. Considering the things I'd done since, though, I'd lost the right to object. I wouldn't say I was bloodthirsty, but I could no longer describe myself as a pacifist without being a raging hypocrite as well.

"When Karanos asked which Maegester school I was going to attend, I told him I didn't know. He suggested St. Luck's and... you know the rest."

I frowned and barked out a laugh. "No, I don't. Hello? Rockthorn Gorge? Cliodna? Why her? Why here?"

I wasn't resentful. Not anymore. But I needed to know more about her since she was a member of the camarilla. Not to mention she'd threatened my life. Maybe.

Ari's expression was inscrutable. Was he mad? Embarrassed? With who? Over what?

"She was my first," he said quietly.

"Your first...?" The words were out of my mouth before I realized what he meant. *Oh.* Never mind. I clenched my jaw and looked away.

We sat in silence for a few minutes and then Ari said, "And that's all I'm going to tell you about her, Noon, because she... doesn't... matter," he repeated. "I never loved her. I was just... talked into her."

"Uh-huh," I said, rolling my eyes, "whatever, Ari." I snorted. "And you can't say she doesn't matter, by the way. She's the Lady of the Gorge, the demon with the second most seniority here. So... let me guess, she played a big part in helping you get elected?"

Ari's silence was all the affirmation I needed.

"You know, she threatened to poison me."

"What?" His voice was sharp.

I told Ari the details of my conversation with Cliodna, and his expression darkened. He stood up and started pacing. Even if Cliodna had just been testing me, it was clear that Ari didn't like what she'd said.

"She knows I would do more than kill her. I would pluck her feathers out one by one, debone her, and *then* kill her."

Ari's signature had become icy. Last year, it might have alarmed me. This year, I just asked him to sit back down. "What good would that do me?" I asked. "I could care less about being avenged. I want to live."

"So does Cliodna."

It was his matter-of-fact delivery that tipped me off. "You've had this discussion with her," I said breathlessly, trying to convince myself it was incredulity I felt, not fear. "You've already warned her not to kill me."

"Cliodna is excitable and high-strung," he said. "But she's not suicidal, and she doesn't do anything that isn't in her own best interests. I made her understand that killing you would not result in a favorable outcome for her."

I sputtered. Ari sounded so pragmatic. Was this the demon side of him? Having seen – and felt – the drakon earlier today, I thought not. That beast's desires were passionate and primitive, whereas the man in front of me sounded cold-blooded and analytical. This time I jumped up, no longer able to sit still.

"When did you tell Cliodna about me? Before or after she helped you get elected?"

I could only imagine the Lady of the Gorge's reaction to discovering Ari's feelings for me after helping him get elected. She'd have wanted to kill us both.

But Ari said, "Before. I told her about you last summer – the day I arrived, almost a year ago. I would have told her anyway, but she sensed your *signare* on me and demanded to know who put it there."

"And you had no trouble telling her."

Ari laughed. "Why should I? I'm not ashamed of my feelings for you. *You're* the one going around telling everyone you're my *ex*-inamorata."

I opened my mouth to tell him it was Fara who'd first called me that, but then decided we needed to stay on track. I walked over to where Nova was napping in a patch of sunlight and leaned against the stone wall of the castle.

"What about Malphia? The only thing the Demon Council seems to know about her is her name. What's her role?"

"She was Potomus' spymaster."

I made a face. "And you kept her on?"

"Noon, if I fired everyone who was dangerous or deadly, you'd go too."

My cheeks flushed and I looked away. I didn't know whether to feel ashamed, offended, or pleased. I cleared my throat and turned back to him.

"Tell me about Yannu. Frankly, he seems like the best candidate for patron. He's Captain of the Guard. He's lived in the gorge for almost as long as Cliodna. He's a bunyip and over half the ranks are bunyips. Why wasn't he elected? Do the people or Cliodna not like him?"

I could hardly blame them if that were the case, although it would be weird to be aligned with Cliodna on something.

"Acheron and Yannu don't get along. Technically, Acheron doesn't get a vote, but realistically, he's got at least three thousand. Over a third of the residents in Rockthorn Gorge consider Acheron to be their primary deity. They follow other demons, of course, both greater and lesser, but their main adoration and devotion belong to Acheron."

"Why doesn't Acheron like Yannu?"

Ari's mouth quirked. "Two totally different life philosophies, that's all. Yannu is all about action whereas Acheron is not. Acheron is, in many ways, like his river – natural, flowing, meandering. He's incredibly powerful. Like his river, he can rage and kill. But most of the time he prefers to be a part of the background, not control the foreground."

"Maybe Yannu is upset that Cliodna and Acheron backed you," I argued. "Maybe he's been vying for the patronship all along. Maybe he killed Potomus and then tried to kill you because he wants to be Lord of the Gorge, not Captain of the Guard."

Ari frowned, not following. "Displodo has bombed the dam when patrons haven't been present too. The dam was the target, not me."

"But the fact that Acheron opposes the dam is well

known, isn't it? Maybe Yannu wanted to make it look like Acheron was Displodo. Or maybe Acheron really *is* Displodo."

Ari seemed to seriously consider my theories, but he looked doubtful.

"If you don't think either Acheron or Yannu are Displodo," I pressed, "then who?"

"Why do you think Displodo is a demon we know?"

I told him Zeffre's theory then – that Displodo was one of the demons in his camarilla.

"Is it true?" I asked. "Were they the only demons who knew you were going to be on the dam that day?"

Ari nodded slowly.

"Do any of them have a reason to destroy the dam… or you?"

He sighed, and I felt the faintest whiff of *melancholia* in his signature. For a moment, it took my breath away. I realized how abrasive my questions must have felt to him. Yes, Ari had hurt me deeply when he lied to me about being a demon. But I was the one who'd broken up with him. I was the one who'd told him I couldn't be with him anymore. I was the one who'd forced him to find a future elsewhere.

Well, he had. And I'd just shot it to hell by telling him one of his new allies might be trying to kill him.

He rolled up the blanket, deep in thought, and then stuffed it, the bottles, and the empty bags back in his pack. *Melancholia* turned to *resolve* and he stood up. "I don't know…" he said finally. "The only thing I'm sure of is that I don't trust them. Not really." He looked over at me then, his expression ambiguous.

"Besides, why do you think Displodo is a demon at all? Maybe he – or she – is human." He looked both patient and impatient, resigned and determined, forlorn and optimistic. Had I not sensed his earlier blink-and-you'll-miss-it moment of vulnerability, I might have responded with a joke about demons being the root of all evil. Instead, I asked about Zeffre.

"Then what about your foreman? I'm betting he knew you were going to be on the dam the day Displodo destroyed it. Do you trust him?"

Ari smiled. "With my life and yours."

My eyebrows rose. "But he was Lord Potomus' foreman. Basically, you inherited him in the same way you inherited your camarilla. How come he alone has your trust?"

"Because he's my uncle."

My jaw dropped. Huh?

Ari laughed, but then sobered. "My aunt died years ago. She was my adoptive dad's sister. Tenacity is Matt's cousin – and mine."

"Tenacity is… Zeffre's daughter?" Even I laughed. And then I teased, "The demon Lord Aristos has an Angel cousin. Ha!"

But Ari's face stayed serious and he walked over to me. "You're wrong, you know," he said quietly. "Zeffre's not the only one who has my trust. My *consigliere* does too."

By late afternoon I felt as if we'd hiked all of northern Halja, but of course that wasn't even close to being true. My legs were burning, and I was sweating and beginning to wonder if Ari was prolonging this patrol simply because it was an excuse for him to be alone with me. But when I saw the *via ferrata* rising up the nearly vertical rock face in front of us, I knew Ari had led me this way with a final destination in mind.

Via ferratas, or "iron roads," were a misnomer. There was nothing roadlike about the iron rungs, pegs, and cable route that had been screwed into Mount Occasus' limestone wall here.

I put my hands on my hips and glared at Ari. "Seriously? What's up there anyway? It can't possibly be worth it."

He smirked and pulled a large paper-wrapped package out of his pack. "Come on, Noon," he said while unwrapping it. "You'll be fine. First semester, I'd have had to carry you up. But now? I'm pretty sure you'd be able to carry *me* up, if you were determined enough."

I snorted my disbelief while Ari pulled a meaty bone out of his bag and tossed it to Nova. She let it drop in front of her and then sat back on her haunches, waiting for me to give the signal that it was okay to start gnawing on it. I wish I could say her behavior was the result of her getting better about not chewing things she wasn't supposed to, but truth is, Ari made her wary. I think it was because he was a demon. In some ways, I couldn't blame her.

I sighed and gave her the go-ahead. Ari handed me a water bottle and I took a few swigs, eyeing the *via ferrata* with trepidation. I didn't have acrophobia, but nor did I have the head for heights that some people did. Rafe and I had done a lot of climbing last semester and, at one point, he'd had to cast me up with three different climbing spells.

Seemingly out of the blue, Ari asked me how another of our former classmates was doing – Brunus Olivine, the MIT who'd shot the cursed arrow at me.

I froze with the water bottle halfway to my lips and then slowly lowered it.

"Is Adikia looking after him," Ari asked, "Or did one of your father's Maegesters take care of him?"

Adikia was the Patron Demon of Abuse, Injustice, and Oppression. She was also the patron of the New Babylon Gaol. She was well known for her love of torture. "Looking after" a prisoner meant boiling, burning, flaying, branding, cutting, and anything else dreamt up by her enforcers' sadistic minds. I wouldn't entrust Adikia with my worst enemy. Still, mercy hadn't been my motivation.

"I took care of him," I said, meeting Ari's stare.

"You killed Brunus?" Ari's tone made it clear that he found the idea pretty unbelievable. But, for once, I wasn't offended that he'd underestimated me.

I'm not exactly sure why I said what I said next. Maybe it was because, without further explanation, Ari would likely think that I'd killed Brunus for revenge.

"He was holding a knife to Rafe's neck," I said.

"So you killed Brunus to protect your Guardian?"

I frowned. Was Ari going to try and make me feel guilty about killing Brunus? I refused to look away. After a moment, Ari did. But when he turned back to me, the full force of his gaze made me feel like the water I'd been drinking had suddenly turned to ice. Instinctively, I took a step back. My foot hit a rock that I hadn't known was there, throwing me off balance, and I fell backward and landed on my rump with a thump. It was such a girlish thing to do that I just sat there, glaring up at Ari, pissed that he'd literally brought me so low. My uncharacteristic clumsiness then led Ari to do what he might not have done otherwise. He offered me his hand to help me up – and I accepted it.

Ari pulled me up from the ground and I stood in front of him, inches away, head tilted back, eyes defiantly narrowed, until he rubbed his thumb across the back of my hand. I shivered and looked down. The warm glow of my skin where Ari had touched me contrasted sharply with the silver patina of Rafe's bracelet. When I looked up again, Ari was staring down at it.

"Is this bracelet a *signare*, Noon?"

His voice was solemn, but not menacing.

"No," I said quickly, shaking my head. There was a lot of meaning behind the bracelet, but it wasn't an Angel's version of a *signare*. Ari's relief was so palpable, it prompted me to admit something I wasn't even sure Ari had a right to know – that I'd kissed Rafe.

It was the shortest, most peculiar admission I've ever made. Rafe had told me to tell Ari "everything." I assume he'd meant that, if I wanted to, that included the fact that we'd shared a kiss... or two... or more.

I wasn't much for kissing and telling. It was poor form. And, besides, Ari and I were definitely *not* together at the time. So it wasn't really any of his business.

So why burden him with my admission?

Because I believed in having "clean hands." I'd accused Ari of lying to me by omission. I wasn't about to do the same thing to him. I didn't know how, or if, my confession would change things between us, I only knew I had to make it.

"Ari... Rafe and I... during my last assignment... down in southern Halja... we... well, he... No, *me*—I kissed him." And then, as if Ari couldn't already sense my conflicted emotions, I added, "Not on the cheek. Not as a friend."

Ari closed his eyes and buttoned up his signature. But his grip suddenly became vicelike and hot as a brand. I tried to pull my hand back, but he held tight.

Nova stopped gnawing and started growling, her hackles rising. Instinctively, I sent a pulse of magic down my arm into my hand. There was a spark and then, thank Luck, the moment before my fireball exploded, Ari released me and stepped back.

We glared at each other.

Nova rose from the ground, tense, ready to strike, her eyes on Ari.

I wasn't going to apologize. Rafe and I had done nothing wrong. Ari would just have to deal with what had happened and move on.

"Why isn't Rafe here now, Noon? Why is he no longer your Guardian?"

"I told you. He said he wanted to train with the Ophanim."

"So he's an oath breaker."

I huffed. "I released him from his vow."

Ari recapped his water bottle, crumpled up the paper wrapping from Nova's bone, and stuffed them both back in his pack. It took longer than it should have, and the entire time I couldn't help feeling he was digesting what I'd said.

I let him. Better here than down below with his camarilla, the entire town, and apparently his uncle and cousin too, watching.

Finally, he looked me in the eye. "There's only one way down," he said, pointing back toward the trail. "You can't get lost. I'll see you tomorrow."

And then he shouldered his pack and started climbing the *via ferrata*.

Luck spare me from jealous ex-boyfriends. Luck spare

me from men who think they're invincible. Luck spare me from *via ferratas*.

Watching Ari climb the *via ferrata* with only one good arm while he was still upset about my revelation was excessively agonizing. I suppose, if you're the kind of person who thinks that girls should be punished for kissing people after their boyfriend has broken their heart, then the next hour was my true *just deserts*.

Needless to say, I left Nova contentedly munching on the bone Ari had so thoughtfully brought for her and followed him up the iron road. I barely spared a thought for my own safety, so focused was I on Ari's arduous climb.

What if he fell?

I couldn't stop him or catch him. Could he even fly with his damaged wing? I became so concerned that I fired up a knife and was just about to cut my palm and make an offering for Ari's safe passage to Verstung, Patron Demon of the Northern Mountains, when I heard his voice.

"Don't," he called out. "Please don't. I'm fine. You're fine. It's not much farther. You don't need to make an offering." It almost seemed like he was trying to convince himself as much as me.

I'm fine.

Was he?

11

THE MAGNA FAX

The *via ferrata* led us up the side of Mount Occasus. At its windy top was a walled plaza surrounding a stone tower that matched the crumbling architecture of the ruined castle below. Perched in one of the tower's crenels was the huge bore of a cannon – the Magna Fax.

"I thought Maegesters and gunpowder didn't get along," I said, pointing to the giant cannon. My pants and tunic pressed against me, as if they were afraid of the wind that pushed them, while daring strands of my hair escaped their binding and flew madly around my face.

"They don't," Ari said, unshouldering his pack. He glanced up at the Magna Fax and then turned to me. "The first lords of the gorge were Maegesters, just like Servius Rockthorn. But after the fifth one died of natural causes within only a century and a half, some residents started pushing for a demon lord. The town's engineer argued against it. Said a demon lord would end up being a bugbear to the town instead of protection against the *rogares*. He told the townspeople he'd build them something that would be more valiant than a Maegester, more enduring than a demon, and more powerful than

Luck himself."

I stepped out of the shadow of the tower and into the light of the setting sun. "Didn't Rockthorn Gorge's early settlers know that mortal arrogance rarely goes unpunished?"

Ari gave me a cryptic look. "The engineer was a practical man who believed in living people more than absent lords. Sound familiar?"

Reflexively, I opened my mouth to say something smart. But I shut it when nothing came to mind. It was true that I wanted to believe the living held more sway over me than the dead, but my life's course had been directed by too many quirks of fate for me to convincingly argue that Luck didn't play his part.

"The engineer told the town he could build the ultimate protector for them out of stymphwax."

"Stymphwax? As in stymphalian birds?" I whistled in admiration. Stymphalian birds were Lucifer's fabled birds of prey. They made basilisks seem like ladybugs and drakons seem like lumbering elephants. Their feathers were hard as mail and their blood and body fluids were hideously flammable. During Armageddon, they'd dive-bombed Lucifer's targets, willfully sacrificing themselves in order to create fiery infernos around their dead bodies. They lived for two things: war and death. They had zero nesting instincts – because they built hives out of stymphwax, which was a thousand times more explosive than they were.

I laughed. "Has the Magna Fax ever been fired? If that story is true, a gunner would be safer waving a lightning rod in a thunderstorm than they would be trying to fire that thing."

Ari smiled, but it seemed as though he was enjoying my amusement rather than agreeing. "The Magna Fax is ensorcelled," he said.

I gave him a wry look. *Of course it was*. My amusement faded. In my experience, ensorcelled objects, while not always cursed, almost always led to bad luck.

"An Angel helped the engineer collect the stymphwax and mold it into the Magna Fax. Then she cast Temper over it. It can only be fired with a slow match made from the pages of her spell book."

"What happens then?" I asked, my voice low and foreboding.

"Gorge legend says the Magna Fax is pre-loaded. That its cannonballs are magically produced when it's lit. The town likes to boast that their 'protector' could level a city... or an invading army. But who knows? You were right to ask; it's never been fired."

"But it could be. I don't see any guards up here, and you don't seem too concerned about someone firing the Magna Fax. Does that mean the Angel's spell book – the cannon's book of matches – was destroyed?"

Instead of answering me, Ari walked over to the low wall surrounding the plaza's perimeter. Beyond him, the view was stunning. Soft, green waves seemed to undulate around us. Nearer mountains shimmered in bright shades of lime and pear, while those farther away dissolved in a distant curtain of greenish-black. To our left the sun was sinking, and its dying light made the Magna Fax look as if it were cast from burnished gold.

"Let me guess," I said, coming to stand beside Ari. "The engineer destroyed the Angel's spell book – because he realized loaded weapons can backfire?"

"No. Town historians claim the Magna Fax was the outpost's only protector for almost thirty years – from the day it was built until the day the engineer died."

I snorted. "Besides the legionaries. In any case, who really knows what happened up here eighteen hundred years ago? We barely know what happened in New Babylon then."

Ari shrugged. "True, but you should know the rest of the story, since you'll be living here for the next six months... or possibly longer."

I glanced over at him, stunned by the brief, blistering swell of *hope* in his signature.

"After the engineer's death, Rockthorn Gorge elected its first bunyip patron. If you believe the old ballads, that first demon lord conceded that the Magna Fax was capable of defending the town, just as it was capable of destroying it. He hid the Angel's spell book – the cannon's matchbook – and then he had an offering bowl installed up here to remind everyone that Rockthorn Gorge was protected by a living demon and waning magic, not a stymphwax machine held together by an Angel's spell."

Whoa. Well, whoever that first bunyip was, he wasn't subtle. Nor did he seem to care for Angels. Were those universal bunyip traits? Because he sounded like Yannu.

"Where was the matchbook hidden? Do you know?"

"It was disguised as the *tabula ansata* on the statue of Servius Rockthorn – the one that's in the center of the rotunda's atrium under the oculus."

"Who else knows that?"

Ari frowned. "You, me, Cliodna, and Yannu." He must have known what I was thinking then because he said, "It's been safe there for millennia."

"Nothing stays hidden forever."

We stared at each other. He blinked first. "Well, what would you have me do? Move it now? That would only draw attention to it. The rotunda has twenty-four-hour guards and a surfeit of shielding spells. Any member of the camarilla – except you – would have a hard time stealing it."

I sighed. That would have to do. For now. Eventually the book would have to be moved to New Babylon for safekeeping. But I had enough to press Ari about today.

I looked around and spotted the offering bowl down on a lower level of the plaza, as well as a bronze plaque at the base of the tower beneath the Magna Fax. I walked over to take a closer look.

TO YOU, THE HARDY SETTLERS OF THE GORGE,

MAY THIS GRAND CANNON DETER YOUR ENEMIES AND ENSURE YOUR FREEDOM AND INDEPENDENCE.

OBADIAH ZEFFRE, FYR 128 AA

"Zeffre?" My voice was laced with suspicion as I turned toward Ari. I didn't believe in coincidence. "Your foreman – your uncle – is a descendant of the engineer who built the Magna Fax?"

He nodded.

"Ari," I said cautiously, knowing how important his adoptive family was to him, "didn't Displodo's legend start in the second century?"

"Yes," he said quietly. "But Nephemiah Zeffre is not a sinner."

I pressed my lips together as a new theory started to take shape in my mind. Maybe Ari had been right when we'd discussed Displodo earlier. Maybe Displodo was human. Maybe Displodo was Nephemiah Zeffre. Maybe Displodo had *always* been a Zeffre. Maybe Obadiah's unfinished legacy – convincing Rockthorn Gorge to eschew demons and declare their independence – had been passed down from father to son for nearly fourscore generations.

I walked across the plaza, down the steps, and stopped in front of the offering bowl. Chalices were everywhere in Halja. Hyrkes used them to offer blood sacrifices to the demons they adored. This one came with the usual knife, bandages, and another inscription.

FOR TO THE DEMONS BELONG DOMINION OVER RIVER, LAND, AND SETTLERS

"Rockthorn Gorge's first demon lord wasn't subtle about his claim," I told Ari, who'd followed me. "Instead of hiding the Angel's spell book, that first bunyip patron should have dismantled the Magna Fax – or at least removed Obadiah's inscription. Foolish, wasn't he? To allow the idea of freedom and independence to fester in followers' minds?"

Ari gave me a funny look, half-surprised, half-amused. I smirked—*should I tell Ari my question was facetious?*—and peered at the river below. From this distance, it looked as thin as my arm.

"Do people still climb up here to offer sacrifices to the Lord of the Gorge?"

Ari nodded and faced me.

"Did you bring me up here so that I could offer a sacrifice to you?"

I'd offered countless sacrifices before. Most of them had been nothing more than a symbolic scratch, but I knew from our time together that Ari had never liked the idea of me doing it. Now, however, his dislike of blood sacrifice took on new meaning. Maybe it was because he didn't like the idea of me giving blood sacrifices to *other* demons.

But even before I saw his face, I knew that couldn't

be right. He stared back at me, his expression a mixture of disappointment and disgust.

"I didn't bring you up here so that you could make a sacrifice," he scoffed, clearly annoyed with me now. "You followed me."

I folded my arms across my chest. "You *were* going to bring me up here."

"Do you really not know me, Noon?" And then, with no warning, he kicked the chalice, smashing it into bits. Large chunks of it sailed off over the cliff while the rest of it fell to the ground in pieces.

I was more dumbstruck than scared. I didn't know what shocked me more, the fact that Ari had just destroyed a relic that was almost as old as the Magna Fax, or the fact that he'd done it using only his muscles and no magic.

But Ari wasn't dismayed, or even out of control; he was simply angry.

"I don't want you to treat me like a demon or a deity," he said bluntly. "That's not who I am." He stared at the river below, his signature a mass of churning emotions. "You asked me earlier why I came here... why I chose to become patron of Rockthorn Gorge." He turned to face me. "I didn't do it for me. I did it for you. I knew if I became Lord of the Gorge, I'd be able to request a *consigliere*. The day after the election, I told Zeffre to write your offer letter."

At first, I didn't know what to say. *He became the patron demon of seven thousand people just to have an opportunity to win me back?* It was almost too much to contemplate. But then I reminded myself that, regardless of the future, I had a job to do *now*.

"Ari, you can't become Lord of the Gorge and then not expect to be treated like a patron. You say that's not who you are – but it is. Regardless of the reason, you chose this life. Your followers are depending on you to keep them safe. Someone out there is a threat – to them, to you. What was it you once said to me? 'You were born with waning magic. You should learn how to use it.' Well, Ari, you were born as a drakon. Don't you think it's time you learned to fly?"

"I know how to fly."

"Then show me."

"*This* from the girl who had her Angel cast Stonewall to keep me ground-bound earlier today."

I said nothing. I didn't need to. I had a feeling silence was my strongest argument to that statement.

Sure enough, after a moment, Ari raked his hand through his hair and gestured futilely between us. "The difference is that I love the part of you that is full of waning magic, but you don't love the part of me that shifts into a drakon – and neither do I."

"I didn't love the part of me that was full of waning magic in the beginning," I said. "*You* taught me to do that."

Ari's gaze met mine again, his face half-golden, half-shadowed. *How appropriate*, I thought.

Was I brave enough to make a deal with a demon?

"Ari, I want to offer you something. But you have to offer me something in return."

I could tell he suspected a trap – and he was right.

"What do you want?"

"I want you to shift in front of me. Here. Now. Without anyone watching or waiting to kill us. I want to see your left wing. I want to see if it can be healed."

"It can't be."

"Nightshade regrew my tooth, you know. And

everyone said that couldn't be done."

Ari laughed. "Impressive, but a tooth isn't bone. And your tooth is what, a half-inch long? My wingspan is almost thirty feet. Even your miracle-working Mederi brother wouldn't be able to grow back something that big."

The sun, and my window of opportunity, was slipping below the horizon. The wind buffeted us from every direction and I had a feeling we were standing on the edge of more than just Mount Occasus. We were standing at the edge of the rest of our lives.

"If you want to keep working together," I pressed, "you're going to have to do this."

"What do you mean? You can't quit this residency." Ari's tone was mostly amused, but there was a hint of apprehension.

"No, but I can work to contract, as they say. Act as your consig during the day and then disappear into my room every night…"

Ari's eyes narrowed and his gaze became calculating. It was pretty clear he was already thinking up all sorts of reasons for me to be wherever he wanted me to be.

"I'll tell you what," I said. "I'll give you an offering. And then you can decide if you want to reciprocate."

"It better not be blood."

I shook my head, suddenly unable to speak, and stepped toward him, shaking. My offering – my gift – was irrevocable. Once given, I wouldn't be able to take it back.

Ari watched me move toward him the way Virtus watched rabbits. I think this morning's melee and our discussions this afternoon had made Ari feel less assured than usual. But it wasn't insecurity I sensed in his signature as much as a need to shore up his position. I stopped walking when the tip of one of my boots hit his and then, before I could lose my nerve, I stood up on my toes and pressed my mouth to his. Instantly, a stinging spark raced from my lips to my navel. I gasped and laughed and he smiled, as if he had all the patience in the world.

I tried again.

Ari's lips were soft and warm, a direct contrast to his rock-solid chest. I raised my arms, clasped my hands around his neck, and leaned into him, deepening my kiss. He tasted like salt and sin, two things that were as addictive as he was. My tongue tingled, my thoughts scattered, and my magic parried with his.

Ari was a very willing, albeit passive, recipient of my gift – until I lowered my heels to the ground and started to pull back. Clearly unsated, he then refused to let me go. He kept his mouth on mine as he wound his good hand through my hair, preventing my retreat. Only when he sensed I was short of breath did he leave off, but his fiery kisses were soon scorching a path down my throat. I froze when he reached my collarbone. I wasn't yet ready for him to venture lower and risk touching my mark, even through the cloth of my tunic. He raised his head. His eyes were glassy and blown, his pupils wide, his expression rapacious.

"Should I shift now, Nouiomo?" His voice was as low as the gorge and just as treacherous. He was sounding a warning note. Telling me the exchange was uneven. I'd given him a kiss, but he would take... Luck knew what. I swallowed, suddenly scared to say yes.

Ari laughed, the sound of it somehow darker and more dangerous than before.

"It's good to know some things haven't changed,"

he said, his mouth hovering over mine. I closed my eyes, breathlessly waiting, wanting, worrying... about Ari and eventide and surrendering to them both. "You're still eager... and reluctant."

Ari's hand reached for mine behind my back and he locked our fingers together. Then, instead of kissing me, he whirled me around so my back was flat against his chest and he nipped at the nape of my neck. My skin broke out in goose bumps and my knees nearly buckled before I finally broke away and turned around.

"If you wait too long, I won't be able to see your wing."

But Ari just shook his head and advanced on me. For once, I didn't mind. I willingly allowed him to press me back until I was one step away from the broken railing.

"You're going to shift one way or another," I warned. When he realized what I meant, he stopped and became serious.

"Come on," he said, stepping back. "We should climb down before it gets too dark."

"I'm not leaving until you shift."

He sighed. "We can't stay up here forever."

"Exactly."

"Noon, the first time I shifted you were petrified, the second, infuriated, the third, cautious enough to incapacitate me. I don't want to repeat those experiences, do you?"

"No," I said matter-of-factly. "Which is why now is a good time."

"The fact is, we don't know how either of us will react. Which is why now is a horrible time. If you panic and run... and fall... I'm not even sure I'd be able to catch you. Not that I wouldn't try, but..."

"The wing, Ari, I know. That's why I want to see it. Yannu told me it was your biggest weakness."

"He did?"

I bit my lip and then admitted, "That or me. He couldn't decide."

But Ari didn't look upset. He just looked thoughtful.

"You won't be afraid?"

I shook my head, making sure my signature was tucked in tight.

White lies didn't count, right?

"You'll wait to climb down until I come back?"

I scoffed. "Definitely not. If you can fly off this rock, I don't want you coming back. It was bad enough watching you climb up here at sunset. I don't think I can take watching you climb down in the dark."

"Listen to you," he said, grinning. "You scale a couple of mountains and suddenly you're a mountaineer."

"Get on with it!" I shouted impatiently. "I wanna see some wings and a tail."

So… he showed me.

And at first, I *was* petrified (it's a pretty startling thing to see) and then I was infuriated (it looked excruciatingly painful; I didn't know who to be angrier with – me, for asking him to do it, or Luck, for making it so painful in the first place). Then I was cautious (although not enough to incapacitate him and, besides, I was no spellcaster) and then, finally, I was curious.

He sat perfectly still as I approached. I'd never been this close to him in drakon form before. My head didn't even reach the top of his back. For the first time since I'd found out what he was, I looked at him – really looked at him.

First off, he was huge. That part, I remembered. It was only one of the many things that made him uber intimidating. And yet... he was smaller than the tower. It made him seem *slightly* more approachable.

His shape was – in a word – wicked. Nearly everything about him ended in a point: his twelve-foot tail, his curved claws, his webbed wings, and the half-dozen lancelike horns that extended from the base of his neck. They rested harmlessly flat on his back now, but I knew those horns flexed as easily as wings or arms. During battle a drakon angled them forward, instead of backward, allowing them to impale the enemy.

I'd seen Ari do it once. To another demon, right before he bit his head off.

I closed my eyes and took a deep breath. When I opened them, Ari's ruby-red eyes were locked on me. He unfurled his wings and, immediately, I saw how debilitating his left wing injury probably was. I made an involuntary sound of dismay and moved toward it to get a better look. His words from last night seemed to taunt me.

I just dropped out of the sky. Crashed into the brush. Broke my wing. And lay there.

The wing jutted out at an odd angle from his side. Its bony framework was a wreck. Underneath the thin leathery membrane, it was easy to see where bones had been broken and had healed unnaturally, re-fusing at irregular connection points. Anger flared, brief and hot. I clenched my jaw.

Stupid, I thought, *so stupid*.

Ari snorted fiery sparks. They glowed against his malachite-colored scales and the stygian sky. But instead of being scared, I just glared. After a while, the drakon's ire dissipated.

It was time for him to go.

Before he flew off, though, there was one final thing I wanted to do. It was somewhat harebrained. Some might even think it akin to poking a bear or a beehive. But I likened it to hugging Nova or taming a hawk. (As if barghests or birds equated to deadly demons – Ha!) Still…

I wanted to touch him.

Maybe it was because I was afraid of doing it and I wanted to conquer that fear. Maybe it was because I wanted to claim the beast as wholly as I had the man, although I realized the selfishness of my desire. Regardless, I reached toward him before I could think better of it.

Slowly, I extended my hand toward his massive drakon heart, giving him time to pull back or fly away. But he didn't move.

My fingers slid gently across slick scales and then I rested my entire palm against his chest. The scales beneath my hand glowed, and their fiery red color spread, until every pointed tip of him blazed against the night sky. He raised his head and breathed fire just as I felt a reverberating magic backlash – the ringing sting of my *signare*'s reciprocity. It was painful, but also exhilarating, and I whooped with joy.

Marking Ari in drakon form was way better than lighting a bonfire.

"Go!" I yelled.

I would've smacked him on the rump if I could have reached it, but he seemed to need no additional encouragement. Without further fanfare, he launched himself off the cliff and into the sky, the downdraft from his wings buffeting my face.

I watched him go, burning brighter than the moon, but flying as erratically as a butterfly.

Yannu was right. The wing was a problem.

And it would have to be fixed.

Later that night, I asked Fara to research ways to heal it and I wrote a letter to Nightshade.

Night—

Remember that tooth you grew back for me last winter? I have another anatomic challenge for you – bones. Specifically, drakon wing bones.

I realize Mederies don't typically heal demons. And that old breaks are usually considered irreparable. But, as you've often reminded me, Demeter is a progressive tribe. If anyone can help, it's you.

Is there any chance Linnaea would grant you leave to come north for a few days?

Your imploring, begging, beseeching sister,

Noon

p.s. I'm enclosing a sketch of the wing.

12

ICHABYE

Ghrun's green turned into Haita's heat as one month passed and then another. Rockthorn Gorge's mountains soared, but unlike the high peaks of southern Halja, they never froze. In fact, during late summer, one could be forgiven for wondering if they were high enough to reach the edge of the sun's corona – it was that hot. Relief from the heat came only every three days or so, in the form of intense lightning squalls that evoked the Battle of Armageddon. I thanked Luck nearly every day that the Magna Fax could only be lit with matches that were safely hidden.

My morning melees with Yannu and his retainers continued. Sometimes against Malphia, Pestis, Kalchoek, and/or Vannis, sometimes not, and never again with Ari. I also left off shaping anything other than traditional weapons. No more pepperboxes or flaming bunyips. No attempts at a blunderbuss or a bigger fire-breathing drakon. Instead, I capitulated and started adding some of the fungible bunyips to my team. It improved my win-loss record, decreased the daily burns and blood, and revealed nothing further of my skills or battle strategies. I'd shown Ari's camarilla enough, those first few days, to establish my right to serve as his *consigliere*. They didn't need to be shown any more of who I was or what I could do until I trusted them – all of them – which was just as well because I had no more tricks up my sleeve. Acting like I was holding back was my last line of defense.

Those sunrise practices started to feel like the bouts at St. Luck's had – painful, monotonous, necessary; something to be endured, not enjoyed. Sometimes, afterwards, I headed out with whatever team I'd chosen that morning for an afternoon patrol. We defended the town against all sorts of *rogares* I'd never heard of before: head crushers, eye gougers, snallygasters, skunk apes, splintercats…

Other days, after the morning melee, I exchanged my leather armor for something lighter and looser. Something that exposed more skin but revealed fewer curves. Something that still covered my demon mark though. It seemed as if Sartabella had consulted my mother in designing my summer workaday wardrobe. My clothing trunk was full of sleeveless, high-necked tops. Not that there was any real risk of Ari accidentally touching my mark, though. After that third night, we hardly touched at all.

Ari modified his initial plan. Instead of spending the months in between my arrival and Frigore Luna working and pretending we didn't really know each another, we worked and pretended our relationship was purely professional. It was almost as much of a farce, but I was a willing participant. Ari had been right when he'd said some things hadn't changed. I was still equal parts eager and reluctant. Once settled in the gorge and assured of his relative safety, I hesitated to change our relationship yet again. As he'd said on the *via ferrata* that third day, he was fine. I was fine. I knew we couldn't live in limbo forever, but that didn't stop me from wondering if we should try. After all, relative safety was difficult to achieve in Halja. Why risk it?

So we worked.

Rockthorn Gorge had a barrister who took care of most Hyrke legal matters, but anything involving a demon was brought before Ari and me. Much of it was mind-numbingly boring. Witnessing promises. Collecting, cataloging, and storing offerings. Drafting deeds, wills, and conveyances. Mediating small disputes. Recording judgments and decrees.

Often, I sat in on meetings. Rockthorn Gorge didn't have almost a million people like New Babylon did, but it was one of the largest outposts in Halja and Ari was a hands-on patron. We discussed imports and exports with Runnos and Eidya, security and border patrols with Yannu and Malphia, the copper and tin mines with Cliodna, the grape and orchard harvests with Bastian, and anything having to do with the Memento Mori project with Zeffre. In time, I learned that the gorge was not nearly as inhospitable as I'd once thought. The town was full of roughnecks and roustabouts but they weren't ruffians or rioters; the mountains were rugged and untamed, but also pristinely beautiful; and the outpost's reputation as a "demonic anthill" and place of historic unrest was only partially true.

By the end of Draugr, the viaduct had been rebuilt and work on the underlying dam had resumed. The construction site was patrolled 24/7 by a team of rotating personnel handpicked by Ari and me. Often, the team included Fara, me, or both of us. At the insistence of Tenacity, Ari had another offering bowl installed outside the rotunda. He forbade blood sacrifices, though, even symbolic ones, and promised instead that any material offerings would go to the families of Displodo's victims.

Weeks went by, and then months, with no other acts of sabotage, but I was still wary. It wasn't just Displodo I was worried about; it was my future. Fourth-semester residencies often turned into permanent positions. Would I be sent back here after graduation? Would I spend the rest of my life in Rockthorn Gorge? As what? Ari's *consigliere*? Or something more?

What would my father say when he found out Lord Aristos was Ari Carmine?

Ordinary kids worried about whether their dad would like whoever they loved. I worried that mine would execute him.

One of the conditions I'd set for accepting this position was that Ari tell my father who and what he was. That he confess to the executive that the new Patron Demon of Rockthorn Gorge was really his former favorite, Ari Carmine, the allegedly human, demon-killing wunderkind who'd gone missing last year and was now presumed dead. Ari had promised to do it by the end of my residency.

Why had I insisted on that condition?

Because, at the time, I'd detested his lie.

Now?

I was starting to think his promise was worse.

───────────

The day after the new viaduct was completed, the Midland Express arrived at Rockthorn Gorge's train station for the first time since before I'd arrived. Along with car loads of New Babylonian Hyrkes anxious to see friends and family, the train brought day merchants, building materials, replacement parts, medicine, a half-dozen horses, one bull, and the mail. No one from my family was on board, but that didn't mean the occasion wasn't marked by an exchange of Onyx correspondence. I sent my letter to Night and received a sealed dispatch from my father and a package from my mother. Sartabella also sent the final item that she'd designed for me – the one she'd sewn after my last fitting while I was on my way up here.

Like the rest of her creations, it was wrapped in paraffin paper and had a label indicating the event I'd need it for. This one was labeled "Test Flights."

Was she out of her mind?! My mouth went dry, my signature zinged with alarm, and I nearly dropped the package right then and there. Luckily, no one noticed my reaction, however, and I was able to hide it later without anyone seeing it.

My father's missive was worse.

DEMON COUNCIL
OFFICE OF THE EXECUTIVE

FOR IMMEDIATE DELIVERY

Nouiomo Onyx

Maegester-in-Training

Office of the Patron Demon

Rockthorn Gorge, Halja

ASSIGNMENT MODIFICATIONS:

1. Update the Council immediately. Use carrier doves if necessary! Scry if you have to!!

2. Submit a detailed report on the status of the dam. What's taking so long?! I don't care that St. Luck's didn't make you an expert on mortar and concrete. It doesn't matter that waning magic doesn't mix with machines. Don't bother telling me that Maegesters aren't engineers or architects. Those are PISS-POOR EXCUSES!

3. Submit a detailed report on the new patron. Include an itemized list of his strengths and weaknesses. Don't hold back. Spy if necessary. I want to know where he came from and whether he can be trusted. Do the people love him? Do you? Enough to spend the rest of your life growing old beside him while he stays perpetually young?

4. Use extreme caution when meeting with Acheron. He arrived, unscheduled and unannounced, in New Babylon recently. His stated purpose was to attempt a renegotiation of the agreement concerning the hydroelectric dam. Put bluntly, he doesn't want us to build it. And then he threatened us with some sort of domesday weapon.

Did my father actually say those things? Well, no. Not exactly. His ten-page, typewritten, single-spaced instructions were much more abstruse, although my rendition of #4 wasn't too far off the mark.

My mother's package was just plain puzzling. She

was a Mederi, but she didn't practice medicine any more. She also didn't garden, at least not in the way that other healers did. There's an old rhyme about a Mederi named Mary who's quite contrary because her garden grows blue roses and red violets. The poet obviously never met Aurelia, because her garden grows black onions, as well as black shallots and garlic.

In any case, it may seem strange that after opening Sartabella's triple-dog-dare-you package and reading Karanos' first draft of what was sure to become the bestselling treatise *Day of Reckoning: 1,001 Ways to Avoid It*, my mother's gift was the one that scared me the most.

It was a spell book.

What, in all of Luck's scorched earth, did Aurelia expect me to do with a spell book? She was more out of her mind than Sartabella.

It was old and tattered, but beautiful in a faded way. On its cover was an infant sleeping in a basket, nestled in the bough of a tree, deep in the center of a forest, thriving at the edge of a world, which was held in the palm of a hand. Its title, *Ichabye*, was scrawled across the top in swirling, gilded letters.

Nonplussed, I'd frowned, and after a quick glance around the train station to make sure no one was watching, I'd cracked it open. But there was no inscription or note, nothing that explained why my mother – a Ferrum, one of the most blue-blooded (and some would say cold-blooded) Host lines of all time – had sent me an Angel prayer primer.

I was tempted to hide it along with the paraffin-wrapped package from Sartabella, but I slipped it into Fara's bookshelf instead. After all, there was nothing sinful *per se* about the book. It was just that, as a member of the Host, I couldn't use it.

Fara found it later that night.

"Noon, did you tell Tenacity she could read my spell books?"

"No…" I would never have done such a thing without asking Fara first.

"Then why is this in here?" she'd asked, pulling it out. She thrust it toward me so that I could see it. I played dumb.

"What is it?"

"*Ichabye*."

"I can see that."

"It's a collection of short, easy children's spells. You've never heard of it?" Thankfully, she didn't wait for me to answer. "Almost every Angel's first spell is one from *Ichabye*."

"Not the Book of Joshua?"

She laughed like she couldn't believe what I was saying. "Noon, you've read Joshua. Can you imagine trying to teach a three-year-old something starting with the Book?"

I gave a non-committal grunt. How would I know how Angels taught their children magic? Mine was innate. I'd been born with the ability to smile, cry, burp, and set things on fire. It was learning how *not* to set things on fire that had been difficult.

But Fara had turned her attention back to her bookshelf and was muttering something about having to have a talk with Tenacity. I knew I'd have to confess, although I wasn't sure what my crime was.

"I put the book there," I said.

Fara turned around. "You did? Why?"

I shrugged. My go-to expression for all uncomfortable situations. "My mother sent it to me."

Fara's eyes widened. "*Aurelia* sent this to you?"

I nodded. She stared at me. Surprise gave way to contemplation and then wistfulness. Maybe she was remembering reading *Ichabye* with her mother.

"You know what 'Ichabye' means?" she finally asked.

I shook my head. This time I wasn't playing dumb.

"Ich is an old way of referring to yourself. And bye is short for 'be wy ye.' Ichabye means 'I'll be with you.' It's one of the most basic, but difficult to explain, faith concepts there is. It's a prayer that invokes protection, grants strength, and repels loneliness. In a way, it's like love, but a little more specific. It's the type of love a person needs at the exact moment the spell is cast."

A thought suddenly occurred to me. "Did you cast Ichabye over me the morning of my first melee when Malphia was attacking me?"

Fara smiled. "See? I just *knew* we'd be a good match." And then she laughed and grinned. She'd said the same thing the day we'd first met, although it had taken me a while to see what came so naturally to her. She handed the spell book to me.

"What am I supposed to do with it?" I asked her. "It's not like I can cast the spells that are in it."

"Love should be shared. If you're not ready for it, give it to Tenacity."

I balked. As she'd just pointed out, I'd read the entire Book of Joshua. More than once. Not to mention countless cases, code sections, horn books, legal digests and periodicals. So it was a little insulting to be told an Angel's ABC book was beneath my reading ability.

But then I realized what Fara might be implying. That I wasn't ready to try casting a spell from *Ichabye*. My blood ran as cold as they say a Ferrum's blood can run.

Had I not told Fara the story of how I came to have waning magic?

I could never try to cast a spell from *Ichabye*! It's not that the Angels' Savior wouldn't listen to me – it's that Luck might hear.

And I could never take that chance.

13

THE MISTRESS OF TEMPTATION

For weeks after the night she'd quasi-threatened to poison me, Cliodna sent invitations to me to visit her in her sanctuary. I came up with one excuse after another. The days grew shorter and the nights longer. Eventide's winds became stronger and cooler. I kept rejecting the Lady of the Gorge's overtures. It wasn't just that Cliodna had slept with Ari (although that wasn't exactly a fun fact), it was that I didn't trust her.

But I couldn't continue to ignore her either. As I'd reminded Ari, she was the demon with the second-most seniority in the gorge. If I was going to work here, I'd have to learn to get along with her. So, after repeatedly telling her I had no interest in sharing or hearing any stories involving Ari, and that I was also uninterested in having her teach me how to shape weapons laced with poison, I reminded her that the only thing she might be able to help me with was repairing Miss Bister's table – the one that Nova had chewed up the morning before I'd left New Babylon. I'd brought it – or rather what was left of it – up to Rockthorn Gorge with me.

Why?

Because I was stubborn like that. And because, if I didn't find a way to repair it, I wouldn't be returning to Megiddo when I returned to St. Luck's, which was pretty hard to contemplate.

The week before Frigore Luna, I finally accepted one of Cliodna's invitations.

Because Sartabella hadn't included any "visit with your ex-boyfriend's ex-girlfriend" outfits, I donned my walkabout clothes. Fara, however, was in a pique about that morning's melee and All Things Demon and recast her glamour. Instead of her usual show-stopping beauty, which would have been perfect for visiting a demoness who valued that above all else, Fara masked herself as the hideous Morridusa from the Daimoneda/Perthius/Megaptera story. Then, her pique still not assuaged, or perhaps because she remembered Cliodna's bitchy remarks regarding barghests, she glamoured Virtus too. In a snap, Fara's feline was transformed into another barghest. Suddenly, her tiger was bigger than a bear, smellier than a sewer, and uglier than a warthog.

She stood in front of me then, her hair hissing, my bag of sticks resting on her hip, daring me to tell her to change the glamours. But I didn't. I couldn't. Because I was sorely tempted to tell her to cast me up with a similar one as well. After all, how likely was it the vain, shallow Cliodna would go out of her way to try to fix Miss Bister's "ruined piece of trash"? It was much more likely that Cliodna would offer me something else – something outwardly pretty but riddled with inner toxicity. And then, when I refused it, she'd declare me as hopeless as the irreparable things I refused to give up on.

Shortly after lunch, we ascended the stone steps of the ruined amphitheater behind the rotunda and made our way to the top of Mount Ortus. Cliodna's sanctuary was an airy pavilion painted in white, gold, and black, with a steepled roof and scores of shapely caryatids. It was as beautiful as the demoness who made her home there.

We were met at the door by one of the handsomest Hyrkes I'd ever seen. He was shirtless and had quintessential six-pack abs, bulging biceps, a sheen of sexy sweat, and a killer pearly-white smile. I had more than my share of men to deal with (Ari was, let's face it, more than a man, and Rafe… well… let's just say out of sight did not always equal out of mind), but I couldn't help staring. I had to will my jaw to stay shut so that I wouldn't say something idiotic. And then I remembered *outwardly pretty but riddled with inner toxicity*. This poor blacksmith or glassblower might be poison-free but that didn't mean he wasn't a trap like everything else Cliodna would offer me.

The man beckoned for us to follow him and led us through the pavilion. Hundreds of birds – hyacinth macaws, scarlet tanagers, golden pheasants, rainbow lorikeets – squawked, talked, and then scattered when we approached. I realized that the space wasn't a sanctuary for humans, or even demons, but rather for birds. There were no cages. There was only shelter, seed, and countless basins full of rippling fresh water.

We passed through various artisan stations until we finally joined Cliodna in the cabinetmaker area. Instantly, I felt guilty. Her dress was wildly provocative – it barely covered her butt – but she'd obviously worn it with our visit in mind since it was made out of wood. Her eyes narrowed when she saw that I was accompanied by Fara-*cum*-Morridusa and two barghests instead of one.

"Charming," she said. "I gather every cabinetmaker under my auspices, ask them to assemble their finest collection of tables, and clothe myself in the most austere robe I've ever deigned to wear and you bring me your bag of trash and three beasts beaten by an ugly stick."

My guilt fled and I almost fled with it. I decided then and there I would never learn to get along with Cliodna no matter how long I stayed in the gorge. She was awful. I couldn't stand her and I didn't want to be around her one more minute than I had to. But her next words stopped me from leaving.

"You're upset because I voice the obvious?" she asked. "You expect me to believe your Guardian chose to glamour herself as one of Halja's most infamously grotesque creatures by accident? Or that she turned her comely cat into a beast known for its homeliness to pay homage to me? No, Nouiomo. She did it because she does not like me. And you didn't stop her because you feel the same."

"Candid words from a demoness whose preferred weapon kills anonymously and remotely."

She sighed. "If I wanted you dead, you'd be dead."

Uh-huh. *Ari* was the reason I wasn't dead, not Cliodna.

"You said you had something you wanted my artisans to look at," she said. "Let's see it."

I motioned to Fara, who upended the bag. The remains of Miss Bister's eleventh-century pedestal table clattered to the floor. The sticks were no longer soggy. Instead, they were covered in some sort of green fuzz. Ugh. I guess barghest slobber didn't react well with rosewood. Cliodna didn't bother to hide her distaste. Her signature pulsed with disgust. To my surprise, she turned toward Fara.

"Can you glamour it?"

"Of course."

Cliodna looked at me. "Then you don't need my artisans."

"I don't want a glamoured table."

"You have a glamoured Angel."

"It's not the same."

"How so?"

I scoffed. "Fara's a person, not a possession, for one thing."

"And for another?"

"It's not my table. It's my dormater's. She doesn't want to pay an Angel to keep glamouring it. She wants her table back, the way it was."

Cliodna gave me a long look before answering. "Sometimes we can't have things back the way they were." I shrugged, and Cliodna pressed her point. "You really expect to turn that… pile of putrid hardwood back into the table it once was without using magic?"

I exhaled and switched my gaze from Cliodna's ice-blue eyes and exquisitely shaped cheekbones to the soft, billowing clouds gathering in the heat-hazed sky.

The Angels tell us that it never rained in Heaven. There was no weather, and *caelum est aeternum* was a truism, not a fallacy. It was only after the apocalypse that Angels experienced storms and loss and transmutation. In Halja, death was a process, not a state. But it meant that all Haljans, including the Angels, truly lived. And living meant letting go. Accepting that nothing lasts forever.

Caelum semper mutans.

"No," I admitted. "I don't. I guess I was hoping…" My voice trailed off. Had I made the right choice in coming here? I wasn't in any immediate danger, but what could I realistically hope to accomplish? Cliodna and I would probably always just barely tolerate each other. Miss Bister's table would be forever ruined. A new, different table might be able to be built from its pieces, but it would never be the same. Even if Cliodna's artisans were able to create a new table – some sort of phoenix-from-the-ashes table – was one more year at Megiddo really worth indebting myself to a demoness who wanted me dead? Probably not.

Cliodna motioned to the artisans who were gathered here. All told, there were twenty or more, a mix of men and women, standing next to every type of table imaginable: dining, bedside, coffee, picnic... pedestal, folding, drafting, nested... oval, square, rectangular, round... The cabinetmakers were just as varied, but one thing the people and pieces they stood beside had in common was that each and every one of them was extraordinarily beautiful.

"Wouldn't it be easier to give your dormater something else? Surely, there's something here that would please her?"

I choked back a sudden burst of laughter, imagining Miss Bister's reaction. Would she accept a Rockthorn Gorge objet d'art in lieu of her eleventh-century heirloom? Maybe, especially if it was delivered and installed by one of Cliodna's Adonis craftsmen.

Cliodna's moniker should have been the Mistress of Temptation.

"And the price?" I asked.

"Spend the night of Frigore Luna with me."

Fara gasped. I stared. I wasn't even remotely tempted now. But Cliodna laughed. "It's not what you're thinking. In fact, I promise, right here, right now, in front of all of these witnesses, not to touch you."

I frowned. That still left poison, explosives, waning magic, and attempting to induce madness as possible murder weapons. But she seemed to sense the direction of my thoughts and said, "I also promise not to harm you, or attempt to harm you, in any way."

My frown deepened. I couldn't figure her out. What did she want?

Again she motioned toward her artisans and their wares.

One night with the Mistress of Temptation in exchange for something that might buy me another year on campus with Ivy at Megiddo – was it worth it?

I shook my head.

"Your collection is beautiful," I said. "But I don't want anything in it."

Fara breathed a sigh of relief, and Cliodna's signature dimmed.

"I want a new table built from the old pieces."

Fara shouted *no* at the same time Cliodna said *done*.

Indeed, I thought. *What had I done?*

14

DOMESDAY WEAPONS

It was a bit eerie, staring at myself.

I squinted at the familiar figure – a 22-year-old female wearing black pants and a short wool cloak. She stood beside a barghest, a tiger, and a nymph, but though her companions were unusual, my gaze was drawn to her weapon – a fiery pepperbox that flickered dangerously in the hazy greenish-gray mist. Hopefully, the woman and her companions wouldn't flicker tellingly as well. Fara and I had argued about the weapon, but she'd insisted the gun would look the most confident – if only because it was the most unpredictable.

The spell was called Simulacrum. Fara had recently learned it and suggested we use it this afternoon for our meeting with Acheron. Considering that the river demon had chosen the Memento Mori dam site as the venue for our meet, I'd readily agreed. Even if my father hadn't warned me to use "extreme caution" when meeting him, I would have anyway. After all, this was the place where a dozen people had lost their lives only three short months ago.

The Hyrke workers who were normally on site had

been sent home. Tonight was Frigore Luna—the night I'd promised to spend with Cliodna—and the Hyrkes were more than happy to have the afternoon off. In their place, hidden in the cliffs, was my team from this morning's melee – three bunyips and one argopelter. Never one to neglect details, Fara had also brought white thorn and marshmallows. (Acheron was a magnus stilio. White thorn was a natural stilio repellent and marshmallows were a nice, non-bloody, offering.)

"Maybe he's wary too," Fara said. "Of coming out into the open. If he senses a handful of demons lying in wait around his suggested meeting spot, what do you think he'll think?"

"That he should have met us at the rotunda tonight," I grumbled. The viaduct was fifteen miles southeast of Rockthorn Gorge. It'd taken us over an hour to get here via handcar on the riverside rail tracks. Acheron hadn't specified that we come alone, but he had specified "middle of the bridge."

In the middle of the viaduct, Fara's nymph simulacrum scratched Virtus beneath his chin while mine raised the pepperbox, took aim, and pretended to shoot a mountain raven. I groaned.

"What is it doing? I don't act like that."

"I think the spell's wearing off," Fara said. "Do you want me to recast it?"

"No," I said, rising up from my crouched position. "Give me the marshmallows. I'm sick of waiting."

Fara, glamoured in the same way as her nymph simulacrum, looked as though she might argue but then relented and handed me the lunch pail Tenacity had given us. After a moment's hesitation, I stepped out from where I'd been hiding and walked toward the viaduct. I stopped when I got to the end, though. I wasn't going to walk out onto it until Acheron showed himself.

Luckily, I didn't have to wait long.

I felt him before I saw him. His signature was sluggish, but also powerful, like the relentless rise of a river during a flood. He crept closer, but I couldn't see him. I whirled around, instinctively shaping my preferred weapon, a simple sword. But the only person standing behind me was Fara, who'd also come out of hiding. She murmured a few words and our simulacrums disappeared just as a giant lizard crawled up over the side of the viaduct. He slithered to the middle, shifted into humanoid form, and waited for us to join him. We had little choice, since meeting with demons like Acheron was part of the job.

He greeted us with a series of clicks and croaks, which we were prepared for. Stilios spoke Ripian, an Aquaian river dialect. They understood the common tongue, but they didn't speak it.

I presented Tenacity's lunch pail to him, suddenly worried it wasn't the right offering. Maybe I should have brought him fish or venison. He raised the pail up to his snout and sniffed. I couldn't be sure he smiled – his grin was permanent after all – but his signature felt pleased and a moment later he clumsily dug out the pail's contents: one s'more, two crispy rice cakes, and a flask full of melted chocolate and marshmallows. He tipped his head back, downed everything in two big gulps, and noisily bleated a half-dozen trumpet calls into the air.

"He liked it," Fara interpreted unnecessarily. Acheron shifted his attention to her then, looking very much like he wanted to eat her next.

"Your nymph glamour may have been a mistake," I told her *sotto voce*. But she scoffed at my warning and introduced us.

Even though I'd been working alongside various demon species for months now, I'd never met a stilio, let alone a magnus stilio. When they shifted into their "human" form, they retained their reptilian hands, head, and tail. His nether region had familiar parts though and, since it appeared that Acheron wanted his body to be as unadorned as his river, I made sure my gaze stayed on his leathery face. The same couldn't be said for him. His beady-eyed gaze roamed freely over my body, lingering here and there. At the end of his mildly offensive perusal, he leaned over and thrust his sharp-toothed snout in my hair.

I nearly thrust my sword in his gullet. Thankfully, sanity prevailed. Ripian was a rudimentary language. Stilios often supplemented it through magical, chemical, and tactile means. Acheron's signature rubbed against mine as he smelled my hair.

Why hadn't I thought to steep last night's bath water with white thorn bark?

His snuffling intensified and the pointy end of one of his teeth scratched my neck. I started to raise my hand, in order to push him away, but then thought better of it. No need to risk losing my sword arm.

Instead, I formed a fiery nose ring in the river demon's nasal septum. The revolting smell of burned flesh told me I'd gone too far seconds before Acheron reached out and grabbed me.

Suddenly, everything and everyone was gone. Fara, our beasts, and my backup team. The riverside railroad. The viaduct and soon-to-be dam.

All of them – gone.

There was only Acheron, me, and the river.

We stood, or rather levitated, a hundred feet above the lower falls. A moment ago, there'd been a solid viaduct beneath our feet. Now, there was only thin air. Before, there'd been a silent heap of dry rocks in the riverbed below us – because the river's water had been diverted during the dam's construction. Now, the formerly dry riverbed gushed with rushing white water. Still holding the delicate chain that I'd fashioned from waning magic and fastened to Acheron's nose ring, I turned toward the river's newly unfettered upper falls.

Rising almost three thousand feet into the air, the waterfall's massive top tier was staggering to behold. It roared louder than a gale-force wind and threw more mist than a Maegester throws magic. A ferocious, unending rumble stuffed my ears and rattled my head while colorful prisms assaulted my eyes. The scattered light beamed in cheerful, wild, riotous contrast to the somber green of the surrounding forest as a seemingly unstoppable flow of water cut a slow course straight through solid rock.

Shocked by the marvel before me, I momentarily forgot to wonder where – or even when – I was, how I'd gotten there, or who I was with. I turned back to the only other living creature I could sense, bursting with the rawness of the place.

Its potential.

Its power.

I nearly dropped the golden chain then, but thankfully, my other senses reasserted themselves and I realized Acheron was still holding me by the arms. He wasn't gripping me tightly or hurting me. But it seemed as though he didn't want to let go.

Me neither.

"Where is everyone?" I asked, fighting the urge to yank his chain as panic began to replace awe. "Where did the viaduct go that we were standing on? The railroad? *Where are my companions?*"

But Acheron just smiled with that changeless grin

of his. And then, with a violent, abrupt shake of his head, he ripped the nose ring out and snorted, spraying me with blood. He looked me straight in the face, bared his teeth, and growled.

Once, during my first semester, a demon had pulled me with him into the ether. When we'd emerged, we'd been in a different place. But *this* didn't feel like *that*. (For one, I wasn't on my knees puking.)

But if Acheron hadn't dragged me through the ether – where was I? Was this place real? Were we in the past? Or was this simply a vision of what Acheron hoped the future would be?

All I knew was that Acheron's signature thrummed with anger and resentment. But I couldn't tell whether it was directed at me generally, because I represented the Council, which wanted to dam his river, or if it was directed at me personally, because I'd just tried to control him with a nose ring. (Disjointedly, I wondered if I'd be able to convince Fara to leave that detail out of her next field report).

In any case, the reason for my offense didn't matter, only that I had offended. I began to sense I'd overreacted. That the scratch on my neck had been an accident. That Acheron, though powerful, was primitive. I couldn't give him what he most wanted – the cessation of the dam project. But I could hear him out.

I stepped back and his hands dropped from my shoulders.

Instantly, we were back on the viaduct. Fara was murmuring the words to a spell I didn't recognize. Nova was growling more fiercely than Acheron just had. Virtus was crouched, his tail lashing, ears back, ready to attack. My backup team had joined us. As had a dozen stilios.

We were surrounded by demons.

I held up my hand. The last thing I wanted was a bunch of *regulare* demons falling into a fight because I failed to control the situation. Talk about failing. I wouldn't just flunk my externship. I'd be kicked out of school, executed, or worse.

"Why did you request this meeting?" I asked. "To show off your shamanism skills? To ambush me? Or do you want to talk about the dam?"

I'd been authorized to offer the river demon a better deal than his current arrangement with the Council, but only in return for his unequivocal support of the Council's plan to turn the viaduct into a dam.

Acheron snarled his response and Fara, who'd left off spellcasting, interpreted. "He'll continue to allow the viaduct but not the dam."

I sighed. "You don't have the authority to disallow the dam."

Another series of roars and croaks. But this time, Fara frowned. "I'm unfamiliar with one of the words he used." She turned to Acheron. "Do you mean 'domesday *weapon*'?"

Acheron appeared to lose his temper then, and one of his stilio minions stepped forward. He was holding a large leather pouch. When Acheron spoke again, Fara paled. "He threatened the Council with whatever is in there," she said.

The minion pulled a book out of the pouch. *Oh, no*, I thought. *It must be the Angel's spell book – the Magna Fax's book of matches. It hadn't been disguised as Servius Rockthorn's tabula ansata. It had been given to Acheron for safekeeping….*

"He called it 'a Maegester's greatest weapon,'" Fara said, her voice ominous.

But then, as if to clarify, Acheron barked out a

single word. Fara looked at me, her expression a mixture of chagrin and relief, and interpreted.

"'The law,'" she said. "I understand what he meant now – a Maegester's greatest weapon is the law. And that book is some sort of law book."

I realized, sometime later, why my father's description of Acheron's appearance before the Council had been so muddled. Even with a good Angel interpreter, the river patron was a difficult demon to understand. The book turned out to be an ancient land survey titled "*Domesday Descriptio.*" Compiled shortly after the apocalypse by a Host scribe, it listed Halja's landowners, their tenants, how much land they held, what was on it, whether it was wooded or cleared, field or fallow, whether it was improved with buildings and, if so, what kinds. Most importantly, however, it contained a record of Lucifer's land grants, the vast majority of which had gone to his warlords, but one of which had gone to the demon standing right in front of me.

"But… how…?"

Acheron's argument that he – and he alone – had the right to control his eponymous river caused a cascade of thoughts in my head that rivaled the lower falls:

1. I'd never heard of the *Domesday Descriptio*.

2. If the book was authentic, and Acheron's claim was true, that would make him over two thousand years old!

3. If Acheron prevented the Council from building the dam, it was the people of Myriostos who would suffer. Didn't he care?!

But when I voiced my concerns, Acheron shook his

massive head. No, he didn't care. And then he let loose an invective stream of roars and bellows. According to Fara, who admitted she only understood about one word in three, Acheron blamed everything on the "King of the Rats" or the "Slum King." *That* was who the river patron wanted the Council to target. *He* was the demon responsible for Myriostos' misery, as well as that of Rockthorn Gorge, since it was the slum lord's fault the dam had to be built in the first place. If he'd only taken better care of his followers—

"Does Myriostos even have a 'Slum King'?" I asked Acheron.

But by then, the river demon had lost his patience. He growled, snapped his jaws, turned on his tail, and stomped off.

"What did he say?" I asked Fara.

She swallowed, switching her gaze from Acheron back to me. Finally, she said, "He'll see you tonight."

"And? That's it?"

She cleared her throat. "He also said you have no idea what Memento Mori actually means."

My face darkened. I knew exactly what it meant. *Remember that you will die.*

Had Acheron just insulted my education... or threatened my life?

15

FRIGORE LUNA

Tonight, you must be Daimoneda not Perthius.

I stared at Sartabella's note and then at the dress she'd made for me. Then I checked the label on the package again.

Yep, it said, "Frigore Luna." As in, "Cold Moon." But this dress was red hot.

Or rather blood red.

Like many Haljan holidays, Frigore Luna had local customs associated with it, but even I knew it had a universal color theme – the night sky. Everyone at the ball tonight would be dressed in blue, black, gray, or silver. Everyone except, apparently, me.

The floor-length moire skirt was a uniform claret and so full I wondered how I'd be able to squeeze in between the myriad statues in the rotunda's atrium, which was where the patron's ball was being held. The entire town was celebrating tonight, but of course not everyone would fit in the rotunda, so a lottery had been held. In addition to Acheron, Ari and his camarilla, their guests, and a handful of *regulare* retainers, two hundred tickets had been given to various Hyrkes around town.

Everyone would be arriving in the next half-hour or so, and I'd be expected to be dressed and ready.

It's not that I'd never worn resplendent dresses before. I had. Once. Maybe twice?

It was that Sartabella was giving me whiplash. After three months of following her previous instructions to "be Perthius" – a brave, heroic Maegester – I was now expected to perform an immediate turnabout and be Daimoneda, the "princess" who was nearly sacrificed to Megaptera, the giant drakon. Maybe I should be thankful I wasn't going to be stripped and chained to a rock somewhere to await Ari's advances, but it was still nervewracking to know that I'd willingly offered myself to another winged creature for the night – and that I'd be going home with Cliodna dressed in this.

"You don't love it?" Fara asked. "Seems like it's perfect for you. Long sleeves and a high neckline." She smirked.

She was technically correct – the top of the dress was long-sleeved with a high neckline, but the material was a sheer illusion. Except for a swirling vine of red rose appliques, I'd look like I was attending the party topless.

Was it too late to stop payment on Sartabella's bill? Not only would the color make me stand out, flowers weren't a typical Frigore Luna motif. Worse still was that, from time immemorial, red roses had stood for only one thing – love. Deeply passionate, all-consuming, head-over-heels-in-love love.

What would Ari think when I showed up in this dress?

Or Cliodna?!

"Is there another dress in the trousseau?" I asked, glancing enviously at Fara's glittery ultraviolet gown.

She shook her head. "I could glamour you."

I stared at my reflection in my room's floor-length mirror. Fara was an excellent glamourist. Maybe finally allowing her to glamour me would be best. She'd certainly enjoy it.

"With what?" I asked her. "What would your glamoured dress look like?"

Fara considered and then shrugged. "Nothing that would be better than this."

"Better? But you were smirking at it a moment ago."

"I wasn't smirking at the dress… I was smirking at your modesty."

"Come on, Fara. How modest can a person dressed in this gown claim to be?"

"Warm, lusty roses for the night we 'celebrate' loneliness and death? Sartabella has your number, alright. You're the only woman in all of Halja with waning magic. You'll stand out no matter what you wear. *You're* the only one who still thinks you're nothing special." Fara walked over to the mirror and tapped on it with her finger. "But be careful about that, Noon. Don't let your modesty mess with your sense of self."

"Well, of course, *you'd* say that," I said, laughing, thinking of all of Fara's hyperbolic glamours. But Fara didn't laugh along with me. Instead she responded with what appeared to be, at first blush anyway, a non sequitur.

"Did you happen to notice the one type of table that was missing from the collection Cliodna showed you?"

I frowned. "No…"

"A vanity table. Don't you think that's odd, considering how obsessed with beauty she is?"

I nodded, my mind only half on our discussion now. I could hear voices out in the atrium and the beginning notes of a song.

"And did you also happen to notice that there wasn't one mirror in her sanctuary? There wasn't even a clear bowl of water. Every reflective surface was rippled with waves."

"So? She's the Patron Demon of Waves and Waterbirds."

"I think there's more to her than meets the eye."

I gave Fara a doubtful look. "She seems pretty shallow to me. Dangerous, yes. Deep, no."

But Fara didn't look convinced. "All I'm saying is, it takes one to know one."

"One what? What are you talking about?" Every now and then Fara talked in riddles and it drove me nuts. But to my surprise, she answered bluntly.

"Something's wrong with her. She's beautiful, but broken. She doesn't like herself. My guess is she can't even look at herself."

I stared at Fara's glamoured image in the mirror and the sounds from the atrium faded. All of my attention was now riveted on the reflection in front of me.

Could Fara? I wondered. *Stand to look at herself?* And then, as if she'd read my mind, she dropped her glamour and the two of us stood in front of the mirror staring back at each other.

I turned to her, not wanting to continue this conversation through the glass, no matter how apropos it may have been. In all the time I'd known her, I'd never asked Fara how she came to have her scars or why she loved such glamorous glamours.

"Fara…" I said tentatively, torn. *Would she want to tell me? Did I have the right to ask*?

"It wasn't a botched spell," she said. Her scratchy voice seemed to grate more than usual. Maybe because I instinctively knew I wouldn't like what she was about to say. "It was a curse – a self-inflicted one."

I inhaled sharply. I couldn't help it.

"What happened?"

"I loved myself both too much and not enough."

Gah, more riddles! "I don't understand."

"The glamoured face I use the most is what I *used* to look like, before the curse. I was young and zealous and someone convinced me that having pride in fleeting pulchritude was a sin. You know what's a sin? Not appreciating it while it lasts. I can glamour you but, tonight, I think you should go as you are. If you don't, you will forever regret not bringing red roses to whoever is waiting for you."

"Cliodna?" I asked, my voice laced with skepticism.

"*Caelum semper mutans. The sky is always changing.*"

But instead of asking her yet again what her cryptic remark meant, I simply murmured "Joshua, fifteen, ten" along with her. It was the closest I'd ever come to saying Amen.

Frigore Luna was observed on the night of the new moon in Ciele, the month of frost. Despite it occurring during the harvest season, it was not a harvest festival. It was an acknowledgement, and forcible delay, of something inevitable, rather than something that had already occurred.

As with most Haljan holidays, Frigore Luna involves fire. On Bryde's Day, celebrants light candles.

On Beltane, bonfires. On Frigore Luna, torches. Tonight, their fire would be a symbolic ward against winter's dark, death, and loneliness.

More than a hundred torches had been installed around the perimeter of the rotunda's atrium. By morning they'd all be gone – claimed by couples on their way to a night of warm companionship, heated coupling, or (for Cliodna and me) a continued game of cat-and-mouse.

Fara and I made our way from my bedroom chambers toward the atrium. We knew our way, but even had we not, we could have found it by following the increasingly loud voices and chilled air. We entered the room and I was momentarily struck by the way in which Tenacity had transformed the place.

Every statue was covered in a gauzy shroud, its identity erased for the night. Instead of the strawmen often used elsewhere, Tenacity had turned the rotunda's sculptures into shadows, half-forgotten memories, and evanescent beings – things that each of us would eventually become. Then she'd partnered with one of Bastian's Angels, who'd cast a frost spell over the entire room.

We entered and Fara announced my arrival. Thankfully, she kept it brief, sticking to my name and formal title. I stepped forward with what I hoped was a confident smile and made my way through the parting crowd, heading for the two strongest demon signatures in the room. One of them I was intimately familiar with. The other I wasn't, but I knew who it belonged to – Acheron.

I found them in the middle of the room, standing next to Servius Rockthorn's statue. Not wanting to interrupt, I came to a stop just inside the circle of pillars surrounding the statue. But Ari looked over and his companion's gaze followed. I have no idea what the river demon initially thought of my blood red ball gown, because all of my focus was on Ari. He looked both ominous and omnipotent. I suppose he would have to, what with Acheron's visit and all. It wouldn't do for the patron of the gorge to look less mighty than the patron of the river that ran through it. Still... I inwardly gulped, almost glad my promise to Cliodna would prevent Ari from tossing me over his shoulder at the end of the night and carrying me back to his chambers.

He was dressed in his most magnificent cloak to date. As long and sweeping as my dress, it was black wool with elaborate gray embroidery and an iron clasp. He walked toward me and, not wanting to appear meek or unsure in front of the crowd, I met him halfway. After months of trying to pretend we were nothing but two professionals working together, it would have been obvious to even the Hyrkes who were present that we were anything but. Ari had finally had enough of keeping me at arm's length and I knew, even before he slipped his hands around my waist, that he wasn't going to do so tonight. He rested his forehead against mine and breathed my name. His fingers tightened on my waist.

"No fair," he murmured.

"What isn't?"

"*You*," he said. "*You* are not fair." He stepped back and his hands moved from my waist to the ends of my unbound hair. Gently, he brushed it behind my shoulders. He stared at my demon mark, which was visible beneath the sheer fabric of my top.

"How much self-control do you think I have?"

"Enough, Lord Aristos," I said, intentionally keeping my voice light. "You're keeping your guest of honor waiting."

I turned toward Acheron then, but slipped my arm

into Ari's, and the two of us walked over to him. I gave the river demon a deep, solemn nod and he stared at me for a few moments, his signature ebbing and flowing with the crowd's energy. His magical aura felt old and complex, more primal than Ari's when he was in drakon form, perhaps more deadly, but also – at least right now – calmer.

Acheron motioned to Ari's heart and then to mine and emitted a long series of throaty burbles interspersed with a few barks. Ari smiled, but his expression was strained. I hadn't realized Ari spoke Ripian, although it made sense. He knew at least a handful of demon languages and he'd spent time here when he was young.

"It's... complicated," he finally told Acheron, whose carnivorous gaze then fell on me. I hoped the river demon wouldn't reach out and try to grab me again. Who knew what fiery restraints I might try to bind him with? Acheron pointed at me again and said something else.

"He's curious about your dress," Ari told me.

"Oh... ah... My dressmaker told me to wear it."

Acheron just stared. I couldn't tell if he was angry or confused. Ari gave me an odd look, and I knew he wasn't translating everything. Where was Fara? She'd picked the wrong time to go missing.

"'Dressmaker' isn't a word he'd be familiar with."

"Armorer. My *armorer* told me to wear it."

Upon hearing my words, Acheron tipped back his head again and brayed. He had to be laughing. His signature was full of mirth.

"Show him your fiery dove," Ari said.

"I'm your *consigliere*," I snapped. "Not your court jester." The words slipped out before I thought better of them. Maybe it was that Ari had commanded instead of asked. Or maybe it was because I was missing half the conversation – the half about me – and it made me defensive. Or maybe I was just tired of having to be polite to demons who issued veiled threats about ending my life.

Thankfully, Ari seemed to understand my unease. "Noon, it's okay. You don't have to. Acheron just thought it was funny that your armorer designed something that looks like *that*. And I thought he'd appreciate seeing that your 'weapons' can be as unconventional as your armor."

Inwardly, I snorted. Acheron had already seen that earlier today when I'd bound him briefly with a bull-worthy nose ring. The river demon snuffled and growled, his toothy grin widening. He pointed at me, thumped his chest, and then motioned toward the torches, but Ari cut him off with a curt, "No."

"What did he say?"

But Ari refused to answer.

More growls and grunts. Ari's signature pulsed once, violently and possessively, before he dragged me away, glaring at Acheron the entire time. The river demon laughed; his great barking bursts loud enough to reach the invisible moon in the dark sky above us. Then he snapped his jaw shut and turned his hungry gaze elsewhere.

The first part of the night passed in a whir of increasing agitation. Drums thrummed, piccolos piped, couples danced, and two by two, people started pairing off and claiming torches. Acheron wasn't the only one drawn to my blood-red-and-roses gown. I swear, if I were an Angel, I would've spent half the night plotting ways to curse Sartabella. No less than three bunyips (two retainers and the Captain of the Guard!) propositioned me. Ari and Yannu nearly came to blows over it, although I could tell Yannu's heart wasn't set on seduction. He was only testing our weak spots per his usual, and Ari was too baited to be objective. Malphia also hinted that she wouldn't mind messing with my mind for the night. And then the Hyrkes started in on me – not as a potential partner, but as a matchmaker. After all, they said, wasn't *that* why I'd worn the dress?

Both Bastian and Rockthorn Gorge's sommelier approached me about brokering an arrangement with Fara. When I asked her, she surprised me by saying, of the two, she'd have picked the demon over the Angel because he was kinder.

"But I'm already promised to someone else."

"Who?"

"Virtus."

Of course. I didn't know whether to roll my eyes or turn pea green with envy.

About an hour after midnight, Ari lost his patience and started pulling me toward one of the torches along the wall. He hadn't left my side all night – and I hadn't complained. His hands hadn't strayed anywhere untoward, but nor had he kept them to himself. In other words, he could be forgiven for assuming our dry spell was over and that tonight we'd resume all aspects of our previous relationship.

Would I have been ready but for my promise to Cliodna? Was I using her as much as she might be using me? And where was she, by the way? If she didn't arrive soon, I wouldn't even have *an excuse…*

I tugged Ari in the other direction but he was

having none of it. His signature swelled with *arousal*, the effect of which wasn't lost on me. It would have been embarrassing, but for the fact that every other person with waning magic had already left. I wrenched my hand from Ari's grip and he turned around.

"Do *not* tell me you're having second thoughts."

Second thoughts? I couldn't afford first thoughts....

"Noon, you know I love that you're equal parts eager and reluctant. But not tonight."

"I'm not reluctant."

"Then you grab the torch."

When I didn't, though, his signature started to crash and I fell apart with it. I grabbed his arm, but instead of pulling him toward a torch, I pulled him into one of the atrium's curtained alcoves. It was as private a space as we were going to get without heading off to his chambers.

"I did something foolish," I said.

He frowned. "What?"

"I told Cliodna I'd spend the night with her."

I could tell from his expression that he would have believed almost anything else but what I'd just said.

Let's face it, I'd done some pretty foolish things. And Ari had witnessed several of them. But this... *this* seemed to take the cake, as they say. I may have pulled off some extraordinary stunts in the last year or so, but my admission seemed to take us back to the day we'd first met – when I'd moronically decided to jump for a boat that had already left the dock.

"What?" Ari repeated, nonplussed.

I started pacing the small area, my skirts rustling as they brushed back and forth against him. He stood completely still, watching me with an incredulous expression on his face.

"I..."

Ugh...

I told him then what I'd done and why. It sounded ludicrous even to my ears.

"A table?! You said you'd sleep with Cliodna if she repaired *a table*?"

"No!" I started rubbing my arms, a sure sign of nerves. "She swore not to touch me – or harm me. And I'm *not* going to sleep."

"Then what are you going to do? What does *Cliodna* want to do?"

"I don't know," I admitted.

Ari didn't say a word. He just kept staring.

"Ari, don't you get it? If I fix the table, I can go back."

"Go back? To St. Luck's?"

"Yes. And to Megiddo."

Understanding was starting to dawn on Ari's face but it was mixed with something else I didn't like – sympathy. He walked back to a bench that was pushed against the wall and sat down. His signature was soft as he patted the seat next to him.

I sat down, smoothed my skirt, and faced him, ignoring the feeling in my stomach. It wasn't a good kind of anticipation I was feeling. It was the bad kind.

"Noon," Ari said softly, "you know you can't ever really go back, don't you?"

I made a half-hearted, noncommittal gesture. Ironically, Cliodna had said something similar.

Sometimes we can't have things back the way they were.

"Are all demons so fatalistic?" I asked, wringing my hands. Slowly, gently, Ari pried them apart and clasped them in his.

"Why is looking forward fatalistic?"

I shrugged and tried to pull away, but he held tight.

"You are the smartest and bravest person I know," he said. "And, most of the time, you make excellent decisions. But when you make decisions based on fear—"

"Fear keeps us one step ahead of the blade," I scoffed.

"Nouiomo, *listen* to what I'm saying. I listen to you when you call me out on my poor decisions. That's what people who love each other do."

I'd been looking at my hands, but with those words, I looked up and what I saw in Ari's face and felt in his signature shattered my self-control. Without thinking, I leaned forward and wrapped my arms around his neck and buried my face in his shoulder.

Ari scooted me onto his lap.

"It's not fear of the next five minutes that screws you up," he continued. "*That* you're able to brush off as easily as my advances." He laughed to show he was half-kidding. "No, it's fear of your own future that sends you scrambling."

I rested my head on Ari's shoulder and he put his arm around me.

"Do you remember what my original plan for tonight was?"

I froze. "Black Gilliflower?"

"Real romantic, right?"

"No."

He nodded. "I think we've moved past it, don't

you?"

"You told me it wouldn't work on you anyway," I said grumpily.

But he ignored my complaint, saying instead, "I'm going to ask you a series of questions. All you have to do is answer 'yes' or 'no.' Think you can do that?"

I hesitated long enough for Ari to laugh and tell me that question didn't even count – did he need to get the truth serum out?

"No. I mean 'Yes,'" I said, laughing just the tiniest bit too. I so wanted this night to be over, but I had to admit, it was nice being curled up in Ari's lap. And I'd already told him everything about *our* relationship. What questions could he ask that he didn't already know the answer to?

"You know I'm a demon now. Don't you?"

I rolled my eyes. "Yes."

"Do you forgive me for not telling you that before Rafe cast Revelare Lucere?"

I didn't answer right away. Not because I didn't forgive him, but because his question brought up all sorts of memories and it took a moment to process. My first night here, I'd told him I wasn't trying to forget, I was trying to forgive, but the truth was, I forgave him a long time ago.

"Yes."

He kissed me then – a sweet, shallow, lingering kiss – before continuing.

"You know we can't go back to the way things were last year, right? I can't go back to Infernus… and, even if Miss Bister allows you and Nova to return to Megiddo this year, it won't be the same?"

I shrugged, but Ari let my evasion pass and pressed on.

"And you know you can't stay at St. Luck's forever." He wasn't even bothering with questions now. He was just lecturing. "And, as reluctant as you were to go to St. Luck's, you're just as reluctant to leave now, aren't you?"

I stubbornly refused to answer.

"See why I thought the Black Gilliflower might be a good idea?"

I harrumphed, not finding as much humor in the situation as Ari seemed to. But Ari placed his hand beneath my chin and tilted my head up.

"Do I make you happy?"

My eyes widened. It was the first question that was truly a surprise. The first had been rhetorical, although I'd answered it, and the rest had been ones I'd been avoiding, but this one was unexpected – and easy.

"Yes."

"Do you love me?"

My first thought was, *how could he even ask?* But then I realized that all the times I'd said I loved him were in my head. Sure, he probably felt it in my signature, but those three words could be mighty reassuring to someone who'd just found out the girl they were in love with was spending the night with someone else.

"Yes. I love you."

"Will you marry me?"

16

REGINA AMORIS

I sputtered.

Had I heard Ari correctly?

"You know," he said, "'I shall take you as mate, for here and ever after, to live and die by your side?'"

Oh, Luck below, Ari was quoting the demon marital vows. When they mated, they mated for life. Spouses were bound by law and magic. *Your debts are my debts, your sins are my sins, your life is my life . . .*

"No!" I cried, jumping up. "You can't give up centuries of your life for me."

But my explanation of why I'd rejected him as well as whatever he was feeling in my signature had him smiling.

"Yes, I can. I already told you. I don't want to be treated as a demon or a deity. But I could probably learn to like it if you were by my side. If my life could be like it has been the last three months... but with you in my bed... growing old with me.

"I don't want to outlive everyone I love, Noon. You, especially."

I resumed my pacing and my red skirt rustled with

even greater agitation than before. Damn Sartabella and her red roses!

"You can't propose to me on Frigore Luna. It's bad luck."

Ari frowned. "I've never heard that."

"Well, it is." I was making it up, but seriously, did Frigore Luna seem like a good holiday for Ari to propose on? "And what will my father say?" I groaned and smacked my forehead. Marriage proposals called for melodrama, right? Would hyperventilating be too much? My fingers started curling inward and I started to feel lightheaded.

But Ari took my turmoil in stride. "Sit back down."

"No."

"Please?"

I stopped pacing, but didn't go near him. I was back to not trusting him. How could he have done this? Asked *that*? And here I'd been worried about taking our relationship from limbo to declared love. He wanted to take us straight to the altar. My vision started blackening at the edges. I really was hyperventilating.

I walked over to the bench, sat down, and put my head between my legs. Ari put his hand on my back.

"Are you okay?"

I shook my head.

He sighed. "If it makes you feel any better, I didn't expect you to say yes."

I raised my head up and looked over at him.

"At least, not at first."

I put my head back down.

"If you were a demon, you'd be the Patron of Reluctance."

I don't know how long we sat like that. Long

enough for the noises from beyond the curtain to grow quieter. Finally, I was able to string enough coherent thoughts together to sit up and focus on what Ari had said.

"Speaking of reluctance… Do you think Cliodna's out there?"

Ari shook his head. "She's not coming."

I brightened momentarily, rashly thinking that might mean I wouldn't have to honor my promise, but then knowledge of the way things worked in Halja and the look on Ari's face brought me back to reality.

"Why not?"

"Because she's hoping what almost happened, will happen."

"Which is?"

He gave me an acerbic smile. "That we'll take a torch off the wall and head back to my chambers. Or, even better, that we don't, but you decide not to meet her anyway."

"But… Why…? *Oh…*"

Ari nodded. "She's hoping you'll renege, which, at best, would make your position here tenuous."

I stood up. It was time to go then.

Ari stood up too. "You only need to spend a few hours of darkness with her not to renege."

I swallowed, suddenly nervous. "Are you worried?"

Ari snorted and glanced away for a moment before turning his gaze back to me. "When am I ever *not* worried about you, Noon?"

Ari insisted on two things: (1) that we wake Fara so she could cast me up with every defensive spell she knew;

and (2) that I not walk up the mountain to Cliodna's sanctuary alone. After some back and forth, I finally figured out that Ari's insistence on accompanying me wasn't because he didn't think I was capable of taking care of myself ("I'm letting you suffer the consequences of your own deal with the devil, aren't I?"), it was that he was superstitious ("It's Frigore Luna, Noon. I don't want you walking *anywhere* alone tonight.")

So he trusted Cliodna a scintilla more than the shadows? I wasn't sure that was reassuring.

Just before I left, Tenacity came running over to me. Embracing her jester role, she'd taken the night's theme to an extreme and had come dressed as a dancing skeleton.

"I heard Fara casting you up. I know where you're going."

"Oh…" Well, that was somewhat unfortunate. My dark-hours visit to the Lady of the Gorge isn't something I'd normally want my herald announcing, but it wasn't a secret either.

"Well, wish me Luck," I said breezily, preparing to step out. But Tenacity's next words stopped me.

"Can I cast something over you?" she asked.

"Uh…" Botched spells were no joke. I didn't want to snub Tenacity but… "Now's not the best time."

"But you're the one who gave me the book."

"What book?" Ari asked.

"*Ichabye.*"

"The prayer primer?" His voice rose in disbelief.

Tenacity nodded and glanced back and forth between us, suddenly looking much less sure of herself. In the month since I'd given Tenacity *Ichabye*, she'd spent nearly every spare moment with it. So far, however, she had yet to successfully cast a single spell. I imagined, even with Fara's guidance, the likelihood of a lowborn Hyrke teaching herself faith magic was pretty far-fetched. But I didn't want to be discouraging.

"It's okay," I said, ignoring Ari. He might feel he was at the end of his rope with me, but if so, he'd just have to make more rope. Besides, Tenacity was his cousin. You'd think he would be a little more supportive.

"What spell were you thinking of?"

She seemed embarrassed now that she'd even approached me.

"You don't need it," she said. "Fara's a fantastic Angel. I'm sure she cast you up with everything you'll need." Tenacity's voice betrayed her sincerity. In fact, it would be fair to say that Tenacity probably hero-worshiped Fara.

"You know what Fara said when she told me I should give you that book?" I asked her.

Tenacity shook her head.

"'Love should be shared.' So if you memorized a spell from it... I want to hear it."

She closed her eyes for a moment and then recited the words.

Night's dark shades will soon be over;

Still my watchful care shall hover.

Let your battle cry...

Be Ichabye

Tenacity's spellcasting voice was the opposite of Fara's – melodious, but also stiffer and more hesitant. Still, there was earnestness laced within it too, and when Tenacity whispered the final word, I felt the spell slip into place. She opened her eyes, looking anxious.

"Well done, spellcaster," I said, grinning at her.

"Your tenacity paid off."

Ari left me when we reached Cliodna's sanctuary. We could both feel her inside the open-air pavilion, so he wasn't technically leaving me alone. And besides, I was going to be fine. Fara's sophisticated, ironclad spells and Tenacity's simple, guileless one felt like plate armor and a never-ending hug, the latter of which would likely prove the most effective against the affliction I felt in Cliodna's signature.

I made my way through the main part of the sanctuary. The birds were quiet; the only sounds were an occasional flutter or flapping of wings and the constant gurgle of the copious bird baths, water fountains, and shallow pools. In other words, the sounds were soothing, but Cliodna's magic and state of mind were not.

It didn't help that there wasn't one tiny flame lit in the entire sanctuary. No torches, despite the fact that it was Frigore Luna. Although… if Cliodna's original plan had been to spend the evening alone, then the warmth of a torch would likely only remind her of the absence of a partner.

Was the Mistress of Temptation lonely?

I snorted to myself. If so, she had only herself to blame. Hadn't she read the white paper on the use of honey versus vinegar?

"You're late." Cliodna's voice came out of the darkness, but faint starlight allowed me to see the barest hint of her outline. It looked like she was sitting behind something – something large and rectangular. Remembering Fara's theory, I couldn't help wondering if it was a mirror. Maybe Fara had been wrong and Cliodna was actually obsessed with her own appearance.

"I thought you would come down to the rotunda."

Cliodna scoffed. "I wasn't in the mood for a party."

"You were in the mood to sit alone in the dark?"

But she'd already turned her attention back to her mirror. Her arm moved and I wondered if she was brushing her hair. I thought about lighting a fireball so that I could see her but figured it would be better not to disturb her. Only my presence was required, not my interest in whatever it was she was doing. So I walked to the pavilion's half-wall and stared up at the night sky, wondering what others in my life were doing tonight. After all, Frigore Luna didn't need to be spent with a lover (ahem, look where I was right now).

I spotted the constellation Leaena and thought of my mother. Rex made me think of my father and Gemini, my brother. Cor, which meant "heart," made me think of Rafe, but only because we'd searched for the White Heart together last winter. Then I admitted, if only to myself, that that wasn't entirely true. But you know what? Rafe had bailed on us before we ever got started, which was probably a good thing since I had my hands full with Ari.

What's more, there was no Amoris Triangulum constellation.

And even if there were, I wouldn't ever wish on it!

"Such chaotic emotions," Cliodna said. "I think *now* would be a good time."

"For what?"

"To paint you."

"Paint me?" I sounded like one of her parrots.

A second later, the pavilion blazed with firelight. Cliodna had lit every single torch held by her shapely caryatids. I saw then that she sat in front of an easel, not a mirror, and that she held a paint brush, not a hair brush. When she saw my dress, her eyes widened. And then she laughed, the sound of it mellifluous amongst the gurgling and burbling, before calling me over so that I could see what she'd been working on.

She'd painted Cygnus, the swan constellation.

Looking up to where it would have been in the sky, I understood now why she'd been sitting in the dark. Behind the fiery torches, the sky was a uniform black. But in Cliodna's painting, it sparkled with color and variation. Whorls of ivory and gold swirled around glowing orbs of light, which twinkled and blinked against a sapphire sky.

Of course Cliodna was an artist, I thought.

Together we stared at the painting until finally, she reached forward, plucked it off of the easel, and motioned for me to follow. She led me through several empty artisan areas, past more birds and bird baths, down a long, twisting set of stairs, until we finally reached a locked door. She pulled a key out of her cleavage and opened it.

I was expecting another studio. Maybe one with a dais or a chaise lounge. Possibly some props or more paint, really anything but what was in there. When Cliodna pushed the light switch, I saw that the space was an enormous gallery, which held what must have been *thousands* of paintings. They were hanging on every inch of wall space. They were stacked to the ceiling in corners. They were piled five, six, seven feet high on the floor. And each and every one of them was of the same thing – Cygnus.

I followed Cliodna into the room, glancing from one painting to the next. All of them were as beautiful as the one she'd painted tonight, but viewed in this context – next to myriad more just like them – they looked more foreboding than beautiful.

Cliodna walked over to one of the walls and leaned her newest creation against it.

Would she continue painting them until the entire room was full?

If so, what then?

Would she build a new gallery?

Or become a full-fledged lunatic?

After a few minutes of subterranean stargazing, she shooed me out of the room, relocked the door, and stuffed the key back between her breasts. Then she reversed our earlier route. We emerged on the first floor of the pavilion and Cliodna motioned toward the spot where I'd been standing before.

She returned to her easel and mounted a fresh canvas. On impulse, I asked if I could see a mirror to touch up my hair and makeup. Cliodna froze only momentarily, but it was enough of a reaction to confirm that Fara might have been right. Cliodna ignored my request and asked instead, "Why did you choose to wear red tonight? It's an unusual choice."

"Frigore Luna is as much about love and warmth as it is about cold and loneliness."

Again she froze, her paintbrush an inch away from the canvas. She looked up at me. "Did the dress make you feel love tonight?"

I shook my head. "No one is going to feel love just because they wear a dress."

Cliodna smirked as if she begged to disagree. I wasn't surprised, since it seemed every piece of clothing she ever wore was designed to evoke a passionate reaction in people. But passion wasn't love – or at least passion wasn't all there was to love.

"What were you feeling when I first said I'd paint you? Just before I lit the torches?"

I frowned. This visit with Cliodna was beginning to feel like a creepier version of the sittings I'd had with Sartabella.

"Don't you know?" I asked. Maybe Fara's cloaking spell was shielding me from the worst of Cliodna's prying.

"I want to hear what you call it. And who you were thinking of when you felt that way."

No way was I telling her that. One, I'd already told her I wasn't going to talk about Ari. And, two, anyone else I loved was even more off-limits as a topic of conversation.

So we spent the next hour or so in silence. It was tense and exhausting. Still, I began to think the only ill effect of the night might be tiredness. That is, until Cliodna finished my portrait.

"Take a look," she said.

I suppose I should have known it was a trap. After all, it's not like I didn't know how dangerous Cliodna was. She loved to lace pretty with deadly. And she had a penchant for temptation, yet she'd offered me nothing – no food, no wine, not even a seat.

So I should have been on guard.

I should have been more careful.

But the whole time I just kept thinking I'd be safe, at least for the night, because Cliodna had promised not to harm me. I'd forgotten that a Maegester needed to be just as much of a wordsmith as a warrior. My precarious state of safety had been based on the definition of one word.

> **Harm** /härm/
>
> *verb (sometimes used with object, i.e. victims who should know better)*

1. to physically injure

2. to intentionally inflict emotional distress

I walked over to Cliodna's easel and stared at the painting that was mounted on it. It was the most beautiful portrait I'd ever seen. My first thought was that it couldn't possibly be me. There was no way I could ever look that... devastating. The red of my dress looked warm and alive against the twilight backdrop. My figure was more sumptuous than the caryatid's next to me and my expression was infinitely more luminous than the torch she was holding. I frowned in confusion as I realized the portrait was already framed. There was even a nameplate.

REGINA AMORIS

Cliodna laughed again, but this time it didn't sound mellifluous. It sounded malevolent.

"What do you see?" she asked.

What did she mean? Didn't she see the same thing I did?

Before my eyes, the painting changed in subtle ways. The red of my dress looked angry instead of warm. My figure looked more salacious than sumptuous. And my expression became anguished. Tormented. Tortured even. Rafe's silver bracelet glinted and a new constellation appeared in the sky – a triangle. But instead of experiencing the anguish and torment I saw on my face, I felt nothing.

"Cliodna," I said, squeezing my eyes shut, "this isn't the portrait you painted, is it?"

Again that laugh. If there was a hell beyond Halja, it would be full of demons laughing like that.

"You were a Laurel Crown contender last year, were you not?" She said. "I know racers have to be exceedingly focused on their own targets, but you must remember some of the things the other racers were sent to recover? Unlike you, some of them were actually successful."

Oh, Luck, no. This could NOT be happening to me. Past experience had taught me that Luck was cruel. But this cruel?

"Is that...? Did I just...?" I couldn't finish my questions. I couldn't form whole thoughts. My mind was starting to shut down because my heart was turning to stone. In a few minutes, I probably wouldn't even care that I no longer had the capacity to love.

Because I'd just seen *Eidolon's Alternate Ending*.

The painting had been Thefarius Ryolite's target. Centuries old, it had been commissioned by the demon lord Nickolai as a bride gift for his inamorata. But the Angel who'd painted it had botched the enhancement spell. No one knew what the original subject had been because everyone who viewed the painting saw something different. Their only shared experience was that, ever after, they were incapable of feeling love.

"Your emotions are as chaotic as when you were stargazing earlier," Cliodna chortled, her tone triumphant. "But I don't think it's love that you're feeling. I think it's recollection. And your memory is correct. Ryolite was my champion last semester, just as you were the Divinity's."

"You cheated," I whispered. "At the *rota fortunae* ceremony. You shaped a poison ring. But that wasn't your best weapon. *Eidolon's Alternate Ending* is."

"But it's not a weapon, it's a gift. Surely you can see that? In fact, it was Nickolai's bride gift to me. *I* was its original subject. He wasn't content with a mere portrait of *rara avis*. No, Nickolai wanted more. Always more. So he had an Angel cast the spell Fairest over it."

Again that laugh.

"My engagement portrait was the most magnificent and terrifying thing I've ever seen. But gazing upon it spared me centuries of heartache, romantic angst, and conflicted agony. Who wants to be tormented by the miseries of love? Honestly, Noon, I've granted you a boon."

And that's when I knew I deserved my alternate ending. Because I'd known how dangerous psychotic demonesses could be and I'd made a deal with her anyway. The question wasn't whether spending Frigore Luna with Cliodna was worth another year at Megiddo. It was whether losing the ability to love was worth another year at Megiddo. And the answer was *definitely not*. But was it too late for me?

In the past, I'd gotten myself out of worse situations than this by using unorthodox tools and weapons. So when I began to feel magic that was darker and more suffocating and loveless than Malphia's had ever felt, it gave me an idea.

Yes, it was an idea that carried some element of risk.

But what choice did I have?

Life was about one step backward and two steps forward, right?

Love was about taking chances and dealing with the potential heartaches, wasn't it?

So I remembered the spell Fara had cast over me that day when I'd nearly succumbed to Malphia's magic. It was the same spell that Tenacity had cast over me just before I came here – Ichabye. I started whispering it.

"Night's dark shades will soon be over. Still my

watchful care shall hover."

"What are you doing?" Cliodna hissed.

Was I trying to cast Ichabye?

You bet I was!

No one knew better than I did how difficult curses were to remove. I was desperate.

"Let your battle cry be Ichabye."

And then I kept repeating the word "Ichabye" over and over again like a mantra. Like a ward against the cold and loneliness. Each time I said it, I remembered someone I loved.

I'll be with you.

I even remembered myself. There were a million and more ways to love and I wanted to experience each and every one of them – regardless of the anguish or torment I might suffer as a result. Because love was life.

I backed away from the easel and opened my eyes. The sky was pink. Twilight had given way to sunrise.

I fled the vile Cliodna and the evil *Eidolon's Alternate Ending* and scrambled down the steps of the ancient amphitheater, stumbling, tumbling, frantically murmuring *Ichabye, Ichabye, Ichabye...*

Did it work?

Was I cursed? Again? With something worse? Something that wouldn't kill me, but would instead require me to live a loveless existence?

Ari was waiting for me at the bottom, just outside the rotunda. From the dark circles under his eyes, it looked as if he'd stood against that pillar, watching, waiting, and worrying, all night. When he saw me, he straightened and I ran to him, my heart and arms wide open. I launched myself at him, uncaring of whether we crashed to the ground or not.

We didn't.

"Ari, I…" But I was through with words. I clasped his head in my hands and lowered his face to mine, kissing him deeply, reveling in the feelings of *warmth* and *love* and *relief* that swirled around us, each of them, all of them, redder and more alive than the cursed shade I'd just escaped. And then I grabbed his hand and headed toward my chambers.

Frigore Luna might be over, but I still wanted and needed what he'd originally offered.

17

FITTINGNESS

Ari's hand burned in mine. I was fairly certain, if I looked down, that I'd see flickering wisps of fire where our fingers ought to be. It wouldn't have been the first time. But I didn't look down. Not because I was scared, but because I really wanted to make it to the bedroom before I lost control. It had been months since I'd unintentionally destroyed anything beyond my alarm clock.

I barely remember racing through the atrium, entering my chambers, and shutting the door. But with the click of the lock, my world went from hazy to uber-focused. Ari pulled me over to the edge of the bed, but instead of tossing me onto it, he paused beside it.

"Does this mean 'yes'?"

I shook my head and swallowed. "I can't marry you."

"Yes, you can."

"But I won't."

He rested his right hand on the swell of my hip. I could feel his restraint. How much discipline it took for him to talk instead of take. Ever so slowly, he moved his hand up the side of my torso until his thumb hit the soft curve of my breast. His gaze sharpened as he gauged how much effort he might have to exert to bend me to his will.

Not much, I'm afraid.

My face flushed immediately and my pulse started pounding. I'm sure, given the intensity of his stare, that he can't have missed the throbbing vein in my throat. My chest rose and fell with my breathing, which now felt labored. I wasn't hyperventilating. I was panting.

This was embarrassing. Wasn't I worldlier now than when Ari had last tried these tricks on me?

I was more sophisticated now. I was smarter, stronger…

Hungrier, hornier…

"Go ahead," I said.

I meant it merely as permission. But the tone of my voice and the tilt of my chin suggested a challenge. Ari answered it as if I'd thrown down a gauntlet. Without any further encouragement, he lowered his mouth to my mark. The shocking sting of his kiss there made me stiffen and gasp. The sheer-illusion fabric provided a barrier, but it was gossamer thin and barely acted as an impediment to his marking me with another *signare*. Not that I cared though – about either the pain or the portent of possession. I was too far gone with the pleasure of it.

Ari rained scorching-hot kisses along one of the red rose vines on my top while his magic ran roughshod over Fara's defensive spells. They popped like bubbles seared by a wild, inexorable wind. His hand splayed against my back as he pulled me closer. I said his name, my voice somewhere between a stuttering croak and a contented moan. I couldn't help it. Ari was hard and soft in all the right places. Both the man and his magic fit me perfectly.

He lifted his head and stared at me, looking dazed with *arousal* and inamorata-lust (a new phrase I'd just coined to describe the near-unbearable sensation caused by feeling your own partner's aching, all-consuming need for you). I pushed his cloak from his shoulders and realized his left arm was in a sling. Remembering anew exactly when, where, and how he'd broken his arm – wing – my signature pulsed with regret, tenderness, and lingering irritation over the fact that he could have prevented the permanent effects of his injury.

But the irritation gave me the willpower I needed to break free from his embrace. I walked over to a chest of drawers and slipped off Rafe's silver bracelet. It didn't feel right to wear it anymore, knowing what I was about to do with Ari. I'd never declared my feelings for Rafe. And Rafe had only said he loved me once. Even then, I hadn't known for sure.

Neither of us is sure anymore if my feelings for you are real. Right? That's what you've been thinking about and wondering... Well, this will give us a chance to sort things out.

Sort things out apart, you mean.

Were we ever really together?

I shook my head, ridding it of the unwanted memory. I didn't want to think about Rafe right now. Wouldn't.

I'd just saved myself from *Eidolon's Alternate Ending* by reminding myself there were a million ways to love. I knew with absolute certainty how Ari felt about me. And how I felt about him. I didn't want to keep him waiting and wanting and wondering what role he would play in my future.

So I placed Rafe's bracelet on top of the chest and

turned around to face Ari.

His expression was guarded. His magic was a little more banked than before.

I wasn't going to make him ask what taking off the bracelet meant to me. And I didn't want to tell him again that, no, I wasn't going to marry him. That I wouldn't. Ever. So I told him the next best thing. That I was his. Just like he was mine. And that he could mark me with his *signare* again and that would have to do.

He stared at me for a few moments, his earlier *arousal* and inamorata-lust replaced by something that was much more difficult to define. It was something that was beyond intractable. It was something akin to a bone-deep rejection of how the world worked. It was something that felt like Ari would defy Luck himself if he was denied what he wanted.

"Turn around," he said.

I gave him a quizzical look but complied. He swept my hair over one shoulder and ran one finger slowly down the row of buttons on my back.

"Do you know how long it will take me to try and unbutton these?"

"Then don't," I said. "Fara's a gap-filler. If she doesn't know a mending spell, she can find one."

"So I finally get to rip your clothes off of you?"

"Only if I get to burn yours off of you."

He laughed and leaned toward me, burying his face in my neck. Every spot rubbed raw by his rough whiskers was soon soothed by the press of his flesh against mine, specifically his shiver-inducing, brain-addling, soft-as-smoke lips. Within seconds I was trembling with aching need and impatient want.

What was he waiting for? Hadn't we waited long enough?!

Ari stepped back and I was suddenly bereft. My back felt chilled and I started to turn around, but Ari's hand on my shoulder stopped me. He moved it to the nape of my neck and then, even more slowly than before, ran his finger down my spine. Buttons fell to the floor, scattering like beads. For one brief, uncanny moment, I worried that Ari had partially shifted or taken some other form with razor-sharp claws. I clenched my fists, hissing as the sharp, erotic burn of his touch from nape to buttocks charred silk and scalded skin, producing ashes, sweat, boneless limbs, and a sinking feeling in the pit of my stomach that making love to Ari wouldn't quite be what it used to be. That being denied what he wanted – whether it was my body for the last fourteen months or my hand in marriage for ever after – had caused the drakon in him to become more possessive and aggressive than it had been before.

Would I be able to control him?

Who said I wanted to?!

It's not like I wanted him to try to control me.

He placed his hand on the small of my back. His thumb slid into the small dimples there as he caressed both curves and cleft with his fingers. Then he moved his hand slowly back up my spine, cooling the burn but upping the ache. He pushed my dress off one shoulder and then the other, letting it fall to the floor. Because of the gown's sheer top, the only undergarment I had on was a pair of lace knickers. I stepped out of the dress and faced Ari.

He'd seen me naked before, of course. Only about a thousand times. But my body was different now. Leaner, more muscled. There were even a few scars and, as a result of the *suffoca ignem* curse and its removal, my demon mark was now much, much darker. I wondered what Ari would make of all the changes. Whether he'd miss the girl with the voluptuous curves who'd been soft and scared. His gaze swept the length of me and his face settled into an expression of rapt wonder that was almost comical. Indeed, he appeared incapable of looking away. Without taking his eyes off me, he kicked my dress out of his way and closed the distance between us.

But I put up a hand to stop him.

"My turn," I said, grinning. But I didn't have nearly the patience that Ari seemed to. Instead of a slow, teasing burn, I vaporized every stitch of clothing he wore except the sling. Torching that had seemed counter-productive. I didn't want Ari focused on his damaged arm. I wanted him focused on me. I smiled sweetly and then gave him the same full-body stare that he'd given me. But the only unexpected things I saw were a few ashes stubbornly clinging to his excessively muscled middle. I knelt before him and gently blew them away.

It nearly undid him. I could feel that I'd finally pushed Ari to the point of almost losing control. And for a man – a demon – like Ari, that was no small feat. He groaned and plunged his hand into my hair. He grabbed a fistful of it and slowly pulled me to my feet with it.

I stood before him a little wobbly. A little drunk on his own reaction to me.

I motioned in mock indignation toward my dress. "You said you'd *rip* my clothes off."

He reached forward, swaying like a giant who'd been clubbed in the head, grabbed the waist of my lace knickers, and pulled. The fine mesh ripped and they fluttered to the floor.

"Satisfied?" he said, his voice nearly a growl as he yanked me toward him.

"Not even close," I said, placing his hand on my heart.

Luckily, Ari was kissing me when his fingertips finally brushed my demon mark. Otherwise, my scream might have woken all of Rockthorn Gorge, whose residents were surely sleeping after their night of debauchery. Involuntarily, I arched my back, but instead of retreating Ari doubled down and flattened his palm against my breast. I bit his tongue, no longer able to keep up the pretense of a kiss, and gasped for breath, shuddering beneath him. He shushed and hushed and murmured how sorry he was over and over again. But I don't think he was. All I could feel in him was this euphoric sense of rightness... of fittingness.

Eventually, he lowered me to the floor and took me there, as an ordinary man might take an ordinary woman. Good thing too, since the bed – and nearly everything else in the room – had been reduced to a smoldering pile of charred wood, ashes, and soot.

IDYLL

Ari
Almost two years ago
And every moment since

He felt her before he saw her. Sitting on the docks in Etincelle, waiting for the morning ferry. She'd been completely buttoned up – with both cloak and cloaking spell. And her face had been half-buried in the cowl neck of her sweater but her signature... well, it had *surged*. To Ari, it had felt like a deep, powerful subterranean stream. One that, once he was caught in, he didn't think he'd ever have the strength to pull himself out of. Nor had he wanted to. Her magic had swirled around him, capricious and strong, almost knocking him over as if it were a dark watery wind. It was only after he touched her that he knew. What he'd felt was just a shadow. A vague, colorless outline of what she might become. He became fascinated, then nearly enchanted. He began to feel like a lapidary, but instead of cutting gems from stone, he was carving light from darkness.

When this girl's signature finally surfaced, what would it feel like? Would it rage like a rock-strewn river? Would it wink and shimmer like moonlight on water? Or would it shine like glass – a glossy sheen atop a deadly force?

Noon's magic had felt like all of those things, and

more. Every time he saw her or felt her, it was different. *She* was different. There was an old Hyrke saying about living happily ever after. "Ever-newer waters flow on those who step into the same rivers." The trick, they said, was to find the river. Most folks from Bradbury picked the Lethe.

But Ari Carmine had picked Nouiomo Onyx.

Part II

Never regret thy fall,
O Icarus of the fearless flight.
For the greatest tragedy of them all,
is never to feel the burning light.

—OSCAR WILDE

18

LUCK IS ON YOUR SIDE

Noon—

Drakon wing bones, huh? I'm sure you're aware, dear sister, that there are only a handful of winged demon species in all of Halja. How you've managed to have run-ins with two of the possible five species out there, I have no idea. But what's wilder still is this…

I recently captured a scarlet augur, which had a broken wing. The presentation was eerily similar to the one you describe – an old break that healed improperly. I don't have the time or the paper to tell you how difficult it was to figure out how to fix that wing.

My point is simply that Luck is on your side.

Linnaea was intrigued enough by my success with the scarlet augur to grant me leave to come north and attempt the same procedure with your drakon. Expect me the week after Frigore Luna.

Your ingenious, masterful, brilliant brother,

Nightshade

19

A SHINING BRIGHTNESS

They say that before the apocalypse, names had magical power, similar to modern-day spells. Followers were told to use deities' names judiciously – or not at all. And demons were told not to share them.

It all seems a bit paranoid now. Countless times a day, Host and Hyrke invoke Luck by saying his name, not to mention the myriad other times greater and lesser demons are called upon by name as followers go about the business of beseeching. But *those* names aren't birth names; they're monikers, chosen by the demon.

To my knowledge, only one demon has ever been granted a birth name.

I woke sometime around noon the day after Frigore Luna. I hadn't slept that late since... since.... Who knew? I felt achy in all the right places. I felt exhausted. Sore. Satisfied.

At least for now.

I sat up and grinned at Ari, who was resting beneath me with his good arm draped across his face. He'd always been like that. Aggravatingly robust after even the latest nights. My gaze traveled the naked length of him, hardly believing the night we'd had. What was it Ari had called me before I'd trekked up to Cliodna's place?

The Patron of Reluctance?

Well, not anymore.

It wasn't just that I'd given as good as I'd gotten last night, it was that now I wanted to apply that audacious spirit to every aspect of my life. Suddenly, I wanted to shape my magic like a fiery drakon and go for a test flight. I wanted to write to my father and request a meeting. I wanted to hang a sign that said *here be drakons* over my bed.

I wanted to slip back under our non-existent covers and test Ari's aggravating robustness.

But my bedroom was a disaster, my barghest needed to be fed, and eventually, someone would come looking for us. I wasn't going to hide the nature of our relationship any longer, but it didn't seem prudent to be found in such a state of dishabille either. Tenacity had been none too pleased about my melting my alarm clock. I could only imagine what she'd say about me torching the entire room.

I started sifting through the wreckage, glad that most of my possessions were in my study or dressing room. The red-roses gown was a casualty of love but the rest of my trousseau had been spared. As had Rafe's bracelet. I bent down and retrieved it from the pile of ashes that had once been my chest of drawers, marveling at its apparent imperviousness to waning magic. In the sunlight, the bracelet gleamed shiny and bright.

How appropriate, I thought, glancing at the inscription on the inside of the bracelet.

BHEREG 9-2-92

"Looks like your former Guardian's cuff is as surprisingly hale as he is."

I turned around to see Ari staring at the bracelet. His voice was laced with slight irritation and grudging respect.

I took a deep breath, remembering that I'd torched my Patron of Reluctance persona along with nearly everything else in this room last night.

"He's not just my former Guardian," I said, handing Ari the cuff. He frowned but accepted it and a moment later asked the question I knew he would.

"Who is Bhereg?"

"You," I said. "*You* are Bhereg."

And then I told Ari the rest of the "everything" that Rafe had told me to tell him. That they were half-brothers and that, upon Ari's birth, Rafe had given him the name Bhereg. The entire tale sounded outlandish, more like a cheap horror novel than the near-unbelievable truth, but Ari listened patiently. Calmly. Even a bit callously.

And then he said simply, "It doesn't matter. Even if it's true, it changes *nothing*."

I would have spent more time contemplating Ari's reaction to the news that he and Rafe had a familial connection if it weren't for the fact that, soon after, Ari made another discovery, one which required a much more immediate response.

LAST CHANCE… LIVE FREE OR DIE

It was another cartoon. This one showed a lit Magna Fax firing a giant meteor toward the Memento

Mori dam. I looked up at Ari. His dark eyes seemed to simmer with the presentiment I felt in his signature. Only a few minutes ago, he'd left my chambers to find clothes in his own dressing room while I did the same. I'd barely had enough time to pull on a camisole and some pants when he'd returned with the threatening note.

"Where did you find this?" I asked.

But instead of answering, he just pulled me into the atrium where Fara was already waiting.

Post-party, the cavernous rotunda was a mess. It reminded me a bit of Timothy's Square after a festival. Wine bottles and overturned goblets were everywhere. Nova had upended a trash can, the statues' shrouds were askew, one of the alcove curtains had been torn from its rod, and every single torch was missing – as well as Servius Rockthorn's *tabula ansata*.

A dreadful, nauseous feeling bloomed deep inside of me. The *tabula ansata* was the Magna Fax's matchbook.

"So what does it mean?" Fara asked, motioning to the cartoon. "That Displodo's going to try to use the Magna Fax to blow up the Memento Mori dam?" Before I could answer, though, she narrowed her eyes and glanced between Ari and me, no doubt noting the absence of Rafe's bracelet on my wrist as well as other more and less obvious signs of our change in status. "Wait—

"Are you two back together now?"

Despite the enormity of what we were facing, I smiled at Ari. "Yes," I said, unequivocally. Suddenly, knowing we were as close as we'd ever been gave me a new sense of optimism. But it faded fast when I explained to Fara that the rotunda's relaxed security last night had given Displodo his chance to break in and steal the Magna Fax's matchbook.

"Huh? What do you mean, 'matchbook'? How can a stone tablet be a matchbook?"

"The statue's *tabula ansata* wasn't made of stone," Ari told her. "It was just made to look like it was, which means whoever has it, now has the key to a weapon that could destroy more than just the dam. A lit Magna Fax could level this town. Instead of a dozen casualties, there could be thousands."

We raced through the atrium and the rotunda's foyer toward the outside where we had a clear view of Mount Occasus, its ancient guard tower, and the Magna Fax.

"Ari, if you shift, you can fly us both up there. We might be able to beat Displodo to the top. Fara, cast a simple levitation spell over me. It will make me lighter and easier to carry. After you're finished, find Yannu. Tell him to round up the retainers and meet us at Mount Occasus. Tell him Displodo found the Magna Fax's matchbook."

"You're going to ride Ari?" Fara asked incredulously. "What… like a horse?"

I glared at her. "No…" Well, yeah, maybe.

Actually, considering Ari's broken wing, my plan was to hang on and hope like hell I didn't fall off. I wouldn't be riding. I'd be flapping in the wind like a flag. I glanced at Ari to gauge his reaction. He looked like he wanted to argue but realized now wasn't the time to be overprotective. My confidence waned. But then I remembered someone who not only thought I could ride a drakon, she'd encouraged me to shape my own. In fact, she'd designed an outfit for just that purpose.

"You're right," I said to Fara. "Forget that plan. It's insane." I turned to Ari. "Fly up without me. I'll meet you there."

He frowned, perhaps suspecting I had another even more ill-conceived plan in mind. But relief over the fact that I wouldn't be clinging to his back while he dive-bombed Displodo, combined with his impatience to get moving *now*, won out. He nodded, backed up to a clear space, and shifted. I didn't stick around long enough to see him take off. Instead, I ran back inside and headed for my blackened bedroom and the thankfully unscorched dressing room beyond.

I reached my trousseau trunk and threw the lid open. It banged against the wall and I rummaged through the paraffin paper-wrapped packages until I finally found the last item that Sartabella had designed for me – the one labeled "Test Flights."

I ripped it open. Inside was a note:

Now, you must ride Megaptera.
You are ready!

The suit wasn't much different than my sparring suit except that there was no fiery red drakon emblazoned on it (guess Sartabella thought it would be redundant considering I'd be riding one), the backplate was much bulkier, and there was a pair of goggles. I changed quickly and nearly bumped into Fara, who'd followed me in.

"So you're going to ride your own magic up there?"

I nodded.

"Okay, well, forget the levitation spell then. Its ceiling is about two feet. What you need is this"—she strapped a leather holster around my waist and thrust a pepperbox revolver into it—"in case you deplete your magic and every bump and booster spell I cast over you."

It was time I didn't have, but I stood as patiently as

I could while Fara spent her *potentia* on me. She bottomed out. Emptied everything she had into and over me. Some of the spells felt familiar. Others felt fresh and new. A few minutes later, I felt invigorated. Charged up. Like she'd just splashed cold water in my face and pumped Thunderbolt straight into my veins. But instead of being a magnet for everyone's attention, I now pulsed with energy and magic.

Just as I was heading out, Tenacity showed up. Her dancing skeleton costume was now a harlequin one. She stood in the doorway, gazing at my destroyed bedroom, mouth agape.

"What happened?"

"Oh, uh… Ari and I happened. I'm really sorry about the room. I'll help you clean it up when I get back."

"Where are you going?"

"To stop Displodo from lighting the Magna Fax," I yelled from the hallway.

Outside once again, I wasted no time trying to shape my mount. I'd done it before. Sort of. Down in southern Halja, I'd shaped my magic into a barghest. I'd dubbed her "Nova," which is where Nova's name had come from. That fiery mount had been short-lived. Rafe and I had ridden her for less than an hour before my magic tapped out. And then I'd been unable to use my magic for a good hour or so after that, which I couldn't afford to let happen today.

Luckily, however, I was stronger than I'd been last semester, and I had the benefit of Fara's spells. Besides, how long could it take to fly to the top of Mount Occasus? A few minutes at most? I'd be fine.

But trying to shape the damn thing proved more difficult than I'd hoped. Five attempts later, Fara was long gone. On her way to find Yannu and round up help.

For what seemed like the hundredth time, I looked up at the Magna Fax. There was still no sign of light or life at the top of Mount Occasus, which was good. We could still pull this off. If only I could *focus*.

Tenacity came out to watch and instead of being a distraction, she became my center. I cast off my growing fears and concentrated on how Tenacity hadn't let her lack of proper schooling stand in the way of becoming who she wanted to be.

She simply *did it*.

What was it she'd said earlier?

I believe in the teachings of Joshua, so the demons call me 'Angel.'

Well, I believed I could shape a drakon big enough to fly so the demons could call me… whatever the hell they wanted. The only thing I cared about was *doing it*.

My sixth attempt roared to life. She literally tipped her head back and bellowed fire upon her birth. Tenacity jumped up from where she'd been sitting and stumbled backward as Megaptera (I had to call her something!) turned her red eyes toward us.

She was terrifyingly beautiful, especially when she stretched her wings and I realized they were perfect. *That's what I want for Ari*, I thought. *I want Nightshade to mend his broken wing and make it perfect again.*

But first things first.

I took a running start and leapt onto Megaptera's back. Effortlessly, I found my seat and gave Tenacity a jaunty wave as Megaptera rose gracefully into the sky—

Ha! It didn't actually happen like that.

Tenacity ended up having to give me a leg up. She beamed when I told her that her old-fashioned, unensorcelled boost was worth ten of Fara's fancy spells. I climbed up and clumsily wedged myself in between Megaptera's lance-like horns, furiously hoping I wouldn't be thrown off if she toggled them forward for battle. I guessed, since they were made from my magic, I could dissolve them if they became a problem, but that made me wonder what else I might not be anticipating.

Enough, I scolded myself. I'd wasted enough time. I probably could have hiked to the top of Mount Occasus by now. I focused on one remaining thought – *up!* Megaptera's haunches tensed and then, a moment later, she launched herself into the sky.

20

MEGAPTERA

Flying a fiery drakon shaped from my own magic was the most amazing thing I'd ever experienced – bar none. I'd climbed to the top of some very high places, stood at the top of other high spaces... Mountains and skyscrapers, bridges and bell towers... I'd ridden in fast cabs, bouncing boats, even on the back of a barghest. But none of it compared to this. *This* was height and speed the likes of which I couldn't have ever imagined. The moment Megaptera took to the sky, my body soared, my stomach dropped, and my perspective of the world changed forever.

Everything shrank and expanded at the same time. Rockthorn Gorge's buildings became smaller as my view opened up. Behind me, the town and its landmarks became model-sized. The river Acheron grew longer as Mount Occasus loomed larger. Wind whipped across my face, stuffed my lungs, and tangled my hair. The air – the sky – seemed laced with something special, a palpable bliss that was more than magical. For one wild moment, I knew I could escape everyone who had ever tried to control me: my father, the Council, St. Luck's... even Ari.

How had he resisted the urge to scoop me up and fly off with me?

Maybe he'd been holding out for this – the day when we could fly off together, as equals.

But the view that tempted me was the view that tethered me. Up here, I felt as if I could see the future – Ari's and mine and the tiny town of Rockthorn Gorge's. In the shadow of Mount Occasus, the settlement looked small and vulnerable.

Live free or die? I couldn't afford to do either.

The flight to the top of Mount Occasus was both regrettably and thankfully short. If it weren't for Displodo's threat and the limits of my magic, I could have stayed in the sky forever. As it was, however, I made it to the base of the guard tower with a decent reservoir of magic to draw upon.

Why hadn't I thought to bring a blade? Firing a pepperbox made from metal might be less risky than firing one made from magic, but how good would my aim be? I'd never fired a real gun in my life.

Too late for regrets. I gritted my teeth and concentrated on descending.

Ari's expression was inscrutable. He stood watching me wrestle with Megaptera, attempting, for the first time, to manage speed, lift, wind direction, and a relatively small landing area. Riding a beast shaped from my own magic was both good and bad. Megaptera was fully within my control – but I had no idea how to fly. I was winging it.

I snorted at my own dumb pun and tried not to overthink my landing. I came in too high and too fast. My signature zinged as I realized the very real danger of falling over the cliff. If I lost my focus and Megaptera sputtered and went out, there was little chance I'd be able to reshape her before I died. Would Ari be able to catch me?

He reached up and I bent over and grabbed his hand. He yanked me from my seat and I fell, crashing to the ground next to him. My shoulder crunched painfully and the wind was knocked out of me. Megaptera dissolved in a downpour of ash and soot. I rolled over, wheezing, trying to catch my breath while expanding my signature.

The only other waning magic users I felt were Ari and two bunyips at the bottom of the *via ferrata*. Their signatures were faint but they buzzed with astonishment while Ari's nearer and stronger one pulsed with delight... and not a small amount of turmoil. I stood up quickly, not wanting Ari to suspect how much shaping Megaptera had taxed me, and tested my shoulder.

How ironic would it be if I'd broken my *left arm? No steel blade, no Angel healer...*

It wasn't broken, though. I stared at Ari while windmilling my arm. He was dressed in borrowed clothes. Presumably he'd checked in with whoever was below and one of them had lent him some gear. I knew we should discuss Displodo first and that I should ask him what he'd learned from the bunyips below, but I couldn't help grinning.

"So... whadya think?" I asked, motioning to the now-empty sky.

Ari struggled for a moment, his emotions at war with one another. Finally, admiration won out. He smiled and shook his head. "That... *that* was incredible. I knew you could do it, but... just... don't fly so high again until you know what you're doing. You, ah...well... You looked like you were riding a winged bull in a maelstrom."

My jaw dropped. True or not, what right did Ari have to criticize *my* flying?! *He* was the one who looked like—

But then he grinned and I laughed and for one single moment it was just us on a windy mountain we'd both flown to the top of. Sunset was hours away, and that strange, foreboding, orange-turning-blue, fiery kisses, bared hearts, and impending gloom-of-night feeling I'd had the last time we were here felt far off.

"Who's at the bottom?" I asked.

"Oleg and Igor. They were patrolling the base when I flew over."

I acknowledged with a nod, but I'd be lying if I said I remembered which bunyips they were. The retainers did *not* go out of their way to distinguish themselves – they were all big, brutish, and tank-like.

Ari and I reconnoitered the mountaintop plaza. We patrolled its perimeter, peeked over the sides of the mountain, and expanded our signatures as far as the horizon, or at least that's what it felt like. Vaguely, I felt a contingent of signatures marching our way, but the mass felt like retainers – a bunch of bunyips and a few other demon species I didn't immediately recognize. Their magic seethed with *expectation*, but it was a battle response I was used to.

Rumbling thunder and a rogue wind gust told me a storm was on its way. *That* made me uneasy. Storms always seemed to presage something terrible. An electric web of light flared in the clouds above one of the western ridges.

"Ari..." I said slowly, turning around, "Did you check inside the tower?" I glanced up at the Magna Fax, which poked out from the tower's crenelated battlement.

"No," he answered quietly, "but I can't feel anyone in it, and how would they have gotten up here without either Oleg or Igor seeing or sensing them?"

I pursed my lips but was careful to keep my signature steady.

"Displodo might not even be a demon," I reminded Ari. "On the other hand, if it's Acheron, he wouldn't have to use the *via ferrata*." He could slither up the side of the mountain.

"You still think Acheron might be Displodo?" Ari didn't bother to hide his skepticism.

We walked toward the guard tower. I shrugged. "Acheron hates the Memento Mori dam project, and I think he'd do almost anything to stop it. He threatened the Council. He threatened me—"

"He did? When?"

I filled Ari in on my meeting with Acheron. With everything that had happened last night and this morning, I hadn't had a chance. But Ari was more interested in Acheron's alleged claim than his alleged threat.

"Acheron isn't Displodo, Noon. He respects the law. He respects the Council. He... respects you."

I gave Ari an incredulous look. "Sure he does." I laughed. "Want to know how I tried to control him yesterday? I shaped a fiery ring and put it right through his nose. Not that it worked."

Beside me, Ari made a strangled noise in his throat. Alarmed, I turned toward him. But no one was attacking him; he just looked dumbfounded. "Noon, you—?"

Ari made some other unintelligible noise. I couldn't tell if he was laughing or horrified. I finally grabbed his arm and put my finger to my lips. We were standing in front of the guard tower. I shaped a sword and pulled the door open. Ari stepped inside, peered up, and then motioned to me.

Inside was a spiral staircase with no handrails, lit only by the meager light from arrow slits in the wall and our swords. We kept our weapons bright as we crept in and up. Boots silent, breath held, we climbed toward the top. I didn't count them, but there had to be as many steps in the tower as there were days in a year. And a year is how long it seemed to take to reach the top. The tower was beginning to feel like a giant mausoleum by the time I reached the last step and emerged onto the roof.

There, crouched in between two merlons, was the Magna Fax. I knew it was only a weapon – a tool, neither inherently good nor bad – yet it seemed an evil thing.

How could anyone build something so powerful and expect it to serve only as a deterrent?

At least one small part of Obadiah Zeffre must have wanted to see his creation put to use, which made me worry anew about his descendent, Nephemiah. How much of the town's original engineer's hubris had been passed down? How much of his zealousness?

The view from the top of the tower was spectacular, but the line of retainers making their way along the trail to the base of the mountain gave us no time to appreciate it. I shielded my eyes from the setting sun and squinted at the approaching figures.

"Can you tell who's coming from their signatures?" I asked Ari.

"Feels like Kalchoek... Pestis and Malphia... and one more I don't recognize."

Well, at least Ari had confirmed my first impression – that there wasn't a pack of *rogares* on their way to meet us. But Kalchoek? And Pestis and Malphia? *Ugh.* I didn't know who would be worse to work with – any one of them or the unfamiliar demon.

"Could the stranger be Vannis?" Hidebehinds could cloak their signatures; maybe they could camouflage them too.

But Ari shook his head. "Doubtful."

I didn't voice the obvious next question: *Could it be Displodo?*

After a brief debate, we decided to split up. I agreed to climb back down to the plaza and meet up with Rat Boy, Fly Girl, and my melee nemesis while Ari stayed up top to guard the Magna Fax.

On the way down, I considered our suspects:

ACHERON*: He wanted the Memento Mori dam project stopped and he wasn't above using dramatically unorthodox means to achieve his goal (he'd threatened the Council and assaulted me... albeit, I'd assaulted him first). He was in possession of an ancient book (possibly an altered forgery of a lost or stolen original?), which he claimed gave him Luck-granted rights over this area. He was also at the rotunda mere hours before Displodo stole the Magna Fax's matchbook.*

ZEFFRE*: Descended from the engineer who originally built the Magna Fax for the very purpose of drastically reducing the town's reliance on demon lords. He was also the foreman of the Memento Mori dam project, which meant he had unrestricted access to the viaduct and building site. And he was Ari's uncle. Other members of Ari's adoptive family (ahem, his mother, Joy) possessed a wickedly fierce independent streak. It wasn't too hard to imagine that Zeffre might be hiding one as well. Maybe he valued his independence over other people's lives.*

MALPHIA: Where to start? Her magic was more than destructive. It felt like a blight on the world. She fought as if her personal mission was to stamp out every bit of light or love, past, present, or future. She'd not only beaten me in my first melee, she'd almost killed me. And she'd continued to taunt me ever since. That said, she was a fan of dark, lonely things – of suffocation and inexistence, not fiery explosions.

CLIODNA: She hated me... and everyone else. Because she was incapable of love. She'd all but admitted she valued people no more than dolls or puppets. And when she toyed with you, poison was the least of your concerns. Still... my conflicts with her were personal. And Cliodna had a lot to lose if the Memento Mori dam project was stopped and the town's ties with New Babylon broken. Most of her miners and artisans would be out of work. Their adoration for her would quickly turn to antagonism.

YANNU: It was true that, after an altogether justified "testing" phase, Ari's Captain of the Guard had seemed to accept me. And yet... I couldn't quite bring myself to cross him off the list. It wasn't (necessarily) that he could have cared less whether I lived or died; it was that he was a bunyip, more than half the ranks were bunyips, and his history in the gorge was longer than Ari's. I had a feeling Yannu had seen himself as Potomus' successor... But would Yannu go as far as destroying town infrastructure, killing residents, and murdering patrons to pursue his ambition?

SOMEONE ELSE: ...

I was beginning to contemplate that last amorphous suspect when I reached the bottom stair. Mulling over my list would have to wait. I pushed open the tower door and found Kalchoek, Pestis, and Malphia waiting for me. Pestis' mouth was closed, so thankfully there wasn't yet a swarm of flies overhead. Her glistening face and lidless eyes stared back at me as I brought the trio up to speed.

"No sign of Displodo?" Malphia asked. I shook my head. *Unless he's you...* She smirked. "You looked like you were going to save him the trouble of killing you earlier."

I gathered she was referring to Megaptera and ignored her barb.

"Who's below with Oleg and Igor?"

"Ungvar."

"Where's Yannu?"

"On his way with more retainers."

I realized then just how isolated and alone I was. Not just on top of Mount Occasus, but in Rockthorn Gorge. Three months of working here and I still trusted only three people – Ari, Fara, and Tenacity.

"Guess who finally had to pick me for her team?" Malphia chortled and then turned her back on me. Pestis just stared, silent and unblinking, creepy and quiet. Her signature reminded me of dying things. Of decay and rot. Malphia's signature was worse, though. If Pestis felt like death, then Malphia felt like the one-two punch of a living hell followed by The End. And Kalchoek? He just felt oil-slick and dirty, as always.

Keeping my signature open so that I could try and sense the presence of another waning magic user was difficult and unnerving. The weather didn't help. The incoming storm made the surrounding green of the mountains look darker than midnight. At least midnight there were twinkling stars and the potential for dreams.

The blackness in the mountains expanded as the increasing gloom prematurely extinguished the fading sun. There were no last rays of yellow-gold hope. The mountain peaks were suddenly the color of tension and fear – a roiling stew of nihility steaming with ash-colored clouds and electric light.

I descended a set of stairs to one of the smaller levels of the plaza. The effects of the others' signatures were less pronounced down here, but my sense of emptiness and unease remained. By the time the rain started, I felt as brittle as a burnt butterfly wing. It occurred to me that Displodo's cartoon hadn't stated a deadline. There was no ticking clock. We'd rushed here to stop him, but he might not come. He could wait five days, five years, or even fifty to use the matchbook he'd stolen.

How long would we be able to triple guard the Magna Fax with guards at the base of the mountain, top, and tower?

A few days more, I thought, ascending the steps and heading back toward the tower to complete my circuit. *That's all. Just until we think of a different plan. Some way to lure Displodo out of hiding. Or a way to convince the residents of Rockthorn Gorge that it was time to dismantle the Magna Fax...*

Something crackled when I took my next step. But when I looked down, there was nothing. I raised my foot and peered at the sole of my boot. There, smashed in the middle of it, was a fly.

Had I just killed one of Pestis' flies?

I grimaced and waited for a telltale sign of irritation to flash in her signature, but I felt nothing. In fact, I couldn't feel her at all anymore, which might have been comforting had my gaze not skipped ahead to the ground in front of me.

It was covered with flies – dead ones.

My signature zinged and I rushed forward, shaping a sword as I ran. Fiery heat exploded in my palm and quickly morphed into a solid, warm, familiar shape. I gripped the hilt of my sword as I raced up a few more steps, rounded a corner, and ran across the largest section of the plaza. Pestis was lying on the ground in front of the tower.

She was as dead as the flies.

21

DISPLODO

Whoever had murdered Pestis had literally torn her limb from limb. And then burned her. As if they'd been inspired by the sick, sadistically twisted people who torture insects. The ones who tear wings off flies or burn ants under a magnifying glass.

Involuntarily, I raised my left hand to my mouth. The smell was awful, but it was also just a natural reaction to seeing something terrible. Lightning flashed and the Magna Fax, high above on the tower wall, flickered. I heard the scuffle of boots on stone and turned around. Malphia and Kalchoek approached simultaneously from different directions. Surprise was evident in both their faces and signatures, but that didn't mean anything. I'd met plenty of demons who were bad actors with good acting skills by now. I squeezed the hilt of my sword and clenched my jaw, bracing for a blow. But it didn't come.

Kalchoek glanced at Pestis, his nose twitching, teeth protruding, eyes gleaming, and then switched his gaze to the rest of the plaza. Malphia just stared at Pestis. Then she looked up at me, frowning, and switched her gaze to the Magna Fax.

Ari—! Immediately, I expanded my signature, but the stone walls of the tower blocked my magic from reaching his.

Was Displodo on his way to the top?

I turned, ran for the door, swung it open, and peered up. I was just about to step inside and start climbing when I felt a sharp, explosive pain in my chest. It radiated outward as if my heart was suddenly pumping burning nitroglycerin through my veins. The shock wave rippled from chest to limbs, pulling them apart as if each had been tied to a different horse.

Was this what the medieval torture of being drawn and quartered felt like?

No – this was worse, but mercilessly quicker. I didn't have time to worry about anything. Not Ari, not my body, not Rockthorn Gorge. Not Displodo... and whether he was actually a she. Whether he was Malphia... or Kalchoek... or Vannis... or Acheron... or anyone else.

There was only pain, not panic – because there wasn't time. I fell to the ground, burning. Vaguely, I realized that whatever magic blast had hit me had probably been what killed Pestis. I no longer felt like a burned butterfly wing. I was beyond that. As I hit the floor, I felt like ashes. Ashes that would have been scattered by the wind if they hadn't been sheltered by the tower. My last thought before darkness took me was of Tenacity – the unorthodox Angel who'd seen me off on my first, last, great flight.

I died with the words to her parting spell ringing in my head.

Ich be wy ye...

I'll be with you...

But I didn't die. I don't know if it was Tenacity's spell or one of Fara's or if Displodo had simply underestimated the amount of magic it would take to kill me or what, but I woke with a splitting head, shattered joints, and flayed skin. Or at least that's what it felt like.

My cheek was pressed against the flagstone floor of the plaza. I coughed, tasting blood, and pushed myself up with my hand, my head swimming. I bit my lip so that I wouldn't cry out and gingerly got to my feet. My eyesight was blurry, my thoughts were in disarray, and my muscles were in open revolt.

Malphia lay beside Pestis. She looked as bad as I felt, but she wasn't dead. I could feel the faint wisp of her signature. It shimmied and swirled, wobbled and twisted, echoing the path of the inky black shadow that was oozing off her body. I remembered from the night we'd all stood around Ari's *rota fortunae* that Malphia's "best weapon" was a black shadow. I gathered that she was either shifting to heal or forming her best weapon, but either way, I couldn't help her.

I turned back around and eyed the tower with a sense of dread. In my current condition, it would take a half-hour at least to reach the top. Distantly, I felt Kalchoek's signature and, beyond that, Ari's.

So Kalchoek *was Displodo?*

I didn't have the time or mental focus to puzzle it out. All I knew was that, once again, I needed to beat Displodo to the top.

The same routes were available to me as before: climb… or fly.

It wasn't really a choice, since Kalchoek was already halfway up. I shuffled outside and took a deep breath, focusing. I couldn't afford worry or panic. They'd be counter-productive. I didn't have time for six attempts.

I tried. But instead of forming a fiery drakon, I just felt like I set myself on fire again. Tears welled, from frustration or pain, I don't know. Probably both. I almost starting sobbing right then and there, but instead I dug my fingernails into my palms, bit my lip hard enough to draw blood, and *forced* myself to concentrate. I formed Megaptera on my second try.

Feeling even more ragged and worn, I climbed onto her back. It was a clumsy, ugly mount but I managed to position myself adequately if not confidently and Megaptera launched herself into the air. Three rotations around the tower's exterior, sensing nothing but the wind and the storm. The smattering of raindrops that I'd barely noticed on the ground now felt like ball bearings aimed at my face. I squinted against the gray haze as I flew round and round on my way to the top. It seemed like a year again but it was only seconds before I reached the battlement.

By then, Kalchoek was already there. Ari took one look at me – Luck knows what I looked like; probably more bloody and burned than he'd ever seen me – and his face reflected true horror. But it was the horror of concern… and conflict. I couldn't be sure – signatures don't allow us to read minds – but he looked like someone faced with an impossible choice. Urge me to jump to the roof and face Kalchoek with him, or urge me to fly off, out of harm's way.

But he had to know it wasn't his choice. Before I could jump, however, Kalchoek threw another waning magic blast at me. I twisted my torso with a hair's breadth of space to spare and nearly lost my seat. Kalchoek's blast singed my chest anew as it sailed past, but there was no direct hit. Megaptera seemed to flicker in time with the cloud that exploded behind me and the rain became fiercer, as if Luck was trying to extinguish my mount.

I had a feeling a second blast from him would be fatal. That no spell, no matter how thoughtfully or expertly cast, would be able to save me.

Behind the battlement, Kalchoek appeared to brandish a scroll. But I knew it wasn't a scroll. It was a page from the Magna Fax's matchbook. My terror increased when I saw its end catch fire.

If Kalchoek used it to light the Magna Fax, where would the cannon's first stymphwax ball go? The mountain ridge opposite us? The Memento Mori dam?

Or the town of Rockthorn Gorge?

Ari and Kalchoek circled each other while I circled them in the sky. The wind, rain, and thunder drowned out my voice. It was dizzying and disorienting.

Why wasn't Ari blasting Kalchoek?

Then I realized that the rooftop was covered with paper – pages from the cannon's matchbook. Kalchoek must have had the book in his pocket and, once he'd reached the Magna Fax, he'd shredded it. Ari didn't want to risk accidentally lighting the cannon. After nearly two thousand years, the wax creation would be far from stable. So Ari was trying to smother Kalchoek by leeching the oxygen from around him, which Kalchoek was resisting, of course.

Well, he'd have a harder time against two of us.

I flew close to the battlement and prepared to jump off, but when I stood in my seat my hand brushed against the pepperbox holstered on my hip. I'd completely forgotten about it. Suddenly, an idea sparked.

Why wait to smother Kalchoek when I could just

shoot him from here?

I pulled the pepperbox out of the holster and aimed it. My unexpected move caught their attention. Ari's eyes widened in surprise, but Kalchoek just laughed and took advantage of the moment. A cold, sinking feeling, wetter than the rain, heavier than the Magna Fax, seemed to descend on me as I watched, seemingly in slow motion, as Kalchoek launched himself toward the Magna Fax's fuse. I pulled the pepperbox's trigger, but I already knew I'd been too slow.

Three things happened almost instantly: Kalchoek touched the burning end of the match to the Magna Fax's fuse; my bullet reached Kalchoek's brain; and Ari threw his own waning magic blast – this one directed toward the Magna Fax itself. I guess he thought to destroy it before it was fired…?

The cannon crackled with fiery heat as the Tempered stymphwax melted into an inchoate ball of searing light and brittle magic. Ari jumped from the roof just as the ball exploded. A blistering shock wave shattered the battlements and slammed into me, knocking me from my seat. Megaptera fractured into a million dark, glinting flakes. I flailed, grasping at nothing, my insides churning with icy fear as I tried to re-form her. Fear metastasized into full-fledged horror as I realized my magic was blown.

As the billowing edges of the explosion raced toward us, Ari started shifting. His chest swelled like a balloon, his muscles bulged and popped, his skin stretched… His wings formed, one snapping open like a sail, the other writhing in the wind… His face contorted with pain… Until he finally emerged from the transformation with his drakon's gaze locked on me.

Ari would have caught me. I know it. And we both would have lived. The wing wouldn't have mattered. It was perfect. Ari was perfect. I don't know why I ever thought it wasn't or he wasn't. Or why I ever thought things could somehow be better. They'd been absolutely perfect. Exactly as they were. There was never any need to go back to an earlier time in our relationship. Or any other point in my life. If only we could have stayed *just like that* forever...

But the Magna Fax detonated instead of firing, and the resulting explosion engulfed Ari. It would have engulfed me too if he hadn't shielded me from it. His claws extended as he reached for me. I reached for him too, screaming, my hands raking the air. I watched as the fire consumed him, first his tail, then his wings, his body, and then finally his head. The last image I have of Ari is his eyes – mulberry red and fiery, warm with love and sacrifice.

I continued to fall down the side of the mountain after that, thinking to die and welcoming it. Ichabye started kicking in and I rejected it. The only person I wanted with me had been turned to ashes before my eyes. Oddly, impossibly, I remembered something Ari's mother had said to me once.

It's not every day you meet the woman your son is willing to die for.

I wondered now as I'd wondered then – *had Joy seen Ari's death?*

I'd said that she couldn't have meant what she'd said. *Because how could someone go on living after something like that happened?*

Thank Luck I don't have to, I thought, just as I felt a rush of magic. Something in the back of my flight suit released. My descent slowed abruptly and forcibly. Once again, I felt a punch in my chest and a loosening in my joints. But it was gentler than Kalchoek's blast had been. I looked up. I was tied to some kind of huge, frameless, silk umbrella.

I would have burned it and continued falling if I'd had any magic left.

22

A DIVINE HELL

Sartabella called it a parachute, I found out later. The name was a pre-apocalyptic meld of two words that meant "to protect against" and "fall." But what I'd really needed wasn't protection against falling, it was protection against falling *in love*. Or protection against my heart breaking *again*. This time, in a way that couldn't be mended.

Ari, Pestis, and Kalchoek-*cum*-Displodo were all dead. The Magna Fax had been completely destroyed, along with the plaza and the tower at the top of Mount Occasus. Pieces of it had fallen into the Acheron River below. Remarkably, Malphia, like me, had survived. Before the explosion, she'd fully shifted into smoke and shadow. For one glittering moment, her story had given me hope that Ari might still live. Maybe he'd done the same…?

But the black spot in my heart that grew larger by the day told me otherwise. Ari might have been able to escape the blast that way, had he not been trying to catch me. If he hadn't tried to save me from falling…

For days, I went round and round what happened in my mind, obsessing about the details. All the things I could have done differently. I knew it was madness. That I shouldn't think about such things. But I couldn't help it. I began to realize Ari's death was my fault.

How could I have been so arrogant?

Why had I thought I'd be able to succeed at what other Maegesters didn't even attempt?

Riding a drakon shaped from my own magic? Firing a gun? Casting a spell?!

I'd been a lunatic to think I could get away with such things.

My actions may not have directly caused Ari's death, but I blamed myself nonetheless. Luck had punished me. I was sure of it.

Because there were no remains, a memorial was scheduled instead of a funeral. Neither were very popular with demons, but because Ari had been the outpost's patron, his would be a large, well-attended affair. Upon hearing of his death, Cliodna had declared herself and all her artisans in a state of mourning until the patron's procession. The announcement had been perfunctory though; it wasn't as if Cliodna was grief-stricken.

True to character, Yannu had taken charge after the catastrophe. He'd assessed the damage, searched without success for any remaining traces of stymphwax, and warned the ranks and the town that there would be zero tolerance for any "aftermath chaos." Ari's camarilla agreed to stay on until a new patron was elected, since it was likely the new lord would have need of their services in the same way that Ari had.

Since Displodo had been revealed to be Kalchoek, the town found itself unexpectedly free of the underlying tension it had lived with for the past year. Sure, in time someone else would likely use Displodo's credo to further his or her own aims again; and in the meantime there was always the chance of a random *rogare* attack; but paradoxically, Ari's death, happening as it did at the same time as that of the town's biggest terrorist, somehow made the town feel safer. Instead of a memorial procession, everyone seemed to be planning a celebratory parade.

And I began to feel as if I were living in a divine Hell instead of modern-day Halja.

A few days after Ari died, I stood on the platform of Rockthorn Gorge's train station awaiting the arrival of the Carmines. Because the town lacked an electro-harmonic machine, Zeffre had sent his brother-in-law a note via carrier dove. It was a brutish way to give him the news that his son had been killed, but there was no way to avoid it and still give Ari's family the chance to attend his memorial service.

I thought about sending a note to Rafe as well. He'd been Ari's brother as much as Matt Carmine had, but then I thought better of it. The Carmines didn't know about Rafe's fraternal relationship with Ari. Ari's death would be shock enough. And Rafe had already attended Ari's funeral once – when he was six. After Rafe had mistakenly thought he'd drowned Ari in the Lethe. Luck knew, I remembered that... or rather I didn't remember it...

I groaned in frustration and blinked, looking around, almost not recognizing where I was. *The train station*, I reminded myself, *in Rockthorn Gorge*.

This was what the last few days had been like. Scattered thoughts. Not much sense. Barely surviving.

Not eating. Not sleeping.

Fara had glamoured me today. I think she'd glamoured me yesterday and the day before too. Said I wouldn't want the world to see me walking around in my nightshirt.

I could have cared less what people saw me walking around in. It's possible I might've burned the world down if my magic hadn't still been depleted.

If it didn't come back, I wasn't sure what I'd do. Not become a healer, that's for sure.

Maybe I'd toil in my mom's blackened garden… bury the pepperbox there… dig up some—

"Noon," Fara said, her voice impossibly rough and soft at the same time, "they're here."

Matt, Ari's younger brother, stepped off the train first. He was currently a student at my undergraduate alma mater, Gaillard University. He was blonde and big, but still had that puckish look so many undergrads have. The last time I'd seen him he'd been jovial – home for Beltane break and looking forward to a holiday known for its *anything goes* attitude.

Now, he looked like he'd literally been deflated. His mouth drooped, his shoulders sagged, and his eyes were downcast. He barely recognized me. I wasn't sure if that was because it had been so long since we'd last seen each other or if it was because of Fara's glamour.

He stepped toward me, looking unsure of how to greet me. Fara intervened and somehow smoothed things over, though I doubt Matt remembers what she said any more than I do. Maybe she asked about their trip? I'm sure she said she was sorry. Everyone was sorry, but what good did that do?

Ari's parents disembarked next. Joy was still small, white-haired, and pink-eyed, but instead of her usual rainbow hues, she was now dressed in colors as somber as mine.

I didn't know what to say to her – this human woman who'd taken in a demon child and raised him to be good and strong and just. Joy wasn't an enigma to me. I'd gotten to know her not just as a mother, but as a woman, last semester. She was what people in Bradbury called *hveit*. Born without magic, she was special nevertheless. Immune to magic and blessed – or cursed – with partial sight. She was a soothsayer of sorts. She also baked delicious beef and onion pie, sewed her own clothes, and lived the life of a traditional, salt-of-the-earth Hyrke. Every time I'd ever seen her, whether in her own modest kitchen or standing next to the most powerful person in Halja, she'd always looked like a clear, bright, preternatural prism. But not today.

Today, Joy leaned heavily on her husband's arm as she stepped out of the train car. Her grief was so severe I realized she couldn't truly have seen Ari's death. At least not exactly in the way it had happened.

Steve frowned at me. It was fleeting and soon passed, but he managed to convey an excess of disapproval in that one second. *He blames me too*, I thought. But for reasons that were older than just a few days ago. I remembered what Ari had said the day we'd first hiked to the top of Mount Occasus.

My parents haven't always agreed on what future I should have.

It seemed clear that Steve had humored both his wife and son about me. That his preference would have been for Ari not to date me. I think he also suspected – and rightly so – that I was somehow responsible for Ari's premature passing.

But he hid it well and embraced me in a great, big bear hug, as he had the first time we'd met. I embraced

Matt after that, trying, and failing, to keep my cheeks dry. I turned to Joy then and forced myself to meet her gaze and accept whatever judgment I saw reflected in her eyes. But all I saw were glistening tears and... sympathy.

It was too much. I selfishly started sobbing on her shoulder. Luckily, Fara didn't let it go on too long before she discreetly cast Serenity over me and I calmed. But the calm felt ephemeral and insufficient and I knew I'd need to find a better way to cope.

23

SIC TRANSIT GLORIA MUNDI

Later that afternoon, the entire town gathered down on First Street. Custom dictated that Ari's memorial procession begin there. For the next four hours the cavalcade would wind its way up through the town's switchback streets, until just before dusk, when it would reach the graveyard at the top of the mountain. The fact that there was no body to be buried was irrelevant. The important part of the ceremony was the procession – and the offerings.

As Ari's court jester, Tenacity had arranged everything. In all, there were a half-dozen participating pageant carts, most of which represented various people who'd played a significant role in the departed patron's life. Over the past few days various residents, both Host and Hyrke, had pitched themselves to Tenacity, arguing that they were worthy of a float, but she'd stood her ground and kept the number at an even six.

Yannu, as Captain of the Guard and Ari's most likely successor, got a float. He'd chosen to decorate his with a bronze bunyip. Despite its relatively minuscule size, the newly forged metal talisman and its accompanying cohort of retainers evoked feelings of protection, strength, and tradition.

Cliodna, the town's unofficial "lady" and past inamorata of the patron, also got a float. She'd taken her lead from Yannu (no surprise there) and adorned her cart with an exquisitely crafted, undeniably expensive, golden drakon accompanied by a trio of beautifully carved, undeniably handsome, golden-haired men. She herself was in full-on swan mode, all *rara avis extraodinaris*. She'd taken one look at me and tsked. Oddly, her sympathy seemed as genuine as her disdain. I ignored her, barely registering that the next two wagons were decorated as a guard tower (for the rest of Ari's camarilla) and a river dock (for his family; a nod to Bradbury, although Rockthorn Gorge's First Street residents also adored it).

As Ari's *consigliere* and most recent inamorata, the fifth wagon was mine, although I didn't want it. I would gladly have given it to any one of the residents who'd approached Tenacity begging for it. But Tenacity tenaciously refused my refusal until Fara gently reminded me that she too was in mourning. Fine. But there would be no fiery drakon on my float to rival Cliodna's golden one. I had neither the desire nor the magic to prove to the town that I could best her. Both Tenacity and Zeffre had been disappointed until Fara came up with a better idea. My cart would be adorned with a statue of Justica, just like Metatron's fabled oxcart. It was the ultimate symbol of Haljan authority and justice.

"Who knows, Noon?" Tenacity said, helping me up onto my float. "*You* might be elected Rockthorn Gorge's next patron." I looked at her blankly, squinting against the dull, gray light. "The first five lords of the gorge were Maegesters," she continued, as if I'd responded to what was obviously a naïve statement born from endearing, but misplaced, loyalty. "Why not you?"

I barked out a laugh, too harsh and loud for the occasion. "Let's see how many offerings I receive."

The sixth and final float was empty. It was Ari's. If all went according to tradition, it would be piled high with votive offerings by the time it reached the town's mountaintop grave site. Tradition also held that whichever float was given the second-most number of offerings would be the departed patron's successor. It wasn't an official election, of course, but by the end of the day, I imagined Yannu's float would be covered in coins, small crowns, clay figurines, lanterns, candles, and spattered blood.

I remember only a few things from the procession: Nova, sitting at my feet; Virtus prowling the edges of our float as if it were *Cnawlece* plowing through the eastern Lethe instead of a pageant wagon weaving its way through Rockthorn Gorge; the uncanny silence of the crowd; the snuffling and snorting of the oxen pulling the floats; and Tenacity's invocation.

Barefoot, clothed in rags and carrying a scepter, she was dressed as the Infinite Man or Crowned Beggar, one of Halja's most powerful alpha-omega archetypes. She climbed up on the Carmines' floating dock and, against the backdrop of First Street's real one, delivered her last ode to Ari in a clear, high voice that easily carried over the rushing waters of the river behind her and the quiet calm of the people in front of her.

> *Today, we hallow the dark Bradbury prince,*
> *Who has ruled us justly and honorably since*
> *He became our young patron—Veneration?*
> *No! We resist.*
> *And yet death insists.*
> *Master of the* rota fortunae... *he was not.*
> *Nor are any of us. We are all caught.*

As Luck spins and weaves and cuts
Our fate, faith, time, and ties.
We remember, but for a moment
Life's brief player, rogare *slayer,*
Gorge lord, member of the demon horde,
Aristos!
Nullum funus sine fidula.

No funeral without a fiddle. She motioned then to someone in the crowd, and a demon stepped forward. Seven feet tall with viridian skin and a sleek, muscled physique, he was a fossegrimen. He bowed to the floats and the crowd and then pulled a violin out from underneath his cloak. Its color was the same greenish-blue as his skin. The tailpiece and fingerboard were made of bone, its scroll was a carved skull, and on its body was a glowing pyrograph – a flaming waterfall… or the fiery outline of a million falling stars rushing toward a single grave.

He began to play and the procession moved forward with a jerk and a halt, frequent starts and stops, the fossegrimen's long, plaintive notes underscoring the clinking of trinkets as they were thrown toward us.

By midafternoon, we'd reached Fourth Street. The sun had barely shown itself and was already creeping away. I stood, leaning against the statue of Justica, dazedly gazing at the crowd, unable and unwilling to recognize any who approached. Luckily, there weren't many. Most threw their initial offerings on Ari's now loaded cart and then approached one of the others. It wasn't that people didn't like me, but… well, Maegesters were lawyers, after all, and not very popular with lay people. The settlers here knew me as Ari's *consigliere* rather than as his inamorata, which was how I'd wanted it. At least it had been, until Frigore Luna.

I closed my eyes, thinking only to rid myself of unwanted thoughts by way of ridding myself of unwanted sights... and sounds. I wanted to clap my hands over my ears and run. *Would that Luck-forsaken fossegrimen ever cease?* My only goal was to make it to the graveyard. Then, people's attention would be elsewhere, and I'd be able to climb down and... do what exactly? Crawl in a grave? My bed? Drown myself in the river? In a sea of tears? Fara would see to it that I didn't. Dear friend that she was, I was tired of having her lead me around and put me through my paces, as if I were one of the oxen pulling these floats.

A deep, dark, cancerous ache was growing inside me. *Excise it or die*, a small voice whispered in my head. It was the voice of survival, and I smothered it.

I opened my eyes, bewildered, furious, and ashamed to be so. *Fourth Street.* ***Still on Fourth Street.***

Acheron was waiting at the lychgate to give the final benediction. He walked toward Ari's cart, now piled high with beads, blades, armor, wine, incense, and what seemed like ten thousand paper lanterns. He cupped his clawed hands together, palms up, thumbs out, and suddenly, there was water in them – headwater from the source of the Acheron River, I was told later.

The river demon thrust his hands toward the burning lanterns and a spray of water fell over them, extinguishing each and every flame. The fossegrimen finally, thank the Lost Lord, stopped playing and Acheron emitted a series of high, chirpy, unintelligible sounds. No one needed them translated. By the time

Acheron spoke the Ripian word for "ashes," the sun had set.

It was over.

I was filled with the most profound sense of... *nothing*. There was nowhere I needed to be. No one I needed to see.

I slipped to the ground, made my way over to Ari's now-dark float, and pushed Rafe's silver cuff into the smoldering heap. Just before someone might have come looking for me, I entered the lychgate and lost myself in the graveyard.

Tonight, I only wanted the company of the dead.

I don't know where I wandered next. It wasn't to Hell because I was already there. But somehow, much later, I found myself on the steps of Cliodna's sanctuary. Around morning, I'd started to realize why she called it a sanctuary. It wasn't just for birds. It was for people like me. Like her. Or, rather, the person she had been.

The Patron Demon of Waves and Waterbirds greeted me at sunrise, her face a perfect porcelain mask. No puffy eyes for her. No snotty sleeves. No cracked lips or splotchy skin. After all, *she* had not spent the night sleeplessly wandering in search of a dead lover who was never coming back.

She gazed at the morning sun and stretched, her gossamer-thin robe ruffling around her like feathers. Fists planted on her bare waist, she surveyed me while I huddled miserably on her doorstep. Her gaze was predatory, but not completely without pity. It was the look of someone who was about to squash a spider... slit a throat... or exact her revenge.

"So," she cooed, crouching down next to me,

"Nouiomo Onyx, you come to me uninvited. Tell me, my pet, which belladonna do you long for – the poison or the painting?"

This time, when I viewed *Eidolon's Alternate Ending*, the painting's subject wasn't a person, it was a place.

Last semester, after I'd been shot with the cursed arrow that had almost killed me, my mother had tried to reverse the curse by dunking me in water from a perennial spring. That swim hadn't healed me, but it had given me eleven visions from my future. Ten of them had come true during my last assignment. The one that hadn't?

A dam with lightning in the sky above it.

I frowned, not understanding the significance of seeing this vision twice. Did it mean completion of the Memento Mori dam was now twice as likely? Or doubly doubtful?

And what difference did it make anyway?

"What do you see?" Cliodna asked. Apparently, she was obsessed with what people saw when they looked at her portrait.

I scoffed. "How many times have you shared this painting since you reacquired it?"

"You're the first."

I nodded and took a deep breath. I felt good. At peace. I *could* breathe again.

"So?" She prodded.

"The finished dam," I said, shrugging. Cliodna looked confused. "I know," I said. "I don't get it either. But I assume it's a good sign. You want the dam finished, don't you?"

Cliodna frowned at the painting, but then quickly brightened. "Better, *caritas mea*? I don't know why you fought it the first time."

We were in one of her subterranean vaults, but this one was much smaller than the one she'd led me to the night of Frigore Luna, and there was only one painting mounted on the back wall – *Eidolon's Alternate Ending*. There was no ceiling in the tiny room, just a stone floor and slanted walls that met at a horizontal seam directly above our heads. The floor and walls were covered in wax. But it was just regular petroleum wax. I remembered that Sartabella had wrapped all of the clothes she'd made for me in paraffin paper to preserve their enchantments. Maybe that's why Cliodna had this cell coated with wax.

In any case, it didn't matter. What mattered was settling my bill and getting back to work.

"What do you want in exchange for this viewing?" I asked, turning toward her.

She really is beautiful, I thought. Her eyes were only a smidge lighter than lapis lazuli, but just as intense. Her eyebrows swept upward in a permanent, regal arch mirroring her impossibly high cheekbones. Her skin was so smooth and flawless, it looked like blush-colored blown glass, while her hair was as white and soft as a swan's underbelly. She was covered in gold chains, river pearls, and another shimmering, translucent gown. As with most of Cliodna's body coverings, there was little to it. Its most notable feature was its collar, a large, lacy, pleated adornment that evoked feathers.

"I want to be the Patron Demon of Rockthorn Gorge. *I* should have been Potomus' successor, but then Acheron endorsed Aristos and—"

"What about Yannu?"

"He'll continue to be Captain of the Guard."

"No, I mean, what about all the residents who support him? I was at Ari's memorial procession. Yannu's float was buried under three feet of offerings while yours… was not."

Cliodna glared at me. I felt it then for the first time. The change. How different I was. I wouldn't truly understand just how much until later, but right then, it felt empowering. Liberating. I gathered that love was an emotion that was so significant, it was one of the underpinnings of a person. Take it away and the person changed more than a little bit. Her emotions, her personality, her perspective. All different.

But that didn't mean everything was different about me.

"I may have lost the ability to love," I said, "but that doesn't mean I've lost the ability to think."

"I certainly hope not," Cliodna said, laughing. "Because I need that brain of yours now more than ever. As a Council representative and the former patron's *consigliere*, you are the obvious choice to oversee the election. Isn't that what you did out in the Shallows last semester? Help elect a new patron?"

I harrumphed. That election had involved one uncontested choice and a few hundred settlers, not two contenders and a town of seven thousand.

"I'm not asking you to do anything *ultra vires*, Nouiomo," Cliodna said huffily, "I'm just asking you to… fix things so that the people *want* to elect me."

"In other words, you want me to be your campaign manager."

She smiled. It was cold, but I no longer cared. "Exactly."

"And then my debt to you is repaid?"

"Yes… but I'm hoping you'll want to stay on."

I frowned.

"As my *consigliere*. There's no reason your future plans have to change."

I stared at her for a moment, conflicted. I had a feeling Cliodna's words would have made me angry or sad or vehemently *something* before I'd been cursed by viewing her painting. But those feelings, whatever they might have been, never surfaced. Instead, I just felt... well, not numb really, but logical. Why *should* my plans change? I didn't necessarily care one way or the other about staying in the gorge after graduation now, but I still wanted to do well in my fourth-semester residency.

My employer was dead. It was in my best interest to align myself with the next patron. And what was the likelihood that Yannu would want my help? I laughed inwardly. He probably couldn't wait to send me packing. And then what? What would happen if I returned to St. Luck's now? Residency unfinished and arguably a failure?

Aligning myself with Cliodna made sense. If I spent the rest of my residency helping her, I'd not only repay my debt, I'd finish with a terrific reference and a future job offer. I gave Cliodna the same cold smile she'd given me. "I can't guarantee your election, only that I'll do my best."

She slipped her arm through mine and led me out of the vault.

"I have a feeling *your* best will be more than enough, Nouiomo Onyx."

24

MORRIDUSA

"Y ou want me to do what?"

Tenacity stood in the rotunda's atrium in a shapeless gray dress, holding a mop and pail.

Honestly, was she trying to look like a chambermaid? She was a court jester!

I sighed. I'd explained everything, in excruciating detail, already. We'd been talking for nearly a quarter-hour. I had other things to do. Time to cut to the chase, as they say.

"Clear out Lord Aristos' chambers. Give everything to the town's poor. Make certain they know the gifts are from Cliodna, their future patron. A team of artisans will be here this afternoon to begin renovations on both his chambers and mine. We need to be ready to host a fete here by Friday. In the meantime, you need to do one more thing: tell your father I need to speak with him."

"My vote is my own, Ms. Onyx," Zeffre said stiffly.

He stood in his kitchen, a small room with only a wood stove, a built-in sink, two chairs—one of which was piled high with books—and an old table covered with an embroidered cloth that was too small and stained to boot. Zeffre himself was covered in dirt and grime.

Did he have to look like a chimney sweep? He was the foreman!

I sighed. I hadn't wanted it to come to this. I had hoped Zeffre either already supported Cliodna or would change his allegiance once I presented him with the reasons why she was the better candidate – or rather why Yannu wasn't.

It was muckraking, to be sure, suggesting that Yannu, as Captain of the Guard, had been negligent in not discovering that Kalchoek was really Displodo before it was too late. And then I'd hinted that there might be other legal problems for Yannu with the Council over the fact that Ari and Pestis had been killed, *and* the Magna Fax destroyed, while Yannu was elsewhere. But then I dispensed with the veiled insults and implied threats and decided to just list Yannu's possible crimes outright.

"Obstruction of justice, conspiracy, criminally negligent manslaughter, destruction of property, theft—"

"Theft?" Zeffre's voice was incredulous, although I don't think it was just that last crime that had his mouth agog and his eyes popping out of his head.

"Of the stymphwax," I explained. "Yannu declared the last of it was completely destroyed, but I'm not convinced." I wasn't about to admit it to Zeffre, but Luck knew *I* knew how easy it was to find a valuable weapon, hide it, and claim you found nothing at all. And then I thought of two more crimes to add to the list.

"Violation of civil rights and electoral fraud."

Zeffre looked at me as if I were the monster Perthius slew in order to save Daimoneda. I laughed and took pity on him – after all, it wasn't his fault he wasn't a lawyer.

"Yannu's zero-tolerance policy for any 'aftermath chaos,'" I explained. "It won't be hard to make a solid argument that he was trying to manipulate the election results by denying people their right to assemble and discuss other candidates."

Zeffre's expression darkened further. In fact, it was fair to say, *he* looked like he would explode. "The only electoral fraud being committed right now is by *you*," he sneered. "Yannu is innocent of those crimes and we both know it. Threatening to bring legal action against him isn't going to get me to change my vote."

"Fine," I said, walking over to the stack of books. Thank Luck, Zeffre finally looked uneasy. Did he think I *liked* to threaten people? If he'd only do what was right…

"For now"—I plucked *Ichabye* out of the stack— "let's forget about *Yannu's* crimes and focus on *Tenacity's* crimes." I thrust the book toward him. "Did she tell you about this?"

Zeffre stared at *Ichabye* and then slowly shook his head. He'd gone from obstinate to mute. Well, I needed him obedient.

"Did she tell you what she did?" My voice was low. Calling it threatening would have been like calling a looming extinction event threatening. "She cast a spell over me. *Your daughter*, Zeffre. *A sham Angel* cast a spell over *me*, the executive's daughter… and this town's demon executioner."

Zeffre's mouth was a thin line now, his eyes no longer wide with surprise or squinty with anger. Instead, he looked scared.

Good. Now we were getting somewhere. Zeffre's

fatherly instincts made him rightfully frightened of the truth behind my words.

"Want to know *when* Tenacity cast her spell over me?"

I waited until Zeffre shook his head before continuing. "The night before Ari died."

I lowered my voice. I could be reasonable. Really, I could be. If only Zeffre would be. "Want to know *who* was standing next to me when she cast it?"

This time, I didn't wait for Zeffre to shake his head. "That's right – *Ari*. Now, I don't *think* Tenacity's botched spell caused his death... but who knows? The one thing I *do* know is that Angels who are accused of killing *regulare* demons get sent to Adikia while the Council and the Divinity sort things out."

We stood staring at each other for a few minutes. Then I walked over to the stack of books and set the Angel prayer primer back on its top. I turned toward Zeffre and he spread his palms wide. It was a gesture of appeal. Then he bowed.

"The Zeffres would be happy to support Lady Cliodna in her bid for the patronship," he said. "As would my crew."

Afterward, I was overcome. I didn't have a word to describe what I felt. Claustrophobia, ennui, exhaustion, imbalance? None of them really described what I was feeling. It was just this massive sense of *wrongness*. Of *unfittingness*.

I couldn't be sure, but I guessed it was because I'd acted against my true nature. That the meetings I'd had earlier with Tenacity and then Zeffre were contrary to how I would have acted before the curse. I clenched my

fists. Well, what was the cure? I couldn't go back there
and tell Zeffre I was kidding. I hadn't been.

When I'd gone to Cliodna the night of Ari's
memorial procession, all I'd wanted was to stop feeling
what I'd been feeling. But I hadn't realized how much I
would change as a result of losing the ability to love. It
wasn't just that I couldn't love anymore. I couldn't relate
to people as I once had. I couldn't empathize,
sympathize, or even care. I even found it difficult to
even think like someone who did.

I decided to try, to the extent I was able, to act as I
might have before viewing *Eidolon's Alternate Ending*.

My first opportunity came later that day while I was
saying my farewells to the Carmines. Once again I found
myself standing on the train platform with Joy, Steve,
and Matt, who looked only marginally better than he had
yesterday. *Didn't the boy realize 'handsome is as
handsome does' meant you had to take care with your
appearance? He looked like the body we should have
buried yesterday.*

As surreptitiously as possible, I glanced at the
station clock. Only a few more minutes and I could get
back to my desk. I had invitations to issue, a press
release to write, posters, push cards, and lapel pins to
design…

Nova, who'd been worse than a burr lately, nudged
my hand with her nose. *Ugh.* I wiped my hand on my
pants and stepped away. Steve frowned.

He blamed me for Ari's death.

"He should have shifted into smoke and shadow," I
said. "If he'd done that instead of trying to rescue me,
none of us would be standing here. Everyone would be
alive and somewhere else now." The train pulled up,
whooshing wind and emitting one long, shrill whistle.
"You know what Ari's problem was? He never gave me

enough credit. He never learned that I could take care of myself. I had a"—I windmilled my hand in the air, attempting to remember the name of Sartabella's failsafe, but quickly gave up—"sailing rig designed for me. *It* saved me. So his sacrifice was unnecessary."

Ari's father started toward me, seething like a red bull. But Joy reached her arm out and stopped him. She was looking more snowshoe hare than white rabbit today. Her boots were scuffed and tufts of her hair were poking out from under the sides of her traveling cap. But her pink eyes were as frosty as ever.

"Until we meet again, Nouiomo," she said softly, and shepherded her family onto the waiting train.

My second opportunity to try to act normal came the next morning when Fara and I were discussing the morning's training melee.

"I don't understand," Fara said. "What's wrong with the armor Sartabella made you?"

"I can't wear armor adorned with a scarlet drakon now," I told her again, exasperated. But she just shook her head and frowned. I was tired of frowns. *Why couldn't Fara glamour herself with a mask that never frowned?*

"What's wrong with you?" she asked.

"What do you mean?" My concern that I wasn't able to act like my old self when necessary ratcheted up a notch. *What would I have done in the past? Bite my lip? Give her a hug? Tell her how much I missed Ari? I didn't.*

Maybe I should just tell her about Eidolon's Alternate Ending? *What was I worried about anyway? It wasn't as if Fara would be able to reverse the curse.*

But something made me hold back. It was that weird feeling of unfittingness. It lingered at the edge of my consciousness like a phantom. I was afraid that if I told anyone what I'd done, the feeling would get worse. That the phantom would creep closer. That I'd go mad.

"Noon..." Fara said hesitantly, clearly unsure of how to say whatever it was she wanted to say.

"Just spit it out, Fara. You're an Angel, for Luck's sake. Aren't you supposed to be an expert on linguistics? How can everyday words fail you?"

She stared at me. I was as sick of people staring as I was of them frowning. She cleared her throat. At least it was a new response.

"You've been acting differently, that's all," she said. "But I know you're still grieving, and likely will be for some time." She paused, and I tried to make my face look appropriately sad. "I can't imagine what you're going through," she continued, "but it's just that... well... I worry—"

"Please don't," I said, cutting her off. "Ari used to worry about me and look where that got him. Look, Fara, what I really need you to do is be the best Guardian Angel you can be. Can you do that?"

She looked upset. But I couldn't tell if her distress was because of the situation (fact is, *Fara* was probably still grieving) or if it was because I'd said something wrong.

So I bit my lip, gave her a hug, *and* said, "I miss Ari."

Did it work? I stepped back and looked at her. She gave me a tremulous smile and nodded. "Me too."

Whew.

I waited a few beats and then said, "That's why I can't wear the old armor. Besides, I'm Cliodna's champion now. I need to be glamoured in bright white. No blood specks no matter how wet the fighting gets, okay?"

"Your signature feels different, *consigliere*."

"Oh, yeah? What did it feel like before?"

"Steel lace."

"And now?"

Rockthorn Gorge's Captain of the Guard refused to answer. We were standing on the stage of the old, ruined amphitheater – the same place where Yannu and his retainers had beaten me the first day I'd sparred here and many times since. This morning, however, I couldn't afford to lose.

Today's melee would be the first since Ari's death. It would also be the first melee—and hopefully the last—in which Yannu would act as Rockthorn Gorge's prospective patron. I'd told Cliodna she had to come. Melees in general might not be her style, but this one sure as Luck needed to be. There were only a hundred or so spectators, but I felt confident that each of them would be effective town criers for our cause if we gave them a newsworthy story.

Around us, beyond the stone steps and the rocky outcroppings, past the Hyrkes standing on the observation platforms and the retainers who stood at the ready, were the mountains of northern Halja. Mount Occasus, obviously, was altered. It looked like a sandcastle that had been kicked. There was nothing left of the tower or the Magna Fax. Instead, there was just a jaggedy peak. The rest of the view had also changed. The warm hues of fall had given way to the starker colors of early winter. Gusts of wind rattled bony trees and the air carried a hint of snow. It was clear and invigorating, but I knew it would soon be laced with dust and the smell of burning flesh. For once, I was impatient to get to that part of the fighting.

As he had for previous melees, Yannu introduced me to the team I'd be sparring against: Oleg, Igor, Vannis, and two bunyips whose names started with a Y.

"No," I said simply.

"You'd rather spar against someone else?"

"Yes, you."

He snorted. I didn't hide my revulsion. Blood was one thing. Bunyip snot was quite another.

"I fought against you your first day here, Onyx. Don't you remember getting your ass kicked?" He leaned closer and spoke lower. "You hold your own for a human girl, but don't push your luck."

I didn't know what I would have felt before. Disgust? Obviously. Yannu was hideous. Fear? If so, I hoped I would have hidden it well. I may not have won many matches, but it wasn't as if I were inexperienced. Determination? Undoubtedly so. And this was the feeling I seized upon now. *I'd held my own?* Ha. More likely, I'd been holding back. I raised my voice and shouted so that everyone on the mountain could hear me.

"I'll be fighting today under the auspices of the Patron Demon of Waves and Waterbirds."

Everyone's gaze turned toward the Lady of the Gorge, who was standing stage right. She wasn't wearing much, although that was nothing new. Her headgear, however, was different than her usual white feather tresses. Today, she wore a tall, spiky, platinum crown with a center ridge piece that came down over her nose. It looked like a short, black beak. On anyone else, it might have looked farcical, but on Cliodna it just looked wickedly beautiful. Her eyes sparkled and I felt her signature pulse with *expectation*.

Yannu looked unimpressed. "Your usual teammates?"

"Yes, but you mentioned five opponents, so I want Malphia too."

Beside me, Fara stiffened. I felt a jolt of surprise run through Yannu's signature. I could tell he was as puzzled by the change in my behavior as he was by the change in my signature. But he motioned Malphia over nonetheless.

"She wants you," he called, grinning.

Malphia joined us with a quizzical look, but otherwise stayed quiet. I guessed she sensed the curse like Yannu did. Since we were all about to form fiery swords and try to kill one another, I couldn't work up the energy to care that I didn't seem able to pull off acting like I had before. Maybe the person I was now was better.

Maybe this time, my team would win in record time.

I pulled Fara and Malphia aside for the pre-melee pep talk.

"Fara, cast Impenetrable over everyone and then glamour Nova."

"Don't you want Cryptid for her?"

I scoffed. "No. We're fighting for Cliodna now. She doesn't do ugly ducklings." I turned to Malphia. "Are you able to stop your usual heinous transformation?"

She blinked her baby blues at me. I wasn't fooled. I'd fought against her before. Once the fighting started, "Pretty Malphia" would vanish as quickly as Vannis, and we couldn't have that. She shook her head, frowning. *Ugh. Enough with the frowns.* I turned back to

Fara.

"Then your biggest goal is keeping the glamours up. I'm counting on you, Fara."

We spent a few more minutes discussing our strategy and then returned to where Yannu was standing with the other team. I could tell part of my plan was working already. With her blonde, unbound hair streaming behind her in the wind, Fara looked like a heavenly comet. Malphia, on the other hand, writhed with dark beauty. Her raven-colored hair swirled around her, nearly indistinguishable from the black tendrils of magic she radiated. Nova now looked like a giant she-wolf with a lustrous silvery-gray coat that contrasted nicely with Virtus' glossy, copper-colored pelt. We faced off against the bunyips and the bristly-haired hidebehind. I almost laughed; it was too perfect.

Beauty versus beastly. Cliodna would love it.

"No deadly blows," Yannu reminded everyone. "The first team to be surrounded loses."

And… it began, similarly to before… yet altogether different.

I didn't allow Vannis even one heartbeat before I pulled a steel dagger out of a hidden sheath and bashed him in the head with the butt of the blade. It wasn't enough of a blow to knock him out, but it was enough to stun him. I shoved him to the ground and plunged the dagger through his right shoulder, pinning him in place. *Then* I knocked him out.

No hiding for the hidebehind, I thought, laughing to myself. The whole maneuver took three seconds – smash, stab, smash. But by the fourth second, Y1 had struck me.

My head rang like a gong and I nearly bit the tip of my tongue off. I literally saw red. But I felt no fear. *Huh.*

Guess love has something to do with that too, I thought. What I did feel was rage – pure, unadulterated battle rage. I channeled it into a furious wave and tried to shape it into an enormous winged raptor. So great was my fury, I expected my flaming bird to be as big as the rotunda was wide. But nothing appeared. It was like the first few times I'd tried to shape Megaptera. But before, I'd had at least a spark of magic to work from. Now that spark was gone. Shaping a raptor – or any other sentient creature – out of fire now felt as impossible as shaping one out of water.

A blade then, I thought. *Even the most loveless Maegesters could shape those.*

By then, however, Y1 had picked me up and was slinging me over his shoulder. It was outrageous. I was beyond furious. I must have looked ridiculous and paltry and stupid and small and weak and—

Meanwhile, Malphia was holding her own against Y2, bless her. She was even looking good while doing it, thanks to Fara, who was standing beside Cliodna. Igor was using a javelin to bait Virtus, who was snarling and looking regally fierce. Oleg, however, had somehow managed to catch Nova in a wire at the end of a steel catch pole. She was struggling mightily, her tongue lolling to one side while gobs of frothy spit oozed out of her mouth. *Ack. She was a mess.*

Feeling almost as rusty as the first time I shaped a weapon, I managed to forge a knife. Uncaring of what internal organs I might hit, I drove it deep into the bunyip's back. Immediately, he roared and let go of me. I crashed to the ground head first, tucked and rolled my way free. I stood up, gripping my blade, as he came charging toward me.

Okay, so shaping fiery beasts or smoky demons was out because, apparently, I needed love to do that. I snickered to myself. *What, then?* Almost without thinking, I ripped the edge of Malphia's signature, reached inside, and scooped out a wriggling, twisting mass of blackness.

Hmm... I'd thrown *dark* magic before, but this felt different. Slick rather than dusty, provocative rather than panicky. Malphia's magic was strong and supple. It knew what it was about.

I liked it very much.

Instead of my fiery knife, I took the black mass of waning magic I'd just stolen from Malphia and launched it into the center of Yl's signature. The bunyip staggered and looked at me with an almost comical expression.

What? I wanted to ask him. *What does it feel like? A heart attack? Ice running through your veins? What lies or half-truths are running through your head right now? What end-of-world scenario are you witnessing?*

I became fascinated by the bunyip's response to my invasive magical plunder. He fell to his knees in front of me with a glassy, faraway look in his eyes. I thought about all the weapons I could shape: a mace, a maul, a war hammer... but then decided simple was best. I threw an explosive fireball toward him and watched, pleased as punch, as he dropped to the ground.

Not dead, I hope. 'Cause that might mean a forfeit.

I turned to see how Malphia and the sweetings were making out with their prey. Malphia was suffering a bit. My magical pillage must have harmed her more than I'd realized. Virtus was looking testy. His ears were back and his tail was lashing. He limped as he circled Igor, who held him at bay with a bow and arrow.

Have I mentioned how much I hate bows and arrows?

So I was already annoyed when I turned my

attention to Nova.

She lay on the ground pawing at the wire around her neck while Oleg stood calmly beside her, holding the catch pole as if it were a leash.

I lost it.

Before he had time to react, I'd walked over to Igor and grabbed the bow and arrow out of his hands. Ordinarily, since it had been made from his magic and not mine, it would have sizzled and faded immediately. Somehow, however, I managed to keep it fueled with my own pique. I notched the arrow, aimed at Oleg, and pulled back on the bow.

"Let her go."

He didn't, so I shot him in the thigh. I was no Mederi, of course, and my formal education had, obviously, been mostly "pen and sword" type stuff, as Tenacity had called it, but there'd been an anatomy lesson shoved in here and there. During the time it'd taken me to steal Igor's weapon and aim it at Oleg, I'd mentally riffled through my options and decided a potential bleed-out would be best. That would give Oleg a one in ten chance of survival and allow me to avoid forfeiting. Harsh? Cruel? Sick and twisted?

Look, I had a job to do. *Beauties versus beasties* wasn't the story I wanted the town criers to tell. It was beauties *beat* the beasties.

Oleg predictably cursed me – in an oafish vernacular, not Angelic prose. And then, perhaps irritated by my extreme sparring style this morning, Yannu *finally* joined the fray by barking out commands.

"Yurik," he called, "you've sparred with Malphia before. Make your fire hotter, brighter, bigger. Igor, if you're going to shape a weapon, use it. No wonder the *consig* took it from you. You deserved to lose it. Now shape something else and subdue that useless, unnatural feline swine. And then start pressing in from the flanks!"

I felt Yannu's exasperation turn to enmity. He was taking the bunyips' defeats personally. *Good.*

As almost always in these situations, things happened quickly after that. Yurik tried to follow Yannu's orders but his attempts at shaping and throwing magic became increasingly fitful. Malphia smothered his final, pathetic attempt at "hotter, brighter, better." Igor, meanwhile, tried to implement his captain's suggestion about subduing Virtus, but I'd had enough. I tossed Igor's pitiful bow aside and shaped a blunderbuss. The relief I felt in knowing I still could was outweighed by my impatience. It was time to End This Thing.

I pointed the gun at Igor.

"Yannu's right," I said in a voice loud enough to be heard by all – no way was I losing the attention of the crowd now. "If you're gonna shape a weapon, you should use it." And then I fired.

My shot only grazed Igor's ear, but the effort was enough to fully and completely enrage Yannu, who grabbed Fara's elbow and started dragging her back into the middle of the melee while shaping a fireball.

Yannu wasn't Captain of the Guard for nothing. If he threw his fireball at any one of my teammates, even Impenetrable wouldn't stop it.

But I wasn't scared. Or even mad. I was pleased. This was exactly what I'd wanted to happen.

"Now, Fara," I called.

Immediately, she cast a spell called Portcullis. Thankfully, it took only three words to cast. Yannu was powerful but obviously still blind when it came to seeing the virtue of Angels. He should have been holding her mouth shut as he dragged her. He wouldn't make that same mistake again, but for now, victory was ours.

A cage of fiery bars formed around Yannu and Fara.

Portcullis was essentially a retrofitted Stonewall. Yannu was trapped, for as long as the spell held, with no way to escape or throw magic beyond its confines. Even better? Unlike Stonewall, Portcullis allowed everyone on the outside to see in. The entire mountainside was now watching, wide-eyed, as I approached the trapped Captain of the Guard.

He jerked Fara closer and increased the wattage of his fireball.

I aimed my blunderbuss.

I wasn't going to waste time asking Yannu to release Fara, because he wouldn't and then where would we be? So, before Yannu could declare another draw, I shouted to Cliodna. "What should I do with him?"

Yannu's eyes narrowed and he squeezed Fara's arm even harder. It was dawning on him that, even if this fight was a draw, he'd just lost. You know what they say – a picture's worth a thousand words. Well, the image of Cliodna's *consigliere* holding a gun on the "jailed" Yannu was worth a thousand votes… at least.

"I've always been a magnanimous patron, Nouiomo, you know that," Cliodna answered. Her voice was a perfectly pitched trumpet call that every one of the hundred on the hill could hear. "Toward my waterbirds, my artisans, my miners – really, *all* of the residents of the gorge." She swept her arms out in a beneficent gesture. "Release my good friend, Yannu, so we can all get back to work. He has retainers to train and you and I have some magisterial matters to attend to, do we not?"

25

PRELUDE TO A CRASH

Cliodna left soon after the melee ended, as did the Hyrke crowd. Hopefully, they'd be crowing about Yannu's defeat until well past noon. Malphia, perhaps correctly sensing that her presence was no longer welcome now that her magic wasn't needed, had slinked off with the rest of the retainers, who were heading out on various patrol assignments. That left Fara, Virtus, Nova, and me awkwardly standing on the amphitheater's stage.

It was awkward because I didn't know how to relate to my old team anymore. Nova's presence, not just on my melee team but in my life, was becoming more and more confusing.

Why had I adopted her in the first place?

She was more albatross than barghest. Not only had she been zero help in this morning's melee, she'd been a hindrance. Fara had been forced to expend valuable *potentia* to keep up her glamour; meanwhile the optic the barghest had created by allowing herself to be leashed was damaging to our campaign. What's more, if I got rid of her, I could return to Megiddo for my last two semesters without even worrying about Miss

Bister's stupid, piece of crap table.

"We need to make some team changes," I told Fara, as she dropped Nova's glamour and started casting healing spells. "Nova's a liability. I need you to find a new home for her."

I felt a ping deep inside of me. A warning. It was that feeling I'd had before – the one I could only describe as *unfittingness* or *wrongness*. It told me I wouldn't have acted this way before. Inwardly, I grew angry. Resentful. Fara finished casting her spell and looked up at me. Her face was full of shock – and judgment.

"And while you're at it," I snapped, "make sure your glamour is always smiling. I want everyone on my team to look supportive."

But instead of smiling, she dropped her glamour and faced me wearing baggy, ill-fitting pants and a faded top. Her scarred face looked concerned. I scowled at her and my sense of *wrongness* ratcheted up a notch.

Was she trying to drive me mad? Why couldn't she just do as I asked?

"Noon, please talk to me," she said. "Forget about everything around us – this assignment, people's expectations, your future… and tell me what you're feeling. I know you're still hurting over Ari. How could you not be? One night's wandering and suddenly you claim you're okay? It's not right. *You're* not right. I can tell."

I gritted my teeth. Maybe the solution wasn't trying to act like I had before. Maybe it was getting rid of the people in my life who wanted me to.

But I wasn't quite ready to throw the wine out with the cork, as they say.

"I'm fine," I insisted. "And you did well today, by

the way. Your glamours held up beautifully." I gave her the smile I wished she'd given me. "*Si fortuna et angeli tui tecum sunt, nemo tibi obstare potest,*" I reminded her. *If luck and your Angels are with you, no one can be against you.*

"Indeed," she murmured, looking contemplative.

A week after I'd first met Acheron, he requested to see me again. My first impulse was to refuse. We'd already met and tested each other's mettle. If anything, my position on the dam had only become more entrenched. Cliodna needed the dam finished more than Ari had. Maintaining the underground conduit would offer her miners diversified employment and the project itself would strengthen the town's ties with New Babylon, the main market for her artisans' upscale armor, jewelry, and furniture.

Yannu, however, was on to us. His expertise might be military matters, but he was no stranger to political tactics. As Cliodna's followers and Zeffre's crew started to make inroads with the undecided Hyrkes, word of his humiliation at my hands began to undermine his support with his heretofore declared followers. All of a sudden, the patronship was in play. The election was contested and it was all anyone talked about. The town's former patrons, both long-time Potomus and short-lived Aristos, were all but forgotten. When you lived in an outpost, memories were short and worries were plentiful. Yannu, sensing an opening, moved into the vacuum created by Displodo's death. He began to sound like the now-dead terrorist, and his calls to put a stop to the Memento Mori dam project became increasingly vociferous. Political expediency might have been Yannu's only reason for now opposing the dam, but his turnabout meant I couldn't say no to Acheron.

I needed the river demon on our side – or at least not on Yannu's.

Prior to our meeting, I'd mulled over venue options. Both the rotunda and the dam were active construction sites. Cliodna's sanctuary was full of birds. *Fox in a henhouse* didn't even begin to describe what might happen if I held the meet there. Feathers would fly, alright. I'd been considering the pros and cons of meeting in one of the town's guard towers when I thought of the old ruined castle. I hadn't been there since my third day in the gorge when Ari had taken me on a walking tour of the surrounding area. So the morning before Cliodna was scheduled to move in to the rotunda, Fara cast me up in the bright white armor I now preferred and we set off.

Thankfully, Fara had been more manageable lately. Her focus was back where it belonged – on compiling field notes, corresponding with New Babylon, casting glamours, and serving as interpreter.

The weather was chilly, windy, and wet. Snow wasn't imminent, but people in town had started bundling up. Our glamours, however, kept us warm and mud-free as we squished our way along the old hiking trail. We reached the ruins around late morning to find that the river demon and his band of stilio minions had beaten us there.

I entered the ground floor of the castle and faced Acheron. His beady eyes stared back at me and his gargantuan snout was split with that annoying perma-grin. I stopped before I was within arm's reach of him. I had no desire to see what this area had looked like before the castle had been built. Forest versus castle... river versus dam... Frankly, who gave a damn? I chuckled to myself, but the laughter died quickly as I felt Acheron's signature. It roiled just below full boil.

Acheron spoke in a series of rapid-fire clicks, squawks, and enraged barks. My signature auto-pooled with *expectancy* as he gestured wildly in the direction of the river. After a few minutes, he paused and softened his cadence momentarily, but then launched immediately back into what could only be a tirade. I didn't need Fara to interpret. I was certain Acheron was griping about the dam and threatening to use his secret "domesday weapon" – the *Domesday Descriptio*, the archaic law book that contained proof of the river demon's allodial title.

I was just about to lecture Acheron on eminent domain, appropriation, and the right of kings when Fara started to frown. *Hadn't I warned her not to do that?* Then, without interpreting anything, she shook her head and said, "But Ms. Onyx killed Displodo."

What...? Was Acheron suggesting that Displodo was still at large? That Kalchoek wasn't Displodo? That didn't make any sense. Kalchoek had been at the top of the Magna Fax with the cannon's matchbook when I'd killed him. If he wasn't Displodo, what was he doing there?

Acheron snorted and snuffled and honked his responses while his minions grew more agitated.

"But *Kalchoek* was Displodo," Fara insisted.

"What did he say?" I demanded to know.

"Lord Acheron is... upset about Mount Occasus' partial destruction. He never liked the Magna Fax and isn't upset that it's gone, but pieces of the plaza now litter his river. He wants them removed. He was sorry to hear about Lord Aristos' death. But not Kalchoek's. He said you're to be commended for finally killing the 'Slum King.' Now that he's dead, Acheron believes the Council will find a proper patron for Myriostos—"

"Myriostos?" I asked, my tone sharp.

Fara nodded. "According to Acheron, Kalchoek was the Patron Demon of Myriostos."

"But I didn't think Myriostos had a patron... Why didn't you tell us?" I snapped, glaring at Acheron.

And then, just as he had during our last meeting, the magnus stilio lost it. Apparently, massive lizards have massive tempers. Fara tried to translate as fast as she could amongst all the roaring and stomping and pointing of clawed paws.

"He says he did," she said quickly, jumping out of his way. Acheron's minions also jumped back. "He says he told the Council and you... He says he thought you understood and that's why you killed Kalchoek..."

My brain was spinning. "So Kalchoek was the Patron Demon of Myriostos, who became this generation's 'Displodo' in order to destroy the dam that would give his followers a better life? Something he couldn't – or wouldn't – give them himself?"

Acheron stopped and stared at me. He barked out a single sound. Even before Fara translated, I guessed it meant, "Yes."

"And you think the Council should find a 'proper patron' for Myriostos now?" I asked, addressing Acheron directly.

He made the same barking sound, accompanied by some effusive snuffling and an impatient gesture toward the river.

"In which event," I continued, "the Memento Mori dam would not have to be built because the new patron of Myriostos would somehow be able to provide the slum with safe electricity through some other means?"

Acheron's head bobbed up and down and his grin seemed to grow wider. His signature pulsed with *hope* and *relief.*

I scoffed. "Lord Acheron," I said, my tone laced with disdain and my signature laced with *finality*, "that is the most preposterous suggestion I've ever heard. It's simplistic and naïve. While at the same time, oddly complicated. Why *should* the Council find another way to provide Myriostos with electricity? There isn't one. The Memento Mori project is underway and no one is going to stop it. Do you hear me? Displodo didn't and you won't either.

"And if you continue to try to do so, I'll bring charges against you. The information you provided to the Council regarding Kalchoek's *rogare* status was confusing at best and intentionally misleading at worst. Who's to say you and Displodo weren't co-conspirators? You both wanted the dam project stopped, if for different reasons. Let's see... I could charge you with complicity, malfeasance, interference—"

Acheron lost his temper again, but I stood my ground. He flailed around the ruined castle, looking not unlike a woman pulling out her hair, and then stomped over to one of his minions. He removed a large book from the minion's messenger bag – the *Domesday Descriptio* – and thrust it toward me. I refused to take it.

Acheron continued his tirade. When he finished, he stood a few feet away, holding the book out to me. I ignored him and turned to Fara.

"He doesn't understand your position," she said. "He's not a *rogare*. He's only ever tried to be a good steward of what was entrusted to him. He says truth, the law, and Luck are on his side."

I shook my head. "Truth is a matter of opinion, the law is subject to interpretation, and Luck is on no one's side but his own."

Later that night, Tenacity and I held a fete in the rotunda's atrium for Cliodna. It was a less crowded, more somber affair than Frigore Luna had been. The softly draped shrouds, crystalline frost, and Rockthorn's *tabula ansata* were all gone, but the torches were back, along with hundreds of rush lights. The statues were on full display and, though I'd been walking amongst them for months now, the Watchman's gaze, the Hunter's aim, and the Warrior's sword all seemed sharper.

People's minds and memories likely would be too. Per my instructions, Tenacity had asked the town's Angel sommelier to serve Black Gilliflower. It wouldn't work on the demons, but it would on everyone else. I warned Fara to stay away from it so that she could keep her glamour intact while I set about targeting unsuspecting Hyrkes. After a few sips of "Veracity," every one of Yannu's followers would tell me something interesting, which could be shared with the world, acted upon to their detriment... or forgotten, provided they promised to vote for Cliodna.

Was I planning to blackmail Yannu's followers? Of course not. Not if they were law-abiding Hyrkes with nothing to hide. But sinners didn't deserve the protection of the law and, luckily, I'd aced Sin and Sanction. I'd received the top grade in that class, which meant I'd memorized *thousands* of arcane, esoteric sins no one had ever heard of. I was fairly confident that each and every one of Yannu's supporters had violated a rule or two at some point in their lives. And tonight, with Black Gilliflower flowing through their veins and brains, they'd tell me which ones and when. I grinned to myself and tried to ignore the prickly feeling of *wrongness* that had hovered at the edges of my sanity since viewing Cliodna's cursed portrait.

How long had Cliodna lasted before she'd gone batty?

How long before I couldn't look myself in the mirror?

How long before I started painting abstract portraits of myself in an effort to somehow recapture the essence of who I'd once been?

How long before—

Ruthlessly, I cut off that line of thought. It wouldn't lead anywhere good, that's for sure. *Time to work*, I thought, blending into the crowd – or at least blending in as much as my bright white glamour would allow.

By late evening, I'd made tremendous progress. My means may have been questionable, but they were effective. Twenty-three additional Hyrkes had been brought 'round and would now be voting for Cliodna, as would their families and servants. I'd started to feel pretty confident about the election, which would be held, per the town's custom, on the night of the next new moon. But as I'd so recently reminded myself, Luck wasn't on anyone's side but his own. So I should have foreseen that the ground game I was so carefully crafting might not end as I wanted it to.

I especially should have foreseen two of the three party crashers who arrived that night.

The first crasher was Yannu. He cornered me (to the extent one can be cornered in a round room) and demanded to know if the rumors were true that I was considering bringing charges against him.

"Is that something the Council's genuinely interested in or are you acting independently?"

"That's rich, coming from you," I said. "Acting

independently? Isn't that what you're calling for now? Be careful, Captain, or someone might mistake your campaign rhetoric for treason."

Yannu bent down and brought his face to within an inch of mine. But there was nothing amorous about it. He was all threat. All Big Bad Bunyip. "I'm not calling for independence. I'm calling for an end to the Memento Mori dam project."

"Which, conveniently, gives you three thousand votes from Acheron's followers, not to mention creating unrest among Cliodna's."

"Why are you the swan's champion now? She was never yours. Do you really think she'd make a better patron than I would?"

I hadn't drunk any Black Gilliflower, so it was easy for me to give an evasive answer. "What the Council is interested in," I said, "is a finished dam. What it is *not* interested in is demon infighting. I assume, if Cliodna wins the election, she'll have your support?"

To my surprise, Yannu didn't answer. I knew he was no fan of Cliodna's, but I honestly hadn't pegged him for a *rogare*. I mean, if a demon like Acheron, who'd lived for two millennia and arguably held allodial title to this area, toed the line, where the hell did Yannu get off staring me down over a Council decision made years ago that mattered little to anyone but a handful of people in a neighborhood far, far away?

I said as much to Yannu, who laughed in my face with zero humor. But at least he stepped back after that, which gave me a break from his bunyip breath (for the record, it's almost as bad as barghest breath). We stared at each other under the light of the waxing moon, our signatures taut with tension. The sounds of the crowd and Tenacity's harpsichord seemed distant and irrelevant.

I looked away first, disconcerted and suddenly angry. At Yannu, yes. But also at myself and the situation I was in. The night I'd cursed myself, I'd told Cliodna that I'd only lost the ability to love, not think. But I was starting to worry that's exactly what was happening. My moral compass had no idea which direction magnetic north was. Its needle was just endlessly spinning. It made it very difficult for me to figure out what was right.

So I decided that "right" would have to be whatever worked best for *me*.

That feeling of *wrongness* advanced and the edges of my psyche started curling inward. My signature felt like a piece of paper being crumpled by a giant. I shoved my way past Yannu and made for the door.

Which, of course, was when I bumped into party crashers two and three.

26

EXODUS

Nightshade," I said, surprised, although I really shouldn't have been.

I stared at the sinister-looking man standing in front of me. *Night's letter*, I thought, remembering. He'd told me to expect him the week after Frigore Luna. He was here to try to heal Ari's wing.

The realization was like a punch to the gut. I had a feeling that, had it not been for the curse, I would have been reeling even more. But there was little time to process the irony of my Mederi brother's too-late arrival. My attention switched to his traveling companion, whose taupe-eyed stare met mine as he murmured a greeting.

It was Rafe.

Rafe. Here in Rockthorn Gorge.

"Noon..." Nightshade began, his expression soft and kind and completely at odds with the rest of his looks, "I'm so sorry. I heard about what happened last week but it wasn't until I met Rafe on the train that I realized..." His voice trailed off as he glanced around the room. "Are you able to step out for a moment?"

Suddenly, stepping out was the last thing I wanted to do. At least, not with these two. I knew why Night was here. I'd invited him. But Rafe?

I opened my mouth to ask *Why are you here?* but then shut it. That would sound rude, wouldn't it?

Maybe he'd heard about Ari's death. But, if so, from whom?

The answer to my question appeared almost instantly. Fara, also glamoured in bright white per my instructions, joined us. "Finally," she said, giving Rafe a hug. She murmured something else, low in his ear, and then stepped back, her expression as falsely bright as her glamour.

This was why Fara had been so manageable lately – she'd been scheming behind my back, calling in Angel reinforcements. Just my luck that said reinforcement had met my brother on the way up here. They'd obviously compared notes and now I wasn't sure who knew what. That curling-in, collapsing feeling I'd been experiencing a moment ago intensified. I was glad none of the three of them could sense the chaos in my signature. I looked down at the floor and took a deep breath.

If only the room would stop spinning...

I wasn't sure what to do or how to handle the situation. All I knew was that Nightshade and Rafe's presence was a danger to me. I was fairly certain that extended interaction with these two would bring about what I'd been trying to stave off all week – my complete descent into madness.

So I sucked it up and got real. Geesh. What choice did I have? (I'll admit, I thought about asking Cliodna to poison them, but I wanted a glowing reference from her, not just an okay one; an exemplary *consigliere* solved her own problems).

I introduced Nightshade to Fara, asked how the train ride had been, and apologized to Night that his trip was in vain. "The drakon I was hoping you'd heal is dead."

The look he gave me told me it was the wrong thing to say. I stopped myself from frowning and instead turned to Rafe to ask how his training was going.

"The Ophanim haven't cleaned you up yet, huh?" I said, smiling at him. "Ripped pants, worn leather… Where's your bindle, Rafe? Look, I know glamours were never your thing, but Fara, as you recall, is rather good at them. She could cast you up right now, you know."

"No, thanks, firestarter," he said, using his old nickname for me. But his tone was steely. He glanced around the room impatiently. "So, how about it, Noon? Can you step out?"

This time I did frown. *Leave now? With them?* Aside from the not-slim risk of madness, I wasn't finished here. Twenty-three Hyrkes was a goodly number, but I'd been hoping to net at least twice that from the fete for Cliodna's cause.

One look at Rafe's expression, however, and I knew demurring would *not* be in my best interest. I nodded and followed them out.

We exited through the front of the rotunda – the opposite side of where the morning melees took place – and made our way down to the river. Virtus and Nova joined us and I had to forcibly suppress my scowl. Fara was supposed to have gotten rid of her by now. The barghest butted her head against my hand and I petted her, resisting the urge to mutter, "Go away!" To my dismay, that disoriented feeling I'd had inside the rotunda intensified.

Rafe, Nova, and I separated from Nightshade, Fara, and Virtus. It wasn't until about ten minutes later that I realized we were heading northwest, toward Mount Occasus and the portion of the river that was littered with pieces of the plaza and tower.

Had I led us this way? Was my mind so addled that my sense of direction was going now too?

I decided to try very hard to behave as I would have before. Which meant I had to think about how I would have acted toward Rafe. It was harder than I thought it should be. My memories of my feelings toward him were muddled. I remembered that he'd left to go train with the Ophanim just days after we'd first kissed. Did that mean I should be mad now, seeing him again? Hadn't I loved Ari? Yes, I had. Of that, I was sure. I wasn't going to forget why I'd cursed myself in the first place.

I glanced sideways at Rafe, trying to figure out what he was up to.

If Fara had asked him to come up here because she thought I wasn't dealing with Ari's death well, then Rafe would likely expect me to start there.

"I'm sorry," I told him, "that I didn't tell you about Ari's memorial procession. I just figured you wouldn't want to mourn his death twice."

Out of the corner of my eye, I saw Rafe nod. Our boots crunched companionably on the gravel. Ari and I had walked here once, side by side, just like this. But Rafe didn't know that, so I didn't need to pretend to be sad about it. To our left the river gurgled, its ripples iced with moonlight, and to our right rose the gorge, steep and dark as a fortress wall. And behind us, Nightshade, Fara, and Virtus had dropped back out of sight.

"You seem to be holding up well," Rafe said, slipping his hand inside his jacket. He withdrew a flask and offered it to me. I peered at it suspiciously. Rafe wasn't Cliodna and had no reason to poison me, but still...

He looked hurt, glanced at the flask for a moment, and then took a swig himself. Again, he offered it to me.

How would I have responded before?

I held off saying something flip like, "Life goes on" and instead accepted the flask and took a sip. It was only a sip, but it was enough. I felt its effect immediately and knew I'd been tricked. The wine was dry and powdery and tasted like pepper. I choked and sneezed, glanced down at my no-longer-bright-white armor, and then glared at my ex-Guardian.

"Black Gilliflower, Rafe? Really?"

I started to turn back toward town, but he grabbed my arm. My signature heated up. At least the ensorcelled wine had stopped the spinning. I felt more clearheaded than I had in days.

"Noon, before you go, just tell me one thing. Do you want to talk?"

I wanted to say no, but the Black Gilliflower running through my veins compelled a different answer.

"I'm scared to." I clenched my fists and looked down. I hated how weak and pathetic I sounded.

"I could cast Fearless over you."

In spite of the situation, I laughed. "I'm not going to ask you if you really know a spell called Fearless."

"You don't need it."

"Why do you have so much confidence in me?"

"Because you're one of the things I believe in." He let go of my arm then, his implication clear. I could either stay or go.

"Is your specialty still Grace?"

He nodded.

"Have you mastered it yet?"

He scoffed, but it was more self-deprecating than scornful. "It's kind of hard when I spend all day, every day with a bunch of militaristic knights."

"Why are you training with them then?"

He blew out his breath and looked at the flask, chagrined.

"Because it was where you and Ari needed me to be."

"Huh? Neither of us told you to train with them."

"Did you tell Ari the 'everything' I told you to?"

"What? Like the 'you and me' everything or the 'you and him' everything?" But before Rafe could even answer, I waved my hand in the air to show it didn't matter. "Yeah, I told him."

"And?"

"Why do you care? He's dead, Rafe."

"What's wrong with you, Noon?"

I wanted to evade like I had when he'd asked "and?" but the question was too specific and the wine wouldn't let me. I groaned. "I'm cursed."

He didn't take my answer literally though. He reached down and grabbed a rock from the trail and threw it across the river. It skipped a few times before dropping in.

"Aren't we all?" he murmured.

"No," I said. "We're not. But I am."

He looked at me then, almost as if seeing me for the first time. He gestured with his hands and I felt the barest whiff of a spell. His face hardened.

"Who did this to you?"

"I did."

He looked pained. Ugh. And here I'd been thinking he was the one person who would understand. Guess I was wrong. I turned to go. He had his answers and I didn't care enough to ask more questions.

"Are you really such a coward?"

Anger was an emotion that came easily to me now, and I felt it exponentially more so than I might have before. My fingers itched to shape a weapon and I wondered idly if Cliodna had ever killed anyone out of rage.

"That depends," I snapped. "Now don't ask me any more questions!" I started walking away.

"Why are you scared to talk to me?" he called.

Against my will, I turned around and answered. "Because being around people from my past makes me feel as if I might… go mad."

We stared at each other, yards away on the dirt path beside the river, but miles apart really. Rafe was an Angel pursuing Grace and I was a firestarter with demon blood and an inability to feel love. How was he going to help me? I didn't even want him to. I was only standing here because he'd tricked me into drinking Black Gilliflower.

I should stick my fingers in my ears and run, I thought. Knowing Rafe, he wouldn't chase me.

But I didn't. At first, I told myself it was because I actually wanted to drink more of the Black Gilliflower. It didn't – couldn't – strip the curse, but it made me more clearheaded. I knew, however, that there was more to my decision than that. I'd cursed myself because I'd wanted to survive. I hadn't thought I could handle Ari's death without numbing my feelings. But losing the ability to love hadn't destroyed my desire to live.

I decided, if I was going to go mad, I wanted a Last Hurrah. One final night where I might be as close as possible to the old me. In the morning, I would wake up and continue on the sociopathic path I'd put myself on, but tonight I could tell my old friend why I'd done the things I'd done and what had led to the birth of the new me – a creature as love- and Luck-forsaken as Morridusa.

I didn't want Rafe's pity. I didn't care if he understood my motives. I just wanted him to witness my story. To be an archivist, historian, and scribe. To be the thing that Angels had been since the apocalypse. In other words, I just wanted him to do his job. Even if he wasn't working for me anymore.

I walked back to him and held my hand out, palm up. He gave me a quizzical look.

"I don't know any spells that can prevent madness," he said matter-of-factly.

"Hand over the flask," I said. "And we'll talk. Tonight only, though. Promise that you'll leave tomorrow."

He hesitated, but in the end agreed.

We continued walking north. As an aside, it's odd to drink wine with the purpose of remaining clearheaded. But that's the way Black Gilliflower works. Several sips later, my body felt buzzy yet my mind was still relatively lucid. When I asked where Fara and Nightshade were, Rafe confided that he'd asked them to give him a chance to talk to me without being interrupted, so they'd gone back to the rotunda.

An hour or so later, we reached the portion of the river where pieces of the old plaza and guard tower had fallen into it. High above us, barely visible in the dim moonlight, was the jagged outline of Mount Occasus. We stood at the edge of the river, on the narrow trail we'd been following, gazing at the wreckage of last week's explosion. The river gushed around the debris, making the area sound like a miniature falls. Piles of rubble, rocks, plaza pavers, and stone blocks were everywhere.

"What happened, Noon?" Rafe took a seat on one of the dry boulders beside the river. Nova lay at his feet and he motioned for me to sit opposite them. Then he slipped his flask back inside his jacket. It'd be the last I saw of it; it was empty. "Fara said Ari was killed in an explosion." Rafe glanced out across the water. "I guess this is where…?" He swallowed and turned back to me.

This had to be more than weird for him. There were so many connections among Rafe, Ari, and I that *crisscross applesauce* didn't even begin to cover it. We'd been a trefoil knot, doomed from the start. If Luck hadn't severed our connections by killing Ari, our futures would have been just as tragic, only in different ways.

But Luck hadn't killed Ari, had he?

I had.

The Black Gilliflower flowing through my veins compelled honesty, apparently in my thoughts as well as my speech.

"Are you familiar with a cannon called the Magna Fax?" I asked.

Rafe shook his head.

"It was a large battle cannon made out of stymphwax and magic. One of Rockthorn Gorge's former engineers created it and installed it on top of the ancient guard tower that used to be there." I pointed to

Mount Occasus' jagged peak. "The night of Frigore Luna, a demon named Kalchoek found the cannon's matchbook. Ari and I were worried that he was going to light the cannon and aim it at the Memento Mori dam… or worse, the town. At the time, we thought he was a separatist."

"What was he, besides a murderer?"

"Myriostos' patron."

"Myriostos?" Rafe looked nonplussed. "The New Babylon slum?"

I nodded. "He wanted to stop the dam project because it will provide safe electricity to the people who live there."

"And that's a bad thing?"

"It is when you're a demon who preys off of your followers' misery."

Instead of responding, Rafe grabbed a stick and started stabbing the sandy dirt beside his feet. I gave him a moment to process what I'd said.

"We decided to try to beat Kalchoek to the top of Mount Occasus so we flew—"

"Flew?"

I arched a brow at him. "Are you going to repeat everything I say? Yes, we *flew*. Ari shifted and I shaped a drakon with my magic."

Rafe's expression was wistful. "I wish I could've seen it."

"Bet you regret leaving to train with the Ophanim now," I joked, but my former Guardian didn't share my levity.

"For many reasons," he agreed somberly.

"Guess you weren't where Ari and I needed you to be after all."

Rafe winced.

"Don't worry," I assured him, "I don't feel bad anymore, so you shouldn't either." He looked at me as if he were trying to decide if I was kidding or not, but he had to know I wasn't. "Anyway, we beat Kalchoek to the top of Mount Occasus, but he arrived later with two other retainers. At the time, I thought he was one of them – just a *regulare* demon working for a modicum of adoration from the Hyrkes here who adore strength above all else. But he wasn't. He wasn't a *regulare*. And he wasn't here to work for the adoration of people who adore strength. He was here to ensure the continued subjugation of the weak.

"Ari and I separated. He went to the top of the tower to guard the Magna Fax and I stayed at its base with the retainers. Before we figured out who he was, Kalchoek attacked us. He tried to kill me by blasting me with magic, but I survived. When I woke up, one retainer was dead, the other was unconscious, and Kalchoek was on his way to the top of the tower. So I reshaped my mount and flew to the top where the Magna Fax was, but Kalchoek and Ari were already fighting."

I paused. *Maybe this was a bad idea. Confessing to Rafe.*

"And?"

But his question wasn't specific enough to compel a response.

I should get up now and leave. How was self-incrimination in my best interest?

"Noon, what happened next?"

I opened my mouth and shut it and then finally said, "I killed Ari."

"*You* killed Ari?"

"Yes," I snapped. "And you're doing it again, by the way. Repeating what I say."

We stared at each other. Rafe's face was partially concealed by his mop of hair. But the portion I could see was angular and set, as if he were carved from the same rock he was sitting on. He reached up and tucked his hair behind his ear and I remembered the most incongruous things about him. How he could cast silent spells... How coarse his hair was, except at the nape of his neck. How his *potentia* seemed limitless... How his clothes were always stained, ripped, or worn. Even now, in the shadows, he looked dirty, dingy... and deadly.

"Why do you think you killed Ari?" he asked. "Did your magic set off the explosion?"

"No... or rather, yes, indirectly, but it wasn't the kind of magic you think. I cast a spell."

"You—"

"YES! I cast a spell."

It took Rafe a while to think of a question that wasn't just dumbly repeating what I said, but he finally came up with, "Which one?"

"Ichabye."

Rafe stood up from the boulder he'd been sitting on and stared out at the river. "But Ichabye would never kill anyone... How did you even learn it? Who taught it to you? Are you sure you actually cast it? Maybe you were just repeating the words... And why then? How would Ichabye have stopped Kalchoek?"

I told him everything then. I told him about my mother sending the prayer primer, Fara suggesting I give it to Tenacity, me agreeing to spend the night of Frigore Luna with Cliodna, the fact that Tenacity cast Ichabye over me before I left and that, later that night, I used the spell to avoid the curse of *Eidolon's Alternate Ending*...

"*Eidolon's*—?!" Rafe ran his hands through his hair and groaned. "Onyx, only you. *Only you* would get yourself mixed up in magic like that. Is that how you cursed yourself? You viewed the painting?"

I nodded. "Twice."

"Twice?" And then we both kind of lost it – Rafe because he'd reached his limit of credulity with me, even with the wine assuring him I was telling the truth, and me because I was sick and tired of him repeating everything! But we calmed down a moment later with no magic shed. We faced each other, hands fisted at our sides. I sat down first.

"The first time I saw the painting," I said, "I stopped the curse by casting Ichabye."

Rafe's eyes were wide but he did not – thank Luck! – say *You stopped the curse?* Gah!

"But not the second time. After Ari died, I..." Suddenly, I didn't want to admit that my grief had driven me to such a desperate act as viewing the famed painting I'd first escaped. But I think Rafe knew.

We sat in silence. Rafe drew in the mud with his stick while I contemplated the moon and inwardly lamented my lack of glamour. Finally, Rafe said, "I understand why you cursed yourself, but I don't understand why you think you killed Ari. Ichabye didn't kill him; the explosion did."

"You're wrong," I said, growing increasingly irritated. I was tired of sitting on this boulder and I was tired of Rafe not understanding. "Casting Ichabye was selfish and shortsighted. I'm Host, Rafe. I'm descended from Lucifer's warlords. There's demon blood in my veins. My father is executive of the Demon Council and my mother is a *Ferrum*. You think Luck would let me cast without consequence?"

But it wasn't just the spell. It was everything. There were so many other things I should have done differently… or not done at all.

I should have figured out that Kalchoek was Displodo much earlier…

I shouldn't have separated from Ari… ever.

I should have said "yes" when he asked me to marry him…

I shouldn't have experimented with my magic… or fired that gun…

I should have let him carry me off…

We should have lived free and died… together.

"You know you're suffering from survivor guilt, don't you?" Rafe asked.

"Not anymore."

"But you were."

"And you would know," I said dully. "Look, Rafe, we've each done things that, in a wild coincidence only Luck himself can have orchestrated, impacted the same person… and now that person is dead. No amount of regret will bring him back.

"So you coped by studying Grace and I coped by cursing myself. What difference does it make to the world whether we suffer or how we cope? Or that we don't? So what if I decided to try to fix myself… and I botched it? Who cares?"—I raised my hand toward him, palm out—"And before you say, 'I do,' *I know you do.* I know that's why you came. The old me would say thank you, but the new me? *She doesn't care.* A situation I'm grateful for, by the way."

Rafe threw his stick into the river, stood up, and walked over to me. "You know no one can master Grace, right?" When I didn't answer his clearly rhetorical question, he said, "Which is why I chose to minor in something."

I frowned. "What?"

"You," he said, like I should already know. "And your story doesn't add up."

My eyes narrowed and I flushed with anger, but Rafe waved off my ire. "I'm not saying you're lying – obviously, you're not. But you're not seeing things clearly either."

I wanted to argue, but how could I? I hadn't been right in the head since Ari's death. First I'd been mentally crippled by grief, now I was psychologically hobbled by a curse.

"Noon… who is responsible for Ari's death – you or Kalchoek?"

I looked away, suddenly conflicted. One part of me wanted to continue my argument that I was the one who was ultimately responsible for Ari's death. I hadn't been able to stop him from dying. There were things I could have – should have – done differently. So my actions or failings had caused his death. Hadn't they?!

On the other hand, Kalchoek had been targeting Rockthorn Gorge's patrons and their dam project for months. Before I'd even arrived in the gorge he'd attacked the dam four times, killed the former patron, and made his first attempt on Ari's life. Under those circumstances, was it logical for me to blame myself for Ari's death?

"Kalchoek," I admitted. "But that doesn't mean I was without fault."

"No one's without fault, Noon," Rafe said, peering pointedly at me. "But that doesn't mean they should be condemned to lead loveless lives."

I said nothing. There was a long, pregnant pause before Rafe continued.

"There's one other thing that doesn't add up – the matchbook. You said Kalchoek found it the night of Frigore Luna. If the celebrations up here are anything like what they're like in New Babylon, you and Ari were probably... distracted." Rafe was no longer peering pointedly at me. In fact, he was studiously avoiding my gaze. But, as before, I said nothing. Felt nothing. Until Rafe finally got to his point.

"My guess is Kalchoek planned to steal the matchbook that night, which means he didn't find it by accident. So how did he know where to look? You left that part out of your story."

Instantly, I felt ice cold. My epiphany happened so quickly I nearly trembled. I'd experienced the intensity of my remaining emotions during the morning melees this week. But the scalding heat of battle rage was nothing compared to what I was feeling now. Because, suddenly, I knew I'd hadn't been fairly beaten; I'd been shamefully duped.

Kalchoek had been Displodo, but he hadn't been working alone.

Why had it taken half a bottle of Black Gilliflower to make me see the truth?

Because of my hereinbefore mentioned infirmities. Because of my addled brain. But now I saw what I should have seen immediately after Ari died. Zeffre's theory – that Displodo was one of the demons in Ari's camarilla – had been close to the truth.

The conversation I'd had with Ari months ago replayed in my memory like a ghostly echo.

Where was the matchbook hidden? Do you know?

It was disguised as the tabula ansata *on the statue of Servius Rockthorn...*

Who else knows that?

You, me, Cliodna, and Yannu... It's been safe there for millennia.

Nothing stays hidden forever...

I smacked my forehead against my palm. "Either Cliodna or Yannu told Kalchoek where to find it," I grumbled.

"Uh-huh, and which demon do you think it was?"

Once again, I found myself wanting to lie. I desperately longed to say *Yannu.* After all, if I could somehow pin Ari's murder on him, even as an accomplice, Cliodna would easily win the patronship and I'd get that fantastic job reference, future job offer, and possibly even a commendation.

But Rafe hadn't asked me what I *knew.* He'd asked what I *thought.* And flawed though my instincts might be now, I'd never once sensed anything duplicitous in Yannu's signature. Oh, there was no doubt he was aggressive, threatening, even hostile at times. And he was probably more of a separatist than he'd like for me to know. But, to my knowledge, he'd never done anything against Council policy.

Cliodna, on the other hand, often felt deadly. She was a swan, but she reminded me of a siren. She'd even warned me that "melees weren't her style" – that any attack of hers would be indirect and/or remotely caused.

I'd heard her, but I hadn't listened.

So I sat in front of Rafe with my jaw clenched shut, not wanting to reveal the extent of my failure.

"Noon?" Rafe prodded, frowning. Was he wondering how I was evading the wine's compulsion? It wasn't easy, that's for sure.

My mouth opened…

If I said *Cliodna*, I'd be admitting that Displodo's co-conspirator had not only deceived me, but victimized me as well. Answering *Cliodna* wouldn't just be embarrassing; it would be humiliating. I'd be disgraced and my future would once again be in jeopardy.

I was just about to speak when I realized I had another option. I stood up and started pooling my magic—

"Don't," Rafe said, his voice unnaturally steely. "Don't even think about striking me."

"Scared?" I taunted, flexing my fingers. Fire raced along their edges.

Rafe nodded. "Of casting a spell over you that you won't want. Now, *tell me*, which demon do you think helped Kalchoek kill Ari?"

Was it my imagination, or had Rafe just laced his voice with magic?

"Cliodna," I said, spitting the name out like it was poison. In a way, I guess it was. "I hate you, you know," I told Rafe, backing away.

"That's because of the curse."

"No," I said. "It's the truth. I wish I hadn't talked to you tonight. I wish I'd *never* talked to you. *Ever*. I wish I'd never even met you. I'm sick of you witnessing my heartaches and heart breaks. I'm sick of you trying to patch me back together. You can't fix me this time," I said, taking another step back. "So just stay away from me."

"What if I could?" Rafe blurted out before I turned my back on him completely. "Not take away your grief, but cure you of the curse – would you want me to?"

I froze. And slowly turned back. "How?"

"Let's just say I've learned stronger love spells than Ichabye, but none of them work on unwilling targets."

Rafe wasn't trying to trick me like Cliodna had. He was telling me up front that he could reverse the curse of *Eidolon's Alternate Ending*. But did I want that? Madness wasn't appealing, but did I really want to be tormented by the miseries of love again?

Who did?

But then again, who wanted to be cursed?

Wasn't it in my best interest not *to be cursed?*

Rafe offered me his hand. I narrowed my eyes at him but stepped toward him and slipped my hand into his. On the ground where he'd been drawing, the fiery blue outline of an endless knot flared to life. He pulled me forward into the middle of the sigil – toward the X at the center of the two interlocking hearts.

"This is going to hurt," he said, "Even more than the last time." Before I could react, Rafe raised his hand and pressed it to my chest.

His touch was infinitely gentler than the knife thrust he'd used to cure me of the *suffoca ignem* curse... and yet infinitely more painful. The instant his fingers brushed my *signare*-marked skin, my heart seemed to blister and pop. Every second of grief I hadn't felt for the past week – over half a million fractured moments – ripped through me like shrapnel. But instead of being blown into me, they were blown out of me.

Their exodus nearly killed me. I couldn't cry. Couldn't breathe. I wanted, ohhowIwanted, wanted, *wanted*, not to feel what I was feeling. My knees buckled and I collapsed. Rafe caught me and held me as I gasped for breath, shuddering on the ground, my vision blurring and my psyche shattering. At least the last time he'd lifted a curse from me, I'd blacked out. Not this time.

Not so lucky. I squeezed my eyes shut, stiffening against the onslaught of tears I knew were coming. In a last attempt to stop them, I kicked the outline of Rafe's sigil, breaking it.

But it was too late.

The curse was lifted and I sobbed in Rafe's arms.

27

PENULTIMATE ENDING

I spent the next two hours clutching at Rafe in a state of near-lethally postponed grief. But eventually anger began to replace sadness. I knew it was only temporary. I knew my feelings of loss, desperation, and hopelessness would reassert themselves eventually, but sometime before midnight my need for revenge galvanized me. I swiped the back of my hand across my face one final time and stood up.

"Will you come with me?"

Rafe didn't even ask where, although I'm sure he suspected. Rafe never seemed to care where I was headed. If I needed help, he gave it and that was that.

"I'm going up to Cliodna's sanctuary," I said.

He nodded. "We should get Fara. It might be helpful to have another Angel along... just in case."

"You want Nightshade to do *what* before we confront Cliodna?!"

"Blind us – but only temporarily," I told Fara, turning to Night. "Can you do it?"

We were gathered in the rotunda's atrium, at its edge, near one of the lit torches. The guests from the fete were gone and it was only Rafe, Fara, Virtus, Nightshade, Nova, and me.

Nightshade frowned. "Healers usually help the blind to see."

"Yes, but I have no desire to view *Eidolon's Alternate Ending* again."

"So your plan is to confront a *rogare* demon – one who's caused almost a hundred deaths and who has masterminded multiple attacks – blind? How will you even climb up the mountain to her sanctuary, let alone survive any battle that ensues?"

"There won't be a battle," I snapped. "Cliodna will either try to trick us or trap us. But she won't have time. The moment I see her, I'm going to kill her."

"But you won't *see* her," Night said, his voice uncharacteristically harsh. He ignored me and addressed only Rafe. "You said you knew how to cure the curse. Can't you just cure everyone again once you're finished up there?"

Rafe shook his head. "I won't be able to cast the cure if I'm cursed."

Night turned back to me. "I'm not blinding you – any of you."

I stared at my brother, frustrated. "Fine," I finally said. "I'll just go by myself. If Cliodna somehow tricks me into viewing the painting again, then Rafe can cure me when I get back."

"No!" Everyone said it at the same time. It might have been funny if it weren't for the fact that I was barely restraining myself from leaving immediately – with or without the Angels, blind or not.

"Wait," Fara said. "I've got a better idea." She ran

to the statue of the Watchman and grabbed its shield. "Use this."

I laughed. "What on earth would I use that for? Your shielding spells are worth a thousand of that – no, a million."

She caught the nearby torch's light and reflected it back in my face. I blinked.

"It's a mirror," she said.

"So?"

"Don't you remember?" She asked me. "*This* is how Perthius defeated Morridusa. Legend says that anyone who gazed upon her face was turned to stone. So Perthius used a shiny shield to slay her."

"I have *never*, in all my life, heard that version of the story," I told her.

She shrugged. "It doesn't matter. It's still a good idea."

"Why don't you just wait for Cliodna to come down from her sanctuary and arrest her then?" Night asked. "It sounds like encountering *Eidolon's Alternate Ending* is the bigger risk."

"It's the two of them together," I said. "And the fact that Cliodna's… canny." I looked in the direction of the sanctuary and continued in a lower voice. "Every minute I spend here is another minute she might escape. I want to destroy *Eidolon's Alternate Ending* – and Cliodna – tonight."

Fara huffed. "*We*. Every minute *we* spend here… You're not going up alone."

I smiled at her. It was brief and fleeting, but it was real. I handed her the shield. "I can shape my own. Rafe, grab the Hunter's shield. Night, if we're not back by morning, catch the first train to New Babylon and tell Karanos what happened."

He nodded, looking as grim as the Watchman.

I hadn't worked with both Fara and Rafe since we'd swum into the murky moat and half-submerged basement of the Stone Pointe keep two semesters ago. The memory was disconcerting, but the spells they were casting me up with were decidedly not. They spared nothing between them and loaded me up with all sorts of cloaking, shielding, and magic-maximizing spells. Since being cursed by *Eidolon's Alternate Ending* would likely turn Nova and Virtus into enemies rather than allies, we left them with Nightshade and then the three of us exited the back of the rotunda.

Slowly—and quietly, thanks to the spells—we crept up the crumbling stairs of the old amphitheater. There wasn't much moonlight, but Nocturne helped us to see in the dark. As we neared the top of the mountain and the outline of Cliodna's pavilion came into view, I glanced at the rest of my team. They weren't simply retainers I'd selected for some morning training melee. They were my friends. *If I lost them too...*

My limbs froze and I stopped climbing.

Was this what I would be like now? More scared and hesitant than I'd been on my first day at St. Luck's?

I mentally riffled through all of the spells that Rafe and Fara knew. Was there one they hadn't yet cast that would clear the gelatinous fear from my veins? Get my blood pumping and my legs moving again?

Ichabye? Before, that spell might have been comforting. Now it just reminded me of Ari, death, and sadness. Fearless? That spell would certainly take away my fear, but I remembered how losing the inability to love had changed me in unforeseeable ways. How even my magic had worked a little differently after the curse. I couldn't take that risk tonight.

Fara and Rafe flanked me. In the dim light, Rafe's wild, hay-colored hair and taupe eyes looked like a puff of smoke and two silver bullets, while his ripped pants and worn leather made him look like a shambling (albeit well-muscled) strawman. Fara, on the other hand, had exchanged her earlier bright white glamour for simple gray fighting leathers. We stood there for a moment, staring at Rockthorn Gorge's version of its evil queen's castle. There were no quips or quotes I felt like making; it was time to simply *do*. I squared my shoulders, told them the plan, and then led us the rest of the way up the mountain.

Unlike the night of Frigore Luna, I couldn't sense Cliodna's presence. But that only meant she wasn't on the first, open floor of the pavilion. We kept our gazes cast downward and snuck past the birds and bird baths. I worried that one or more of the macaws might squawk an alarm, but they stayed mute. In fact, it was eerily quiet. No cooing, flapping, or splashing. *Some guard birds they were*, I thought, leading the Angels past a cold forge, inert spinning wheels, and empty work tables. Out of the corner of my eye I watched for easels, frames, paintings, the color white, bare skin, or feathers. Finally, we made it to the narrow, twisting stairwell that led to the sanctuary's subterranean vaults. Inwardly, I snorted.

Every Luck-forsaken time! Couldn't one of my assignments end without me venturing into a demon's dark hidey hole?

The birds' unnatural stillness bothered me. Cliodna had seen me walk out of the fete with two strangers. And, since I hadn't returned or spoken to her since, she might have guessed that something was up.

Would she try to attack us?

Just before we reached the bottom of the stairs, we stopped and Fara cast Simulacrum. Instantly, a duplicate trio of us descended the stairs and walked right. I gave Fara a thumbs up, hoping the ruse might draw Cliodna out from wherever it was she was hiding in the same way it had drawn Acheron out.

But it didn't. After waiting on the stairs for an uneventful quarter-hour, we tiptoed into the lower hallway and stopped at the first door. I'd warned the Angels to touch as little as possible in the sanctuary – especially doorknobs – in case they were coated with poison. Within moments I melted the lock, kicked the door open, and braced for an attack.

But there was none. Our shiny shields told us that this room was little changed since I'd last been in here. It still held a thousand or more of Cliodna's starry self-portraits, each of which appeared chaotically distorted in the warped reflection of our shields. We backed out of the room, made our way to the next door, and repeated our entry procedure. This time, however, I didn't just brace for an attack, I formed a sword. Because this second room was the wax-walled vault where I'd been cursed by *Eidolon's Alternate Ending*.

As soon as we entered, the golden bronze of my shield flashed white and my signature zinged. I nearly looked up so that I could face the demoness head on, but Rafe issued a warning.

"She's not here, but *it* is," he said. "I can feel it."

"Me too," Fara said, her voice shakier than ever. "It feels… awful."

I peered more closely at my shield, fascinated despite everything. In the reflected image of the painting, a young woman with snow-white hair and a gossamer gown cradled a small cygnet in her hands. She looked lovely, sweet, and ethereal. It was almost impossible to imagine she was a demon.

It was Nickolai's bride gift to me. I was its original subject. He wasn't content with a mere portrait of rara avis. *No, Nickolai wanted more. Always more. So he had an Angel cast the spell Fairest over it.*

Near the door, Fara made a strangled sound and Rafe said, "We have to destroy it."

I approached the painting sideways, keeping my gaze glued to my shield. Out of the corner of my eye, I saw the gilded edges of the painting's frame. In its middle was a whorling mass of blackness, a glint of silver, and a splotch of red. The desire to face the painting head on was nearly irresistible. Whether it was the spells the Angels had cast over me earlier or my own sheer will, I don't know, but I managed to keep my gaze averted long enough to get within arm's reach of it. By then, however, my sword felt as if it were forged from lead. I could barely hold it, let alone lift it. So I tried to blast *Eidolon's Alternate Ending* the old fashioned way – with a big, ugly, undisciplined fireball. But my waning magic felt as weak as water vapor.

I glanced over at Rafe and Fara. "A little help?" I said, gritting my teeth and straining against the painting's corrosive effects on my magic. For a split second, I worried that the painting was even more powerful than any of us had ever thought. That it had tongue-tied the Angels and that its next move would be to force us all to drop our shields and look at it directly. Thankfully, however, my Angels responded immediately. Fara cast Ichabye while Rafe cast something that felt so bold and daring it could only be Fearless.

Strength returned to my arm and I raised my sword and plunged it into the middle of *Eidolon's Alternate*

Ending. An unholy shriek sounded from the end of the hallway as my fiery sword oozed into the painting, bubbled across its blackness, and consumed the centuries-old, hateful thing. I had never felt such joy in destroying something. But my joy was short-lived.

Because destroying the painting had alerted its owner to our presence. As charred pieces of the painting's frame fell to the floor, I turned to the doorway of the small vault and saw Cliodna standing there.

28

SWAN SONG

If it hadn't been for the shriek and the birds, I wouldn't have known it was her. In the past, Cliodna's hallmarks had been beauty, bare flesh, and bright white. The creature standing in front of us was none of these things. She was revolting in a way that made "melee" Malphia's macabre battle visage seem merely bleak. If *this* is what she turned into when threatened, I understood now why Cliodna insisted melees weren't her style.

Her pink skin was now bone white with deep fissures. Her dark eyes were blood red, and instead of a wisp of clothing, she wore black rags smeared with birdlime and dead birds. A maggot-ridden raven was the centerpiece of a twine choker tied around her neck, a dozen swallow skulls rattled at her wrist, and bird claws pierced her ears and nose. Her signature was no longer flighty or volatile... it was positively unhinged. Magically, Cliodna felt 100% birdshit crazy.

Thank Luck we'd come up with some kind of plan before entering. I think that – and Fara's melee practice – was the only reason she was able to cast Portcullis as quickly as she did. Almost instantly, a fiery cage formed around the swan demoness. She glared at us from behind the bars, her expression so calculating it gave me goose bumps. The Angels dropped their now-useless metal shields and faced Cliodna with me. But she didn't even spare them a glance.

"Did you think destroying the painting would cure you?" she spat out, her voice echoing discordantly.

"No, things happened the other way around," I said. "I was cured and then I destroyed it."

Cliodna shrieked again. Fara twitched, but Rafe stayed preternaturally still. Behind us, *Eidolon's Alternate Ending* was a pile of ashes covered with melted wax.

"Tell me why you helped Kalchoek."

"Who says I helped him?"

"Ari told me you were the only other person who knew where the Magna Fax's matchbook was hidden." A lie, since Ari had told me Yannu also knew, but I wanted to see what she would say.

She stared at me, her expression cunning. For a moment, I thought she might try to attack us despite Portcullis. *Was she more powerful than I thought?* But then her expression softened and she tamped down some of the vileness roiling inside her signature. "Nouiomo... *caritas mea...* what happened? You left the fete – that wonderful party – why? Things were going so well... Until *he* showed up." She switched her focus to Rafe and I became scared for the first time. "Who is he?"

"An old friend."

"I think he's more than that."

I ignored her comment and pulled the vial of waerwater out from under my shirt. I removed the chain from around my neck and held it out toward Cliodna.

"You know what this is?"

"I know poison when I see it."

"The last demon I gave this to lived. Confess and your trial can be drinking it, instead of fighting us."

A spark flared in her signature – a foul, muddy feeling that was too tainted to be called hope.

"But most demons who drink it die, don't they?"

"It's your only chance. If you fight us, you'll die." Another lie. Not the part about dying if she fought us, but the part about drinking waerwater being her only chance. There was no way I was letting her walk out of here.

She glanced up and around, surveying the cage that Portcullis had built around her, and then threw a huge blast at the bars, which momentarily eclipsed her behind a fiery mass of heat and light. She recovered quickly though, grabbed the bars of the cage, and tried to burn her way through. Her paper-thin skin caught fire as clenched the bars tighter and tighter.

I should have killed her then. Portcullis prevented Cliodna's magic from reaching us, not vice versa. But I demurred. Perhaps because, even more than I wanted her dead, I wanted to know why – *why* had she done it? Why had she partnered with Kalchoek? Why had she plotted to destroy a dam that she would have benefitted from? Why had she conspired to kill almost a hundred people, *including Ari*?

My desire to rid the world of her narcissism and deceit and callousness was nearly overwhelming, but she let go of the bars and said, "Fine. I confess. I helped Kalchoek."

"Why?"

"The patronship, Noon," she said. "It's always been about the patronship. I am *sick* of being the patron of lapping waves and water fowl. I deserve better. I deserve *more*."

"I think we deserve *more* of an explanation than that," I said, barely keeping control of my magic. And then I realized—

"It was you," I said, my voice full of horrified wonder. "*You're* the one who told the Angel to cast Fairest over your engagement portrait. It wasn't *Nickolai* who wanted more. It was *you*."

"I've always wanted more, Noon. Haven't you? I've always longed to be more beautiful, more powerful, more adored. *Who doesn't?* Yes, it was me who hired that bungling Angel centuries ago, but he paid for his ineptitude. I poisoned him. Just like I poisoned Nickolai when he refused to marry me."

I stared at her, but it wasn't her appearance that frightened me anymore. It was *her*.

"When Kalchoek came up last summer to try to talk Potomus out of building the dam, the bullheaded bunyip refused to listen. But I told Kalchoek not to worry. *I'd* stop the dam project – if I became patron. The *rattenkönig* was surprisingly quick to understand that Potomus had to die. And that 'Displodo' should take the blame."

"But you didn't become patron. Ari did. Didn't you help him get elected?"

Her face twisted with rage. I gathered the memory of Ari winning the patronship wasn't a happy one.

"Once Acheron backed Ari, there was no way I could win," she admitted. "So I plotted. And planned. I convinced Yannu to take Kalchoek on as a retainer and I became a member of Aristos' camarilla – so I could learn how to best kill him. I might have spared him... maybe... for a few decades or more... But he was too besotted with you – his human whore. I wanted to kill you both."

And then she stopped. I waited for her to continue, but she didn't. That was it. The whole of her confession. When I made no move to either execute her or hand over the vial, she prodded.

"I upheld my end of the bargain, *consigliere*. Now, uphold yours. Give me the waerwater."

Why did I give it to her? Why didn't I just kill her?

Because, at the time, I didn't have a good reason not to. Giving it to her was the law. So I tossed her the vial. It clattered to the floor and she walked over to it, picked it up, and uncorked it.

My memory of what happened after that is a bit blurry. Nightshade explained later that, sometimes, when patients suffer a traumatic injury, they experience confusion about what happened immediately after the event. There's some long, formal name for the condition – which I've intentionally forgotten. All I remember is this:

Cliodna picked up the vial, uncorked it, and threw its contents right in my face. Because Portcullis was made to keep demons and waning magic in, it didn't stop the waerwater, which hit the left side of my face and blinded me in that eye. The searing pain was agonizing, but that's not why I did what I did. I did it for Ari. And for the hundred others Cliodna was responsible for killing.

I formed a fiery sword and hacked her to pieces.

When it was over, Rafe and Fara led me out of the sanctuary's basement. The left side of my face was in ribbons and there was so much of Cliodna's blood splattered on me that I could barely see out of my other eye.

Nightshade healed me in Fara's quarters. As he'd

said, healers usually help the blind to see. And he did. He cured the blindness in my left eye, but was unable to fully restore its natural color. Similarly, and miraculously, he was able to heal all of the damage to my brow and cheek, except for a small scar. Fara offered to glamour me and Rafe offered to find a restoration spell, but I forbid them.

Those fixes sounded too much like Fairest.

Rafe left at dawn. He might have stayed, he said, but he'd promised me otherwise. Part of me wanted to release him from that promise. He'd cured me of the curse I'd brought on myself and helped me past the roughest patch of my recovery. But I knew keeping him in the gorge would be substituting one crutch for another. And besides, I had Nova.

Nightshade, however, refused to go. He'd come to mend a drakon's wing, he said, but if he couldn't do that, he'd at least make sure his sister's mind, body, and spirit were properly set. He'd conducted open heart surgery on me once. He imagined this new trio of things I'd tried to break would also heal, with time. For now, however, I felt raw and vulnerable. As if I were a snake recently molted, a chick freshly hatched, or a colt just born. My legs were wobbly and my future even more so. But it was *my* future once again.

The first order of business post-killing Cliodna was to tell Yannu what I'd done and why. I explained that the Patron Demon of Waves and Waterbirds had conspired with Kalchoek so that he could keep the miserable residents of Myriostos under his criminally negligent thumb while she could finally become the patron of something other than "lapping waves and water fowl." Yannu was enraged and disgusted. In his eyes, I was almost as much of a sinner as Cliodna, since I'd served as her *consigliere* and campaign manager. The fact that I'd only worked for her for a week, and that I'd been cursed while doing it, wasn't seen as a mitigating circumstance because I never mentioned *Eidolon's Alternate Ending*. That part of the story was personal and not much of an excuse anyway.

The day after Rafe left, Yannu was declared the new Patron Demon of Rockthorn Gorge.

Which meant it was probably him that started the process of running me out of town. But it could have been any number of others: Zeffre, Malphia, Acheron... Really, anyone I'd threatened with the law or bullied with my magic. I tried to right the wrongs I'd committed in the week since Ari's funeral, but my heartfelt amends and earnest apologies didn't change my new status. I was officially *persona non grata* with the people of Rockthorn Gorge. Within a few days, I'd packed my bags and said my goodbyes to the one person who was still speaking with me, Tenacity. After hearing that I'd killed Cliodna, she'd forgiven my sins, saying she'd suspected something similar to the truth all along – that Ari's death had affected me so deeply I'd ceased being myself for a time.

The first day of the first week of Fyr, Nightshade, Fara, Virtus, Nova, and I clambered up onto the Rockthorn Gorge train platform to await the next train back to New Babylon. By then, the trees were bare and specks of snow and ash dotted the air. On the leeward side of the platform a steel-drum fire pit burned, and on the windward side, a vendor hawked apple cakes and cranberry tarts.

Minutes before our train was scheduled to arrive, a

man carrying an enormous crate approached us. I tensed, immediately recognizing him as one of Cliodna's beefcake craftsmen. He set the crate down in front of me, withdrew a crowbar from his utility belt, and cracked open the crate. Inside was a table.

"Her ladyship left instructions that, in the event of her death, I was to deliver this to you and finish it according to your wishes."

The round pedestal table appeared to be an eleventh-century reproduction pieced together from planks of unfinished oak and bits of greenish-black rosewood – the chewed-up and spit-out remnants of my former *dormater*'s table. There was no paint, stain, or varnish on it, although that didn't mean the table wasn't adorned with something else.

"I can't accept it," I told the craftsman.

"She said you'd say that, and she wanted me to assure you that it isn't poisoned."

I raised an eyebrow at him.

"Or cursed."

I gave him a sardonic look. By this time, everyone but Virtus had gathered around the table and its packing box. Night had a quizzical look on his face, but Fara knew what it was: my ticket back into Megiddo – *maybe*, if it wasn't a trick.

Fara frowned and then glanced at me. I couldn't tell what she was thinking, but it wasn't anything good. Still, she confirmed that the table wasn't cursed.

I nodded. I didn't feel any magic radiating from it either. I looked at Nightshade. "Is it poisoned?" He leaned toward the table, waved his hand over its top and down its pedestal.

"No," he said simply.

What was wrong with it, then?

With a dramatic flourish worthy of an Angel, Cliodna's craftsman pulled a paintbrush, palette, and paints out of his backpack. Even before Fara warned me, I'd already guessed the trio of tools was ensorcelled.

"Let me guess," I said, "They're cursed with a spell called Born Yesterday."

The craftsman smirked. "She said you wouldn't go for it, but that I should try – for old times' sake. Melees—"

"Weren't her style," I finished for him. "I know."

He winked in response, reached into the crate, and spun the top of the table.

"*Faber est suae quaeque fortunae*," he said. *Every woman is the artisan of her own fortune.*

29

PRODIGAL DAUGHTER

They're already in there." Faustus said. "Third door on your left."

I nodded to my father's intake clerk and walked down the hall toward the door.

I'd like to say that by mid-Fyr I was back to my old ways, seamlessly reinserted into the daily rhythms of St. Luck's, looking forward to finals, and generally enjoying my return to the city, my friends, even Megiddo perhaps.

But I wasn't.

It had been two weeks since my return, and my future looked bleak. Formal and informal accounts of what had transpired up north had trickled down to the faculty and my father. I'd offered little evidence to refute anyone else's assessment that I'd acted poorly during my residency, especially with respect to the patron's death and the week after. St. Luck's had suspended me and I'd moved back home to dig in my mother's blackened garden, just as I'd said I would. I thought about giving Miss Bister the unfinished *rota fortunae*, but I knew she wouldn't want it. In fact, I knew she would hate it. So I left it in my mother's garden, which might seem like an odd thing to do, but it fit right in next to the broken mirror and rusting knives that I'd previously left there.

I managed to harvest an entire wheelbarrow's worth of black onions, shallots, and garlic before the summons came.

DEMON COUNCIL
OFFICE OF THE EXECUTIVE

FOR IMMEDIATE DELIVERY

Nouiomo Onyx

Onyx Estate

Etincelle

You are hereby summoned to appear before the executive at noon today to discuss your possible expulsion from St. Lucifer's School of Demon Law.

The summons commanded that I appear before my father, but that didn't mean I'd get off easy. The fact that he hadn't handed it to me over breakfast said as much, although we weren't much in the habit of chatting over eggs or oatmeal. No, expulsion from a demon law school was, obviously, a huge deal. So I was taking it seriously. I'd left Nova in Etincelle and I'd come dressed in my best cloak. Still...

I wasn't sure how vociferously I would defend myself. After all, the summons had said we were going to discuss my possible *expulsion*, not *execution*.

Maybe I deserved to be kicked out of school...

I knocked on the door and entered.

Inside was a fairly nondescript conference room. One wooden table, six large chairs, and three windows overlooking the delivery boys and bicycles waiting outside the Office of the Executive. I wondered if one of them would soon be delivering a message regarding me.

My father was seated at the head of the table, his signature cloaked and his face expressionless. Three other people were there: Waldron Seknecus, St. Luck's dean of demon affairs; Ralla Wolfram, my faculty advisor; and Donald Shivel, the dean of student affairs. Shivel was the only Hyrke in the room and I couldn't help wondering what his presence meant. Usually, MIT matters were handled between my father's office and St. Luck's Maegester faculty members.

I nodded to each of the men and slipped into the empty chair opposite my father – the one at the other end of the table. To my surprise, Karanos turned to Shivel and said, "You requested this meeting. You have a quarter-hour to present your reasons."

The dean looked momentarily taken aback, but his expression settled into a determined look as he turned to face me.

"You may recall, Ms. Onyx, from my welcoming speech during your first-year orientation, that I assured the Hyrke students at St. Lucifer's that they would be safe – that each and every Maegester-in-Training accepted at the school had been thoroughly vetted, that their previous demon experience was substantial, and that their discipline and self-control were absolute.

"None of this was true for you, however. You were never vetted, you had zero experience before coming to our school, and you've always had discipline and control issues." He cleared his throat and glanced at Karanos. "While I recognize that humans with waning magic must, by law, be trained as Maegesters, there are other schools which may be better suited to you. Other institutions where you can continue your education and training without endangering—"

"—Are you truly suggesting that we expel St. Lucifer's second-year *Primoris*? Over what? The death of yet another patron up in Rockthorn Gorge?" Seknecus' voice was soft, but his signature was as hard as ever.

"Personally, I think Ms. Onyx should be given a commendation for killing one of the *rattenkönigs*," Wolfram said. "Although"—he turned to me—"I did make it clear that getting the hydroelectric dam built was your priority. Yannu has now withdrawn his support for the project and Acheron is backing him, which means the people of Myrios—"

My father cleared his throat. Wolfram pressed his lips together, his sense of social responsibility clearly at war with his sense of self-preservation. "This is Dean Shivel's fifteen minutes," Karanos said. "Let's let him have it."

Shivel narrowed his eyes, perhaps wondering – as I did – if my father was just humoring him. I'd never thought of my father as being in my corner. He'd gone out of his way during my time at St. Luck's to show his impartiality, but as Shivel's next words showed, maybe it hadn't been enough to combat rumors of nepotism.

"Grave allegations have been brought against your daughter. I was assured, *by you*, Karanos, that when she declared and we allowed her to remain at St. Luck's – arguably the most prestigious demon law school in all of Halja – that there would be no favoritism." My father leaned forward, perhaps to respond, but Shivel doggedly pressed on. "Last year, she killed a fellow student during the Laurel Crown Race. This year, the patron she was working for died under her watch. Multiple complaints have been brought against her. These latest by two of our seniormost northern *regulares*. The new patron of our country's most populous outpost accused Ms. Onyx of dereliction of duty, reckless endangerment, breaking the town's rules of engagement, destruction of property, electoral fraud, and extortion. The overlord of the area's complaint was simpler, yet more condemnatory. He accused her of 'willfully ignoring the law.' Under those circumstances, how can we allow her to stay?"

Shivel's face was red. I didn't need to sense his nonexistent signature to know he was fired up. Hearing his take on what had happened, albeit based entirely on the biased correspondence sent to him by the pair of demons I'd most wronged, made it sound as if expulsion would be too good for me. Even if I'd been in the mood to defend myself, what could I have said? Arguably, each of those accusations was true.

"Noon?" That was it. One word – my name. That would be Karanos' only defense of me. Under the circumstances, it was probably more than I had a right to. My father was offering me a chance to defend myself. Would I take it?

"It's true," I began slowly, "that I should have been more aggressive in my search for Displodo. I should have figured out who he was months ago. I should have foreseen that he might try to use the Magna Fax and that catastrophe would be the result. I was reckless, not just on the day the patron died, but also during training. I took risks in shaping unorthodox weapons and sentient creatures… I sidestepped the former Captain of the Guard's rules of engagement by encouraging my Guardian to cast experimental spells. As for the rest…"

It was all true. I had no defense, only an explanation, and even that would require I tell them more truths than I was willing to share.

"So you admit that you 'willfully ignored the law'?" Seknecus asked, his tone incredulous.

My father responded before I could. "If she did, then the Council did too. Acheron's allodial title claim is, quite frankly..." Karanos struggled for a moment before finally finding the right word. "...inconvenient, since it gives him the legal right to prevent the Memento Mori dam project."

Everyone fell silent. I was fairly certain, in that moment, that Karanos wished I'd burned the *Domesday Descriptio*, Luck and the law be damned.

"The one demon's statement we don't have," Seknecus said, turning to me, "is the most important one. Would the past patron have agreed with these allegations? If your former employer was here, what would *he* say?"

I could've lied. It wasn't as if I'd been forced to drink Black Gilliflower. Or that I hadn't already perfected the art of lying by omission at the end of assignments. But I didn't want to, any more than I wanted to tell the truth.

Suddenly, my throat closed up and tears threatened.

"He'd say..."

Do I make you happy? Do you love me?

I buried my face in my hands.

"He'd say..." My voice was scratchy and rough.

Noon... you know you can't ever really go back, don't you?

I shook my head and looked up, my eyes dry. "He'd say I was ready for whatever comes next."

Karanos stared at me, his expression a weird mixture of pride and defeat. After a moment, he nodded and said, "Recommendations?"

Shivel wasted no time suggesting – again – that I be expelled.

"Demote her from *Primoris* to *Postremus*," Seknecus suggested.

"I've got a better idea," Wolfram said, his signature pulsing with an emotion that could only be described as *Eureka!* "Community service." He grinned at me. His whole demeanor was so at odds with the meeting we'd just had that I instantly became wary.

"Not Adikia, okay?" I said. "I realize beggars can't be—"

"—Adikia?" Wolfram made a sound of disgust. "Luck, no. *Myriostos*."

"Myriostos is a place, not a patron."

"It's a place that needs a patron."

"You're suggesting I oversee another election? After I've just been accused of electoral fraud?"

"No. I'm suggesting you become the patron of Myriostos."

I stared at Wolfram. "Me?! Aside from all of the other problems with that idea, there's the fact that I'm human."

Wolfram shrugged. "So were the first five lords of Rockthorn Gorge. There's no law that says a patron has to be a demon. That's just how it usually works. But you never bother with how things usually work, do you?" He turned to my father, completely ignoring the shell-shocked Seknecus and the outraged Shivel.

"Give her until the end of her fifth semester to improve things in Myriostos. *She* can figure out how to get them clean water and safe electricity. *She* can find ways to reduce the crime and disease."

"And if she doesn't?" Karanos asked.

"Then Dean Shivel can decide her fate."

Well, that would certainly put an end to Shivel's complaints of favoritism. Presumably, all options would be open to him. He could decide execution instead of expulsion. Or that I work for the horrid Adikia... for the rest of my life. I shuddered.

Karanos and Seknecus exchanged a look and then my father turned to me. "You said you were ready for whatever comes next. Are you ready to become the patron of New Babylon's biggest slum?"

The circus had come to town. Or, rather, that's what I felt we looked like as we waited in front of the gates of Myriostos.

After my meeting at the Office of the Executive, I'd left looking like I knew what I was doing. But as soon as I was out of sight, I had a quiet little meltdown in the alley behind the train station. For two years, I'd trained to be a Maegester. Now I was supposed to become a patron? I had no idea how to solve Myriostos' myriad problems.

If you were a demon, you'd be the Patron of Reluctance.

Not anymore though, right? A bracing gust of wind and a deep breath had ridden me of most of my panic. The logical place to start was *there*, I'd decided – in my new home.

So I'd spent the afternoon gathering my unofficial camarilla, borrowing a wagon, buying supplies, and then transporting them from the heart of the city, through Ragland and Paradise, to Myriostos. It hadn't been easy, even with two mismatched beasts pulling my wagon. We'd traveled twenty-five miles, which is why we'd stopped in front of the gate – to give Nova and Virtus a break.

My wagon was stocked not only with firefighting equipment and other items I'd need, but also food and drink from Marduk's, which I planned to share with my new neighbors: meat pies, hard cheeses, baked apples, kettle corn, a barrel of wine, and four jars of Thunderbolt. Fitz, dressed outlandishly as always in a punky-looking velvet suit with a flower boutonniere I'd already blackened, had been pushing Ivy since Victory Street to drink one.

"You'll be able to read over a thousand words a minute."

"No."

"You'll be able to *write* over a thousand words a minute."

"No."

"You'll be able to—"

"No!"

This time, she'd had enough of Fitz's prodding. She tossed her Armed Conflict casebook at his head. He ducked and it sailed through the air, nearly hitting an arriving rickshaw. The passenger – a young woman in a red corset, checkered mini-skirt, and striped tights – jumped out. She grinned, waved to me, ran over to Fara, and gave her a big hug.

"Who is *that*?" Ivy asked.

I laughed, as much from Fitz's expression as Ivy's tone. *Oh, boy.* Francesca Cerise had broken it off with Fitz not four days ago. Even if he hadn't been rebounding hard, this girl would have captured Fitz's attention.

"Tenacity," I called, hopping down from the wagon. "What are you doing here?"

"Yannu dismissed me from his court," she said, picking up the casebook. "But I heard you might be hiring…?"

"Who told you that?"

"Your father."

"You went to the Office of the Executive to try to find me?"

Her freckled face fell.

Ah. "You didn't go there looking for me, did you? Who were you hoping to work for?"

"Ionys," she said, biting her lip. Ionys was the Patron Demon of Wine, Winemaking, and Vineyards. He had three hundred formally trained Angels on his payroll. I didn't think she'd pick up many skills working for me that would help her land a job with him, but nor did I think either one of us should be underestimated.

"The accommodations won't be what you're used to," I warned her. "And you'll have to learn to work with this to get everyone's attention," I said, tossing her a jar of Thunderbolt. "No fire-breathing here."

She caught the jar and nodded, her gaze now glued to the electric bolts flashing inside of it. I walked over to her and traded her three more jars for the casebook.

"Lead the way then," I said, motioning toward Myriostos' main street. I stepped back to stand beside Fitz. "Watch this," I told him, pointing. Tenacity began a series of cartwheels, handsprings, tucks, and aerials – all while juggling the four jars of Thunderbolt. Fitz's eyes grew as wide as the rising moon.

Watch a woman become the artisan of her own fortune.

And then I stepped out of Paradise and entered the gates of Myriostos.

ACKNOWLEDGEMENTS

Many thanks and much gratitude to:

Betsy Mitchell, who helped with content and copy editing. Betsy was subjected to an early version of the manuscript and her comments were extremely helpful. If not for her, the story of Noon's time up in Rockthorn Gorge would still be full of plot holes, inconsistencies, and a less-than-satisfactory ending. http://betsymitchelleditorial.com/

Rebecca Frank, who illustrated and designed the cover. I heard this may be Rebecca's last illustrated cover. Sadness! But kind of neat that Noon might be her last cover illustration. She is still designing beautiful photo manipulation covers. To see more of her work, visit her at http://rebeccafrank.design/.

Roxanne Rhoads, who has helped with publicity and promotion for all of the Noon Onyx books. Roxanne is always a pleasure to work with. Prompt, professional, and friendly. http://bewitchingbooktours.blogspot.com/

Joan Havens, who has assisted with the Latin translations in all four Noon novels. I did not take as many liberties with the translations this time, but any errors – or apparent anachronisms – are entirely my fault. The Latin phrases I use are often Roman quotes, but every now and then the phrase is just a simple translation, i.e. *Nullum funus sine fidula. No funeral without a fiddle. "Fidula"* is a Late Latin word for "violin," an instrument the Romans didn't have. But since Halja isn't based on any one place or time, both Joan and I felt its inclusion was consistent with my pastiche approach to worldbuilding.

Meredith Bond at Anessa Books, who formatted both the digital and print versions of this novel. Because my first three books were traditionally published, this part of the publication process was new to me. What a job! Merry was wonderful to work with. If you are an indie author who wants to avoid the myriad sticky wickets of formatting, check out her author services at http://www.anessabooks.com/.

All of the bloggers who interviewed me, allowed me to guest blog, spotlighted the series, participated in the cover reveal, reviewed the books, and/or helped to spread the word about the series in other ways – you are all fantastic, terrific, and awesome! Authors rely on a healthy network of supporters to let the world know about their books. I continue to be humbled and amazed by their enthusiastic support.

My friends and family, who continue to assist me in ways both big and small. If writing a novel is a labor of love for the author, than for those close to them it is an exercise in patience, indulgence, and fortitude.

MY READERS!

Especially to those of you who contacted me and said you wanted a fourth book. *Pocket Full of Tinder*, for many reasons, was the toughest of the four books to write. I'm excited that it's finished and that I can finally share it with you, but my excitement is tempered by my knowledge of the story's saddest event – and by the uncertainties of self-publishing. In many ways, I feel like Noon at the end when she steps out of Paradise and into Myriostos.

*Watch a **writer** become the artisan of her own fortune...*

If this story moved you, inspired you, made you laugh, cry, or think... please share your thoughts with others! Review the book on Amazon, Goodreads, and/or wherever you hang out online.

Writing a review continues to be one of the most effective ways you can help support an author whose work you want to see more of.

http://www.goodreads.com/book/show/31373111-pocket-full-of-tinder

Attributions:

"The wise build bridges and the foolish build dams." – Nigerian proverb

"Fall down seven times, stand up eight." – Japanese proverb

"Terror is dreadful, but necessary." – *Journal d'Autre Monde*, 1794

"Ever-newer waters flow on those who step into the same rivers." – Heraclitus

"*Faber est suae quaeque fortunae*." – Appius Claudius Caecus (The original phrase was *Faber est suae quisque fortunae*.)

The inscriptions on the plaque beneath the Magna Fax and the offering bowl at the top of Mount Occasus were inspired by the dedicatory inscription on the Colossus of Rhodes.

The first two lines of the spell Ichabye are from an alternate version of the traditional Welsh air, *All*

Through the Night. The original English lyrics were written by Sir Harold Boulton in 1884.

DISCUSSION QUESTIONS

1. *Humpty Dumpty*: Part I opens with the famous English nursery rhyme. Do you think its inclusion is a reference to a character, relationship, or something else?

2. *Impermanence*: Everlasting change and forward motion (versus stasis and/or reversal) are twin themes in the novel. How were these themes woven into the story? Were there particular scenes, sayings, or dialog that seemed to underscore the overarching theme of impermanence?

3. *Memento Mori*: *Remember that you will die.* It's a dark little saying with an egalitarian message. Its point? In death, we are all equal. Thoughts?

4. *Ichabye*: In each book, Noon's mother has given her a "growing gift." (In *Dark Light of Day*, it was an evergreen. In *Fiery Edge of Steel*, it was seeds and medicinal herbs. In *White Heart of Justice*, it was gardening tools). Why do you think Aurelia sent Noon an Angel prayer primer?

5. *Icarus*: Part II opens with Oscar Wilde's well-known quote about the tragic Greek hero. What allusions to this myth are included in the novel? Do you think one particular character embodied Icarus more than the others? If so, who and why?

6. *Names Have Power*: Chapter 19's title was a reference to Ari – his birth (Rafe gave him the name Bhereg as an infant), death (he was killed when the Magna Fax exploded), and life. Do you think names have power? If so, how? Do you think names can impact a person's life, future, or fate?

7. **Guard the Guards**: Who did you think Displodo was? Did you suspect Kalchoek? Was Cliodna's involvement a surprise?

8. **Worst Enemy**: Which characters were their own worst enemy? Who and how? Are some of those characters more sympathetic than others? If so, why?

9. **Is Love the Ultimate Panacea?** Ichabye saved Noon twice. Rafe cured Noon of the curse of *Eidolon's Alternate Ending* by casting a love spell. Do you think Cliodna could have been cured? Why or why not?

10. **The Ending**: *Watch a woman become the artisan of her own fortune.* Do you think Noon was referring to Tenacity? Or herself? What do you think is next for Noon?

TRIVIA

Myriostos: Was named after the asteroid 10000 Myriostos because the neighborhood has 10,000 people in it.

Memento Mori falls: Was inspired by Multnomah Falls in Oregon.

Kalchoek: A near-anagram of Kalk Hoek (Chalk Corner), which was the name for a shell midden near Collect Pond, New York City's main source of drinking water circa 1700. The pond became polluted, then it became a landfill, and then finally it became one of the world's most notorious slums – Five Points.

The ancient amphitheater: Rockthorn Gorge's melee arena was inspired by the Theater of Pergamon and the observation decks were inspired by Clingmans Dome Observation Tower in the Great Smoky Mountains.

The Magna Fax: Inspirational seeds include the Colossus of Rhodes, the cannon used in the Siege of Colchester, the Sixth Labour of Hercules, and the Icarus myth.

Domesday Descriptio: The real _Domesday Book_ was commissioned in the 11th century by William the Conqueror.

Frigore Luna: This fictional holiday was inspired by All Hallows Eve and the Chinese Moon Festival.

Cliodna's Cygnus painting: Inspired, obviously, by the constellation, but also by Vincent Van Gogh's _The Starry Night_. That painting's subject (the night sky), the artist's history of mental illness and self-mutilation, and the fact that it was painted in an asylum made it an interesting inspirational source for Cliodna's self-portrait.

ABOUT THE AUTHOR

Jill Archer writes dark, genre-bending fantasy from rural Maryland. Her novels include *Dark Light of Day, Fiery Edge of Steel, White Heart of Justice*, and *Pocket Full of Tinder*. She loves cats, coffee, books, movies, day tripping, and outdoor adventuring.

She also loves to hear from readers! Email her (archer@jillarcher.com), subscribe to her newsletter (http://eepurl.com/bAzF7n), and/or find her online here:

Website: http://www.jillarcher.com/

Blog: https://jillarcherauthor.wordpress.com/blog/

Twitter: https://twitter.com/archer_jill

Facebook: https://www.facebook.com/jillarcherauthor

Goodreads: http://www.goodreads.com/author/show/5782149.Jill_Archer

Are you new to the series? Find the first three books here:

Dark Light of Day (Noon Onyx #1)

https://www.amazon.com/Dark-Light-Noon-Onyx-Novel-ebook/dp/B007A9KSMY/

Fiery Edge of Steel (Noon Onyx #2)

https://www.amazon.com/Fiery-Edge-Steel-Noon-Novel-ebook/dp/B009NY48SO/

White Heart of Justice (Noon Onyx #3)

https://www.amazon.com/White-Heart-Justice-Noon-Novel-ebook/dp/B00EOARZP0/

66774749R00222

Made in the USA
San Bernardino, CA
17 January 2018